COMES THE DAWN

IRINA SHAPIRO

Storm
PUBLISHING

Ebook ISBN: 978-1-80508-154-8
Paperback ISBN: 978-1-80508-155-5

Previously published in 2016 by Merlin Press LLC.

Cover design: Debbie Clement
Cover images: Shutterstock

Published by Storm Publishing.
For further information, visit:
www.stormpublishing.co

ALSO BY IRINA SHAPIRO

Wonderland Series

The Passage

Wonderland

Sins of Omission

The Queen's Gambit

Comes the Dawn

ONE

APRIL 1689

London, England

Feeble moonlight streamed through the narrow window of the cell, casting a silvery pall onto the stone floor. The flame of a single candle threw shifting shadows onto the walls, giving off barely enough light to see by, the tiny orange orb the only warmth in the chill of the prison. The night outside was utterly still, as if even the wind was too wary to blow, but the air inside the cell crackled with tension, an electric current coursing between the two men facing each other across the small space, both braced for a confrontation.

Hugo studied Max's features. He hadn't seen Max in several years, not since the showdown in the Paris mine when Max had kidnapped Neve and Valentine and lured Hugo to what he hoped was his own execution. Things didn't go according to plan, at least not for Max, but Hugo had to admit that on some level he was relieved that he hadn't killed Max that day since he didn't want the man's death on his conscience. But oh how he wished never to lay eyes on him again. How was it possible for a man he barely knew to harbor such hatred against him and pursue him across time and space?

Max hadn't changed much physically, but something had shifted in his demeanor. There was a watchfulness that hadn't been there before, a strange sort of resignation almost, which left Hugo wary and confused. Max's presence in Hugo's cell was inexplicable, but then again, most things Max had done since their unfortunate meeting years ago in the twenty-first century had been beyond comprehension. Max was driven by a madness which had been nearly impossible to detect behind his urbane exterior, his need to possess Neve bordering on obsession. Was this why he was here now, to gloat over Hugo's helplessness as he once again made a play for his family?

Hugo balled his hands into fists, ready to beat the man to a pulp, but he discerned no outward hostility from the other man, just a sense of expectation, so he took a step back and forced himself to relax.

"Have you come to finish me off?" Hugo asked calmly. "Or just to gloat?"

"Neither, actually," Max replied, holding up both hands to show Hugo that he held no concealed weapon. His expression was strangely bland, which irritated Hugo even further.

"Then why are you here?"

"I had to speak to you. It's rather important."

"Well, say your piece then," Hugo said with a shrug. "I can't imagine what we have to say to each other at this juncture."

"Hugo, I've wronged you, and I wish to make amends," Max began, but was interrupted by Hugo's harsh laugh. This really was too much.

"You must be joking," Hugo spat out. "I'd like you to leave now."

"Hugo, please, hear me out." Max spread his hands in a gesture of peace, but Hugo was in no mood to listen. The man had unimaginable gall. Perhaps Hugo would be more inclined to listen if they were on even terms, but Hugo's position of helplessness infuriated him. He was locked up, unarmed, and entirely without resources, unable to defend himself or his family.

"Go away, Max," Hugo growled, suddenly furious. "You've tried to kill me twice. You've kidnapped my wife and child, and now that I am finally where you want me, you wish to make amends? I find that difficult to believe. Just know this: if you do anything to harm Neve or my children, I will haunt you from beyond the grave." Hugo winced at the absurdity of this ludicrous statement. Was that the only thing left to him? Making empty threats?

"Will you just shut up and listen?" Max retorted, his patience at an end. "I realize you're angry, and you have every right to be, but I've had a lot of time to think, Hugo. I've always imagined myself to be special. I ridiculed the very notion of God, believing myself to be too superior to need such an obvious delusion. Faith was for those who were less fortunate than I, for those who needed a higher being to pander to, a fairy tale to make their pitiful lives more bearable. I took everything for granted and thought that my money and position could pave the way for anything I wanted. And it had, until I met your charming wife," he added sarcastically. "Coming to this godforsaken century made me realize that I am nothing, and it's a painful truth to face up to. I am a coward, a bully, and a man no one loves. I have nothing and no one to go back to. The only person who ever loved me was my mother, and even if she is still alive, she won't be for much longer."

"What's your point?" Hugo asked, still annoyed, but also mildly curious. This wasn't the overly confident, pompous man he'd met before, who wore his superiority like a shield. This man appeared more human, more vulnerable; unless this was all an act designed to win Hugo's trust before striking the fatal blow.

"My point is that I want my life to count for something," Max explained patiently. "You are the better man, Hugo; you always had been. Maybe that's why the woman I fancied myself in love with gave up everything to follow you to the past. She knew right away that you were the one who deserved her love, not I. She saw something in you that she knew I lacked—moral fiber, honor, strength of character; all the things women yearn for but rarely find."

"That's very touching, Max, and I applaud your newly found humility, but I don't see what you are getting at," Hugo replied. He was thoroughly confused but hated to admit it. Max was up to something, but damn if he knew what that was, and he hated the feeling of trying to maintain his equilibrium on shifting sand.

Max removed his cloak and shoved it at Hugo. "I want you to put this on and walk out. Go back to your family and keep them safe."

"Are you mad?" Hugo was growing angry again, his patience growing thin. This was all a trick, the purpose of which he had yet to work out. Max was as cunning as ever.

"No, I am not. I think I am truly sane for the first time in my life. Hugo, go back to the twenty-first century. Take over my life. Be Lord Everly."

Hugo stared at Max, whose eyes glowed with an inner light Hugo found difficult to reconcile with the old Max. He seemed to be overcome with fervor, like a martyr offering to die for his convictions. He'd spoken of God earlier. Perhaps he'd found the solace of religion, but that still didn't explain this largesse.

"Even if I accepted, which I won't, how could I get away with it?" Hugo asked, a tiny pinprick of hope growing somewhere in his soul. He could never take Max up on his offer, but there was something else he could do. An idea was taking root in his mind, the pinprick now growing bigger and brighter.

"People believe what they want to believe. If you say you

are Maximillian Everly, people will believe you, even if, deep down, they have their doubts. There are only three people who can disprove the claim: my mother, my physician, and my dentist. I have never been fingerprinted, and the doctors are bound by laws of confidentiality. They cannot reveal any information unless subpoenaed by the courts. Only my mother would know for sure."

"I am sorry, Max, but your mother is gone," Hugo said softly. "We had a visit from Simon a few months back."

"You've met Simon? He knows about the passage?" Max gasped, his gaze suddenly more alert.

Hugo could see a momentary flash of pain behind the eyes. Max had obviously cared for Simon, although Hugo wasn't sure if he realized that the housekeeper's brat he'd lorded it over was really his half-brother.

"It would seem so. He escaped from his own wedding."

Max suddenly chuckled, his face alight with amusement. "That's Simon all right. He went back, did he? Good, this is no place for him. Anyway, Hugo, this is your only chance. I am willingly giving it to you. Take it before I change my mind."

"Max, you are offering to die in my place," Hugo retorted. "I must admit that I am somewhat taken aback by your pangs of conscience at this late stage, but you don't understand what you're suggesting. This is not a game."

"Don't talk to me of games, Hugo. I am the one who was sent down to a sugar plantation. I still have marks on my back as a souvenir of the flogging I received, and I agreed to be buried alive and ingested puffer fish poison to facilitate my escape. I know this isn't a game, but having gone through all that to save my life, once safe, I realized that life is actually quite worthless. I've thought this through."

"This is absurd. I won't do it," Hugo hissed as the muffled sound of footsteps echoed in the corridor outside. The guard was coming back.

"Yes, you will. You will do it for Neve, because she doesn't deserve to be a widow. I have never known love like that, Hugo. If I had a woman who loved me as much as Neve loves you, I would do anything to stay alive. I would sacrifice anything, including a man who wronged you."

"What is it you're really after, Max?"

Max hung his head for a moment before answering, his breathing labored. "Redemption. I want redemption."

Hugo opened his mouth to reply when they heard the jangle of keys outside the door.

Their eyes met as Max pushed the cloak into Hugo's hands. "Go."

"I'll be back in three days, Max. I need to see to my family and try to figure out what evidence the Crown has on me, but I will be back. You have my word. I'm not prepared to let you sacrifice your life for me."

"That's my decision to make," Max replied as he sat down on the cot.

"No, it isn't."

"Just go."

Hugo threw on the cloak, pulled the hood up over his head, and followed the guard out the door, his heart thumping painfully against his ribs.

The corridors were illuminated by the faint light coming from several sconces, the flames of the torches flickering and casting eerie shadows onto the walls. This part of the Tower wasn't beneath ground, but it felt like a tomb; the inmates buried alive, their chances of regaining freedom practically nonexistent. The next time most of them walked out of this prison would be to face their executioner. Some received a pardon, but Hugo wouldn't be one of them—not this time.

His insides twisted with guilt, but he forced himself to walk on, his eyes glued to the stone floor until he was outside in the fresh April air, walking through the gates and out to freedom.

Max's horse was tethered outside, just as he said, but Hugo chose not to ride. He led the animal by the reins, needing some time to walk and come to terms with what had just occurred. He still doubted Max's motives. Could a person truly have such a drastic change of heart?

Even if Max were repentant, Hugo couldn't accept his sacrifice. What kind of man would that make him? He supposed many would, especially given their past history, but this just wasn't right. To kill Max during an altercation would have been honorable; to simply condemn him to death wasn't.

But Max had given Hugo a welcome reprieve, an opportunity to see to Neve and try to discredit the evidence against him. He would return in three days as promised, and set Max free, perhaps to return home to the twenty-first century.

Hugo smiled bitterly as he imagined himself as Lord Everly in that distant future. How sweet it would be.

* * *

The streets were deserted and nearly pitch dark, the overhanging top floors of Tudor houses that stood shoulder to shoulder like a line of soldiers casting the streets of Blackfriars into deep shadow. Narrow alleyways gaped like open mouths, their dank breath stinking of refuse and rotten vegetables. Only the light of the moon lit Hugo's way as he walked in the direction of the Strand.

The night was still, but a slight tang of the Thames hovered in the air, bringing with it the smell of wet mud, which couldn't overpower the scent of new grass and flowers that grew stronger as Hugo left Blackfriars behind. What was it about spring that made a man so acutely aware of his desire to live? Somehow, dying in the dead of winter never seemed as devastating as it did when the world was bursting with life, the cold and dark of winter replaced at last by sunlight and color.

Hugo hesitated for a moment before knocking on the door of Brad's house. He could see a narrow chink of light glowing between the shutters on the ground floor. Someone was still awake, and he hoped it was Archie. He was desperate to see Neve, but talking the situation over with Archie would help him put things in perspective, and maybe come up with a feasible plan of action before facing his distraught wife. He needed to reassure her, not inform her that he would be going back to the Tower in three days' time, and this might be their last goodbye.

Hugo took a deep breath and knocked softly on the door. He felt momentary relief when he heard Archie's heavy footsteps, but the relief was quickly replaced by surprise as Neve, Frances, Brad, and Jem filed into the foyer, all talking over each other, their faces alight with joy at seeing him.

"Hugo," Neve flew into his arms, her face tearstained and wan, but her eyes shining with happiness. "Did they let you go? Was it all a terrible mistake?" She looked so hopeful, so relieved, that Hugo's throat tightened with regret.

"No, it wasn't, love. I'll explain later," he mumbled, loath to tell Neve that he was still under arrest and would have to go back.

Hugo was spared further questions when Jem flew at him and wrapped his arms around his middle.

"Jem, what are you doing here? Is your father with you? Did you come for the coronation?" Hugo's heart swelled with joy at the sight of the boy. He'd missed him so much since his father had taken Jem to live with him. Jem wasn't Hugo's son, but he would always be his first child, the first person who truly needed him and gave him unconditional love. Losing Jem had been painful for them all, but most of all for Hugo since he'd had no choice in the matter. To insist on keeping Jem would be to deny him a future he deserved, but Nick Marsden, although a good

friend and honorable man, could never love the boy as
Hugo did.

Jem shook his head against Hugo's chest but made no reply.
Hugo bent down and kissed the top of Jem's head, the curls tick-
ling his nose. Last time he'd held Jem, his head had reached just
above Hugo's waist. He was a child no longer. He was thirteen
now, practically a man.

Hugo held him at arm's length, studying his face. There was
just a shadow of fuzz on his upper lip, and he'd grown at least a
foot since they had said goodbye in Paris. Jem's voice was still
that of a boy, but it wouldn't be long before it changed, and all
traces of the child were gone forever.

"I'll deal with you later," Hugo said softly. "I'm happy to see
you, Jemmy."

"Hugo, there've been some developments," Brad said
quietly as they all trooped into the parlor. Frances went to get
some refreshments from the kitchen while everyone took a seat,
eager to hear what Hugo had to say. He wasn't even sure where
to begin. To try to explain Max's visit defeated even his imagination, so he turned to Brad.

"What's happened, Brad?"

"Someone made an accusation against Neve. An ecclesiastical committee is already in Cranley, ready to arrest her as soon
as she returns. I've come to warn her."

Hugo stared at Brad, his mouth open in shock. An accusation of witchcraft? He expelled his breath and took a seat by the
hearth, suddenly exhausted. They'd returned to England less
than four months ago, and already their peaceful existence in
Rouen was nothing but a distant memory. Would they never be
able to just live their lives without the constant threat of danger?

Hugo waited until Frances handed around cups of ale and
set down some bread and cheese on the sideboard. He gulped
down his ale and held out his cup for a refill. He was hungry,
but food would have to wait. Five pairs of eyes were boring into

him, waiting for an explanation and some reassurance that Neve wouldn't have to face trial.

"Right," Hugo began. "I have been granted a three-day reprieve, the reasons for which I am still trying to understand."

"A reprieve from the Tower?" Archie asked, his eyes round with incredulity.

"In a manner of speaking. I must use this time to discover what evidence the Crown has against me and try to discredit it. We also have to figure out how to deal with this baseless accusation against Neve," he added. Hugo still couldn't believe this was real. Who would make such an accusation at this stage? And why?

"Neve must remain in London," Brad chimed in. "She will be taken as soon as she returns."

"I have to go back to the children," Neve protested. "I can't stay away indefinitely. There's nothing the committee can do to me. There's no proof of anything."

"Proof is not always necessary," Hugo replied, reminding Neve of her time in Newgate. "Proof can be fabricated, as we all know."

Neve shook her head stubbornly. "I must go back, Hugo. I must be with the children."

Hugo looked at the expectant faces. They assumed he had a plan, and one was forming in his mind, but he needed a little time to finesse the details.

"Brad, I'd like you to escort Neve and Frances back to Surrey. Archie, I need you to remain in London, and Jem, go with Lady Everly. Brad, you can send a message to me with Jem. It's not safe for me to remain here, so I'll be at the Black Dog in Blackfriars. Now, I need a few minutes with Archie, if you don't mind."

Hugo pulled Neve into his arms as everyone began to file out of the parlor. There was so much he wanted to say to her, but the words simply wouldn't come, so they just stood together, her head on his shoulder, his chin resting on her golden curls.

Neve finally broke the embrace and looked up at him. "Is this it, Hugo? Is this the end?" He could hear the fear in her voice but couldn't bear to lie to her.

"I don't know, but I will do everything in my power to keep you and the children safe."

"And will you keep yourself safe as well?" she asked, already knowing the answer. "How did you get out?"

"I left Max in my place," Hugo replied with a smile.

"That's not even remotely funny."

"No, it's not, but it happens to be true. I'll explain when I come up. I didn't want to say anything in front of everyone. Go get ready for bed; I'll join you presently." Hugo planted a lingering kiss on Neve's lips before finally releasing her. "Go," he whispered.

Archie closed the door behind Neve and turned to Hugo, his face filled with determination. "What's the plan?" he asked without preamble. "What would you have me do?"

"Go home," Hugo replied as he reached for some bread and cheese.

"Home?"

"Go back to Cranley, but keep your presence a secret. You can stay with your father; his farm is remote enough that no one will know you're there. Find out who made the accusation against Neve and what evidence they have," Hugo clarified as he chewed slowly. His mind was going in circles, but he needed to organize his thoughts and come up with a viable plan. He pushed his plate aside, no longer hungry. "There are three reasons why someone would make an accusation of witchcraft," Hugo theorized as he began pacing in front of the hearth, something he frequently did while formulating an idea. "One: The accusation was made by a religious zealot who sees evil behind every bush. Two: Neve is somehow a threat, and this would get her out of the way. And three: This is done out of revenge, either against Neve or myself. Once we know what we are dealing with, we'll decide on a course of action."

"What course of action did you have in mind?" Archie asked, still considering the three choices.

"A zealot would be the hardest to dissuade, but if this is, in fact, a case of revenge or jealousy, there is always a financial angle to pursue. Everyone can be bought at the right price. If the accuser can be paid not to testify, the case would very quickly fall apart, and Neve would be safe from persecution."

"I can't think of any religious fanatics in Cranley, can you?" Archie asked, his brow furrowed.

"No. I wager this has nothing to do with witchcraft at all," Hugo mused as he helped himself to another cup of ale. "Just make sure that Neve stays out of your investigation. The committee must not learn of your efforts on Neve's behalf. The accuser must withdraw their accusation without any hint of interference – understand?"

"Of course," Archie replied. "And what will you do in the meantime?"

"I'll start by having a friendly chat with Henry FitzRoy," Hugo replied, his voice suddenly laced with anger. "He's the only person who could have betrayed me, and, like myself, he has much to lose. Henry is playing both sides, pandering to his cousin Mary while still maintaining his loyalty to his uncle, Mary's father, James II. At this stage, he believes an armed invasion by James is a real possibility and must convince James of his loyalty should James reclaim the throne."

Of course, Hugo knew this wouldn't happen and William and Mary would rule for years to come, but Henry FitzRoy, illegitimate son of Charles II, nephew to James II, and cousin to Queen Mary, did not. Revealing his double dealing to Mary, who was no doubt already suspicious, being the clever political consort to her husband for years, would destroy any credibility

Henry had at Court and possibly force Mary's hand in having Henry incarcerated for treason. Hugo had no wish to see Henry arrested, but he would blackmail him if it came to that.

"Watch yourself," Archie advised unnecessarily. "He's a duplicitous bastard."

"That he is," Hugo replied. "But everyone has a weak spot, and I know Henry's. Get some rest, Archie," Hugo said as he turned toward the door. "This might be my last night with my wife," he said sadly. "I want to make sure it's memorable for us both."

TWO

His Majesty, King William III, sank into a comfortable chair in front of the hearth and stretched his booted feet out to the fire, enjoying the warmth. He'd been attending to royal duties since rising at dawn, and his back ached from sitting on the throne, his posture erect and shoulders rigid as he saw petitioner after petitioner, followed by a session with his advisors, and a never-ending supper which left his bowels groaning with indigestion.

The king's steward, Wilf, placed a cup of hot milk at his master's side and retired discreetly to the corner to await further instructions, his day not over until William was tucked into bed. William reached for the cup of milk and took a sip, sighing with pleasure. He drank wine and brandy all day long, but his drink of choice was a simple cup of hot milk with a teaspoon of honey mixed in. It soothed the nerves, as well as his irritated throat. Having to talk all day left William nearly mute by the time he finally came up to bed, a time when Mary liked to discuss the events of the day. Mary had retired early, pleading a headache, and William was more than happy to spend a few blissful minutes alone before his guest arrived.

It was nearly midnight, but Jurgen Van Houten was a man

who favored the night and felt most comfortable under the cover of darkness. William smiled at the thought of his old friend. He'd known Jurgen since the two were hardly more than children. Jurgen was the youngest son of the head groom at the palace where William grew up. He'd been something of a troublemaker then, and the perfect secret ally for a boy whose life revolved around duty and sacrifice. Despite the differences in their stations, Jurgen never treated William as a royal scion, but more as a timid friend who needed gentle prodding to loosen up enough to allow a little bit of fun into his otherwise overly structured life.

William had often snuck out to meet Jurgen in the stables after midnight, and the two had adventures together which seemed wild and exciting at the time but were really nothing more than acts of rebellion more appropriate to peasants. As they reached their adolescence, the adventures had taken on a somewhat different character, but Jurgen assured William that a man had to have real experience of certain aspects of life rather than just acquired knowledge or advice from his elders. William hadn't disagreed, but still blushed with embarrassment when he recalled some of the situations he'd allowed Jurgen to lure him into. Still, he had fond memories of those times, and the experience he'd acquired had served him well, as had the brotherly camaraderie of his only real friendship.

These days, Jurgen was a prosperous businessman who owned several merchant ships, as well as a sugar plantation in the West Indies. William was sure that Jurgen dabbled in slavery and owned several brothels in his native Holland, but he didn't judge. Jurgen was the only person in his life who wasn't intimidated by his station and had the courage to tell William the truth when asked for counsel. And tonight, William could use the advice of a trusted companion.

William smiled as the door opened to admit his friend. Jurgen hadn't changed much over the years. He was still slight and lean, his dark hair worn long, and his pointy beard thick and wiry above the intricately embroidered navy-blue doublet. Jurgen favored dark colors, preferring to appear sober rather than frivolous. His dark eyes twinkled with merriment as he spotted the glass of milk in William's hands.

"Wilf, bring me a brandy. A large one," he added as he took a seat opposite William and folded his hands in front of his lean stomach. "Hard day?" he asked William.

"You might say that, old friend. I'm afraid I'm in need of your advice," William replied as he drained his cup of milk and handed it to Wilf, who had come in on quiet feet with the brandy.

Jurgen's eyes slid to Wilf, but William waved a hand in a gesture of dismissal. Wilf had been with him for nearly a decade, a faithful retainer who knew how to meet his master's every need and keep his mouth shut. Wilf never gossiped, his loyalty absolute. And for that, William treated the man with the respect he deserved and rewarded him handsomely at least once a year to remind Wilf of his gratitude.

"We can speak freely," William assured Jurgen, seeing the look of apprehension on his friend's face. Jurgen valued his privacy, and for good reason, but he had nothing to fear from Wilf.

Jurgen shrugged in acquiescence and turned back to William. "Might this be about the traitor Everly?" Jurgen asked as he took a sip of his brandy and crossed his feet at the ankles in an effort to get more comfortable.

"It's been less than two days since Everly's arrest and already all of London is buzzing with the news. Having been one of Monmouth's conspirators, he's viewed as something of a hero, so I must tread carefully. Executing a man who risked his life to bring about a Protestant monarchy will not only turn him into a martyr but will be the worst possible way to begin my relationship with the British public and nobility. I must rule with a firm hand, but being seen as a despot is not my objective. Besides, the evidence against the man is scant, to say the least."

"You can always release him," Jurgen offered half-heartedly.

"Which would make me seem weak and overly trusting," William countered, "inviting my enemies to plot against me with no fear of reprisal."

"So, if you won't release him and you dare not execute him, what do you propose to do with the man?"

"I can try to obtain more evidence to support the accusation, but as it appears now, it might need to be fabricated, which is dishonest and not the way I choose to rule. I consider myself an honorable man, Jurgen, not someone who orders an arrest and then provides the evidence to support the accusation."

William sighed with frustration, still annoyed with Mary for making the decision to arrest Everly in haste. Had she sought his counsel, he would have advised her to have the man watched, his correspondence intercepted, until they had the proof they needed. But now it was too late, and Everly was already in the Tower, awaiting a trial which would be nothing short of an embarrassment.

"There is another way, Will," Jurgen said, his eyes crinkling with humor as he watched his friend battling with his conscience. Jurgen always found William's desire to be honorable something of a joke, not being encumbered with such a sensibility himself. Sometimes William wondered if Jurgen even had a conscience, or a fear of God, but always felt guilty for thinking such uncharitable thoughts.

"And what way is that?" William finally asked, knowing he wasn't going to like the answer.

"The way in which you can claim total deniability," Jurgen replied. "Why not leave it to me?"

"What have you in mind?"

"Nothing you need to concern yourself with," Jurgen replied as he rose to his feet. "I'll see to everything."

It wouldn't be the first time William had allowed Jurgen to get him out of a difficult situation. He'd taken the blame more than once when William was caught sneaking out of his bedchamber, or returning just before dawn in clothes that were soiled and reeking of cheap perfume and tobacco smoke.

"All right, old friend, and I thank you. Dealing with Everly's possible treason is not something I relish."

William clapped his friend on the shoulder as he laboriously rose to his feet. Wilf was instantly at his side, ready to assist him with preparing for bed. William yawned widely and stood still as Wilf began to undress him.

THREE

Archie left London after midday to ensure that he didn't encounter Lady Everly and Frances on the road. They needed to remain ignorant of his presence in Cranley, allowing him to go about his business unobserved. The only one who'd been entrusted with the secret was Jem, since he could keep Archie abreast of what was going on at the big house without anyone noticing. Few people paid attention to adolescent boys, so Jem would be virtually invisible. Lord Everly had tried to persuade Jem to return home to his father, but Jem was adamant about remaining with the Everlys. He wished to help, and judging by his obstinacy, things at home were not nearly as rosy as Nicholas Marsden had led Hugo to believe in the few letters that he'd sent since taking Jem away from them.

Archie felt sorry for the boy, but his practical nature prevented him from supporting Jem in this foolishness. He'd been given an opportunity few base-born children could even dream of, so whatever caused his dissatisfaction with his new family, it would be best to put it aside and make the most of his good fortune. Archie was certain that Lord Everly shared his view, but under the circumstances, he was in no position to take the time to reason with Jem or deliver him back to his father. Jem would have to sort things out for himself, but for now, he'd be a great help.

By the time Archie made it to Cranley, it was already growing dark, the village settling in for the night. Warm, yellow light glowed in some windows, but most had already been shuttered to keep out the cool night air. Archie glanced up at Everly Manor, sitting proudly on its ridge. One window was lit on the ground floor, but otherwise the house looked dark and forbidding. The children's nursery faced the back of the house, and that's likely where Neve was at this moment. She wasn't the type of woman who entrusted the rearing of her children to servants. She spent as much time with the children as she could, more often than not sending the servants away as she bathed the children and put them to bed. She reminded Archie of his own mother, who'd been kind and gentle, and often sang him to sleep when he was frightened, or simply wished to spend a few extra minutes alone with him. The memory of his mother always brought a tightness to Archie's chest. She was long gone now, the sound of her voice no more than a whisper on the wind.

Archie shook his head stubbornly as if to chase the memories away, then turned his horse northward, toward his father's farm. The little house looked as forlorn as ever, the single window the only beacon of light in an otherwise darkened landscape. There were some sounds from the animals in the barn, but Cecil the dog didn't so much as raise his shaggy head as Archie dismounted and saw to his horse before going to the house. He knocked softly, so as not to frighten his father who seldom had any visitors. Archie's childhood friends, Bill and Arnold, looked in on his da regularly and helped him around the farm, but aside from them, no one ever bothered with the old man anymore.

"Archie, my boy, what a pleasant surprise," Horatio Hicks

exclaimed, clearly pleased. "Come in, come in. I was just about to sup. Will you join me? I'm afraid I've only got the mashed neeps to offer you, but there's some bread, cheese, and ale."

Horatio had been hale and hearty in his day, but now, on the cusp of seventy, although still wiry, he looked thinner than ever, his skin a waxy yellow in the candlelight. His once-red hair was mostly all white, and the cornflower-blue eyes which had many a girl in the village sighing after him had become faded and rheumy. Archie felt a pang of worry, seeing his father so diminished. It'd been only a few weeks since he'd seen him last, but the decline was noticeable, and rapid.

"Are you all right, Da?" Archie asked. "Are you struggling for funds?" Archie couldn't remember the last time he'd seen his father eat meat.

"Oh aye, son. 'Tis not the lack of funds that's bothering me; 'tis me teeth. They're loose, and the gums are bleeding something awful. It's too painful to chew, so I make do with porridge and mashed neeps. A bit of bread soaked in milk does quite nicely for breakfast."

Horatio set down two bowls full of buttery turnips. Archie would have preferred some beef or even rabbit stew, but he was hungry, so this would have to do. He tore off a hunk of bread and spread some butter on it.

"Da, you need to eat certain foods to prevent scurvy, which is what you have. Her ladyship says that eating onions, carrots, cabbage, and oranges will stop the bleeding and strengthen your gums."

"And how does her ladyship know of such things?" Horatio asked suspiciously.

"I don't know, but she's very knowledgeable," Archie replied.

"So, am I to eat an onion the way I would an apple? Just bite and chew?" Horatio guffawed.

"No, Da. But you can make onion soup, for example. Add

some chunks of stale bread before you eat and let them absorb the broth; it's quite tasty. The French eat it all the time."

"I don't hold with French ways, my boy, but if you say it will help me keep the teeth in me mouth, I'll try it. I suppose adding some onions and cabbage won't be too much of a hardship. Never had an orange though. That would be a treat." Horatio wiped his bowl with a piece of bread and drained his cup of ale. "So, what brings you here, Archie? Why are you not with your wife? A lovers' quarrel?"

"No, Da. I need to stay with you for a few days. Someone's made an accusation of witchcraft against her ladyship, and I need to ferret out who without giving myself away."

"Yes, I've heard of that. There's talk in the village. Is she back then?"

"Yes, she returned this afternoon," Archie replied, watching his father to see what he could learn.

Horatio's face clouded with worry. "They'll be arresting her come morning, mark my words. Those examiners have been at the inn these past two days, just biding their time, waiting for something to do. They'll be happy now." Horatio shook his head. "You should go over there, Archie. Tell her to leave while she still can. She should take the children and go."

"Da, his lordship has been arrested for treason, and her ladyship's got nowhere to run. This is her home, and the home of her children. She wishes to prove her innocence."

"Oh, Archie, 'tis not an easy thing to do." Horatio sighed. "This was before your time, but there was a witch fever in England not long before the outbreak of the Civil War. There was a man. Oh, what was his name?" Horatio scratched his stubbled jaw noisily as he tried to recall. "Oh, yes. Matthew Hopkins. He was believed to be the most effective witch hunter. Hundreds of women were put to death because of his findings— innocent women, most of them."

"How did he prove them to be witches?" Archie asked, curious.

"Oh, he had his ways. Some said he had some sort of retracting prong that he pushed into moles and warts and such. If the woman felt no pain, then she was proclaimed a witch. And, of course, there was the swim test and torture. A body will confess to anything to stop unbearable pain."

Archie sat back in his chair and gazed thoughtfully at his father. "Da, are you suggesting that they'll torture Lady Everly?" He'd heard stories as a lad of women practicing black magic, but he couldn't recall any witch trials in Cranley during his childhood, nor did he believe that Reverend Snow would permit Neve Everly to be tortured. Reverend Snow was a good man, an enlightened man, not some backwater fire-and-brimstone preacher. He had great respect for Lord Everly and would do what he could to prevent a miscarriage of justice.

"Make no mistake, Archie. These men will get what they came for, one way or another. Lady or no lady, your mistress will not escape their brand of justice unless the accusation is withdrawn, and fast. Once the trial is underway, superstitious fools will come forth and give evidence of her witchery. Some will think they are serving God, and others will simply take joy in the spectacle, it being the greatest entertainment this village has seen in decades."

"Would people who've known Lord Everly and his lady really make up such lies?" Archie asked with disgust, but he already knew the answer. They would, especially since Hugo and Neve had recently returned from France, a place as close to the immoral dens of Hell as any Englishman could bear to imagine. Not many would cast the first stone, but they would be happy enough to join in once the fun had begun. "Da, is there anything you need doing while I'm here?" Archie asked as he pushed away his empty bowl.

"Wouldn't say no to some firewood. There's a pile of logs needs chopping out back."

Archie nodded and rose to his feet while his father collected the dirty crockery and poured some water from a jug to wash the plates.

Archie stepped outside into the cool April night. The sky was clear and vast, the nearly full moon rising above the tree line in the distance. A legion of stars filled the spring sky. Archie set the first log on the chopping block and balanced the axe in both hands. Physical work was always a good way to release some of his nervous energy. The conversation with his father worried him, especially since Hugo wasn't there to look after his family. If anything happened to the Everlys, Archie would never forgive himself.

By the time he finally came up with an idea, Archie had a sizeable pile of chopped wood. It might not work, but it was a starting point, which is exactly what he needed at the moment. It was too late in the evening to put his plan into action, but tomorrow would do just as well. All he could do at the moment was stack the wood, put away the axe, and get some sleep.

FOUR

APRIL 1689

Surrey, England

Archie rose well before dawn and helped himself to some leftover bread and cheese before slipping quietly from the cottage. His father was still asleep in the curtained alcove, which held the bed in which his parents had slept since the day they had wed all those years ago. Now, his father slept there alone, his shrunken form barely taking up even half the mattress. He snored lightly, but at least he wasn't wheezing, which Archie supposed was a good sign. Aside from the scurvy, he seemed to be in fine health.

The air outside was fragrant with new grass and rich earth, the sky clear. It promised to be a lovely day, the type of day when everyone found an excuse to step outside, if only for a few minutes. Archie debated taking his horse, but then decided that he would go on foot. It wasn't far, and he would be less conspicuous should anyone happen to be on the road at such an early hour.

Archie cut through the fields and followed a wooded track

in order to approach his destination from the back. The shutters were thrown open, the windows of the house already alight, and smoke curling from the squat chimney. Archie positioned himself behind the barn and settled in for the wait.

The sun rose majestically behind the scrim of trees to the east, painting the world a violent red before beginning its ascent, the rays going from crimson to a peachy gold, when Archie heard the banging of the door and the slap of bare feet on the ground as three children erupted from the house and made for the privy. The two younger boys went in together, arguing noisily as they did their business.

"'Urry up in there, me feet are freezin'," the girl outside called as she hopped from foot to foot. Her dark hair spilled down her back in tangled coils, and her breath came out in white puffs as she blew on her hands.

The two boys finally emerged and ran back to the house, giggling as their sister took a deep breath of air before stepping into the stinking privy. Archie waited patiently until she'd finished and emerged into the chilly morning, pulling her shawl tighter around her shoulders.

"Tess," he whispered, nearly giving the poor girl an apoplectic fit. She whirled around, her face a mask of terror as her eyes searched for the sound of the voice. "Shh, 'tis only me, Tessy."

"Good God, Archibald Hicks, what in the name o' the Good Lord are ye doin' skulkin' behind privies at the crack o' dawn?" the girl demanded, her cheeks flaming with indignation. She was no more than eleven, but she was so slight that she looked to be as young as her brothers, who were under the age of ten.

Tess Henshall bore a striking resemblance to her sister Ruby, who worked as a maid at Everly Manor, and Archie thought she'd be a pretty young thing someday, a fine prize for any lad. Tess wasn't as timid as Ruby, and whereas her sister was pale, Tess was glowing with good health.

"I'm sorry; I didn't mean to startle you, Tess, but I need to have a quiet word."

"So, ye couldn't wait 'til I was all dressed and proper?" she demanded in righteous outrage.

"I don't want anyone to know I'm here, least of all your siblings."

"Right, what'ye want then?" Tess was rubbing her arms with her hands to keep warm, so Archie pulled off his cloak and draped it around her shoulders as he pulled her behind the barn out of sight of the window, where he could see Mistress Henshall going about her morning chores.

"I just need a moment of your time, Tessy."

"Go on then."

"I need to get into the rooms of the clergymen who are staying at the inn." Tess worked at the King's Arms as a maid-of-all-work. She cleaned rooms, peeled vegetables, and took out chamber pots. The poor girl hardly saw the light of day with starting just after dawn and finishing at closing time. The Henshalls had always been poor, but since the death of Master Henshall, the family was barely surviving, and the number of children to feed didn't help matters. The three older girls were already employed, and the boys went into the village every day, earning a pittance by hiring themselves out to anyone who needed help. Mistress Henshall didn't have the means to pay for apprenticeships, so the boys didn't stand to better their fortunes.

"And 'ow do ye mean to do that, I ask ye?" Tess demanded.

"Do they not leave their rooms?" Archie asked.

"They take their meals in their rooms," Tess replied testily. "And I ain't riskin' my employment."

"Do they not go out at all?"

"They've gone to the church to consult with Reverend Snow, otherwise they keep themselves to themselves. Why do ye need to get in there anyhow?" Tess asked, curious as ever. Ruby wouldn't have asked; she was too timid.

"The less you know the better," Archie replied. "What can you tell me about them?"

"Not much."

"What are they like?" Archie persisted.

"Well, I don't know, do I?" Tess answered testily. "I can't tell much about 'em from the contents o' their chamber pots."

"Come, Tess, you must be able to tell me something."

Tess shrugged irritably. "They're old."

That wasn't saying much since to a girl of eleven; Archie was probably old as well. "Do you know their names?"

"Aye, I 'eard Master Reeve addressin' 'em. There's Bishop Cotton. 'E's got a room to 'imself, and seems to be in charge," Tess replied thoughtfully. "'E called for hot water twice. Likes to wash, unlike the other two. Bishop Hargrave is the oldest. 'E smells," Tess added, "and 'ardly 's any teeth. 'E eats mostly bread soaked in milk since 'e can't chew meat. Seems a bit 'ard o' 'earing too."

"And the third man?" Archie prodded.

"The third 'un is the youngest. Bishop Oswald. 'E frightens me," Tess confessed, shuddering at the memory of Bishop Oswald.

"Why?"

"I can't rightly say, but there's somethin' about 'im. A cruelty in 'is eyes, I suppose. 'Is mouth is always pressed into a thin line, and 'is eyes dart about the room, as if tryin' to find sin in every corner. I 'eard 'im say to Bishop Cotton that Mistress Reeve is tryin' to bewitch 'im."

Not surprising, Archie thought grimly. Mistress Reeve was a handsome woman in her mid-twenties. She had a friendly

nature and tried to make everyone feel welcome and at ease in
her husband's inn. If a man claimed that she tried to bewitch
him, then likely he found himself lusting after her and couldn't
admit that the fault lay with him and not with the young
woman. A man like that could be very dangerous, especially to
Lady Everly, who was beautiful and often too outspoken.

"And what did Bishop Cotton reply?" Archie asked
carefully.

"'E said that they might examine Mistress Reeve after the
trial, if the situation called for it."

Archie was taken aback by the response. Were these men
planning to start a witch hunt in Cranley? His thoughts
instantly turned to Frances. He knew people whispered behind
her back. There was talk of her having relations with Hugo
before her marriage to Archie, and the fact that she'd lived for
several years in France, where every woman was believed to be
licentious, hardly helped.

"Can you signal to me when they leave if I hide out behind
the inn and let me in by the back door?" Archie demanded with
a renewed sense of urgency.

"Makin' a habit of skulkin' behind privies, are ye?"

"All right, smart mouth," Archie growled, "I'll make it worth
your while." He held up a sixpence coin. He had to get into the
rooms and see what he could find out about these men and what
evidence they possessed. He had to discover who had made the
accusation against Neve to have any chance of helping her.
"Get me in and this coin is yours."

"And if ye don't find what ye're lookin' for?" Tess asked
suspiciously as she eyed the coin greedily. A sixpence was a
fortune to a girl like Tess.

"The coin is yours anyway. Just get me in and alert me if
they come back. That's all I ask. Do we have an agreement?"

Tess was about to answer when her mother came outside

and bellowed, "Where are ye, Tess? I need yer 'elp with the little 'uns before ye leave for work."

"I got to go. Be behind the inn 'round noontime."

"Thanks, Tessy," Archie said with a smile and vanished into the woods.

FIVE

I watched silently as the flaming orb of the sun began its ascent over the line of trees outside the bedroom window. I'd purposely left the shutters and the bed hangings open, suddenly terrified of the dark. There were times when I enjoyed our private little world where nothing mattered but Hugo and I in our great bed, but today wasn't one of those days. I drew strength from the solid little bodies of my children who snuggled next to me in sleep. Hugo didn't approve of taking the children into our bed, but he wasn't here, and I needed whatever solace I could get. I wasn't sure what this day would bring, but I knew it wouldn't be anything good. I tried not to think of Hugo and what he'd been up to since I left London with Frances yesterday. I would never have left him if it weren't for the children, and now my heart was torn in two, one half here with my babies, and the other with my husband, who was once again in mortal danger.

I half expected someone to come and drag me away last night, but despite my state of nervous expectation, no one showed up. Perhaps word hadn't reached "The Inquisition" that I was back in Cranley, although in a small village where gossip normally spread like wildfire that was highly unlikely. No doubt something would happen today; I was under no illusions. I knew what happened to women accused of witchcraft in the seventeenth century. My only hope was proving my innocence and relying on the good people of Cranley to come to my defense. No matter what happened, it couldn't be as bad as being thrown into Newgate Prison and left to die without any hope of release or trial. I had survived that, if only just, and I would survive this.

Hot tears rolled down my cheeks, my tear glands completely indifferent to my bravado. I was scared—terrified—and I had good reason to be. The outcome of the trial had nothing to do with either justice or truth, and everything to do with prejudice, ignorance, and superstition, not to mention a desire to inspire fear and terrify the masses into submission. The Church was good at that.

I nearly jumped out of my skin as the door handle slowly turned, and a ghostly presence appeared in the room.

"I'm sorry; I couldn't sleep," Frances said as she climbed into bed next to the sleeping form of Michael. "I'm scared, Neve."

I reached out and took Frances's hand. It was cold and small in mine, her face drawn and gray in the peachy light streaming from the window. "How much time do you think we have?" I asked.

"Not too much. Ruby said that the members of the committee are staying at the inn. They'll be here today."

"Can I ride my pony today?" Valentine asked sleepily. "Is Archie back?"

"No, sweetheart, Archie isn't back yet, but maybe Joe can take you out riding this morning."

"But I want Archie," Valentine protested. "I don't like Joe."

"Archie will be back soon, Valentine," Frances said

patiently. "How about we take a walk after your riding lesson and pick some wildflowers for Mama? Would you like that?"

"No," Valentine said simply. "Maybe Michael wants to pick flowers. He's still a baby," she stated with derision. This made Michael, who'd just woken up, cry.

"Not a baby," he wailed.

I put my arms around both my children and drew them to me to hide my tears from them. They were still so achingly young and innocent. What if they lost both Hugo and myself? There were so many orphans, and the only blood relative my children had was the accursed Clarence, who wanted nothing to do with us and would probably rejoice if any tragedy befell us. I could never trust him to look after my children. My only hope, should the worst come to pass, lay in Archie and Frances. I knew that I could trust them with my life, but somehow, at this moment, the thought wasn't comforting. I wanted to see my children grow up; I wanted to share their triumphs and wipe away their tears. I knew that every mother felt the same, regardless of station or the century in which she lived, but so many were carried off by disease, wars, and, as might be in my case, rigged trials.

"Hungry, Mama," Michael complained, now that he'd stopped crying.

"I have an idea. Let's have breakfast in bed today," I suggested.

"Oh, yes," the children said in unison. They thought it was a fun game, but in some strange attempt to block out reality, I refused to get out of bed. As long as I was in bed, I was safe, untouchable.

"I'll tell Cook," Frances said as she slid out of the big bed.

"Thank you."

Frances gave me a warm smile. She understood, but I could see that she was more frightened than she was letting on. Frances was a different person when Archie was around, but when separated from him, she tended to regress to the frightened, insecure girl she'd been when we had first met her. I wished that Hugo would have sent Archie home with us, but knowing Hugo, he had his reasons for asking him to stay on in London. I trusted his judgment, but without a man about the house, I felt as vulnerable and exposed as Frances.

* * *

It was mid-morning when they came. I smoothed down my skirts and patted my uncovered hair, suddenly self-conscious of my appearance. Would it make any difference to these men how I looked? Would appearing sober and demure influence their opinion of me, or were their minds already made up, their decision made? My hands shook as Ruby knocked timidly on the parlor door and announced the visitors.

"Come," I called out, wishing that I could climb out the window and run for my life. I was glad that the children weren't in the house. Valentine was in the paddock with Joe. Once she got on her pony, she forgot her pique at not having Archie to teach her, and Michael was in the meadow, picking flowers with Frances. Both children had been subdued, even after our breakfast in bed, instinctively sensing that something was wrong. Valentine gave me a great big hug before going off with Joe, her eyes full of worry. She was very perceptive for a child of three.

I was surprised to see Reverend Snow rather than the grim men from the diocese. He looked uncomfortable as he entered the room, his wide brown eyes gazing at something just beyond my shoulder rather than straight at me, which was a sure sign that he was here against his better judgment. I liked Reverend Snow, and thought him a good and kind man, but today I burned with resentment against him, furious that he would believe such tripe about me and summon the men from the ecclesiastical committee.

"Reverend Snow, please have a seat," I offered coolly. "Can I offer you some refreshment?"

"No, Your Ladyship, but I thank you." The reverend remained standing, his hands tightly clasped in front of him. He radiated tension and regret. "My lady, this is not a social call, much as I would like it to be. I don't know if you've been informed, but an accusation of witchcraft has been made against you."

"By whom? I have a right to know," I demanded, suddenly outraged now that I heard the words spoken out loud.

"I am not at liberty to say. Once an accusation of such conduct is made, I must report it to the bishop. I had no choice in the matter," he added apologetically. "I hope you understand."

I inclined my head. Did I understand? The man had known me for years, had offered me counsel when I needed it. Could he really believe that I was Satan's familiar and practiced the dark arts?

"I don't believe a word of it," he exclaimed vehemently, as if he'd read my thoughts. "Lady Everly, I know you to be a good, God-fearing woman, and I will state as much at the trial, but you must beware. People are frightened, and they will say anything when they feel threatened, or when they believe there will be no consequences to their actions, at least not to them personally."

"Are you here to arrest me, Reverend Snow?" I asked calmly, despite the erratic banging of my heart.

"I am here on behalf of the committee. I asked to be the one to speak to you. Since there're no facilities for detaining prisoners in Cranley, I have asked the committee to allow you to remain in your own home until the trial, which will be in three days' time. I ask that you do not leave the village, or the house, for that matter. I've brought Mark Watson with me. He will remain here with you until the trial. I've asked him to be respectful and unobtrusive. Perhaps he could sleep in the kitchen, or anywhere else you deem appropriate."

"So, am I under house arrest?" I asked, suddenly wishing I could just throw both men out. I knew Mark Watson from the village. He was a burly man in his late thirties, one who could restrain me with one arm tied behind his back. We'd never actually spoken to each other, but he always appeared taciturn, his anger barely contained. They'd picked the perfect man for the job. Mark Watson would have no qualms about doing what was necessary to keep me from leaving, particularly if he'd be handsomely paid.

"In a manner of speaking, yes. Please comply with this order. It will only make things worse if you don't. The trial will be held at the church after Sunday service."

"And am I not allowed to seek evidence which might help me, or round up witnesses who would speak on my behalf?" I asked, astonished by the unfairness of the situation.

Reverend Snow shook his head. "If anyone wishes to speak on your behalf, they must come forward of their own accord at the trial. And I can't imagine what evidence you might present to disprove an accusation of witchcraft. All I can advise is that you appear respectful, composed, and try to maintain your dignity. Any outburst on your part will result in ill will toward you, which might sway the judges' favor." Reverend Snow backed toward the door, clearly as eager to leave as I was to be rid of him. "Good day to you, Lady Everly, and my heartiest sympathies on his lordship's arrest. I had hoped he would be here in your hour of need."

"As had I," I said, barely holding back the tears.

SIX

Archie sprang to attention when he saw Tess emerging into the yard behind the inn. This was the fourth time she'd come out, but, before, it'd been to empty out chamber pots, hang out the washing, and go to the privy herself. She'd kept her eyes firmly averted from where he waited, her shoulders stiff with tension. Archie was bored of sitting in one spot, but he had to be within range of the back door of the inn to spot Tess coming out.

She looked around furtively before giving a small wave. Archie was beside her in seconds.

"They've gone to the downstairs parlor for their midday meal. There are quite a few patrons t'day, so it might take longer than normal to get served. Ye 'ave a 'alf 'our, at best. Follow me," she said as she led him into the inn and up the dim stairs to the rooms above. "If they catch ye, I'll say I'd never seen ye. Understand?"

"Yes."

"These two rooms 'ere." Tess unlocked the rooms and motioned for Archie to enter. "I'll be back when the church clock strikes the 'our to lock 'em again. 'Urry!"

Tess disappeared down the stairs while Archie searched the

first room. The inn was a small one, the rooms cramped and dark. A small window which faced the front yard was so grimy as to barely let in any light. Archie looked around. Other than two cloaks and hats, he saw nothing of interest. There were no folios which might contain documents, or anything else in writing. The two clergymen who shared this room didn't bring so much as a clean shirt. The room stank of stale sweat and unwashed feet. The bed linens were rumpled and gray, the bed not nearly large enough for two grown men to share.

Archie gave up and moved on to the other room. This one was a trifle larger, with a window that faced the back of the inn. The chamber was cleaner, and the bed was neatly made, likely by the occupant himself. The window was partially open to allow some fresh air to ventilate the room. This man appeared to be more fastidious, his cloak hanging on a peg and his fresh linen neatly folded and stowed in a small leather satchel. Archie looked beneath the garments, but there was nothing else in the bag. A small bar of lye soap and a hairbrush were placed next to the ewer and basin, and there was a well-thumbed Bible on the pillow, but there was nothing else of a personal nature. Archie turned on his heel in frustration. Did these clerics not bring anything in writing? There wasn't so much as a pot of ink or writing paper.

Archie stilled as he heard heavy footsteps on the stairs. It couldn't be Tess, so it was either the innkeeper or one of the clergymen. He pressed his ear to the door. The steps were growing closer, and since there were only two rooms in the passageway, they were heading toward one of the rooms. Archie looked around in a moment of panic. There was nowhere to hide. The only avenue of escape was the window, which was barely large enough for Archie to squeeze through. He crawled through the window, cursing silently as his shoulders got momentarily stuck in the narrow frame, then laid himself flat on the pitched roof, praying for purchase as he dug his heels into a slight indentation. If he moved an inch, he would slide straight down into the yard, feet first. He'd have sprained ankles at best, broken bones at worst. And he would most likely be caught snooping.

Archie held his breath as he heard a movement right next to his head. A pale hand appeared for a moment before the window was pulled shut and locked from the inside. Archie remained still, pondering what to do. He saw Tess emerge from the inn, looking about her like a frightened rabbit. She must have seen the man heading back upstairs and couldn't find a way to warn Archie.

"Psst," Archie hissed.

Tess looked up, her mouth opening in shock when she saw Archie plastered against the roof. She was about to say something when a gruff voice called out to her from inside.

"Tess, where are ye, girl? There's vegetables as needs peelin', and slops to be fed to yon pig. Get yer sorry arse in 'ere this minute."

Tess threw Archie a look of apology as she disappeared back inside.

Archie shifted his weight and yelped in surprise as the heel of his boot came free and he slid down the pitched roof, crashing onto his left side painfully. The yard beneath the roof was littered with wooden splinters, pebbles, and heaps of refuse which would be shoveled into a bucket and fed to the pig. Archie felt a wooden splinter digging into his ribs as his face scraped against something hard and sharp. His shoulders were bruised from squeezing through the narrow window, and his left ankle throbbed painfully.

"What the devil was that?" the innkeeper bellowed from somewhere inside.

Archie got to his feet and hobbled for cover. A trickle of blood ran down his cheek and his left side hurt like hell, but he didn't think anything was actually broken. Archie massaged his sore wrist as he hid behind a thick oak just as the publican exploded into the backyard. He looked around in confusion, then noticed the disturbed patch of mud where Archie had fallen. The innkeeper looked up, shrugged, and went back inside just as Archie slid down to the ground and leaned against the tree for support. Every inch of his left side throbbed, but he didn't care about the pain. He'd found nothing of value, which was concerning since time was running out.

Archie saw Tess's anxious face peer into the yard, her eyes scanning for him. She looked relieved when she failed to spot him, and emerged into the yard with a bucket full of slops for the pig. At least she didn't get caught helping him, which was something. He wouldn't want to be responsible for Tess losing her place. At eleven, she was helping to support her family. He'd have to stop by later and thank her for helping him.

Archie allowed himself a few minutes to recover before laboriously getting to his feet. It was a long walk to his father's farm, and would take him at least two hours in his condition, especially since he had to stay off the road.

"Damn it all to Hell," Archie cursed as he stepped onto his injured foot. He found a stout stick and used it to take some of the weight off his ankle as he ambled along. He needed to come up with a new plan for helping Lady Everly.

SEVEN

Hugo pulled his hat lower over his eyes and stepped into the soupy fog of the April morning. The Black Dog was a small and dingy inn with two tiny rooms situated in the rafters, and a publican who served only a greasy stew and cheap ale all week long. It catered to the lower orders and reeked of rancid meat, spilled beer, and loneliness, but it suited Hugo just fine. He needed to lose himself among the anonymous throngs of London until it was time to return to the Tower, and no one paid any heed to the patrons of the Black Dog. During the day, it was frequented by ferrymen and stevedores who came in for an affordable dinner, and at night, it was filled with men who wanted a bit of company, but had nowhere else to go.

The street was already roiling with activity, the road full of wagons, riders on horseback, and women going about their morning shopping. Hugo kept away from the walls for fear of having a chamber pot upended on his head, or stepping into a pile of refuse concealed by the shadows created by the overhanging upper floors. He was dressed like a tradesman, but he didn't need to smell like one, especially when about to confront Henry FitzRoy, 1st Duke of Grafton.

Hugo walked along briskly, his hands thrust into the pockets of his leather doublet. In truth, he wasn't sure what he hoped to accomplish. Even if Henry owned up to the truth, there wasn't very much he could do at this stage. Withdrawing his statement would do little to exonerate Hugo since the damage had already been done. The best he could hope for was to discover exactly what their Royal Majesties had on him and attempt to discredit the evidence. Hugo growled in frustration as he increased his pace. Neve was alone in Cranley, facing a trumped-up accusation of witchcraft, and he was powerless to help her. Archie would do what he could, but Hugo felt a maddening helplessness which stoked the fires of his anger.

Damn Henry FitzRoy, damn the Marquise de Chartres, and damn James II most of all for the coward that he is, Hugo thought savagely. The web of political intrigue which he'd been surrounded by since adolescence seemed to have become even more intricate and twice as dangerous, making Hugo feel like a trapped fly about to face the spider. He'd put his life on the line repeatedly, and what had he accomplished except disgrace, attempts on his life, and the need to constantly look over his shoulder? And now his wife was threatened, his children vulnerable, and his estates in danger of being confiscated if he were pronounced guilty, leaving his son with nothing to inherit but shame and poverty.

There was a time when Hugo longed to return home from the twenty-first century, believing his rightful place to be at Everly Manor and at the side of the king he served, but now Max's words kept ringing in his ears. "Go back to the future, be Lord Everly. Take over my life." Max had no idea how tempting his offer was. To live a life of peace and religious freedom was a reality Hugo could only dream of. Even if by some miracle he managed to talk his way out of this charge, there was still the accusation against Neve and the never-ending political wheeling and dealing which was nearly impossible to avoid for a man of his standing. Perhaps if he didn't know what the future held, he'd be more driven to change the present, but the die was cast, the history books printed, and nothing could be done to undo the events of the past few months. The consequences of James's actions would reverberate throughout history, resulting in several failed rebellions and countless deaths, but at this stage, Hugo no longer wanted any part of that story. He just wanted to live in peace with his family—a dream which was slipping away at an alarming rate.

Hugo finally reached the duke's London residence and looked around for a suitable spot to wait for Henry FitzRoy to make an appearance. Hugo had imagined this encounter from every angle and decided that a sword wouldn't do him much good. Instead, he had brought a flintlock pistol and a dagger, neither of which he planned on using. The pistol wasn't even primed or loaded; it was simply for show, since Hugo had no intentions of shooting Henry FitzRoy. He had enough problems without killing the man in cold blood. However, he did wish to speak with him, and that in itself presented a problem. Hugo couldn't very well call at Henry's house since he was presumed to be in the Tower, so he had to await his opportunity.

Two hours later, there was still no activity. Henry was a night owl, so it was reasonable to assume that if he went out, it wouldn't be first thing in the morning. It was now well past noon, but the house looked almost uninhabited. Had Henry decamped to France? Hugo wondered. He stepped from foot to foot, tired of standing.

If an interview with Henry produced no results, he would need to figure out a different way to clear his name, but at the moment, nothing at all came to mind. Short of requesting an audience with the royal couple, there was nothing he could do, and even if he were granted an interview, there was nothing he could say that would prove his innocence.

Hugo tensed as he saw a fine carriage come around the

corner and roll up to the house, the coachman dressed in the livery of the Duke of Grafton. He must have just come from the carriage house behind the manor. This was Hugo's chance, as long as the carriage wasn't for the duchess. He left his vantage point and walked in the direction of the vehicle. The coachman paid him no mind, so Hugo stopped just behind the carriage as he waited for Henry to emerge from the house. Hugo noted with satisfaction that this was one of the more luxurious models, with doors on both sides. Most carriages were limited to just the one door, but Henry FitzRoy had to have the latest style from France.

A few moments later, the door opened and Henry finally emerged, dressed in a suit of aquamarine satin, cream-colored hose, and a wig which hung nearly to his waist. His shoes boasted shiny red heels, which were complemented by red bows at the front. He carried a silver-tipped walking stick, which would make for a very nice weapon should he decide to bash Hugo over the head.

Hugo pulled open the door of the carriage just as Henry's servant pulled it open on the opposite side and the two men got in simultaneously, Henry eyeing Hugo with undisguised horror.

"Everly, I was told you'd been arrested," Henry gasped as he made to open the carriage door to step out.

"Don't you dare get out, FitzRoy. Instruct your coachman to drive," Hugo demanded as he trained a pistol on Henry.

The Duke of Grafton visibly paled, his hand shaking as he used the walking stick to knock on the roof of the carriage. The vehicle began to move down the street, its progress slow and stately due to the midday traffic.

"Their Majesties claim to have evidence of my treason, evidence they could have gotten only from you," Hugo spat out, disgusted with the fop before him. "Did you volunteer it, or did pressure have to be applied?"

"Hugo, I am sorry, truly I am, but I had no choice. My

cousin gave me an ultimatum. It was either your head on the block, or mine."

"Ah, so the choice was obvious," Hugo replied sarcastically.

"What would you have done?" Henry demanded, suddenly angry. "I'm in a precarious position, Hugo, torn between my cousin, the Queen of England, and my uncle, the exiled king who hopes to regain the throne. Betraying Mary can result in death and the forfeiture of my lands and titles. Turning my back on my uncle can have very much the same outcome should he manage to gather enough troops and gold to mount a successful attack."

"So, you sacrificed me to save your own skin," Hugo said dispassionately. "And what do you think Mary would do if she suddenly came into possession of evidence of *your* treason?" Hugo asked nastily.

"You have nothing, Everly."

"Don't I? I have about as much as you did when you gave me up. Evidence can be conjured up, just as it can disappear. Wouldn't you say?"

Henry shook his head, making his curls sway like a curtain. "Hugo, the evidence I gave to Mary is flimsy at best. The letter could have been written by anyone, anyone at all. There's no signature, and no seal. You can fight this, and you can win. William and Mary would never sign an order of execution without granting you a trial. I believe you have a fair chance of walking away from this unscathed."

"I see you've given this some thought," Hugo mused, lowering his gun. "How very considerate of you."

"Hugo, killing me will accomplish nothing. And it's not as if you were innocent, is it? I don't know how you managed to get out of the Tower, but you can stay and fight to clear your name, or you can escape to France, as you have before, although I'm not too sure of the welcome you'd receive from the king or the Marquis de Chartres. He needs you in England, not cooling your heels in France while playing the courtier at Versailles," Henry FitzRoy sneered. "Now, would you be kind enough to get out of my carriage? I am on my way to see my cousin, Her Majesty Queen Mary. Shall I send her your regards?"

"By all means," Hugo replied sourly as he opened the door and jumped from the carriage, which was barely moving. The last thing Hugo saw as he turned to walk away was Henry Fitz-Roy's self-satisfied smile.

EIGHT

Hugo laid the pistol on the table, removed the dagger from the shaft of his boot, and sat heavily on the bed, his head in his hands. The meeting with FitzRoy had been an utter waste of time, and he felt humiliated and upset by the other man's dismissive attitude. As things stood now, the royal couple had no choice but to try Hugo; to release him would make them appear weak and gullible. So, he was back to square one. He had one more day until he had to return to the Tower, but he had no plan.

Furthermore, he was worried sick about Neve. Hugo knew that Archie would do everything in his power to keep Neve from coming to trial, but the way things were going, it was entirely possible that he would be unable to stop the proceedings. Hugo longed to be with Neve, but instead, he would molder in the Tower while awaiting the mockery of a trial which would probably send him to the gallows. He supposed that being a nobleman would at least ensure that he was beheaded rather than hanged, a more noble and dignified death, in Hugo's opinion, but then again, if convicted of treason, he might be sentenced to death by drawing and quartering, something he wouldn't wish on his worst enemy.

Hugo sat up and uncorked the bottle of brandy he'd purchased the night before in a fit of despair. He took a large swig, and then another, before resolutely returning the bottle to its place. He jumped to his feet, grabbed the dagger and left the room, suddenly in a hurry.

NINE

Late-afternoon shadows had lengthened into evening, a miasma of gloom settling on the house. Even the children were subdued. They'd had their supper in the nursery and were now quietly playing, too overcome with the atmosphere to fight and argue as they usually did. Neve sat in the front parlor staring into the fire, an open book on her lap. She didn't appear to be frightened, just pensive and weary. Her lips were pressed together into a thin line and her eyes were hooded, her gaze unfocused.

The servants had been jittery since Reverend Snow's departure, unnerved by the unexpected installation of Mark Watson. They floated on silent feet, their gaze averted as they served the evening meal and laid the fires. Frances suspected that Neve knew exactly what they were thinking. A person didn't need to be guilty to be judged so, and in their eyes, she had already been condemned, and so had Frances by association. She suspected that the servants already questioned her relationship to the Everlys. Hugo presented Frances as his ward, but the people in the village and on the estate were well aware that no ward had existed before Hugo's mysterious disappearance a few years ago. There was talk of witchcraft then, Neve being the one suspected of spiriting Lord Everly away with the help of Satan. Frances knew of Neve's ordeal in Newgate Prison after Lord Everly's sister Jane had accused her of witchcraft and paid some thugs to arrest her without a warrant, deliver her to the prison, and leave her there without any hope of a trial.

And then Lord Everly had returned from France, the place most Englishmen thought was right next to Hell itself, being the den of iniquity and lewdness. She'd heard the whispers in the kitchen when Polly assumed no one was listening. Polly thought that Frances was Lord Everly's mistress, a cast-off lover who'd been married off to Archie for the sake of convenience. *If only Archie knew*, Frances thought. If anything befell Neve, Frances would be next in line. Oh, how she wished Archie was back. He'd taken her from the convent and within a space of a few hours went from being a threat to becoming her champion and protector, the one person in the world who would do anything for her. Lord and Lady Everly had taken care of her and loved her as a daughter, but Archie was her husband, the man sworn to protect her, the man she trusted with every fiber of her being. The servants were suspicious of him as well, despite the fact that he'd grown up near Cranley and had been one of them his whole life. The only one who remained unaffected by all the speculation was Ruby.

Frances called for Ruby as soon as she returned to her bedchamber under the pretense of needing her help, but what she wanted was to talk to Ruby privately. Archie had taught Frances to be vigilant, and to always be acutely aware of everything that went on around her. He had taught her to notice signs of danger and discontent in those close to her, especially servants. He'd also taught her how to fight during the years they'd spent in Rouen. Frances knew how to use a dagger. She'd protested when Archie had first suggested teaching her, but now she was glad. She wasn't planning on stabbing anyone, but it was good to know that she wasn't completely helpless, not like she'd been before when Lionel beat her and raped her, and she thought she'd had no recourse. Perhaps if she'd been the woman she was now, she simply would have killed him in his sleep and saved herself, but forewarned was forearmed, and she would never allow anyone to abuse her again.

Frances turned when Ruby entered the room and smiled at the girl to put her at ease. She always looked a little unsure of herself, but tonight she was noticeably jumpy, her eyes darting around nervously. "Ye called for me, Mistress Hicks?"

"I just wanted to talk to you," Frances explained, gesturing Ruby to a chair.

Ruby perched on the end, her back rigid. She wasn't accustomed to being treated like a guest, despite Frances's attempts to befriend her. She was a waif of a girl, just about Jem's age, and treated unfairly by the other servants, who assigned her the lowliest tasks and left her out of their gossip due to her age. But Ruby was no fool, Frances knew that, and she picked up on everything that went on in the house. Sometimes being invisible was an asset.

"Ruby, what do you know of Mark Watson?" Frances asked without preamble. Ruby had lived in Cranley all her life, as had Mark Watson, so she was bound to know something of the man, even if only by reputation. The man scared Frances, and she hoped that Ruby would allay her suspicions by telling her that he was a good man.

Ruby shrugged and looked away for a moment, gathering her thoughts. "He's a rough man, Mistress Hicks. He's docile enough when sober, but 'e has a black temper when drunk, and gets violent. He keeps company with the blacksmith," she added, shuddering. Frances had heard stories of the blacksmith's legendary temper. He wasn't a man to be trifled with, and his brute strength, acquired through years of hard work, made him dangerous when provoked.

"And does Master Watson have a wife?" Frances asked. She

couldn't recall if he were married from seeing him on occasion at church.

Ruby blushed to the roots of her hair, and her lip began to tremble.

"What is it, Ruby?" Frances asked gently. "Has he done something to hurt you?"

Ruby shook her head stubbornly. "No' me."

"Who then?"

"Mark Watson had a wife, but she died years ago. He tried courtin' me mam after Da died. Mam were still grievin', but said she needed a man about the place, 'specially with all us children to take care o'. Master Watson were kind at first; chopped wood, brought buckets o' water from the well, even played with the younger boys, but then 'e changed once 'e thought Mam and 'e had an understandin'."

"In what way?"

"He'd get in a temper and curse at Mam and me younger siblings, callin' 'em useless vermin. Mam tried to soothe 'im with sweet words, the way she did with Da, but he'd get more abusive, 'is anger fueled by 'er attempts to calm 'im. One night I saw 'im hit Mam in the face after she said somethin' to displease 'im. She began to cry, and 'e called her a stupid cow and stormed off, slammin' the door. Mam banned 'im from the house after that, said she didn't need no brute about the place to lord it over us. We were that glad. He frightened us, and we all knew what would happen should they wed. We'd feel the sting of his belt more often than no', mistress, and more besides."

"More?" Frances asked, confused.

"Tessy and me, we saw the way 'e looked at us. We were just eight and ten then, but 'e watched us when Mam wasn't lookin', 'is eyes undressing us. A few times 'e followed me to the privy and pulled the door open, hopin' to catch me with me skirt around me waist. It wouldn't 'ave stopped there."

"Did you tell your mother?" Frances asked, horrified. She

knew only too well what it was like to be a helpless child stalked by a grown man.

"Oh, aye. Mam 'ad noticed it too, and that were part of the reason she sent 'im away. He never forgave 'er and spread vicious lies about 'er in the village. But people 'ave known me mam since she were a girl, so no one believed 'im. She's a virtuous woman, and 'ad no man about the place since Master Watson."

"I see," Frances said thoughtfully. "Thank you, Ruby. Just give him a wide berth for the next few days."

"I will, that," Ruby replied. "May I go now?"

"Of course."

Frances sat on her bed and chewed on her lip. She was afraid to have Mark Watson in the house, especially during the night when she would be alone. She'd seen the way he looked at her, as if she were fair game. His gaze had been insolent and lewd at the same time, and intimidating. He'd never dare look at her if Archie were here, but Archie was in London, and she felt exposed and vulnerable. She'd known as soon as she looked at the man that he had a cruel temper. There was something in his stare that reminded her of Lionel. He'd been mild and charming when they had first met, but changed immediately after the wedding, subjecting her to the kind of cruelty her thirteen-year-old self could never have imagined. Now she was older and had more experience of the world, she knew that many violent men hid behind a placid mask that they presented to the world, and according to Ruby, Mark Watson was one of them.

Frances had passed him on her way to the stairs after leaving the parlor. He'd requisitioned a chair, and positioned himself by the door—a constant reminder that they couldn't leave. No wonder the children were so quiet. They were frightened by his presence.

Frances sprang to her feet, picked up a candle, and made her way downstairs. She shouldn't leave Neve alone with a man like that, not at a time when Neve was alone and helpless. They'd sleep together tonight, safe in the big bed with the children, and tomorrow maybe Archie would come home.

Frances avoided looking at Mark Watson as she hurried past him toward the parlor and opened the door. Neve was still sitting in the same spot; the book opened to the same page. Jem sat across from her, his eyelids drooping as he stared into the fire. It was upsetting to see Neve so withdrawn, but it was even stranger to see Jem so subdued. The boy who came back wasn't the boy who left them in Paris.

Frances set down her candle and took a seat on a settle, suddenly feeling even more deflated. Until that moment, she had hoped that everything would resolve itself, but she suddenly realized with a flash of unexpected clarity that nothing would ever be the same.

TEN

APRIL 1689

London, England

Max watched the last streaks of the peachy sunset fade into the gathering darkness, the first stars beginning to twinkle in the dusky sky. He couldn't open the window, but a fresh draft seeped in, dispelling the fetid stench of the cell. The guard would bring supper just after sunset, so at least there was that to look forward to. The food was barely edible, but Max was hungry and bored. The hours passed with glacial speed, the day dragging on for what seemed like a week. When he'd been here last, he feared imminent death, so the time seemed to conspire against him and go faster, but now that Max was waiting for Hugo to return, two days felt like a fortnight.

Max left the window and sat down on his cot. He'd purchased a candle after using up the one left by Hugo but didn't bother to light it just yet. He needed to conserve his supplies since he'd paid for food and wine. He didn't need the light anyway. What was there to see save the grimy walls and sooty beams? Max stretched out on the hard bed, folded his arms behind his head, and indulged in a bit of fantasy. He wouldn't go back to the future until he knew exactly what befell Hugo Everly. He had to admit that he felt a twinge of pity for Hugo, but if Hugo's arrest resulted in a death sentence, Max had nothing to lose and everything to gain.

The pangs of conscience that had tortured him for the past few years would finally be appeased, as would God. Max had come to realize with an unwavering certainty that everything that had befallen him since coming to the past had been the result of his attempt on Hugo's life in the twenty-first century. He'd tried to take the life of a man who meant him no harm, an offense against God, and God had promptly dispensed justice. Max had paid for his sin by being sent to Barbados, where he had nearly died while buried alive, and then he had attempted to kill Hugo once again in Paris. Max was convinced that the only reason God had allowed him to survive the mortal injury Hugo had inflicted on him in that Parisian mine was so that he could finally understand the error of his ways and find a way to atone.

Two days ago, Max was ready to die in Hugo's place, and was convinced that sacrificing himself was the only way to appease an angry God, but now that Hugo had rejected his offer, he felt lighter and more hopeful. Perhaps he wasn't meant to die after all. He'd learned his lesson, tried to make amends, and had given Hugo an opportunity to see his wife and try to disprove the evidence against him. Once Hugo was back, Max would be free, in every sense of the word. The slate would be wiped clean, and he would be able to finally start living his life in a way it was intended to be lived. He would make every effort to be a good and kind man. He would help others, give to charity, and offer forgiveness instead of plotting revenge. Perhaps this whole ordeal had been for a reason. He'd learned and grown as a human being. He was no longer the selfish, self-absorbed man he'd been in the twenty-first century, who yearned for power and influence. He'd stop trying to control everything and allow God to show him his purpose.

Life truly was a wonderful journey when one stopped trying to influence the outcome and simply surrendered control. It had a plan of its own, and Max was suddenly sure that his own future was just about to begin. Even if Hugo managed to accomplish what he set out to do, Max would return to the future with a clear conscience. He was suddenly full of plans and ideas. Once the media circus caused by his return began to die down, he could do anything he pleased. He could rekindle his political aspirations, travel, make an effort to find a suitable woman to marry, or do nothing at all and allow destiny to take its course. It had so far. He'd never known the kind of pain and fear he'd experienced since coming to the seventeenth century, but he'd also never felt as alive or as connected to the universe. In some ways, he couldn't wait to see what was in store for him next.

Max stared at the dark ceiling as he crossed his feet at the ankles. Strange that had he not overheard the conversation about Hugo's arrest, he might have already been back in the twenty-first century. Instead, here he was, at the Tower of London, once again playing a vital role in the life of his hero/nemesis. It was a shame really that he couldn't tell anyone about what had happened to him since opening the passage in the crypt, for surely they'd cart him away to some out-of-the-way institution and throw away the key. Perhaps once he got back, he could share his stories with Simon, since he now knew about the passage anyway and had visited the Everlys only a few months ago.

Max was deeply saddened by the news of his mother's death, but there was a part of him that felt a twinge of relief. His mother had loved him, and wanted the world for him, but she had also been demanding, demeaning, and at times cruel and indifferent to his feelings. She had done her best for him, but Lady Naomi Everly hadn't been possessed of an emotional nature. She was a woman who still believed in honor and duty at the expense of one's own desires and had viewed his illness as a stain on the family name rather than a condition which made him vulnerable and unbalanced.

Upon being informed by Max's schoolmaster that Max was exhibiting some unseemly behavioral issues, she had promptly found the best psychiatrist in London, who had diagnosed Max with Histrionic Personality Disorder, and had Max on medication within days. Max had to admit that the meds did help. He no longer felt as emotional or out of control, but to some degree, they also altered his personality. He was meant to be taking them for the rest of his life, but he often skipped days or reduced the dose, believing that he wasn't doing any harm. Well, perhaps his obsession with Neve and his quest to find the passage had been the result. Maybe even his attempt on Hugo's life since Max allowed his paranoia to control his actions.

But what a hoot it would be to regale Simon with tales of his escape from Barbados and his plan to kill Hugo in the mines of Paris, making him one of the first corpses to grace the eventual Catacombs of Paris. It was like something out of Alexander Dumas, Max mused. He'd always admired the Count of Monte Cristo. And now he'd had his own adventure, one that would make for an exciting book.

Max suddenly sat up, his mouth open in an O of surprise. That's it; that's what he would do. He would write a time-travel adventure. He'd always been good with words, and no research would be needed. He could describe life in the seventeenth century in painstaking detail, giving his story a harsh realism that so many fantasy novels lacked. He would tell his own story, his hero a cross between James Bond and the Count of Monte Cristo.

"What an idea!" Max breathed to himself as he swung his legs off the cot.

He heard the echo of footsteps in the corridor. Supper was coming, and with it a flask of wine. He needed a drink to celebrate this genius idea. Perhaps he could purchase some paper and ink and start writing in the morning. It would help pass the hours till Hugo came.

Max rose to his feet as he heard the scrape of a key in the lock and reached for tinder and flint. He'd have light while he ate his supper. It used to take him a dozen strikes to light a candle, but these days he was a pro. He produced a spark in seconds, and a tiny flame sprang to life just as the door opened and two men came in, closing the door silently behind them. Max opened his mouth to inquire about his food when he realized that neither man looked like a guard. They were well dressed in suits made of fine fabric and adorned with wide lace collars, and expensive footwear with jeweled buckles and chunky heels. The candlelight glinted off silver buttons and sword scabbards.

There was something foreign about the men. They appeared to be Dutch, which Max supposed wasn't that surprising since they were countrymen of the new monarch. Perhaps they'd come to interview Hugo or inform him of the trial date.

Max suddenly stiffened. There could be another reason for this visit; the men might have been dispatched to interrogate, rather than question. Max was all too aware of the methods of torture available at the Tower. He had been repeatedly beaten and tortured when here last, and the memory made him take a step back, his heart suddenly beating hard against his ribs despite the outward aura of calm.

The taller man hung back. He appeared to be in his forties, with gaunt features and a receding hairline. He had light, slanted eyes which were fringed by nearly colorless lashes. A thin scar ran the length of his cheek from the outer corner of the eye, past the prominent nose, and to his mouth, and gave him a sinister appearance. The shorter man was younger and more handsome. He wore a suit of black velvet, which matched his jet-black hair and dark eyes. A thick, pointy beard looked incongruous against the almost unnatural paleness of his skin. Had he been clean-shaven, he would have looked much younger and less severe. Max was momentarily distracted by the large teardrop pearl which swung rhythmically from his left earlobe, the movement of the pearlescent orb mesmerizing as it reflected the flame of the candle.

Max tore his eyes away from the pearl and focused on the man's face. His unwavering gaze caught Max's attention. Whereas the taller man looked somewhat blank and indifferent, the younger man studied Max is if he were taking an X-ray. His stare was penetrating and speculative, as if he had an idea of some sort and was trying to ascertain whether it would work.

Max hung back, unsure of how to react to this unexpected visit. Whoever these men were, he had to pretend to be Hugo, and hope that his ruse was successful.

The younger man appeared to be satisfied with what he saw and finally came forward, a friendly smile now on his face. He no longer looked as somber as before, but the smile never quite reached the eyes, making Max wonder what the man was about.

"Lord Everly?" the man asked as he held out his hand. It was surprisingly calloused, given the man's prosperous appearance, and the handshake stronger than Max expected. The man squeezed Max's hand with a vice-like grip, nearly making him wince. Perhaps Hugo had found another man of law to defend himself, Max speculated, but this man didn't look much like a lawyer.

"Yes. Who do I have the pleasure of addressing?" Max asked.

The man bowed elaborately, extending one foot and

opening his arms wide, as if Max were a royal and this man his humble courtier.

"My name is Jurgen Van Houten," the man replied courteously, "and this is my associate, Master Jan Van Orden. We were sent by His Majesty, King William III. He wishes to apologize for any inconvenience caused and hopes you are being treated well during your stay. If there's anything you require, please let me know, and I will see that you get it."

The man made it sound as if Max were staying at a swanky hotel rather than being detained at His Majesty's pleasure in the Tower of London.

"His Majesty believes in your innocence, and is working to secure your release. It should be no more than a few days," Van Houten continued.

"How kind," Max replied, astounded by this speech.

So, Hugo would be set free. He must have put the time Max had granted him to good use. If the king believed him to be innocent, then the release was imminent. Several years ago, Max would have found this maddening, but now he smiled happily. It was all happening as it should.

"Would you join us in a cup of wine, Your Lordship?" Master Van Houten asked as his companion produced a small bottle and three cups.

"Yes, thank you," Max replied, accepting a cup of very fine claret. The men drank a toast to Their Majesties, then the cups were refilled for another round of drinks.

"If you wouldn't mind, Your Lordship, perhaps you could write a short note to the king, letting him know that you look forward to being free and wishing him the best in his reign."

Van Houten produced writing paper and a quill with a small bottle of ink. Max scrolled a few lines and signed Hugo's name with a flourish. He'd seen Hugo's signature before and had no difficulty in copying it.

"His Majesty will be most pleased," Van Houten said as he

accepted the note and returned Max's cup to him. "One more toast before we go. Your health, Lord Everly," Van Houten exclaimed, raising the cup in a toast.

"And yours, sirs," Max replied, draining the cup. The claret tasted strange this time, and Max was surprised to find a bitter residue on his tongue. What had the man added to his cup while he was busy writing?

Max gazed at Van Houten in surprise as his vision blurred and his limbs turned to lead. The cell swam before him, the ringing in his ears blocking out all other sounds. Max was sure there had only been one candle, but now he saw dozens of tiny flames, all hovering like hungry, licking tongues in his peripheral vision and making him dizzy and nauseous. Van Houten seemed to be saying something, but his mouth moved soundlessly, like an actor in a pantomime. The other man, Jan Van Orden, stood watching Max, his head cocked to the side, a look of impatience on his face. Neither man moved to help Max.

Max inched toward the cot and collapsed on it heavily. He tried to speak, but all he could produce were a few gurgles which didn't resemble any actual words. His mind was still working, but his body didn't respond to any commands, and he just lay there like a sack of potatoes. Max closed his eyes for a moment to block out the candle flames, which seemed to be multiplying and floating above his face. He might have drifted off to sleep had the sound of breaking glass not startled him out of his stupor. Max forced his eyes open. His eyelids felt heavy, and he could only open them to mere slits. He turned his head toward the sound, feeling as if he were underwater.

Van Houten had used the three-legged stool to break the window. He chose a large shard of glass and examined it carefully before approaching the cot. He sat down next to Max and gently brushed the hair out of Max's eyes. The gesture was so tender that it nearly made Max cry. The man was looking at him with kindness, his lips stretched into a small smile, the kind a mother might have on her face while watching her baby sleep.

Van Houten took Max's hand. The other man approached the cot and pushed up the sleeve of Max's shirt, exposing his wrist. Max tried to cry out in protest, but no words came out. His heart, which should now be hammering frantically, seemed to be hardly beating, as if fading away. Van Houten grabbed Max's hand harder and drew the glass across his wrist. Max felt a momentary pain before blood welled above the cut and began to flow into his hand, which Van Houten had released, and onto the stone floor. Van Houten repeated the procedure with the second wrist, then carefully placed the shard of glass on the floor just beneath Max's hand.

Max's mind was now as sluggish as his body, a strange languidness taking over as he tried to understand why these men had come to kill him.

"Not Hugo," he croaked, his voice barely audible.

"What did he say?" Van Orden asked.

"What does it matter?" Van Houten shrugged. "The deed is done." Van Houten leaned over Max and looked into his panicked eyes. "I am sorry, Your Lordship, truly I am." He planted a kiss of benediction on Max's brow, laid the note on the table where it couldn't be missed, and left with his companion, taking the wine and cups and closing the door softly behind him.

Bitter tears slid down Max's temples and into his hair as the lifeblood drained out of him. He might have been able to stop the bleeding if he were able to find the strength to rise, but his limbs felt like iron bars. He was very nearly paralyzed, only his mind was still working, if at a much slower pace. *Why?* it kept asking. He could feel blood trickling down his hands and onto the floor.

He wasn't sure how much time had passed, but suddenly his body no longer felt leaden. He was floating. It was a pleasant feeling. He was weightless and free of pain, which could only mean one thing.

"Heavenly Father," Max mouthed soundlessly, "please forgive my sins and accept me into your loving embrace."

He closed his eyes moments before his heart ceased beating.

ELEVEN

Hugo woke from a fitful sleep, his head aching dully. And little wonder; he'd finished off the bottle of brandy last night before falling asleep still fully dressed. His clothes were wrinkled and sweaty, and the air in the room smelled stale and alcoholic. He'd spent hours the day before walking the streets in an effort to come up with some semblance of a plan, but nothing presented itself. Tonight he would be returning to the Tower, having accomplished very little of value. He'd written several letters: one to Neve, two to his children, should he never get the chance to see them again, and another to Archie. He had meant to write one to Brad as well, but found himself feeling so gutted after writing to Valentine and Michael that he'd succumbed to melancholy and turned to the drink. It had been a moment of weakness, but he supposed he was allowed one, under the circumstances.

Hugo forced himself out of bed, took off his rumpled shirt and poured some water into the basin. He washed his face and then his upper body with cold water before putting on a clean shirt. Shaving was pointless since he couldn't shave in the Tower for lack of a razor, and suddenly appearing clean-shaven would only alert the guards that he was up to something. He brushed his hair and cleaned his teeth. There was a heel of bread, some cheese, and a bit of ale left over from the day before, but the mice had gotten at the cheese, and the bread was surrounded by droppings. He needed to eat something to settle his heaving stomach, so he grabbed his hat and coat and made his way downstairs.

The smell of fresh bread and porridge nearly made him ill, but he accepted a bowl from the innkeeper's daughter and held out his cup for some ale. The girl poured the drink and then returned with half a loaf of bread, which she placed in front of Hugo.

"Was there something else, child?" Hugo asked when he saw the girl's air of suppressed excitement. He had no time for idle chatter. He had to come up with some sort of plan by midday, or all was lost, but the girl was obviously bursting to tell him something, and it was always good to listen, in case she had some useful information.

"Haven't ye heard, sir?" the girl exclaimed, glad of a chance to gossip. "The traitor Everly did away with himself last night. All o' London is talking o' it," she announced with glee, glad to have gotten to him first.

Hugo nearly choked on his porridge. "He did away with himself? Are you certain? How?" He must have misheard, but the girl was nodding vigorously, eager to tell the tale.

"Oh, aye. They say 'e left a suicide note, wishin' Their Majesties a long and happy reign and sayin' that 'e was lookin' forward to finally bein' free. They say 'tis written in 'is own hand and signed."

"How did he do it?" Hugo demanded, astounded.

"Smashed the window and used a bit o' glass to slash 'is wrists. They say the floor was covered in blood by the time the guard found 'im. Proves 'e was guilty, if ye ask me," the girl added wisely. "Took the coward's way out."

Hugo gripped the edge of the table as a wave of vertigo assaulted him.

"Are ye quite well, sir?" the girl asked.

"Yes, thank you. A bit too much brandy last night; that's all."

"Well, ale is the best remedy for what ails ye. And bread. Absorbs all the evil humors, it does. Here, let me help ye."

The girl tore off a chunk of bread and held it to Hugo's mouth as if she were feeding a child. He dutifully accepted the bread and began to chew it slowly as the vertigo receded somewhat. Another piece of bread was shoved into his mouth, but he hardly noticed. None of this made any sense. He needed to find out more.

Hugo forced himself to finish his breakfast, then rose to his feet and stumbled from the inn. No one paid him any mind as he walked toward the Tower. A gentle rain fell, turning the streets muddy and the stone walls slick with moisture. He expected to see gawkers in front of the gates, but no one was about, the gates firmly shut. Thick gray clouds floated above the fortress, the thunderous-looking mass almost pressing down on the tall towers. There was nothing to be learned here, so Hugo walked toward Westminster Abbey instead. People always congregated there, more interested in finding shelter from the rain and gossiping than in praying.

There were several dozen people inside the abbey. No service would be performed until sext at noon, so people sat in the pews talking, conducting business, or simply waiting out the rain. Someone had actually lit a small fire in the nave, using an old metal pot as a means of containing the flames. The fire also provided some illumination, since the interior was shadowed in gloom, hardly any light filtering through the stained-glass windows on such a dreary morning. Several people stood about, holding their hands out to the welcome warmth. Hugo joined the group, standing silently as the fire warmed him.

"Have you heard the news then?" one of the men asked him. The man was clearly poor, but his clothes were mended in places and relatively clean. He had an intelligent face and educated speech. Perhaps a tradesman who'd fallen on hard times. Hugo wanted to hear the news, but he needed facts, not idle gossip, and hoped this man was in possession of the true story.

"No, what news would that be?" Hugo asked, noncommittally.

"Lord Hugo Everly committed suicide last night." The man actually looked upset as he shared the news, so Hugo judged the conversation worth pursuing.

"Aren't you sorry to hear the traitor's dead?" Hugo asked.

"Traitor? That man was no traitor, and I find it hard to believe that he would take his own life."

"He left a note, he did," another man chimed in. "Signed it and all."

"So what? Notes can be forged. Everly was a brave man, a man of principle. I can't see that he would kill himself before the trial," the first man protested.

"Unless he was guilty. I'd say doing away with yourself is the ultimate admission of guilt," an older woman said, shaking her head.

"Perhaps he was murdered," a young lad, who appeared to be the woman's grandson, piped in, his eyes huge with curiosity.

"Anything is possible, lad, anything," the first man said.

"Don't be daft, Harry. What would be the point of killing the man? He'd be executed soon enough, if guilty. Why hasten his end?" the woman argued.

"To discredit him further, and deny him a Christian burial," the man named Harry said with disgust.

"I wonder if his widow knows yet," the young boy said, warming up to the subject.

Hugo felt a sudden stab in the gut. He'd been so preoccupied with learning about Max that he hadn't thought of what effect his news would have on Neve. She might not have heard yet, but she would soon enough. News traveled quickly, passed from person to person, traveler to villager, and so on. People who left London this morning would spread the news far and wide by tomorrow, and it would reach Neve's ears soon enough. What would she think when she heard that he'd committed suicide? He had to get to Cranley as soon as possible. There was nothing more to be done in London.

TWELVE

Liza stared hard at the note, trying to make out the words. She knew her letters, but this person's handwriting was virtually indecipherable, what with all the loops and curlicues. She glanced up irritably at the boy who'd delivered the note.

"What's it say then? I can't make heads or tails of it."

The boy looked uncomfortable, torn between passing on the message and revealing that he knew what it contained. There was no seal, just a ribbon tied around the scroll, but Liza had correctly surmised that the boy had read the message.

"It says that you are to appear at the trial of Lady Everly this Sunday at the church of St. Nicolas."

"Whose signature is that?" she demanded. It didn't look like the note had been written by Reverend Snow.

"Bishop Cotton. He's in charge."

The boy turned on his heel, eager to leave, but not before Liza grabbed him by the arm.

"Wait a moment. Does this mean the Everlys are back in Cranley?" she asked, suddenly nervous. What if they found out somehow that the accusation had been made by her before the trial? Hugo Everly would find her and rip out her entrails for denouncing his wife. He was a man of admirable restraint, but if Liza knew anything about Hugo Everly, it was that he wouldn't take kindly to a threat against the mother of his children. Every man had a breaking point, and this just might be his.

"Just her ladyship. Lord Everly has been arrested for treason. Haven't you heard? He's being held in the Tower."

"Arrested for treason?" Liza breathed, shocked to the core. Hugo Everly was the most honorable man she knew. The accusation against him couldn't be true, but it certainly made her life easier. Not having him at the trial would guarantee her own safety, unless....

"And what about Archie Hicks? Is he back?" Liza asked fearfully. Archie Hicks didn't have the restraint of his master and wouldn't hesitate to silence her. He hadn't actually killed anyone, as far as she knew, but he was capable, of that she was sure. Liza was a woman of keen instincts, and she knew a threat when she saw one. She'd heard that Archie had married Lionel Finch's widow. God only knew what led to that match, but even love, if that's what it was, couldn't tame the fire that burned within him.

"Not that I know of, but his wife is. She's holed up in Everly Manor with her mistress," the boy replied, desperate to get away.

"Has Lady Everly not been arrested?" Liza persisted.

"No, she's under orders not to leave the house. They have someone keeping an eye on the place should she decide to flee. Are you done with the questions now? I have to get back."

"Right. Thank you," Liza said as she released the boy's arm and stepped back into the house.

This news changed everything. She'd be safe until the trial, with Hugo and Archie out of the way, but she'd planned to approach Hugo just after the trial, after his wife had been convicted and her fate hung in the balance. He'd pay any amount then to have her withdraw her testimony, but Hugo wasn't there and had problems of his own. If Liza hoped to get any money, she had to approach Neve Everly directly. If Neve paid her off, she would simply withdraw her accusation before the trial, or, better yet, take the money and still testify. Kill two birds with one stone, one might say.

"Avis, I need you to look after Johnny for the afternoon. I must go to Cranley," Liza called out to her sister, who was spooning porridge into Johnny's mouth.

The younger girl looked up, clearly annoyed. She likely had plans of her own. If Avis had it her way, she'd be betrothed before the summer, and dreams of a June wedding already clouded her flighty mind. Of course, having one less mouth to feed would be a blessing, but if Liza were honest, Avis was a big help around the house and with Johnny. She genuinely loved the boy, as did her other sisters. They doted on him, which in some small way made up for the fact that the boy would never know his father, a duplicitous captain who'd deceived Liza and promised marriage. Too bad he already had a wife and children up north.

"What, again?" Avis moaned. "Do you have a lover there or something?" she demanded sourly. "I've plans of my own, you know."

"I must appear before the committee ahead of the trial. To give my statement," Liza lied.

Avis just shook her head. They'd argued bitterly over what Liza was doing, Avis taking the side of the Everlys. "Liza, what goes around, comes around. You send that woman to her death, and the Good Lord will see to it that you meet a sorry end," Avis said wisely. She was only eighteen, but at times she sounded like an old woman. However, her warning gave Liza the creeps.

"Oh, shut your trap, Avis. I didn't hear you complaining when I came back from London flush with coin. Lived like a princess you did. Got a new gown and shoes, and even a warm cloak for the winter. If you feel so righteous about it, then I just won't share my windfall with you. How does that sound, you shrewish little minx?"

Avis didn't reply, but Liza saw the look of uncertainty in her eyes. She'd hit a sore spot; she knew that. Avis was a vain little thing, and would take anything given to her, and more. She was resentful of the unfairness that befell her through an accident of birth. She truly was beautiful, and had she been born into a family of higher standing might have made an important marriage, or, at the very least, lived in comfort. As things stood, the best Avis could hope for was the son of a farmer, and although her intended was besotted with her and would give her a good life once they wed, Avis always dreamed of what might have been, and grabbed at anything which might give her a taste of the finer things in life.

"Fine, go," Avis spat out. "But be back by nightfall."

"I will. The roads are dangerous after dark."

* * *

This time, Liza didn't stable her old nag at the inn livery but went straight to Everly Manor. Neither Hugo nor Archie were there to manhandle her, and she wasn't intimidated by the women. She knocked on the door, bold as brass, and waited until Harriet let her in.

"You again. I wonder you have the nerve to show your face around here," Harriet hissed. "His lordship is not here."

"It's your mistress I've come to see. On urgent business. She is allowed visitors, is she not?" Liza asked, directing her question to Mark Watson, who sat by the door, looking bored and irritable.

He nodded and turned back to examining his nails. Liza was of no interest to him.

"What possible business could you have here?" Harriet fumed.

Liza had intended to approach Harriet and urge her to testify against Neve but changed her mind. Harriet was timid, and too God-fearing to lie, especially when she had nothing to gain and everything to lose. Now she wouldn't need her support anyway. This would all be over before it began.

Liza swept past Harriet and Master Watson and walked straight to the parlor without being invited. She took a seat, proud of her own insolence. She was as good as Lady Everly, wasn't she? God only knew where Neve Ashley had come from. Not like anyone had ever heard of who her people were. Liza wouldn't be made to feel insignificant by the likes of her; she held the woman's future in her hands, and she would enjoy watching her squirm.

Liza waited patiently in the parlor until Lady Everly finally walked through the door. She looked pale and tired, but her head was held high, and she fixed Liza with a look of such loathing that Liza felt as if something had just walked over her grave.

Lady Everly closed the door and positioned herself in front of Liza. She didn't sit, but stood with her arms crossed, eyes blazing. "What now, Liza? Haven't you harassed us enough?"

"This is not about my son," Liza replied defensively.

"Oh? So you admit that he wasn't fathered by my husband?" Neve demanded, her tone full of derision.

Both women knew that Liza had lied when she'd accused Hugo of fathering Johnny. She'd only wanted to extort money, but the ploy hadn't worked; Hugo had thrown her out, and Neve had threatened to take Johnny away and send him to Holland to act as a servant to her distant relations. Well, this time her plan would work. Lady Everly's life was truly in danger, and she'd be singing a different tune once she found out that Liza held her sorry existence in her hands.

"I'll make this brief," Liza snarled as she rose to her feet and drew herself up to full height. She was a few inches taller than Neve Everly, and stared her down, which made Liza feel superior. "If you give me twenty crowns, I will withdraw my testimony and there will be no trial on Sunday. If you don't, I will make them believe that you are the Devil Incarnate. You will hang, or be burned, but you will not talk your way out of this one, especially with your fancy lord not being here to protect you this time. Come to think of it, you might even meet your maker on the same day, what with him being accused of treason and all. Wouldn't that be something? You can go to Hell together—you burned to a crisp, and him missing a head."

Liza watched with great satisfaction as Neve opened and closed her mouth like a landed fish. Two bright spots of color appeared on her pale cheeks. "You bitch!" she spat out.

"Not all of us marry rich. Some of us have to struggle just to survive. All you had to do was give me some money for my Johnny, and I would have left you alone, but you were too mean to part with a few coins. Well, now your life is on the line. Will you still deny me?"

Liza allowed herself a small smile. She was enjoying this very much. Lady Everly looked as if she was going to be sick, her face deathly white, except for the unnatural crimson blush staining her cheeks. She was furious though, that was obvious. Her eyes blazed in a way that made Liza want to take a step back, but she wasn't backing down, not this time. She would get what she came for. Twenty crowns was enough to see her family fed for the rest of her life, and she'd put aside something for Johnny's future as well. A good apprenticeship would ensure that he was set for good. He'd learn a trade and make a life for himself, and he'd have her to thank for it, not his worthless father who didn't care if his son lived or died.

"Yes, I will deny you," Neve Everly replied hotly. "I don't believe for a moment that you will ever stop. People like you are like parasites who feed off others. Even if I give you the money, you will come back for more. So, do your worst, Liza Timmins, and see where it gets you. Now, get out of my house before I have you thrown out. I am still mistress here."

"It's your funeral," Liza replied spitefully.

Things hadn't gone as she expected, but the trial wasn't until Sunday, and Neve would change her mind. Once she had time to think it over, she'd see that a few coins were a small price to pay for her freedom. What were twenty crowns to someone as wealthy as her?

"Give my regards to your children," Liza added for good measure as she stormed out past young Jem, who gaped at her in amazement. "What are you looking at, you little bastard?" Liza spat out as she swept past him. Why had he come back? Did his father no longer want him? Liza wondered. Probably had a legitimate son now and had no need for this worthless little guttersnipe. Served him right, knowing who his mother had been. No man in his right mind would believe that any child she bore was his. Margaret had bedded so many men, that it'd be a wonder if she herself knew who had fathered her brat. And to think that they were cousins. Margaret never had time for Liza, she was too busy bewitching every man in the vicinity.

Liza was angry and frustrated as she galloped away from Everly Manor. This was her third attempt at extortion this year, and she hadn't seen so much as a half-crown for her pains. Well, Neve had two days to change her mind. Two days.

THIRTEEN

Jem made himself scarce after Frances rushed to the parlor to comfort Lady Everly. Neve was shaking with fear, tears of rage sliding down her cheeks. Now she knew who her accuser was and was helpless in the face of such hatred and ill-will. Frances convinced Lady Everly to sit down and took a seat next to her, putting a protective arm around her shoulders. The two women sat huddled together, their heads bent as they spoke quietly, so as not to be overheard by Master Watson, who sat just outside the door. Frances was pale as well. She was different when Archie wasn't about, timid and frightened.

Jem's heart squeezed with sorrow. Lady Everly and Frances were the only two women in this world whom he truly loved. Lady Everly had been a mother to him before his father came to Paris to fetch him, and Frances was the closest he'd ever had to an older sister. She teased him, called him names, and frequently told him to go away, but he knew in his heart that Frances cared for him, and would spring to his defense if anyone so much as said a word against him. She'd cried when they'd said goodbye in Paris and made him promise to write to her—a promise that he hadn't kept. But he loved her with all his heart, as he loved Archie, who, in Jem's opinion, was the only man worthy of Frances's affection. This family, although not his own by blood, was the only family that was real and worth fighting for.

Jem took a final peek to make sure that Frances had the situation in hand before slipping out of the house and making for the stables. Mark Watson watched him go, his face a mask of indifference. Jem wasn't under house arrest, so was free to come and go as he pleased. Archie had given him clear instructions. He was to give him a daily report of what went on in the house and alert him to any possible developments. Neither Frances nor Lady Everly knew that Archie was in Cranley, but Hugo had entrusted Jem with the secret so that he could act as go-between if need be.

"Going for a ride?" Joe asked as Jem asked for a horse to be saddled.

"Yes, it's a fine afternoon," Jem replied. He hated lying, especially to Joe, who was always kind to him, but he couldn't break Lord Everly's or Archie's trust.

Jem hung around until Joe saddled the horse, and took off, purposely heading in the wrong direction until he was well out of sight of the manor house. Then he rode hell for leather to Horatio Hicks's farm a few miles away. He hoped Archie would be about because this news couldn't wait. Jem's heart pounded with excitement. He knew who the accuser was, so now Archie would be able to stop Liza from hurting Neve Everly. Archie would know what to do; he always did.

Jem found Archie outside, chopping wood. He looked somewhat worse for wear with a bruised cheek and a sprained wrist bandaged with linen, but he didn't allow his discomfort to stop him. Archie hacked at the wood as if the logs had personally offended him, taking out his helplessness and fury on the firewood.

Archie set down the axe and watched as Jem brought the

horse to an abrupt halt and slid off, nearly falling on his behind. Jem righted himself, then gave up on any pretense of dignity and ran toward Archie.

"Archie, it's Liza. She's the one who spoke up against Lady Everly."

"How do you know this, Jemmy?" Archie asked, turning all his attention to the boy.

"She just came by the house. Demanded that Lady Everly give her twenty crowns to stop her from testifying."

"How did Lady Everly respond?" Archie demanded. He was seething with anger, shoulders tense, hands on hips, lips curled in a snarl.

"She threw her out, but she is scared, Archie. Very scared," Jem replied.

Archie nodded as he turned toward the house. "Jem, go back and keep an eye on the women. You are the man of the house until Lord Everly returns. I'll take care of Liza."

"What will you do to her?" Jem asked with interest, trailing after Archie. He'd missed him so much, and he wasn't ready to leave and go back to Everly Manor. The atmosphere there was so melancholy. He just wanted to spend a few moments in the company of his idol.

"Silence her," Archie replied as he reached for his weapons. "Now, go."

Jem mounted his horse and turned toward home, but then changed his mind and decided to go for a ride instead. He'd missed the Everlys and thought of them constantly while living with his father and stepmother, reminiscing about the days aboard the ship to France and the months after that. He never thought of the day Hugo was shot while walking with Jem by the river; that memory was too painful. Instead, Jem often remembered how they went out for morning walks and ate fresh crepes while watching the boats on the river.

Archie had taken him on outings too, and he sometimes

tagged along with Frances and Luke Marsden and was treated to a cup of chocolate and a pastry at a brasserie Frances liked. Jem even missed his lessons, which he shared with Frances. They used to make faces at each other while Hugo's back was turned and made jokes once the lecture was over. Those were good days, days when he felt like he was really a part of the family. Jem knew that Hugo Everly could never legally adopt him and make him his son and heir, but he also knew that he was loved like a son, and that had been enough. He hadn't even realized how happy he'd been, childishly assuming that life as he knew it would go on forever.

But now, everything had changed. Lord and Lady Everly had problems of their own, and whereas before he was treated as one of the family, now he was underfoot. Lady Everly was too polite and preoccupied at the moment to ask him to return home, but she would as soon as the trial was over, and he would have to leave. Lord Everly had his own son now, and a daughter. Jem wished he could have met the little girl who died. He'd have liked to know Elena. She sounded like a feisty little thing. Michael was a sweet boy, but he was too babyish still. He reminded Jem that he had his own brother back at home, another squalling baby who usurped his place. Still, he would go home in time, but not before he'd completed the task Lord Everly had entrusted him with. He would see Lady Everly's name cleared, and then go to London with Archie to help the master in his hour of need.

FOURTEEN

Liza looked anxiously at the purpling sky. Already, a few tiny stars twinkled up above, and a crescent moon, pale, but clearly visible, was hanging in the twilit sky. The coming night quickly replaced daylight; the woods along the road already shrouded in darkness and strangely forbidding where only a little while ago they were picturesque and filled with birdsong. Another half-hour and the road would be swallowed by darkness, and she still had another hour to go at the very least. The horse was tired, and was barely ambling along, more interested in the grass at the side of the road. Liza dug her heels into the flanks of the animal, but it barely registered her annoyance and continued at the same slow pace.

Liza wasn't frightened exactly, but she didn't wish to be alone on the road after dark. There'd been some tales of robberies of late. Not that she had anything worth stealing, but as her mother always said, God took care of those who took care of themselves, a sentiment Liza wholeheartedly agreed with. She resigned herself to getting back later than expected and allowed her thoughts to return to Neve Everly. What if she refused to pay? The whole ruse had been instigated to get money, but if Liza got nothing, sending the woman to her death would only diminish her own chances of ever seeing Heaven.

There were times when Liza wholeheartedly wished she was a Papist. How easy they had it; all they had to do was go to confession, show some remorse and their sins were forgiven, if not erased. Liza had a list of sins to confess, and she wished for forgiveness. She wasn't exactly contrite, but she did regret some of her choices. At least she didn't do away with Johnny, as she had planned. Something had stopped her from drinking the potion that would expel him from her womb. Liza would have liked to see Captain Norrington rot in Hell for all eternity, but she did love her boy, and everything she did was for him. Perhaps most folk wouldn't understand her motives and condemn her without reservation, but Liza was a single mother who was also now responsible for her three flighty sisters, two of whom would need feeding and clothing for years to come. Liza needed the money, desperately. Neve Everly had to come around. Would she really risk her life just to thwart Liza? It didn't seem very likely, but one could never tell how far someone was prepared to go. Had someone told Liza when she was a girl that she'd stoop to blackmail and extortion, she would have called the person a knave and shunned them for the rest of their days. But here she was.

Feeling a small pang of guilt at her own evolution, Liza decided not to dwell on her character. She'd done what she had to do to survive. Of course, a better person might have chosen a different path, and would choose the path of righteousness even now, but it was too late to change course. She'd have her money, come Hell or high water, and she'd live comfortably and provide for her son.

Liza was so caught up in her own internal argument that at first she didn't notice the mounted rider who emerged from the trees just up ahead. She reined in her horse, peering into the gathering darkness. The man's hat was pulled down low, but his hands were loose on the reins, relaxed. He didn't appear to be carrying a pistol, or even a sword. Not a thief then. Probably just a fellow traveler.

Liza stiffened with apprehension as the stranger drew closer. There was something familiar about the man's posture, but there was nowhere for her to go but forward. Even if she turned around, she'd never get away on her old nag. The horse was barely moving. Liza gasped as the man suddenly dismounted and grabbed the reins of her horse, forcing her to stop. He used one arm to pull her down, turning her away from him and holding her in a steel vise against his chest. Liza could feel his breath as he bent his head lower, brushing the stubble of his beard against her face. She now knew exactly who it was. Archie Hicks, God damn his eyes.

"What'd you want then?" Liza demanded, infusing her voice with false bravado. She was scared, terrified even.

"If you were a man, I'd slit your throat from ear to ear," Archie replied as a sharp blade pressed against her exposed throat. "It would give me great pleasure, given your perfidy, but you have a son, and I will spare you for his sake."

"That's very generous of you," Liza answered sarcastically, but grew silent as the blade pressed deeper into her flesh, drawing a thin line of blood. Liza could smell its metallic tang and sucked in her breath with fright.

"Don't tempt me," Archie replied, his voice full of venom.

Liza grew silent, knowing what was good for her. Archie wasn't governed by the same rules as God-fearing men; he was a born killer, which made him attractive to some women. They sensed the ruthlessness beneath the veneer of civility. Liza had to admit that if Archie wasn't holding her at knifepoint, she might have been quite aroused herself. She'd always found him attractive, if not a very good prospect financially, and had no doubt that a night with him would be most gratifying. That mouse he'd married wasn't woman enough for him; that was obvious.

"What do you want from me?" Liza whispered, ready to offer him her body in return for her freedom. She thought he might be game.

As if reading her thoughts, Archie loosened his hold and shifted his hips, breaking the full-body contact between them. He still held the knife to her throat though, the steel digging into her flesh. "You will go home, take your boy, and leave these parts for good. If you appear at the trial on Sunday, or if I *ever* see you anywhere near Cranley again, I swear that I will kill you. You know me well enough to know that I don't make idle threats. Do we understand each other, Liza?"

"Yes, we do. You will never lay eyes on me again, Archibald Hicks," Liza replied and meant it. Having a dagger held to one's throat was a sobering experience, and the thought of Johnny growing up without her was enough to frighten Liza into agreeing. Being poor and alive was better than being dead and buried, and, in either case, there wasn't much holding her here these days. Her sisters were old enough to fend for themselves. Avis would soon marry, and the other two would have to find employment and start paying their own way. Liza could no longer support them. She'd leave them the house and everything in it and go to London. There were more opportunities there. Perhaps she'd even find a man to take her on and be a father to her son. Her bid to get money out of Lady Everly had clearly failed, and testifying at the trial at this juncture wouldn't line her pockets or win her any friends. It was time to acknowledge her failure and move on before she got seriously hurt.

"Now, get back on your horse and be gone," Archie said as he released her.

Liza turned to face him, their eyes meeting in the dim light of the evening. "Thank you for giving me another chance, Archie," she purred. "I really mean that." Liza arched her back in an effort to make her breasts appear larger and gazed at him from beneath lowered lashes. Perhaps if she got him into bed, he'd be more amenable and change his mind about having her leave for good. Just in case she changed her mind and wished to stay.

"Just go," Archie said. He didn't move from his stance in the road until Liza's shadowy form disappeared from view, then mounted his own horse and turned toward Cranley.

FIFTEEN

I shut the door behind me and collapsed into a chair before the empty hearth. I was still shaking, my mind going round and round in circles. Despite Frances's words of comfort and unfailing support, I now knew I'd done the wrong thing. I had allowed my anger and defiance to prevail, and now I was in even greater danger than before. Liza was a venomous shrew, and now that I had humiliated her twice—no, three times— would do her utmost to get revenge. She'd never forgiven me for "bewitching" Hugo, as she saw it, and my refusal to accept her son as Hugo's had left her bitter and angry. We all knew that the boy wasn't Hugo's, but Liza had chosen to play her trump card, and couldn't accept defeat. The accusation of witchcraft was a last-ditch attempt to hurt me and extort money from the man whom Liza saw as hers. She couldn't have him, but she could take the only thing from him she saw as worth having—money. If he didn't pay up, she would destroy his family by condemning the mother of his children to death.

I was fairly sure that Liza didn't really believe I was a witch, although an uneducated girl could easily perceive some of the things I'd done as witchcraft. Everyone knew that I'd helped

Hugo escape arrest in the spring of 1685. I'd tricked Captain Norrington into allowing us into the church, then led Hugo through the passage in the crypt, taking him to the twenty-first century to avoid certain death. Of course, even in my time this would be seen as magic. I knew that time travel was possible, but most people would still see it as the stuff of science fiction. Liza knew firsthand from her lover that Hugo Everly had vanished from the church, and that he had been with me. She was clever enough to put two and two together, and in her mind it added up to witchcraft.

The incident had been largely forgotten after our long absence from England, but when reminded at the trial, the people of Cranley would only too readily recall the mysterious circumstances under which Hugo Everly had avoided arrest. Everyone would believe Liza, partially because there was no other explanation, and partially because it made for good theater. This would be the most exciting and entertaining thing to happen to the villagers in years, and every man, woman, and child would turn out for the trial, if only to enjoy the performance. The burden of proof wouldn't be on Liza but on me. Anything Liza said about me during the trial would be taken as gospel; she wouldn't need to substantiate her accusations.

My twenty-first-century mind told me not to give in to blackmail, knowing that the blackmailer would come back for more, but this was the seventeenth century, where an accusation of witchcraft by one person was sufficient reason to try to execute someone, sans proof. Twenty crowns amounted to a fortune in this day and age, but I was sure that it had been Liza's opening bid. She would have settled for much less, had I actually been willing to pay her off. Hugo and I had the money, and I should have just paid the woman to make this trial go away, but I had been too livid, and too principled, to give in to her demands. And now she had gone off in a huff, more determined than ever to destroy me, and my family. Of course, there was no guarantee that Liza wouldn't take the money and testify anyway. There was no one here to stop her. Hugo was under arrest, and Archie was in London.

Frances and I were on our own, and the menacing presence of Mark Watson didn't do much to lift our morale. The man hadn't done anything untoward, but there was something sinister about him, and I was almost certain that he'd volunteered for the task. I thought I guessed the reason but prayed that I was wrong. I'd seen the way Mark Watson looked at Frances. He wanted her, that was obvious, and with Archie away, Frances was woefully helpless. I tried to comfort myself with the idea that Watson hadn't tried anything with Frances thus far, but my gut instinct told me that it was just a matter of time until he got her alone somewhere. I'd instructed Jem to keep an eye on the man and alert me should he see anything suspicious. Jem had readily agreed, but there was something odd in his manner. Perhaps he was frightened of Watson. Jem was jittery and unusually silent; no longer the boy I had known. It brought me some comfort to have Jem with us at this time, but I missed the funny little boy who worshipped Hugo and Archie and would gladly sell his soul for a sweetie. I hadn't seen him sneak into the kitchen even once, and he seemed to have little interest in his food these past few days. He was withdrawn and watchful, but I suppose, under the circumstances, that wasn't odd at all.

I buried my face in my hands, allowing myself a few moments of unobserved despair before going back downstairs to face Frances and the children. They kept asking when Papa would be back, and every time my composure cracked a little more. I had no idea what was going on in London. There was no way for Hugo to send word, so the silence was absolute. I had to have faith in my husband and wait, but I didn't have much time. Tomorrow was Friday, and the trial was set for

Sunday morning. Perhaps I could ask Jem to go up to London and find out from Archie what was going on.

The only person I could still rely on was Bradford Nash. I knew that he'd come if I called him, but in view of Hugo's arrest and the upcoming trial, I'd advised him to keep his distance for his family's sake. Brad and Beth would be at the trial, but until then, there was nothing they could do to help.

"Right. Get hold of yourself," I said out loud and leaned back in the chair with my hands resting on the arm supports. I closed my eyes and began to do breathing exercises in order to clear my mind and calm my spirit. I was no good to anyone in this state. I needed to regain some semblance of control over my feelings and present a serene and confident façade to my children, even if I felt as if I were walking on a tightrope suspended over a cliff. After a few minutes, the exercise began to help, and I felt the tension flowing out as my body relaxed into the chair. A few more minutes and I would be ready to go downstairs.

I finally rose to my feet, patted my hair into place and smoothed out my skirt, ready to return, when there was a timid knock at the door of my bedroom. I assumed it was Polly or Harriet, come to light the fire and the candles since it was almost dark outside, and the room was lost in shadow. I opened the door to find a white-faced Frances, her eyes huge with panic, the flame of the candle reflecting in her pupils.

"Frances, what is it?" I cried. Had that bloody man harassed her in some way? I was ready to storm downstairs, give him a stern warning and threaten to report him to Reverend Snow when Frances cut in across my furious thoughts. Her voice was low, and I had to strain to hear her.

"There's a man at the door, Neve," she said as her eyes filled with tears. "He says he's delivering his lordship's body."

I grabbed on to the doorjamb as my legs gave out from under me, refusing to support me any longer. Frances tried to grab my elbow, but I slid to the floor and pressed my forehead to the cool wood. My eyes were wide open, but I couldn't see a thing or hear what Frances was saying. My mind shut down, refusing to accept what I'd just been told. It was as if a great chasm had opened up in front of me, ready to swallow me whole and pull me into a bottomless darkness from which there was no return.

I lay on my side and pulled up my knees, curling into a fetal position as Frances knelt by my side. She set down the candle and tried to rouse me, but my eyes fixated on the flickering flame, drawing me deeper into my trance. There was something so peaceful and cleansing about that flame. It was the only thing that kept me from falling into the darkness; the flame was life.

SIXTEEN

I wasn't sure how long I lay there, but no human being is able to keep thoughts away for long. A tiny voice began to protest, telling me that I must focus, if only for the sake of the children. If I didn't go down, the man would come inside, and perhaps say something in front of the children about their father being dead. And where was Archie? Why hadn't he brought Hugo home? Was Archie hurt? We had to find out, for Frances's sake. The thought clearly hadn't occurred to her yet, but if Hugo were dead and Archie wasn't the one to bring him to me, then he was either dead, incapacitated, or on the run.

I forced myself to sit up. Frances had long since stopped trying to talk to me but continued to kneel next to me in stupefied silence. I got to my feet, picked up the candle, and walked out of the room. It was like an out-of-body experience. I could see and hear things, but I felt as if my body were still upstairs lying on the floor. Frances was behind me, still silent as she followed me to the door.

Mark Watson stood aside, allowing us to pass unchallenged. He'd heard the news. For once, the man had a look of compassion on his face, but it was more for Frances than myself. I floated past him and down the steps toward the wagon. A plain pine box rested in the bed of the wagon, its light color at odds with the gathering darkness and gray boards of the transport. I stared at it, unable to believe that my Hugo was inside. No, my mind kept repeating, but I would have to deal with my grief later.

I tore my gaze away from the coffin and fixed it on the man standing by the wagon, his hat respectfully held in his hands. He was middle-aged, with a full head of graying hair, thick eyebrows over shrewd dark eyes, and the body of a boxer. He wasn't very tall, but he gave off an aura of brute strength. He looked like a man who was on intimate terms with death.

A teenage boy, possibly his son, still sat on the bench and held the reins loosely. He looked around with interest as if he'd never been to the country. He had the same build as his father, but his eyes were young and innocent, his smile tentative as his gaze finally settled on me.

"Where do ye want 'im, Yer Ladyship?" the man finally asked, clearly eager to be done with this gruesome task and return home. It was already dark outside, and the journey back to London would take several hours. The roads weren't safe after dark, but this man looked like someone who could take care of himself. I noted the butt of a pistol visible on the bench next to the boy.

"What happened?" I asked, realizing that the man probably had no idea. He was just someone hired to deliver the body to its family. But he must have heard the gossip in London and surely knew more than I did, which was nothing.

"Suicide, ma'am," the man answered gruffly. "Slit 'is wrists with a bit o' glass." He looked at his scuffed boots, giving me a moment to absorb the news. Suicide was the least honorable kind of death. Even people who'd been executed received more respect. Suicide was a coward's way out, and a person who chose to take their own life was not only frowned upon by their fellow man, but also forsaken by God. The man expected me to be overcome by shame and felt sorry for me.

It's not Hugo, it's not Hugo, it's not Hugo, I kept silently repeating to myself as I tried to keep a lid on my horror.

I directed the two men to bring the coffin into the dining room and set it on the table. Only a few months had passed since my baby's coffin had stood in exactly the same place and I felt as if I were going to faint. I dug my nails into my palm in an effort to distract myself from the grief that was about to engulf me. *It's not Hugo,* I thought again.

Frances thoughtfully slipped the man a coin and closed the door behind him and his assistant. I heard the crunch of wheels on gravel as I stood staring at the pine box. The coffin wasn't nailed shut, just secured with a leather strap. I knew I had to look, but every cell in my being just wanted to run from this room and never return. Suicide. Hugo would never commit suicide; I was sure of that. He regarded suicide as a mortal sin, but a little niggling fear still remained. Everyone had their breaking point; perhaps Hugo had reached his.

Frances stood across from me holding a candle, her face pale and frightened. Mark Watson made to follow us into the dining room at first but thought better of it and returned to his post by the door to give me a bit of privacy. I was grateful for that, at least. I couldn't bear to have him watching me as I performed this morbid task.

"Do you want me to do it?" Frances asked.

"No. This is something I have to do, but I would appreciate it if you stayed. I can't bear to do this alone."

"Of course, I'll stay. Oh, I wish Archie were here," Frances moaned.

I wished Archie was there as well. His solid presence would make this easier somehow, even if my worst fears were realized. I finally sucked in a deep breath and unbuckled the strap, pushing aside the lid of the coffin as Frances leaned closer, illuminating the corpse with her candle.

Unnaturally pale face. Dark lashes fanned against lean cheeks. Wavy dark hair sprinkled with gray. Generous mouth framed by several days' stubble. Yes, it could be Hugo, but it wasn't. I let out a breath I hadn't realized I'd been holding. Great sobs tore from my chest as I beheld Max. I hadn't seen him since that day in Paris when he'd abducted me and Valentine from the garden of our house and taken us into that awful tunnel in the hope of trapping Hugo and leaving him there to die. And now Max was dead. None of this made any sense, but I sighed with relief, thankful that I wasn't looking at Hugo's remains. Why would Max kill himself? And where was Hugo? I was desperate for answers, but I wouldn't get any from Max, save one.

I glanced at his hands which were folded over his chest. I hated to do it, but I reached into the coffin and lifted one hand, turning it over. A jagged gash nearly half an inch thick marked the wrist. The blood had congealed and looked like a smiling red mouth. I grabbed a bowl from the table and vomited into it, unable to contain my horror. My forehead was clammy, and I could scarcely catch my breath as I sucked in air to subdue my heaving stomach. After a few minutes, I finally judged it safe to set down the bowl and return to my task. I replaced Max's hand on his chest and closed the lid.

"Neve, are you all right?" Frances asked, her brow furrowed with concern.

I nodded. I'd always thought that to be the most inane question ever. If someone needed to ask you if you were all right, clearly you weren't. How could anyone be all right when faced with the possibility of being a widow, and then having to open a coffin and look upon a dead body, praying all the while that the man inside wasn't your husband but some other poor sod? I felt a deep sorrow settle over me as I walked from the room. I wasn't permitted to leave the house, but I needed a bit of fresh air. I felt as if I were suffocating.

"Frances, I'm going out into the garden for a moment. I need some air."

Frances nodded but made no move to follow me. She went to join the children instead, who were in the parlor with Ruby. They were playing a game and were shrieking as Ruby chased them around, her cheeks flushed with the effort. I saw Valentine give Michael a push just before the door closed and heard Frances reprimanding her for being unkind to her little brother.

Mark Watson sprang to his feet as I stepped out of the dining room, but he refrained from saying anything as I grabbed my cloak and stepped into the twilit garden. Everything was in bloom, the shrubs and flower bushes bursting with new life. There were no flowers yet, but the garden would be full of flowers any day now. The air smelled of new grass, earth, and woodsmoke; a wonderful smell that always made me think of spring in the countryside.

I wrapped my arms about my middle as I walked between the plants. My mind was in turmoil, but after a dozen turns around the garden, I finally began to calm down, and reason started to set in. Despite my relief at the body not being Hugo, there were other things to consider. If it were believed by the authorities that Max was Hugo, then that meant that Hugo was officially considered dead. The king and queen would have been advised of Lord Everly's death in the Tower.

I sat down heavily on a wrought-iron bench, suddenly too tired to keep walking. Was this a sacrifice of some sort? It didn't make much sense. Max would know that by killing himself, he would also be killing Hugo in the eyes of the world. Hugo would become a nonentity, a ghost. Besides, the Max I knew would never sacrifice anything for anyone. He might have seen the light and wished to atone for the wrong he'd done us, but this was going too far. There was still a chance that Hugo might have been proven innocent, so why jump the gun? Had something happened in the Tower to cause Max to take his own life?

The more I thought about it, the less sense it all made. Did Hugo know Max was dead? Did he have a plan of some sort, and would he put it into action before the trial on Sunday? My head ached from the terrible tension brought about by this day. I rose to my feet laboriously, ready to go back inside. Out of the corner of my eye, I saw Jem walking toward the house from the stables. He'd gone out for a ride, and I hadn't even noticed. Jem needed to return home to his father, and that was yet another issue that would have to be addressed, but not now.

"Hello, Jem," I called out, trying to sound as normal as I could. "You must be starving. I think Cook has some fresh meat pies; perhaps she'll give you one to tide you over until supper."

Jem looked startled by my sudden appearance, but he smiled back. This wasn't the boyish smile I remembered; this was the smile of someone on the cusp of adulthood, a smile meant to hide other powerful emotions.

"I'm not hungry," Jem said and walked away.

SEVENTEEN

Archie sat on the narrow bench and leaned against the side of the house as he gazed up at the starry sky. His father was inside, clearing up after supper. More mashed turnips and bread. Archie hadn't been able to eat much, but he felt no hunger. What he felt was anger, confusion, and loneliness. He wished he could just ride over to Everly Manor and see Frances, but he needed to stay out of sight until after the trial. He'd had no further instructions from Hugo, so the original plan was still in effect. At least he now knew who he was up against and was fairly certain that Liza had taken his threat seriously. If she had, then the trial couldn't go forth, and Neve was safe.

Seeing Liza again had been difficult. The woman was a snake in the grass, and he'd felt an overwhelming desire to kill her. It took all his strength not to. She was a mother, after all, and to deprive her little boy of his only parent would be a cruel thing to do. But, if Archie knew anything about human nature, it was that people like Liza didn't just go away. She'd betrayed Hugo to Lionel Finch and nearly had him killed, and now she was after Neve. Was it a personal vendetta of some sort, or had Liza fallen on hard times and simply wanted to find an easy way to make some money? Jem had said she'd asked for twenty crowns. That was a bold move. Perhaps if she'd asked for less Neve wouldn't have been as outraged, but Lady Everly was a woman of strength and character; she would never buckle to threats or blackmail. Archie almost wished she had.

Paying off Liza would have bought them some time, so he could have returned to London to find Hugo. Hugo needed him, especially at a time like this. Hugo was as resourceful and courageous as any man he'd ever met, but there were things Archie was better at. Despite his best attempts, Hugo could never quite drop his clipped upper-crust elocution or act the thug. Even dressed like a tradesman, the nobleman beneath stood out in a crowd of common men. Hugo needed Archie to go where he couldn't, and carry out tasks which might be distasteful, although to give Hugo his due, he would do whatever it took to clear his name and keep his family safe. And part of working as a team was following orders, so Archie couldn't leave, even now that he knew that Liza had been taken care of. He had to keep an eye on the women and make sure they were safe.

At least Frances isn't in danger, Archie thought, *for now*. Associating with a known witch could have repercussions, and if Neve were to be found guilty on Sunday, all eyes would turn to Frances, who would be found guilty by association. There was already talk in the village, and Frances's natural beauty didn't help her cause. Women were jealous creatures, suspicious of anyone who had the power to take what was theirs. Frances hardly ever went into the village, but Archie had seen the men looking at her in church, and so had their wives. Frances made most of the village women look drab and coarse, and they, in turn, hated her and spoke ill of her.

And, of course, there was Mark Watson to consider. He was in the house with the women, according to Jem, and Archie knew the man well enough to be concerned. He'd known Mark since he was a lad, and Mark had always had a volatile temper and a disregard for natural law. He'd often pursued other men's wives, and there had been talk of him forcing himself on the cooper's daughter about ten years back. Mark had denied the accusation strenuously at the time, but the girl had gotten with child, and her son, who was now nine, bore a striking resemblance to Mark. If Mark Watson so much as looked at Frances or Neve the wrong way, he'd geld him, Archie decided.

Archie suddenly froze, his body going rigid, his legs tensing in preparation. He was ready to lunge at whoever was out there in the darkness. He heard the snap of a twig, and his hand instantly went for his dagger. It wasn't in his boot though. He'd taken it out when he came back and left it next to his sword. Archie looked around for something to use as a weapon. He slowly reached for a piece of split log. It wasn't ideal, but it was something. He balanced the wood in his hand, ready to strike if need be, when he heard a low whistle. Archie relaxed and tossed the wood down as he rose to his feet, a smile of relief on his face.

Hugo melted out of the darkness. He looked tired and stern, his clothes dusty from hours of travel. Archie didn't normally show Hugo much physical affection, but he grasped him in a bear hug, thrilled to see him alive and well. Hugo hugged Archie back, clapping him on the back.

"Is all well?" Hugo asked as they drew apart.

"Come inside and I'll fill you in. You look like you could use a drink and some food, although my father lives on pottage and turnips these days."

"Pottage will be just fine. I'm famished."

Horatio Hicks showed no surprise at seeing Lord Everly in his home. He welcomed Hugo, offered him a cup of ale and a bowl of pottage, then took his pipe and a pouch of tobacco from the mantel. "I reckon you two need to talk, so I'll just have a quiet smoke outside," he said and let himself out.

Hugo wolfed down the food as if he hadn't eaten in days, drank the ale in one long swallow and held out his cup for a refill.

Archie waited patiently. He felt an irrational surge of joy. Hugo was back. Now they would be able to return home to their women and get on with their lives. Perhaps he'd see Franny tonight. A warm glow spread through Archie's chest at the thought of climbing into bed with her and taking her into his arms. It wasn't even the promise of making love, but the need to be close to her, and to know that she was safe, and he was there to look after her.

Hugo pushed aside the empty bowl and leaned back in his chair, his face slightly more relaxed now. "Archie, Max is dead," he announced without preamble.

"What? How?"

"The gossip on the street is that it was suicide. I have other theories myself."

"You think it was murder?" Archie asked, stunned.

"I do, but I can't prove it, especially now that I'm officially deceased. All of London is abuzz with the news. Tell me what's been happening here."

Archie quickly filled Hugo in on the events of the day. "Liza won't be troubling you again. But what are you going to do now? Go back to France?" Archie asked. His stomach clenched with anxiety. The reality of the situation was beginning to sink in, and with it, dread. They'd only been back in England for a few months. Archie liked France, and the years in Rouen had been unexpectedly happy, but he longed to remain in England, close to his father. If he left now, he might never see him again. Horatio was failing; Archie could see that after living with him for a few days. It wasn't just scurvy that had caused him to lose weight and appear more frail. There was something else, Archie was sure of it. There was a wheezing in the chest when he slept, and the way his father grew breathless after performing the smallest of tasks. Horatio Hicks was ill, and not long for this world.

Hugo studied Archie for a long moment, his head cocked to the side as if he were considering something. Archie noticed the tell-tale tremor in his left hand. He was anxious because he hadn't told him the whole truth of the situation. An unexpected thought suddenly popped into Archie's head. Was it possible that Hugo had killed Max himself? It didn't make much sense, but there was always method to Hugo's madness. Or perhaps it had been self-defense. Max had made several attempts on Hugo's life. Could be that he decided to try one last time.

Hugo finally seemed to come to a decision. He leaned forward, and Archie instinctively leaned toward him, eager to hear what Hugo had to share with him. He didn't like feeling left out, as if Hugo didn't trust him.

"Archie, there is something I must tell you," Hugo began, his voice low. The window was open and sweet smoke from Horatio's pipe drifted into the house, reminding the two men that they weren't quite alone. "I hoped never to have to reveal this to you, but I think the time has come. You will find it shocking and fantastical, but you've known me for most of your life. I would never lie to you."

"You're scaring me now," Archie said, attempting humor, but sounding like a frightened little boy instead. He'd known Hugo since he was seven, but he'd never heard him use that particular tone of voice, nor had he ever noticed that expression. It was as if Hugo were afraid of sharing what was on his mind, or very apprehensive at the very least. "Come, you can tell me anything. You know that," Archie prompted.

"Do you remember when I came across Neve walking toward the manor from the church and nearly ran her down?" Hugo asked.

Archie wasn't sure what he'd been expecting, but it wasn't a reminiscence about meeting the love of his life for the first time. Archie silently nodded.

"She hadn't been in sanctuary; she'd come through a passage in the crypt—a passage from the future. Neve was born in the twentieth century, and she had taken me to the future when she saved me from arrest in 1685. When people said there was magic involved, they weren't too far off the mark. I went to the future, Archie, where I met Max. He is from the future, too. He was Lord Everly in 2013."

Archie stared dumbly at Hugo. He knew Hugo would never lie or play a dirty trick on him, but this was just too much to swallow. He had no idea how to reply. He didn't believe Neve was a witch, but he did believe in witchcraft in general. Some women had that gift and used it for evil. There were times when he thought Margaret had been a witch. There hadn't been a man who'd been immune to her type of primal sexuality. But Margaret wasn't evil, just selfish and misguided. Had she been a witch, she'd have healed herself when she'd fallen ill, or conjured up some gold to make her life easier. And Neve.... He'd never seen any evil in Neve, nor had she ever done anything to hurt anyone, but now that he knew this about her, he could never view her in the same way as before. What other powers did she possess? Perhaps Liza had known something, and there was truth in her accusation.

"Archie?" Hugo prompted.

"I don't know what to say. I admit I find it difficult to believe, but if you tell me it's so, I will say I believe you."

"Archie, I never planned to share this with anyone, for fear of putting Neve in danger. You know how people feel about things they don't understand. To be honest, I don't really understand it myself, nor does Neve. Traveling through time is not common in the future, but it's often explored in films."

"In what?" Archie asked, unfamiliar with the term.

"Films are moving pictures that tell a story," Hugo replied absentmindedly.

"Will you tell me something of this future you've seen?" Archie asked, leaning even further toward Hugo. Perhaps hearing more would help him to understand, if not to envision the world Hugo was speaking of.

"I will, but not right now. I'm telling you this for a reason, Archie. Now that I am believed dead, and Neve has been accused of witchcraft, there's every reason for us to leave, and instead of going sideways, I intend to go forward."

"What, to the future?" Archie gasped. "All of you?"

"Yes. We will go to the twenty-first century, and I'd like you and Frances to come with us."

"No," Archie shook his head like a horse chasing away flies. "No."

Hugo inclined his head in mute understanding. He hadn't expected Archie to agree, but he had to make the offer. He didn't think that Archie would change his mind. This was his time and place, and in truth, Archie belonged here, and Frances would remain with Archie, which was as it should be.

"Archie, since you won't be joining us, I have a few requests to make of you."

"Anything." Archie looked relieved, as if Hugo could have forced him to go with them. Taking care of ordinary things was something he could understand, and he would focus on that instead of the extraordinary knowledge Hugo had just shared with him.

Of course, to be fair, Archie needed some time to process the information. Hugo had some difficulty accepting the truth when faced with the future, even when shown running water and electricity, not to mention speeding cars. Archie only had Hugo's word for it, and although he struggled to believe him, on some subconscious level, he probably thought that Hugo had lost his mind.

"Please see that Max gets a decent burial. I know that the Church will refuse to bury him in consecrated ground, but perhaps you can convince Reverend Snow that it was murder rather than suicide."

"And how am I meant to do that?" Archie asked, balking at the request.

"The reverend knows that I'm Catholic. We've never discussed it, but he is aware of my faith. He also knows that, as a Catholic, I would never take my own life, it being a mortal sin. Perhaps he can be persuaded that the circumstances of my death are murky at best."

"I'll do what I can. What else?" Archie asked. He suddenly felt as if he were going to be sick. What would he do with himself once Hugo left? He'd been in Hugo's service all his adult life. He supposed he could find new employment with another nobleman, but he didn't want to work for anyone else. Hugo was a friend, a mentor, a brother. And what of Frances and her devotion to Neve and the children?

"Archie, I need to make sure that Clarence Hiddleston, my nephew, inherits the estate, but only after we've safely gone. If, for any reason, our venture fails, then Michael will still be the heir to the title and estate. I need you to keep an eye on Everly Manor until you know for sure, and then you can contact Clarence."

"Beastly little twerp," Archie said with feeling. "And what am I to tell people about Neve and the children?"

"Tell them that Neve decided to return to France, or go back to her people in the Netherlands. That's where people believe she was from. It really doesn't matter."

Archie stared at Hugo through a mist of misery. "You are really going," he said, more to himself than to Hugo. "You are really leaving."

"Archie, I must. There's nothing left for me here, and I must think of my family. My children will be better off in the future where they can be safe."

"What's it like then, this future?" Archie asked, suddenly really curious.

"It's miraculous, Archie."

Archie sat in mute silence as Hugo described the life he had seen. Archie had a hard time imagining the machines Hugo spoke of, especially the flying ones, but he could almost envision a place where people were free to worship as they pleased, and there was less disease and suffering.

"There are some important details to work out, but we should be ready to go soon. Before Sunday. And now, I must go see my wife," Hugo said as he rose from the table. "I suppose now that I'm officially dead, it's safe for you to return to Everly Manor. You can create a diversion while I sneak into the house. No one must see me alive, least of all Mark Watson."

"Right," Archie replied, still bemused. This was all proving to be too much for him.

EIGHTEEN

I carefully removed Michael's wooden horse from his grasp as he finally fell solidly asleep. He carried that horse with him everywhere and reached for it first thing in the morning when he woke up. Valentine didn't have such attachments, at least not physical ones, but she constantly asked for Hugo and Archie, the two men in her life who meant everything to her. Lately, she'd warmed to Joe a little, the groom who took her out on her pony every day, but she tolerated him more than liked him. Archie was the only person whom Valentine ever tried to please, possibly because he wasn't impressed with her tantrums or demands. When Archie finally doled out a word of approval, Valentine swelled with pride like a balloon and glowed for hours.

She never tried as hard to please Hugo, but then again, she didn't need to. Hugo doted on her the way he'd doted on Elena. She was his little girl, his princess, the daughter who could do no wrong. At times, I'd wished he was sterner with her, but at the moment, I would give anything to have my family back together. I pushed away the nagging thought that my children might never see their father again. I simply couldn't bear to think along those lines. I kept them out of the dining room where Max's coffin still rested. Seeing Max would break their hearts since they would believe him to be their father, and I was in no position to tell them otherwise.

My morbid reverie was interrupted by a desperate cry coming from downstairs. Cook and the rest of the servants had already gone up, having finished their tasks for the day, and would all be in their rooms on the top floor of the house. Perhaps one of the girls had come downstairs for something and saw a mouse. Nevertheless, I had to investigate.

I was still fully dressed, so I tiptoed from the room so as not to wake up the children and made my way downstairs. I should have taken a candle since the downstairs was nearly pitch dark. Harriet always closed the shutters for the night, and all the candles had been extinguished, save the ones by Max's coffin. I walked down the stairs slowly, mindful of missing a step, then stopped. I thought I heard something coming from the dining room, which was the last place I would have expected any commotion under the circumstances.

I inched forward, certain that I'd heard sounds of a scuffle coming from within, and pushed open the door a crack. A tall candle burned at Max's feet and one at his head. In the flickering light, he looked as if he were asleep, his white face reminiscent of a vampire resting in his coffin. I heard a strange sound and stepped deeper into the room. Mark Watson's back was to me, but I clearly saw Frances. He'd pushed her up against the wall and had one hand over her mouth as he groped beneath her skirts. She was making strangled noises and trying to throw her attacker off, but Watson was a big man, and one in the throes of lust. Frances looked terrified, her eyes huge in her pale face. She must have seen me because she suddenly stopped struggling, giving the game away.

Mark Watson uttered a profanity and released her as he spun around to find me standing behind him with a poker at the ready. I was breathing heavily, my blood roaring in my ears with fury. I would have happily buried the poker in the man's gut if he so much as moved.

Watson wasn't the brightest light, but he was smart enough to perceive the imminent threat. He saw it in my eyes. He raised his hands and slowly stepped away from Frances. "Just a bit o' sport, Yer Ladyship," he explained, a crooked smile on his face. "She misses 'er husband, is all."

"So, you thought you'd step into his place?" I demanded, my fury increasing tenfold.

"A woman needs a man to keep 'er happy," he replied, licking his lips.

"She doesn't look very happy to me," I spat back.

"Few women are eager for it, me lady, but once they are on their back, they tend to enjoy it." Mark Watson was still holding his hands up in surrender, but the look on his face was one of insolence.

I gaped at the man, stunned that he would speak to me that way. He'd been respectful enough for the first two days, but now things had changed. In his eyes, I was a widow, with no man to protect me. Lord Everly wouldn't be coming back, and if Archie showed up, Mark Watson would deal with him. Archie and Watson were well-matched physically, and Watson had the support of the villagers, especially the blacksmith, who was a particular friend of his. He was no longer intimidated by my position and thought he could take what he wanted, which in this case was Frances. Not for the first time, I realized what a curse beauty could be. Had Frances been plain, she might have had a much happier life, or at least a safer one. Being a beautiful young woman made her a target in this century where men often took what they wanted regardless of whether consent was given or not.

I motioned for Frances to move away from the wall and get behind me. She scurried over. I could hear her ragged breathing as she stood behind me. I could only imagine the memories Watson's assault would have brought back to her. Frances wasn't crying, but I could feel her terror without even looking at her.

I wasn't sure what possessed me, but I advanced on Watson, the fear and anger of the past few days overtaking all reason. I felt an emotion that I had only experienced once or twice in my life—pure bloodlust. I was gratified to see fear in Mark Watson's eyes as he realized that I wasn't just bluffing.

He backed away and held his hands out in front of him to ward off the attack. "It won't 'appen again, Yer Ladyship. I swear," he stammered.

I bared my teeth in a vicious grin as he bumped into the wall. There was no place for him to go. I held the poker with both hands and pushed the tip into his stomach until I felt the resistance of hard muscle. Watson was strong and could probably overpower me quite easily if he grabbed the poker, so I had better make this count. I pushed the poker harder, hearing him gasp as the sharp iron tip scratched the skin.

"Neve, don't," Frances moaned behind me. "They'll kill you for sure."

I knew she was right. As much as I wanted to cause injury to the man, hurting him would only make the case against me stronger. I couldn't afford to face charges of aggravated assault as well, but there was one thing I could do. Mark Watson believed the stories of witchcraft, being the ignorant sod that he was. I'd seen him make the sign of the Devil behind my back, sticking out the pinky and forefinger to represent horns. All I had to do was confirm what he already suspected to frighten him off.

"If you ever lay your hands on Mistress Hicks or anyone in this house again, I will kill you. And I will do it without laying a finger on you. I will summon my familiar and watch him suck the soul from your body as your blood flows from your veins. Do you hear me?" I growled, hoping I'd sounded convincing.

Watson knew exactly what I was implying. He went white to the roots of his hair as he glared at me. He looked defiant, but I could see that he was scared.

"Witch," Watson hissed under his breath. "Ye are no' long for this world." He lunged forward and grabbed the poker, easily yanking it out of my hands and turning the tip toward me. An ugly smile spread across his face as he advanced on me. I suppose I should have been afraid, but all I felt was overwhelming anger. I didn't back down but stood in front of Frances like a lioness protecting her cub.

"Go on then," I goaded him. "And see what happens."

He advanced slowly, torn by momentary indecision. He had complete power over Frances and myself at that moment, but my words had made an impact. I could see the conflict playing out on his face, but his desire for violence won out. He seemed to make up his mind as he approached us. Mark Watson was now in front of the door, his back turned to the corridor as he leered at me. He held the poker like a spear, raised in his hand with the tip pointing at my heart. I couldn't be sure he meant to use it, but the rational part of my brain told me that he could very easily murder me. I was completely helpless against him, and it would be easy enough for him to explain what had happened, and describe in detail what I'd threatened him with.

I wished Frances would do something, or distract him at the very least so that I could grab something to defend myself with, but she was frozen with fright. I heard her gasp behind me, but assumed it was just fear.

Mark Watson gave her a curious look, his eyes sliding away from mine in surprise. Frances held out a shaking hand and pointed to something behind Watson with one finger, her mouth forming an O of surprise.

A hooded figure materialized behind Mark Watson, a

dagger in his hand like an avenging angel. He held the blade to Watson's throat with his left hand while he applied pressure to the man's wrist to force him to drop the poker. Watson stood frozen, unsure of who was behind him, but terrified to the core of his being. As far as he knew, no one was in the house besides us and the female staff. His eyes grew huge in his face and he trembled visibly.

"Ye've summoned yer familiar," he whimpered, giving me an imploring look. "Please, Yer Ladyship, I meant no harm."

"I did warn you," I replied with great satisfaction.

I could see Archie's impish grin behind Watson's head. He was enjoying this. He must have heard what I'd said as he'd approached the door, and decided to use it to his advantage. He pressed the blade harder to Watson's throat, forcing him to cry out.

"Leave this house at once, or you will suffer the consequences," I said, my voice low and full of foreboding. "Release him," I said to Archie.

Archie slowly removed the dagger as Watson spun about and dashed past him with a shriek of terror. I heard the pounding of footsteps on the stone floor of the foyer and then the slamming of the front door. He would either run home and keep the incident to himself, or go straight into the village and cry "Witchcraft!" I didn't know the man well, but I'd seen the swagger in his step and the cockiness in his eyes. To admit that he'd been bested by a woman would do no favors to his reputation in the village. I concluded that Mark Watson would go home and rationalize what had happened until he could justify running away and screaming like a little girl, making himself out to be the wronged party.

"Are you all right, Your Ladyship?" Archie demanded as he sheathed his dagger, pushed back the hood, and came toward me. He was speaking to me, but his eyes were on Frances. He needed reassurance that she hadn't been accosted by Watson, so

I nodded and stepped aside, leaving the two of them together. I heard Frances's cry as she flew into Archie's arms. Archie's tone changed from gruffness to a whisper filled with longing as he took her into his arms. "Franny," he breathed, "you are safe now."

NINETEEN

My legs felt like lead as I trudged up the stairs. I wanted to ask Archie why he came alone and what had happened to Hugo, but the news would keep. Archie and Frances deserved a few moments together. Archie would come and talk to me when he was ready, and I needed a stiff drink to steady my nerves. Now that it was all over, my hands shook, and my heart raced, making me lightheaded. I had no doubt in my mind that Mark Watson would not have just given up. He would have hurt me to get to Frances, confident that there would be no consequences.

I couldn't help wondering if Reverend Snow was blind to Watson's temper, or if he'd chosen him as my jailer with precisely that penchant for violence in mind. I hoped the former. I couldn't bear to think that the spiritual leader of this community would condone Watson's behavior. I still hoped that Reverend Snow would speak out on my behalf at the trial, but the hope was fading fast. I would truly be on my own in there, but the knowledge that Archie was back gave me a modicum of peace.

I took a deep breath before gently turning the door handle, for fear of waking up the children. I was suddenly exhausted, and all I wanted was to climb into bed and snuggle up next to them. Their warm bodies and sweet childish smell always soothed my senses, and I longed to lose myself in sleep. I needed rest to face whatever tomorrow brought. There was only one more day before the trial. I splashed an inch of brandy into a glass from the decanter Hugo kept on the mantel and swallowed it in one gulp. The brandy burned its way down my gullet but didn't seem to do much to calm me. I considered a refill, but then changed my mind. What I needed was sleep.

It took me longer than usual to undo my laces and remove my gown. Normally, I didn't need any help undressing, but tonight my hands just wouldn't work, and I had to struggle with several knots before I could finally remove the bodice. The skirt was easier. I sighed with relief as I pulled my night shift on and climbed into the high bed. The children were sound asleep, Valentine's arm protectively around Michael. She teased him during the day, but when her defenses were down, she was really quite sweet. I blew out the candle and closed my eyes, but images of Frances's frightened face and Mark Watson's leer danced before my eyes. I was physically tired, but my mind was overwrought. I was glad that the room wasn't completely dark. The light from the fire illuminated the dark corners and made me feel slightly safer, although it was just an illusion.

I was just beginning to calm down when the door handle slowly turned, and I shot up like a jack-in-the-box, suddenly terrified. Archie wouldn't just come in without knocking, and anyway, I'd heard him and Frances go to their own room some while ago. What if Watson was back to finish what he started? I hadn't locked the front door after he ran from the house, I realized. I'd been too shaken. I'd assumed that Archie had locked up, but he might have forgotten as well.

I stared at the door, wondering if I had enough time to find a weapon. The only thing to hand was Michael's horse. Much good would it do me. *A candlestick*, I thought frantically as I looked about me. I'd left the candle on the mantel. I was help-less. I nearly jumped out of my skin as the door opened and a dark shadow entered, the face concealed by the low brim of the hat. My heart began to pound, but this time it was with joy. I didn't need to see the face; I'd know him anywhere.

"Hugo," I squealed as I slid out of bed and straight into his arms. He looked tired and unkempt, but otherwise unharmed. I clung to him for what seemed like an hour, needing to feel his solid presence and the beating of his heart. Hugo just held me against him, his stubbled jaw rough against my temple. He didn't say anything, but there was no need. He was alive and free, which was all that mattered.

Hugo lowered his head, and I raised my face to his kiss. Suddenly, I couldn't think straight. A roaring fire burned in my belly as I tore at Hugo's clothes. He didn't require much prompting. He shrugged off the cloak and yanked at the laces of his breeches as I pulled off his shirt. Hugo laid me down on the rug in front of the hearth. He kissed me hard and pushed up my shift. His hand reached between my legs, but I brushed it away. I was more than ready. He understood my need and plunged into my body, stifling my cry with his mouth. Hugo might have taken his time, but I slammed my hips against his, matching him thrust for thrust. I didn't want tenderness; I wanted unbridled sexual fury.

Our lovemaking was frenzied, the tempest over in a few short minutes. Hugo rested his head against my shoulder as I wrapped my arms around him. I felt as limp as a rag doll, but my womb still vibrated with the aftershocks of Hugo's efforts. He lay still, his breathing ragged, his heart thumping against my breast. Hugo groped for his cloak and pulled it over us should the children suddenly wake. Neither one of us seemed to have the strength to say anything, so we just lay by the dying fire until the flames turned to embers and the room grew colder.

"Come to bed," Hugo finally said as he pulled me to my feet and handed me my shift. "I'm exhausted."

Hugo tucked me in, gave me a tender kiss, and then climbed in on the other side next to Michael. I smiled as I saw him breathe in the child's sweet smell. Hugo kissed the top of Michael's head, then leaned over and kissed Valentine. He gave me a tired smile before falling into a deep sleep. I began to drift as my mind finally let go and allowed me to rest.

TWENTY

Frances stared at Archie in mute incomprehension. Was he making a joke at her expense? No, he couldn't be. Archie looked deadly serious as he related his conversation with Hugo. Silent tears began to fall as the reality of the situation finally began to sink in. They were leaving. Forever. There would be no letters, no visits, and no connection of any sort.

Archie pulled Frances against his chest and stroked her hair, gentling her the way he would one of his horses. "It will be all right, Franny. We'll miss them, but it's you and me now, and that's all we really need."

"No," Frances shook her head against him. "No."

Archie kissed the top of her head. "Franny, they don't have much of a choice. They would stay if they could; you know that."

"The children," Frances sobbed.

"I know you'll miss the children, but they'll be better off where they are going. They'll have better chances of survival, and grand opportunities. Or so Hugo says," Archie added, unable to picture the world Hugo spoke of so eloquently. It all sounded like some laudanum-induced dream, a landscape full of sound and color, and strange machines, which would dissipate as soon as the drug wore off.

Frances drew away from her husband and looked up at him, her tear-stained face a picture of misery. "And what of us, Archie? What will we do without them? Where will we live?"

"We can do anything we want, my love. Hugo owes me some wages, and I have some money put by. We'll have enough for a fresh start. We can stay here in Surrey, or we can go to London or Paris. You loved it in France. We can buy a little farmhouse somewhere and just live off the land. What do you think of that?"

"I think that's the most fanciful idea you've ever had," Frances replied, smiling despite the tears. "I've never met a man less suited to farming than you, Archie."

Archie smiled guiltily. She was right; he hated farming. He found it to be tedious, backbreaking, and utterly boring. The most exciting thing to happen to a farmer, and not in a good way, was the loss of crop, or a sickness among the animals.

"You love it, Archie, the intrigue and danger of serving Lord Everly," Frances observed.

"I do not," Archie protested half-heartedly.

"You do. You come alive when something is brewing. You are not a man content with dull manual labor. If you were, you'd move back home and run your father's farm. His health is failing, and he's hardly in a position to keep the farm going for much longer. But you need adventure and excitement. You'd die a little each day if running the farm was your whole life. And so would I," Frances added, shuddering with disgust. Spending her days cooking, mending, and looking after the animals was not a life she could embrace happily.

Archie gave Frances a perplexed look. Did he really crave excitement that much? He supposed he did. Frances was right; he did come alive when something was afoot. He enjoyed the anticipation, the planning, and the pounding of blood in his veins when there was even a hint of danger. Archie was born to be a soldier, his father said that often enough, but Horatio Hicks had forbidden his son to take up arms after he'd witnessed the slaughter of the Civil War in his youth.

"What about the New World then?" Archie asked, suddenly excited by the idea. "We can sail to Virginia, or Massachusetts Colony, and start afresh. They need men like me there. They need men who can wield a sword as well as plant a crop. There are attacks from the Native Indians. I hear they are fierce warriors," Archie said, his voice full of awe.

"Good grief," Frances exclaimed as she pushed Archie away. "Are you mad? I am not going to America to be surrounded by Puritans or slaughtered by Indians, Archibald Hicks, so you can just put that brilliant idea out of your mind."

Frances turned her back to Archie and pretended to go to sleep. Archie moved closer to her and pressed himself against her back as he wrapped his arm around her and pulled her closer. "Come here, Franny," he whispered in her ear. "We don't have to go to the Colonies, but we can pretend that I am a savage and have captured a beautiful white woman and taken her prisoner. Hmm, what will I do with her?" he asked playfully as he pressed his hard length against her back, moving his hips provocatively.

Frances giggled and turned to face Archie. "You really are a terrible rascal," she said as she pulled him toward her for a kiss.

TWENTY-ONE

Archie watched silently as shifting shadows passed over Frances's sleeping face. Even in repose, she looked tense and unhappy, her eyes moving rapidly beneath the lids. He thought that making love to her would help her relax, but the impending separation from the Everlys was uppermost in her mind. He couldn't blame her. He didn't feel the same emotional dependence on Hugo as Frances felt toward Neve, but he would feel bereft once they'd gone, he knew that.

Archie turned onto his back and stared at the embroidered canopy, his eyes unseeing. He'd meant to tell Franny of Hugo's offer, but somehow the words didn't come. What if she wished to go with them? As her husband, he had every right to make the decision for them both, but he'd promised himself that he would never behave like a tyrant and meant to keep his word. If Frances wanted to go, he'd have to at least consider the possibility.

The very idea was exciting and disturbing at the same time. Hugo had regaled Archie with tales of the future as they'd walked toward Everly Manor this evening. Archie was fascinated by descriptions of machines and computers and horrified by stories of modern warfare. To think that soldiers no longer fought face to face, but from a distance, killing thousands without ever engaging them man to man. Archie tried to picture a gun that shot dozens of bullets at the same time, one after the other. Or a missile. To shoot a weapon that would detonate countless miles away with exact precision boggled the mind. How was such a thing possible?

Hugo said that people no longer used horses for travel, but rather as a quaint tourist attraction. Tired old horses pulled old-fashioned carriages for the amusement of middle-aged couples and small children around a park, while everyday people traveled in metal capsules propelled by motors that accelerated to impossible speeds. And they'd been to the moon! "Impossible!" Archie groaned as he turned over again, unable to get comfortable. There was a part of him that would like to see all these amazing things for himself, but he couldn't honestly consider the possibility.

Archie knew himself well enough to realize that the one thing holding him back was fear, not of the unknown, but of the known. He knew one thing for certain—in the future Hugo had described there was no place for someone like him. What would he do? How would he support his family? He had no skills beyond sword-fighting, and Hugo had mentioned that swords were obsolete. Men no longer wore weapons at all, except those who enforced the law and those in the military, and they were weapons the likes of which Archie had never seen.

Archie knew how to farm, but to do that, he'd need funds to buy land, livestock, and equipment. He had some money put by, but would that be enough to ensure a livelihood in this strange new world? And Hugo did mention something about the need for identity papers. That had been a big problem when Hugo had gone to the future the last time; he didn't officially exist. Archie scoffed at the idea. Why would anyone want to be written up that way? A man was entitled to his privacy, and his secrets. He had no wish to be a number, or a name on some government list where someone would know all there was to know about him. He liked his relative anonymity, liked the freedom to choose his own path.

Frances might feel differently though. Hugo had spoken of amazing scientific advances, things Archie couldn't begin to wrap his head around, but he said that modern medicine was miraculous. Frances wanted a child so desperately. Perhaps those future physicians could help her conceive. But that would require funds and identity papers as well. No one would accept two people who might as well have dropped from the moon.

Archie gave up on sleep, and slid quietly out of bed, so as not to disturb Frances. He pulled on his breeches and a shirt, and went downstairs, his bare feet making virtually no sound on the wooden floors.

Two candles burned in the dining parlor, one at the head, and one at the foot of the coffin. Hugo sat in the corner, lost in darkness.

"Couldn't sleep?" he asked as Archie sat down next to him.

"No, too much on my mind. What about you?"

"Same. I thought I'd keep Max company before his final journey. I can't help but feel responsible for his death."

Archie shrugged, although the movement was lost in the dim light of the room. "He made his choices, just as you made yours. Stop blaming yourself for other people's decisions. You didn't kill Max any more than you killed your sister."

"No, I suppose not," Hugo agreed reluctantly.

Hugo was a born leader, Archie knew that, and as a leader, he tended to imagine himself responsible for the people who came into his sphere, whether he was or not. Hugo likely felt responsible for him as well, but Archie was a grown man. He could take care of himself. He was young and strong and would have no difficulty finding new employment.

"We'll be all right, you know," Archie said. "You needn't worry about us."

"I know you will, but I will miss you. In this life, a man should consider himself lucky if he knows one person he can truly trust. I've been blessed to have known you and Bradford. I can't help wondering if I'll ever meet anyone who will be as genuine or trustworthy."

"Are you going to tell Master Nash where you're going?" Archie asked.

"No. I trust Brad with my life, but there's no need to burden him with this knowledge. Let him believe that I'm dead. It will be easier for him that way. Brad has a life here, a family, and an estate. This is where he was born, and where he will die. Why shatter his view of the world with something he can never really understand?"

"So, why have you told me?"

"You are different, Archie. Your understanding of the world is more fluid. You've seen and done more than Brad, and you've blood on your hands. Brad is still something of an innocent, who believes in good and evil, God and the Devil. You know there's much in between, as does Frances. Few men have experienced as much suffering as that girl has. I wanted to give you both a chance at a better life, and a safer future."

When Archie remained silent, Hugo continued.

"Archie, I will explain to you where the passage is and how it works. I know you don't require the knowledge, but just in case."

"In case of what?"

Hugo shrugged. They both knew they'd never see each other again.

TWENTY-TWO

I woke at dawn. I felt unusually languid, having enjoyed a night of uninterrupted sleep. Recently, my sleep had been fitful and plagued by bad dreams, but last night, I was finally able to rest, safe in the knowledge that Hugo was home.

The children were still asleep, their breathing even and deep, but Hugo was already up and fully dressed. He was writing something, but looked up when I softly called his name.

"No one can know I'm here," he whispered, "least of all the children. I'll bide in Archie's room until they are dressed and at breakfast."

I nodded. Hugo would fill me in later, but for now, I had to follow his instructions. With Max lying in state downstairs and believed by the servants to be Hugo, explaining his presence would be somewhat difficult.

I lay back down as Hugo slipped out of the room. The children would sleep for at least another hour, and then I would take them downstairs and leave them in the care of Frances. In the meantime, I could just savor my contentment.

A few minutes later Valentine sat up, looking about frantically. Her face glowed with expectation, but then her features crumpled as she glared at me with disappointment.

"What is it? Did you have a bad dream?" I asked as I pulled her into a hug.

Valentine pushed me away, her eyes full of suspicion.

"Where is he?" she demanded. "Where is Papa?"

"What do you mean?" I asked carefully.

"Papa was here. I know it. I heard his voice, and he kissed me while I slept."

"Darling, Papa is not here, but Archie is. He's downstairs having breakfast. He came home last night."

Valentine shook her head stubbornly. "I know Papa was here. I felt him."

I glanced away. I hated lying to my daughter, but I couldn't tell her the truth, not yet. First, I needed to find out what Hugo had planned. Having Valentine or Michael blurt something out could ruin everything.

"Papa will be back soon," I promised, hoping that no one had mentioned anything about the coffin downstairs in Valentine's presence. I would have a lot of explaining to do if she were told her father was dead by one of the servants.

"I don't believe you," Valentine mumbled petulantly as she slid out of bed. "Wake up, Michael," she called out.

Michael complied without a word of complaint. He allowed me to help him from the high bed and stood patiently while I dressed him for the day. Valentine liked to dress herself, but still needed help with her stockings and the laces at the back of her gown. She yelped as I brushed out her hair and braided it, pinning it up in a hairstyle much too grown up for a three-year-old. Michael grabbed his horse before I escorted them downstairs. Valentine was still upset, but her face brightened when she saw Archie, who picked her up and tossed her in the air, making her squeal with delight.

"Me too," Michael whined. "Me too."

Archie set down a squealing Valentine and scooped up Michael. "Of course, you too. Are you not afraid?"

"No, lift me up high," Michael demanded, which was surprising because he'd always been afraid. He hooted with joy as Archie tossed him up a few times, nearly making my heart fail when I thought he wouldn't catch him in time.

Frances stood in the doorway of the parlor, her face pale and her eyes filled with sadness. She watched Archie as he played with the children, her hand subconsciously going to her belly. Was it possible that she was pregnant, or just wishful thinking? I knew how much Frances wanted a baby, but I was sure she would have told me if she suspected she was with child. Frances would be too overcome with joy to keep such news to herself. Perhaps her pallor had to do with last night's incident. I had no doubt that Mark Watson would come back this morning, with reinforcements.

I was about to reassure her that she was safe when Harriet appeared at the foot of the stairs, her arms laden with firewood.

"I just need to go upstairs for a while," I stammered and ran up the steps to preempt Harriet walking into my bedroom and finding traces of Hugo.

"Come, let's have some breakfast," Frances said to the children and led them away.

"Archie, you come too," Valentine commanded as she grabbed his hand.

"I already had breakfast, but you can persuade me to have another one," Archie replied as he was dragged along.

* * *

"What now?" I whispered to Hugo as soon as I returned to our bedroom and locked the door behind me. Hugo had returned to our room, safe in the knowledge that the children were downstairs.

"Now, I have a bath," Hugo said. "I'll hide in the garderobe, so Ruby doesn't see me. Just call for some hot water. We'll talk once I feel human again."

I waited patiently, trying to appear nonchalant as Ruby brought bucket after bucket of hot water for my bath. Ruby barely made eye contact as she entered the room, shocked as she was by the news of his lordship's death. No one knew quite what to say, so I just let the matter hang over the house like a miasma. First, I needed to talk to Hugo. There were many things to discuss, but as long as he was alive and with me, they could all wait.

I locked the door once again after the final bucket of water was upended into the tub and called to Hugo to come out. He stripped off his clothes and stepped into the tub, sighing with pleasure as the hot water rose above his chest. I soaped a wash-cloth and began washing him. Normally, he would protest, but this morning he just sat there and let me take care of him. He was preoccupied, which was quite normal under the circumstances.

"Hugo," I called to him softly. "Now what?"

"Hmm?" he mumbled. He'd been lost in thought, his eyes half closed as he leaned back in the copper tub while I soaped his chest and shoulders. "Neve, I told Archie the truth about where you came from," he finally said.

My hand stopped in midair. I wasn't sure what I had been expecting him to say, but it certainly wasn't that. Hugo had never shared my secret with anyone, for fear of putting me in terrible danger. I trusted Archie with my life, but never expected Hugo to tell him the truth. Was that why Frances looked so forlorn? Had Archie shared the truth with her last night?

"There is only one reason why you would do that," I speculated, my voice trembling with emotion.

"How do you feel about going home?" Hugo asked, his eyes

now fully open and watching me intently. He was no longer relaxed, but sitting up in the tub, his face tense.

I had suppressed all thought of the twenty-first century over the past few years, concentrating only on the present, but Hugo's words released something within me, and a flower of hope bloomed in my breast, beautiful and amazing. "Really?"

"Really. It's time for us to leave."

"But, Hugo, what of all the things that prevented us from staying there before?" Hugo's lack of legal identity made life nearly impossible for us. He was even worse off than an illegal immigrant, since those people at least had a valid identity and a verifiable past. Without any kind of identification, Hugo had been unable to work, to receive medical care, or to get married. He had been a pariah, much as he would be now that he was believed to be dead in his own time.

"Neve, Max said something to me the last time we spoke. He suggested that I take his place. He said something about never having been fingerprinted, but I didn't really comprehend his meaning. He also mentioned something about his dentist and physician. I know it was important but couldn't extract the full meaning from his remarks. Do you know what he meant?"

"Yes, I do," I replied happily. For some reason, knowing that Max had given Hugo his blessing meant the world to me. I knew that being the honorable man Hugo was, he wouldn't feel right about assuming someone else's identity, but since Max had encouraged him to do it, Hugo was more willing to accept the possibility of this new life. "What Max meant was that without fingerprints, the police can't prove that you are not Max Everly. His doctor and dentist are the only two people who can disprove your identity, but they would not be able to do that of their own accord. The doctor-patient relationship is confidential. They cannot violate that unless there's a warrant from the police or a court subpoena."

"So, Max was in earnest?" Hugo asked, still amazed that his archenemy would genuinely wish to help him.

"Yes, he was. If we can figure out a way to explain your disappearance, you would be able to step into Max's shoes and take over his identity," I explained, getting more excited by the minute.

"But what about you?" Hugo asked.

"How do I explain being gone for nearly four years and then turning up with two children? That's something we'll need to work out. Oh, God," I said, the penny dropping at last, "now I know what Simon meant."

"About what?"

"Simon knew that Lord Hugo Everly died in 1689. He'd either seen the grave or had found something in the history books. He gave me his card and invited me to call him should I ever need his help. He knew, Hugo. He knew I'd be coming back, but he couldn't bring himself to tell me that I'd be coming back alone."

"It was kind of him to spare you. He's a good man, Simon," Hugo replied as he rose from the tub and reached for a towel.

As Hugo dried off, I had a sudden thought which nearly ripped my innards out. Frances and Archie. We would have to leave them behind. We'd never see them again, never know what happened to them, unless they left some kind of communication for us to find in the future.

Frances and Archie were the closest thing I'd ever had to family. My foster parents had been good people, but I'd never felt the kind of closeness with my foster mother Linda as I did with Frances. Frances was the sister I never had. She was my best friend, my confidante, my support system, as I was hers. How could I just leave her behind? And Archie was Hugo's closest friend. They were from different social classes and backgrounds, but no two men were more devoted to each other.

What would Archie do without Hugo? And where would they go once Clarence took possession of the estate?

I hadn't realized I was crying until Hugo drew me to him and held me tight. "I offered for them to come with us," he said softly. "I know it would be difficult, but Archie is used to manual work. It would be easier for him to adjust, and as Lord Everly, I would be able to take care of them."

"What did he say?" I gulped. I wanted to hear that Archie had agreed readily, but by this point, I knew him too well. Archie wouldn't easily accept the notion of traveling to the future, nor would he relish the idea of being completely dependent on Hugo. He was dependent on Hugo now, but by choice, not from necessity. He was a capable man who would inherit his father's farm after his death. It wasn't much, but it was property which would be his and he could pass on to his children.

"He said no, but he was in shock. Perhaps he'll talk it over with Frances and change his mind," Hugo replied, but I could see from his expression that he didn't hold out much hope of Archie coming around.

TWENTY-THREE

I watched from the window as Hugo's tall shape vanished into the woods behind the house, his black cloak billowing like a sail in the breeze. He'd stay with Horatio Hicks until it was time for us to leave, since no one could know that he was still alive.

Hugo had stood by the window for a long time after his bath, watching the children playing outside with Archie, an expression of such tenderness on his face that it nearly broke my heart.

"I thought I'd never see them again," he'd said softly. "I've been blessed with another chance. What have I done to deserve such luck?" He tore his eyes away from the children and looked at me, a knowing smile on his face. "I met you, and it changed my life."

He pulled me to him, and we just stood there for a bit, savoring this moment in time when we were together, and at peace. He didn't say a word, but I knew he was thinking of Elena, as was I. If only she'd lived long enough to come to the future.

"You must go before anyone sees you," I said, wishing we

could just remain in our safe little universe forever. So much was about to change.

"I'll see you tonight, as planned," Hugo had said as he'd given me a parting kiss.

"Tonight."

We had decided to leave this evening when the church was sure to be deserted. The church in the twenty-first century was bound to be empty as well. Not many modern-day people went to church on Saturday night; the pub was their preferred place of worship. We needed the cover of darkness for our plan, and it was imperative to get away before the trial began tomorrow. A few more hours and we would be gone, if everything went according to plan.

Mark Watson had arrived an hour ago. His eyes were fixed on the toes of his boots as I came down the stairs, but he was now armed with a sword, and I saw the hilt of a dagger sticking out of his boot. I was sure that he hadn't told anyone of what had occurred last night, but he was still visibly shaken.

He'd gazed up in surprise when he saw Archie. "Yer back," he exclaimed, his expression one of apprehension. I could see the wheels turning in his feeble brain. Either it had been Archie who had held him at knifepoint last night, or Archie had returned this morning, and Mark had indeed experienced something otherworldly.

I noticed a twitch of Archie's lips as he bid Mark a good day. "Yes, I just returned this morning," he said nonchalantly. "Left London as soon as they opened the gates and rode hell for leather. Missed my wife, you know," Archie added with a touch of menace.

Mark Watson had noticeably blanched but said nothing and took his seat by the door. At least he didn't bring anyone with him. Having more guards would complicate our escape.

I finally stepped away from the window and looked around the room. There was much to do, but my preparations had to be clandestine since I didn't want the servants or Mark Watson to suspect a thing. I pulled open the trunk containing my gowns. I'd need some fabric. Having lived in the seventeenth century for years now, I'd been forced to learn to sew, and now I was grateful for the skill. I'd make some modern-day clothes for us. We wouldn't win any fashion awards, but at least we wouldn't look as if we were wearing Halloween costumes in April. Hugo, especially, had to look right, in case someone saw him and recognized him as Max Everly. We'd have a lot of talking to do, and having to explain away period clothes would make things that much more difficult. I had no plan beyond getting to Simon, but there was a good chance that he might not be in Cranley, or unable to help. There was the hunting lodge where Hugo and I had hidden out before, but now we had two small children, so we'd need to see to their needs before anything else.

I selected a gown of soft, claret-colored velvet. It had a simple scoop-neck bodice and fitted sleeves. Paired with a knee-length skirt, it would look like an ordinary dress. All I had to do was shorten the skirt, which was voluminous enough to leave me enough fabric to make a simple dress for Valentine. Michael still wore gowns much of the time, as was the custom for little boys, but he'd need trousers and a shirt. Dressing Hugo was the bigger problem. Men's fashions of the time were so elaborate that there wasn't a single garment that wasn't satin, silk, velvet, or damask. Coats were embroidered, and breeches were knee-length and often ornamented with bows, not something Hugo could wear to the twenty-first century. I couldn't even find any simple dark-colored fabric for trousers.

I closed the trunk, then left the room and went down the corridor to what had been Jane's room while she'd resided at Everly Manor. Jane had been in mourning for her husband when I met her, her gowns made of sober dark cloth. Perhaps she'd left something behind. I felt like an intruder in the room that had once belonged to Hugo's sister, but I pushed aside my reservations and went to work, searching the room. Jane had taken her trunk when she returned to her estate in Kent, but she left behind her black cloak. She'd taken the heavier, fur-lined winter cloak, but this was a lighter one, worn in spring and fall, the cloak she had been wearing when she lured me into a trap and watched me hauled off to Newgate Prison. I hadn't realized that she'd returned to Everly Manor for her things, but she must have, since the cloak still hung on a peg in the garderobe. I looked at the garment with distaste. The fabric was something like gabardine, lined with gray silk. It would have to do.

I took the cloak back to my room and spread it out on the floor, scissors in hand. I had to get this right since I wouldn't have a chance to correct my mistake. I would cut out the patterns, then have Frances help me with the sewing. She was a deft hand with the needle, her stitches small and neat. We only had a few hours to get everything ready, but no one would be surprised if I stayed in my room all day. After all, I was officially in mourning, and I didn't even have a proper gown for the occasion. Tomorrow, I would be expected to appear at the church and face charges against me, but today, I would be left alone.

I consulted the paper where I'd written down Hugo's measurements. I was glad I'd had the presence of mind to take them before he left, since I couldn't use any of his clothes as a sample. Hugo had stood patiently while I measured and remeasured, needing to get the numbers right. I would have to make a button-fly since I didn't have a zipper, and that would be a challenge. I'd never done this type of sewing before. It was much easier to make a baby gown or mend an underskirt than create something from scratch. I took a deep breath and began to cut.

It took me over an hour, but by the time I was finished, I had the patterns for Hugo's trousers and a dress for Valentine. Michael's clothes would have to wait. I hid everything in the trunk and went downstairs in search of Frances. Everyone was seated at the large table in the kitchen, since the dining-room table was otherwise occupied at the moment.

"When is Papa coming back?" Valentine whined as I entered the kitchen. I was actually starving, so would take a short break for lunch, I decided.

"Soon, darling," I lied, earning a reproachful look from Harriet. People didn't lie to children about death. Losing a parent, or both, was so common that children as young as Valentine were acutely aware of death all around them. I knew that the servants expected me to take the children into the dining room and have them say goodbye to their father, but they didn't dare to criticize me openly, and I instructed them to keep the door to the dining room shut just in case one of the kids wondered in.

I nodded to Jem who was seated across from me. He looked sullen and pale and didn't return my greeting. Frances and Archie were next to him, their expressions sober. We made small talk while Polly set steaming dishes on the table. Today's midday meal was leftovers from last night, but no one minded. Food was not to be wasted, and a hot meal was still preferable to a slice of bread and a hunk of cheese. We all helped ourselves and tucked in.

"Archie, would you mind going to see Reverend Snow? A burial must be arranged, and since I'm not allowed to leave the house, it falls to you to reason with Reverend Snow," I said.

Archie threw me a knowing look. "You know what he will say."

"Yes, I do, but do what you can. Frances, I would greatly appreciate your help in sewing some mourning clothes for myself and the children. Perhaps we can do this in my room. The light is better there."

"Of course," Frances mumbled.

"Jemmy," I said softly. "It has been wonderful to see you,

but I think it's time you returned to your family. Your father must be worried sick."

I needed Jem to leave but wasn't sure how to convince him to return to his family without it seeming like I was kicking him out, which, in fact, I was. Jem was a curious boy and would get in the way of our plan and ask too many questions. Besides, I really did sympathize with Nicholas Marsden. I knew that whatever his shortcomings, he loved his son and wanted to make him happy, and harboring Jem the way we had been wasn't fair to his father.

Jem got the idea that he could simply stay with us, but as a mother myself, I couldn't allow that. He had to return to his family, and his own future. I could understand Jem's reluctance to deal with his stepmother and new baby brother, but he wasn't the first child to feel resentful when a parent remarried or when a new baby was introduced into the household. As much as I loved him, I had to let him go, for his own sake.

* * *

I glanced at Frances as we settled by the window with our sewing. She was stitching the dress for Valentine, while I worked on Hugo's trousers. They were looking more like skinny jeans than dress slacks, but they'd have to do. Frances sat with her head bent over her sewing, a closed expression on her face as she stabbed the needle into the velvet.

"Aren't you going to say anything?" I asked Frances after a prolonged silence. I was instantly sorry.

Frances's eyes filled with tears. She tried to say something, but the tears just slid down her cheeks, dripping onto the little dress and leaving dark spots.

She shook her head, unable to speak.

"Won't you change your mind?" I asked gently. "Are you certain?"

"About what?" Frances croaked. She let the dress fall to her knees, unable to sew with shaking hands, but continued to stare at it.

"About coming with us."

Frances raised her tear-stained face to me, gaping in genuine surprise.

"He didn't tell you, did he?" It was more of a statement than a question. I'd put my foot in it, and now I'd come between Frances and Archie.

Frances shook her head as she averted her eyes again. My first impulse was to tell Frances to defy Archie, and let him know her own desires, but I bit my tongue and continued sewing. It wasn't my place to interfere in their marriage. If Archie kept things from Frances, he had his reasons. I knew him well enough to know that he would die for her without a second thought. Archie loved Frances with a fierceness one rarely saw in real life. Perhaps he thought he was protecting her, or maybe he was protecting himself.

Archie was a man of his time. Going into the unknown would be daunting, to say the least, especially when he'd be fully aware of his limitations. I was sure that Hugo had painted a realistic picture, having faced difficulties himself when I spirited him into the future. Perhaps Archie already had a plan for their future, and, of course, there was his elderly father who'd lost his wife and grandchildren to illness, his daughter to God, and would be heartbroken to lose his son and daughter-in-law as well, especially if they vanished without any explanation. I hadn't seen the elder Hicks since the wedding, but Archie had mentioned that he was suffering from scurvy and perhaps some other ailment. By seventeenth-century standards, Horatio Hicks was a very old man, and although Archie hadn't said as much, wasn't expected to last much longer.

Frances and I continued to sew in silence, each lost in our own thoughts. We were consumed with melancholy, but there was also love. There was an unspoken bond between us, something that would transcend the centuries and last for as long as we both lived. I reached out and took Frances's hand, and she grasped it with her cool fingers, her eyes full. I knew that I had her support, no matter what, as she had mine. We weren't related by blood, but our experiences over the past few years bonded us for life, and neither one of us would ever be able to fill the hole that would be left by the other's absence.

TWENTY-FOUR

"Reverend Snow was sympathetic," Archie said as he faced me across Max's coffin, "but the answer is no. Since Lord Everly's death is clearly a suicide, he cannot be buried in consecrated ground."

Archie was stating the case in the most diplomatic way possible, but I knew the reality of what a burial at a crossroads entailed. Self-murder was viewed as a crime against God, so the perpetrator was condemned not only in this life, but the next, the promise of Heaven or any kind of divine forgiveness denied them for eternity. A person who committed suicide was not only barred by the Church from having a Christian burial, but had a stake driven through the heart and was buried at night by moonlight with no mourners present. Frequently, the grave was desecrated with rubbish and dung right after the burial as a sign of disrespect. There was no sympathy for anyone who took their own life, no matter the reason, and their families bore the shame for generations to come. In some extreme cases, the suicide's property was forfeit, leaving the family destitute. If that were to happen, Clarence would not inherit, and the future we'd left behind would be altered forever.

"Is there nothing more than can be done for Max?" I asked, already knowing the answer. But I was fairly certain that Max hadn't been buried at a crossroads. If that were the case, Simon would never have seen the gravestone. I'd been to the village in the twenty-first century and drove around, not only by myself but with Max. Had someone been buried at a crossroads and there was still a marker, I would have seen it, and Max would have pointed it out, especially if it was his mysterious ancestor. Of course, all traces of the grave might have been long gone by the twenty-first century, and perhaps the family chose to conveniently forget that bit of history and pretend that it never happened, seeing it as a dark stain on the family name.

Archie shook his head. "Reverend Snow knew Lord Everly quite well and doesn't truly believe that he would be capable of taking his own life, no matter the circumstances, but unless there is some proof that he was murdered, the body must be buried at a crossroads. You, as his wife, may put a marker on the grave in due time."

I nodded in understanding. I suppose that was the best we could hope for. At least there would be a clue for future generations, a tangible reminder of a man who'd lived and died violently. I wasn't at all sure how the gravestone had appeared in the cemetery, but for the time being, that wasn't really important. Somehow it came to be there, so I would just let history take its course. "I suppose we'll just have to accept that," I replied. "When can Max be buried?"

"Tonight at midnight," Archie replied as he eyed Max with distaste. "I am to deliver the coffin to the gravediggers who will be waiting at the crossroads. There are to be no mourners."

I nodded miserably, mentally asking Max for forgiveness. He didn't deserve this; no one did.

"There's something else, Neve."

"What more could there be?" I asked warily. It was only three in the afternoon, but I felt completely drained. Hours of sewing had given me a terrible headache, and the strain of the past few days had left my nerves thrumming like guitar strings.

"There are two men from the village who've been engaged to watch the manor house to make sure you don't make your escape before the trial. Mark Watson let it slip to Reverend Snow that he thinks you might try to get away tonight. They will take turns watching, one person from that copse of trees behind the house, and one from the churchyard. Should you try to leave, they will raise the alarm. Hugo was able to avoid detection, but the whole village will be up in arms if they see you leaving with the children the night before the trial."

"I see. What do you propose, Archie?"

"A few drops of laudanum will put Watson to sleep for the whole night, and the watchman behind the house will see nothing from his vantage point. I will take care of the man in the churchyard."

"Surely you don't mean to kill him?"

"No, just knock him out for a short while. That should give you enough time to make your escape. You must leave after dark, and as quietly as possible. All goodbyes should be said before you go. I will see to Max's burial," Archie added.

"Understood." The thought of saying goodbye to Frances brought tears to my eyes every time, but it would have to be done, and with the minimum amount of fuss. If I'd learned anything from being Lady Everly, it was that walls had ears when you dealt with servants. I didn't expect Ruby, Harriet, Polly, or Cook to betray us, but one honestly never knew. People did inexplicable things in the name of religion, or when motivated by financial gain.

* * *

We had until nightfall to prepare for our departure. Archie had engaged Jem's services in distracting the graveyard watchman, not so much because he needed his help, but because it would help to get him out of the way. I couldn't tell Jem the truth, but I did explain to him that we would hide in the crypt until Hugo came to get us, at which point we would make for the coast and take a ship to France. He was crestfallen to know that we were leaving, this time without him, but he understood. He nodded stoically when I told him of our plan, his eyes glued to the floor.

Frances would make sure that the servants were upstairs when we left the house by the front door. I wasn't too worried about the grooms, since the stable was behind the house and the front door not clearly visible, even should they come outside, which they rarely did after dark.

Normally, I put the children down for a nap in the afternoon, but I allowed them to play through nap time in the hope that they would be tired by nightfall. I'd prepared a tincture of valerian to put in their milk with supper should they be overexcited, but hoped not to have to use it since valerian root had a terrible smell and bitter taste. The children would make a fuss and most likely refuse to drink the milk. I was cautious of using laudanum on children, but if the situation was dire, I'd add a drop of that instead. Having the children sleep through our escape would be easier, especially once we came out on the other side. They might be frightened by the lights and traffic, and having two hysterical toddlers wouldn't help our cause.

The remaining hours flew by with breakneck speed, as time usually does when one is nervous and filled with dread. I barely ate my evening meal, pushing the food around on my plate instead to give the appearance of having eaten. My stomach was in knots, my head pounding with a vicious headache, which had only intensified since that afternoon. Thankfully, the children were spent, their little heads drooping like wilted flowers as they ate their own supper before the adults. They were ready for bed, which was a blessing. I would take them upstairs after supper while the servants cleaned up and had their own meal.

It grew fully dark just after seven in the evening. It was time to put our plan into action. Archie and Jem were already at Horatio's farm with Hugo, having left directly after supper. I told the children to say goodnight to Ruby as I took them upstairs. They were drowsy, but still bickering between themselves as they normally did at bedtime. I dressed the children in their new clothes and quickly changed myself while they sat on the bed, watching me with suspicion.

"This gown is strange, Mama," Valentine complained sleepily as she gazed down at her exposed knees. She was wearing hose, but the hem came to mid-thigh, something unheard of even in clothes for children. Michael seemed pleased with his trousers and shirt, happy to say goodbye to the frilly gown. He stuck his legs out experimentally, smiling at me in wonder.

"What are you wearing?" Valentine asked indignantly. She was staring at my knee-length dress. "Is that a shift?"

"No, darling. It's a type of dress. Don't you like it?"

"No. I like a long train," Valentine said, her attention already on something else. She was yawning widely, so it was time to leave unless I wanted to carry both children all the way down the ridge.

As if on cue, I heard a cry from Frances's room.

"Ruby, Harriet," she called out. "Come quick. I've overturned the tub."

Frances had called for a bath right after supper and had intentionally spilled the water. It would take all spare hands to clean up the mess before the water seeped between the cracks in the wooden floor and began to drip into the room below. I heard running on the stairs as Ruby, Harriet, and Polly trooped to Frances's room with rags and buckets. I waited until the servants were occupied before putting cloaks on the children and sneaking down the stairs. Michael was holding his carved wooden horse as he held my hand. Valentine was protesting loudly. Luckily, the door to Frances's room was closed and the maids were talking between themselves, which drowned out her voice.

Frances was already in the foyer, waiting for us. The prone figure of Mark Watson was just behind her, his chin resting on his chest as he snored softly. He'd be asleep for hours yet, so we had no reason to worry that he'd wake up.

Frances kissed the children, then straightened up quickly, so they wouldn't see the tears swimming in her eyes. Valentine had finally grown quiet, confused by what was happening. She couldn't possibly understand, but she sensed that this was an important moment and clung to Frances's legs like a drowning man to a bit of flotsam. Frances bent down and kissed the top of her curly head. "Be a good girl for your mama," she whispered. "She will need your help."

Valentine nodded silently, her eyes huge with worry.

"I'm sleepy," Michael whined as he pulled on my hand. "Want to go to bed."

"In a few minutes," I replied absentmindedly.

The moment I dreaded had come, and suddenly I wasn't sure I could say goodbye to Frances without breaking down. Our eyes met over the heads of the children, silent tears streaming down our faces. There was so much to say, but neither one of us could bear to say it. There were moments in life when words were inadequate, and this was one of them. We embraced silently, clinging to each other for a long time. For a quick second, I remembered Frances as she had been when I'd first met her in the house of Josiah Finch. She had been so slight, so frightened and confused. At least I was able to take comfort in the knowledge that I was leaving her in a better place than I'd found her. Archie would look after her and keep her safe, and Hugo made sure that they would receive a tidy sum which would help them pursue whatever life they chose.

"Be safe. Be happy. Remember us," Frances whispered.

"You too, Franny. You will be forever in my thoughts. I love you," I muttered through a sob.

We finally broke apart, and all too soon, I was out the door, pulling the children along as we made our way down the ridge while Frances went back up to keep an eye on the servants. Thankfully, the children were both silent, their little legs pumping to keep up with my pace. They were tired and cranky, but understood that something momentous was happening, and for once went along without the usual noisy complaints.

The church loomed up ahead, its dark shape barely visible against the sky. Several candles would be lit inside, but the light seeping through the windows couldn't be seen from my vantage point. I hoped that Archie and Jem had already dispatched the watchman.

"Where are we going?" Valentine finally asked. She was slowing down, intimidated by the darkness and sounds of the night. She was never out after dark, and looked around fearfully, squeezing my hand with all her might. Michael just trudged along, indifferent to our destination. He was sleepy and kept tripping over his feet. I swung him up into my arms and continued on down the hill, the leather purse full of jewelry in my cloak pocket banging against my leg.

"I want to go home, Mama," Valentine whispered. "I'm scared."

"We're going to meet Archie. He's waiting for us by the church."

"Why? What's Archie doing in the graveyard?" Valentine squeaked.

"Hiding." I said the first thing that came to mind, but Valentine instantly perked up.

"Is this a game?"

"Yes, and you must be very quiet."

"I will." She put a finger to her lips, suddenly a little more alert.

Michael was already asleep, his head resting on my shoulder. He was heavy, and my back ached with the strain of carrying him as I made my way down the hill.

I peered into the darkness. The crescent moon silvered the gravestones in the cemetery, but I could see no human figures. All was silent and eerie. I instinctively slowed down, worried that something had gone awry. A dark shape suddenly peeled itself from the wall and came toward me, the face indistinguishable in the shadows.

Valentine gasped with fear, but Hugo swung her into his arms and kissed her on the cheek. "It's only me, sweetheart."

"Papa," she breathed happily as she wrapped her arms around his neck. "I'm wearing a strange gown," she whispered.

"I'm sure it's very pretty. Mama made it just for you."

Valentine didn't respond. She was already half-asleep.

We walked beneath the arch and entered the silent graveyard. I finally spotted Archie and Jem, standing beneath a yew tree. One of the men from the village sat leaning against the thick trunk, his head tilted to the side, his eyes closed. His chest was rising and falling as he slumbered.

I tried not to cry as I hugged Jem. He was as tall as I was, and our eyes met over Michael's head. I expected Jem to look sad, but what I saw in his eyes was anger. I suppose he felt that we were deserting him, which was justified, but he was no longer our responsibility. He had a family of his own, and there was no way we could have taken him with us. Jem didn't say anything, just hugged me loosely and stepped aside.

Archie came next. His arms felt strong around me, and I momentarily rested my head on his shoulder, afraid that I would break down. He held me away from him, his blue eyes dark in his face.

"God keep you," Archie said huskily. He looked as if he were about to cry, or maybe it was just the effect of the moonlight shining through the furry branches of the tree.

I watched as Hugo shook Jem's hand. "Thank you for your help tonight, Jemmy. You've grown into a fine young man. I will miss you." I expected Hugo to hug Jem, but he didn't, treating him like a man rather than a child.

Jem stepped aside, giving Archie his turn.

The two men just gazed at each other, a world of words in their eyes. I knew they wouldn't get sentimental and was surprised when Archie put his arms around Hugo and Valentine. He kissed Valentine's forehead tenderly, then clapped Hugo on the back as he pulled away.

"If you change your mind..." Hugo began.

Archie shook his head. "Go with God," he said instead.

"Keep Frances safe."

"You know I will," Archie replied as he turned to Jem. "Let's go, Jem," Archie barked.

Jem threw a last look in our direction as he trudged after Archie, sullen as ever.

TWENTY-FIVE

We entered the church. The building was absolutely silent, as if the very stones were holding their breath. Two large candles flickered lazily next to the altar, casting just enough light for us to see by. As we made our way down to the crypt, I was suddenly overcome with trepidation. What if the passage no longer worked? What if we wound up in a different place and time? What if we went backward instead of forward? I had no reason to think that we would, but who knew? Anything was possible. Who was to say that the passage opened up only between this time and the twenty-first century, and how were we to be sure if time flowed the same way in both places? What if we went back to a time when Max was still in residence, or what if we overshot the mark and wound up in 2020 or even later? My heart raced as these questions overwhelmed me.

My breath came in ragged gasps as I felt my way down the darkened stairs. I suddenly felt an irrational panic, probably because I knew there was no way back. If the passage didn't work, we couldn't return to our seventeenth-century life. Max, who was believed to be Lord Hugo Everly, would be buried in a few hours, his funeral followed by my witch trial. We only had a short window to make our escape before our disappearance was noted. Mark Watson wouldn't stay asleep forever, and the man in the cemetery would be coming around soon. We had enough money to flee the country and settle somewhere else, but Hugo would be a ghost, a nonentity, and the accusation of witchcraft would prevent me from returning to England anytime in the near future. How had this happened to us? How did we end up in such peril?

Hugo turned and laid his hand on my arm. "Have faith," he said quietly. "All will be well." His voice seemed to echo in the empty crypt, giving the illusion of more than one person speaking. It was as if a chorus of whispers was assuring me that my fears were unfounded, but I still needed convincing.

"How can you be so sure?" I hissed, suddenly terrified as we stopped in front of Bruce the Knight's tomb and the entrance to the passage.

"I'm not sure, but we've survived worse. We are alive, healthy, and have our children and money to live on. Whatever happens, we will land on our feet."

I nodded, absorbing the wisdom of Hugo's words. He was right, of course. Even if we wound up too far in the future or went back in time, we were together, and we had enough funds to keep us afloat for a while. We would figure things out, and make the situation work for us.

"Ready?" Hugo asked as he shifted Valentine in his arms to free his hand.

"Yes," I whispered.

I found myself holding my breath as Hugo pressed the knob in the center of the six-petalled flower. The panel opened, revealing the narrow passage. It smelled just as it had before, of mustiness and dry dust. A cool draft seemed to creep out of the passage, like the dank breath of a hidden cave. I glanced at the children who were deeply asleep in our arms and followed Hugo into the void.

TWENTY-SIX

PRESENT DAY

Surrey, England

Hugo and I stepped into the crypt as the panel slid shut behind us. Several dim bulbs burned, illuminating the stone undercroft. I looked around in confusion at the ladders and buckets propped up against the opposite wall. Tools were scattered on the floor, sloppily left behind by the workers who were probably eager to get home at the end of the day. The far end of the crypt looked as if it was under construction, the mortar between the large rectangular stones fresh and still damp. The carvings snaking around the walls appeared to be intact, but the wall had definitely been reinforced. A border which hadn't been there before ran around the bottom of the wall, possibly to prevent seepage during heavy rain or snow. Bruce's tomb was draped with heavy canvas to protect the ancient effigy from possible damage. A *Daily Telegraph* had been carelessly left lying on the tomb.

Several empty coffee cups and a wrapper from someone's lunch had been tossed into a bucket next to the plinth, the smell of coffee making my mouth water with longing. I hadn't had a proper cup of coffee since leaving France.

Hugo reached for the newspaper and looked at the date. He smiled happily and nodded to me in reassurance. We were in the right time. I breathed a sigh of relief as we turned toward the stairs.

The modern church was lit up like a Christmas tree compared to the dimly lit building we'd just left behind. Electric lights illuminated the nave and shone on the stained-glass windows, which looked breathtakingly beautiful after the high narrow windows of the old St. Nicolas, which left the interior in gloom even on the brightest days. There was no one about at this time of the evening, and everything was unnaturally quiet, the sound of outside life not able to penetrate the thick walls of the church. Our footsteps echoed on the stone floor as we rushed toward the door.

"Locked," Hugo said as he turned toward me. "Let's try the side door."

Thankfully, the door leading into the graveyard wasn't locked. Someone would need a key to enter from the outside, but the latch opened easily enough from the inside. We stepped outside, breathing in the fragrant April air. I smiled as I inhaled overtones of modern life. There was just a hint of petrol, and the smell of commercial fertilizer which had been used to mulch the flowers in the cemetery quite recently.

Now that we were where we needed to be, we had to implement the second half of the plan. We settled the children on a bench, eager to set them down after holding them for so long. I removed my cloak and used it to cover their sleeping forms. Hugo would wait with the children while I walked into the village. I gave Hugo a quick kiss before making my way out of the graveyard and toward the nearest pub. I would call Simon first. If he didn't answer, we'd go to the hunting lodge and wait till morning instead of descending on Stella Harding, who I didn't expect to have a favorable reaction. I wasn't sure if Simon had told his mother about his sojourn to the seventeenth century, but even if he had, she might not be pleased to see us. Stella had been inordinately fond of Max, and hearing of his death would not only come as a shock, but might provoke anger against Hugo, whom she would see as being responsible.

The Richard Onslow pub was crowded and noisy on a Saturday night, the patrons talking loudly as they enjoyed a meal in the dining room or stood at the bar. A young man nearly splashed me with beer as he tried to maneuver his way toward a group of friends, four tankards held in front of him to keep them from being knocked over. I couldn't help remembering having drinks at this very pub with Max all those years ago when I first came to the village for my job. We'd sat in the snug, me with a glass of dry white wine, Max with a pint of bitter. I couldn't keep from glancing at the snug, irrationally hoping to see Max having a beer and talking to an acquaintance, but, of course, the snug was occupied by strangers who were laughing loudly at something one of them said. I turned and pushed my way toward the bar.

The publican was kind enough to let me use the telephone when I told him that my car had broken down outside the village, and my mobile was dead. He didn't remember me, but I remembered him. He was a ginger-haired man in his forties, with a pretty blue-eyed wife who was currently serving someone in the dining room.

"Sure thing, pet. Phone is over there. Do you need a number for a local garage?" He glanced at his watch. "Oh, but they will be closed now. We do have rooms upstairs. You can stay the night."

"Thank you, I'll just call my brother to come get me," I assured him as I pulled out Simon's card. I dialed the number and listened to it ring, praying all the while that Simon would answer. Contacting Simon was essential to our plan.

I was just about to hang up when Simon finally picked up.

"Hello," he said, sounding extremely annoyed. "Who is this?"

I realized that he wouldn't recognize the number and assume it was a wrong number or some sales call.

"Simon, it's Neve," I explained, suddenly worried that his offer of help hadn't been in earnest and just something he'd promised on the spur of the moment.

"Blimey. Where are you?" Simon exclaimed, all irritation gone from his voice.

"I'm at the Richard Onslow. Hugo and the children are at the graveyard. Can you help us?"

"I'm on my way."

I hung up, thanked the publican, and stepped into the cool April evening. Only then did I breathe a sigh of relief.

TWENTY-SEVEN

Simon was as good as his word and met us in the graveyard in record time. He grinned broadly as he gave me a warm hug and shook Hugo's hand. He looked delightfully casual in a pair of jeans, a navy-blue jumper and suave loafers. His light hair was tousled, and his eyes sparkled with mischief.

"All right?" he asked as he took stock of our appearance. Hugo's clothes would not pass scrutiny in daylight, but he looked passable in the dark. I had to admit that after wearing yards of fabric for several years, I felt surprisingly naked in my short dress. I had fashioned a pair of panties out of a petticoat, but I didn't have a bra and felt scandalously unbound with nothing on beneath the sheath. My stockings came mid-thigh and were held in place by a ribbon. I'd pulled the pins from my hair before going into the village, and my hair hung past my shoulders and moved gently in the breeze. I couldn't recall the last time I'd worn my hair loose, since married women normally wore their hair up. Only young, unmarried maidens could get away with leaving their hair unbound. It felt strange to feel it brushing against my neck.

I was glad that Simon didn't ask any awkward questions, the

time for talking would come; just not now. He scooped up Michael and Hugo lifted Valentine into his arms while I picked up the discarded cloaks and followed the men out of the grave-yard and up the ridge. The house looked surprisingly dark, only the front parlor windows lit up with what appeared to be candlelight.

"I thought the children might be frightened by the light," Simon said by way of explanation as he led us into the darkened foyer. "Shall we settle them in the parlor for now?"

Simon pushed two sofas together front to front, creating an enclosed space where the children could sleep without falling off. I covered them with one of the cloaks before following Simon and Hugo into the kitchen. We could hear them as long we left the door open. Simon flipped on the light, invited us to sit down, and went about making tea, his movements clumsy.

"Let me," I said as I took the kettle from Simon, filled it, and set it on the hob.

Simon took out a tin and arranged scones on a plate. "Mum baked these only this morning. Apricot walnut," he elaborated as he set the plate on the table.

I prepared the tea and set steaming mugs before Hugo and Simon before making one for myself. Simon added a splash of milk while Hugo took his black. I inhaled the wonderful aroma of black tea, eager for my first sip. I hadn't had tea in months.

"I must admit, I wasn't expecting to see you, old boy," Simon said as he took a sip of his tea. "I noticed the gravestone for Hugo Everly a few months ago and assumed... well, you know."

"Simon, the gravestone is for Max," I explained, "but he isn't actually buried in the churchyard. He will be buried tonight at a crossroads just outside Cranley. There must have been a marker at some point, but it's long gone now," I added, seeing the look of incomprehension on Simon's face. There was a glimmer of pain in his eyes as the meaning of my words sank in. He'd loved Max long before he knew that Max was his older half-brother. He'd learned to live without him these past few years, but the hope that Max would someday come back was still alive despite our assurance that Max had died in France.

"So, Max is really dead? What happened? Why will he be buried at a crossroads?" Simon asked, looking at Hugo.

"Max was believed to have committed suicide," Hugo said gently, "but, of course, he was mistakenly identified as me."

"Right." Simon set down his cup. There was a slight tremor in his hand and a bit of tea splashed onto the table. He was understandably upset. The brother he loved would not even get a Christian burial, much less his own gravestone. Max fell through the cracks of history, his fate of little interest to anyone but us.

"Simon, where is your mother?" I asked carefully. I hoped to distract him from the news of Max's death with practical concerns.

"Oh, Mum went to Dr. and Mrs. Lomax's house for supper. They play bridge every last Saturday of the month. She'll be back soon, though. Don't worry, she knows everything," Simon added. "Have you some sort of a plan?" he asked.

"Nothing to speak of. Our only goal was to get to you," I added, hoping that Simon hadn't changed his mind about helping us. I felt much safer now that I wasn't faced with a trial in the morning, but we were now in the twenty-first century with two small children, no place to stay, no ready money, and no prospects. I was just about to point that out to Simon when the front door slammed, and Stella Harding walked into the kitchen.

Mrs. Harding gazed upon the people at her table, set down her handbag, unbuttoned her coat, and gave Simon a look of reproach. "You should have made sandwiches. They must be hungry."

"We are fine, really," I said, wondering if that was her only concern. "Shall I get you a cup of tea?"

"Might as well," Stella said as she pulled out a chair and sat at the head of the table. She looked just as I remembered her. There were a few more strands of gray in her dark hair, and a few new wrinkles, but she was well-groomed and smartly dressed, with a colorful silk scarf to brighten her otherwise somber dark dress. Her face was set in stern lines; she wasn't a woman who smiled easily, but I didn't feel any hostility from her, just curiosity. "Just the two of you, then?"

"The children are sleeping in the parlor, Mum," Simon said.

"Good." Stella accepted the tea, added milk and sugar, and gazed at Hugo and me with an air of expectation. "Have a plan, do you?"

"Not as of yet," Hugo replied.

Stella nodded as if she'd expected his answer.

"Well, I think it would be a good idea to take Neve and the children to London," Simon began. "They can stay at my flat while Neve sorts herself out."

"Simon has no idea what to do with me since I was meant to be dead," Hugo added helpfully, making Simon smile in embarrassment.

"Yes, he did show me the grave," Stella said as she took a sip of tea and crumpled a piece of scone absentmindedly.

"Max suggested that I take his place," Hugo explained carefully, watching Simon and Stella for their reactions.

"Did he now?" Stella asked, clearly shocked. "That doesn't sound like the Max I knew."

"No, I don't suppose it does, but he'd changed since we last saw him in Paris. He'd mellowed somehow," Hugo said, his expression thoughtful as he tried to describe this new Max. "I think he'd found God."

Stella scoffed. She seemed shocked by this revelation, but

quickly composed herself and looked around the table. She was focused on the present. I suspected that she would mourn Max later, in private, but right now, she had to figure out what to do with us.

"It's a good idea about Neve and the children, but Hugo must remain here. If he is to pass for Max, he needs to be coached. The accent is wrong, and he barely knows anything about the man he hopes to impersonate. Simon and I can help him," Stella suggested, speaking of Hugo as if he weren't there.

"But, Mum, how do we explain Max's disappearance? He's been gone for over three years now. No one can go off the grid for that long; it's impossible," Simon pointed out, concerned.

"It's difficult, but not impossible," Stella replied. "I'd given this some thought when I still hoped that Max might return to us. We could hardly say that he'd gone to the past, could we? So, I'd come up with what I thought at the time was a plausible idea. It might not be readily believed, but it's better than nothing."

"What's your idea?" I asked, curious to hear Stella's plan. Having to explain a three-year disappearance had stumped me ever since we decided to return to the future. I could reenter my life if I needed to, but explaining Max's reappearance was beyond the scope of my imagination.

Stella looked around, refreshed her tea, then reached for another scone as we all sat in silence and waited for her to speak. I thought Stella Harding to be a humorless woman, but I noticed the little smile playing about her lips. She was actually enjoying this, which somehow made it easier. At least she wasn't hostile. She took a sip, grimaced, added another splash of milk and finally spoke.

"The late Lady Everly's father left her an estate in the Scottish Highlands when he died. Naomi hated the place for some reason, and sold it just as soon as an acceptable offer came through. An American couple from the Midwest. They turned the place into a guest house, but, as far as I know, have never been able to turn a profit, with the location being too remote to be of interest to tourists."

"Mum, get to the point," Simon moaned.

"Have patience," Stella admonished him and went on. "There was a small cottage on the estate. It belonged to the gilly, but the man didn't wish to stay on after the Americans took over. Moved to Inverness to be closer to his daughter. He sold the cottage to Roland Everly, who used it when he went salmon fishing and shooting grouse in Scotland."

"You mean it was his love nest," Simon said with disgust.

Stella didn't reply, but I saw her wince for just a moment. Simon had hit his mark. Stella had been Roland's lover for nearly twenty years. He must have taken her there from time to time when she had some vacation time and could reasonably explain the absence to her employer, who probably knew that her husband was carrying on with the housekeeper all along.

"Did he ever take you there?" Simon demanded, his face twisted with distaste. "You were only his mistress for nearly twenty years."

I felt sorry for the lad. He seemed to feel a lot of bitterness toward his parents and, with Roland being gone, could only take it out on his mother.

"He did, as a matter of fact," Stella replied tartly. "The place is quite remote. It's wired for electricity, but there's no phone, TV, or internet. The electric bill still comes every month and is paid from the business account associated with the museum."

"You never had the power shut off," Simon said, his face alert. "You were waiting for Max to return."

"Yes. Roland always kept the place stocked with food and supplies, and I'd arranged for a local grocer to make a delivery once every few months, bringing non-perishable goods such as tea, coffee, canned soup, et cetera. I thought that if Max ever returned, we'd be able to prove that he was holed up there."

"Is that where you went all those times?" Simon asked, amazed by his mother's craftiness.

"Yes. I stowed away the supplies and made sure that the old Range Rover was in working order. If anyone had gone out there, they'd assume someone was in residence."

"You're a clever old girl, aren't you?" Simon exclaimed proudly.

"I just wanted to protect Max. I promised Naomi before she died that I would look after her boy should he ever return."

"That's kind of you," I said. "Max would have been happy to learn that he wasn't forgotten by those who cared about him."

"So, Neve, you and the children go to London, and Hugo will remain here. We'll keep it quiet for a few days while we coach him, then we'll call the police and tell DI Knowles that Max has returned to us. The official story will be that Max had suffered a breakdown of some kind and went off to Scotland, where he's been for the past three and a half years. Once the media scrutiny subsides, the two of you can be reunited. We'll figure out how to introduce the children into the equation later."

"What if no one believes this story?" Hugo asked.

"They might not believe it, but they won't be able to disprove it. Max dabbled in writing at one time, did you know that?" Stella suddenly asked. "Wrote a spy novel."

"Was it any good?" Simon asked.

"Absolute rubbish," Stella replied with a grin, "but we can say that Max was in Scotland, working on his novel. And we have his efforts to prove it."

"Do you really think we can pull this off?" Simon asked. "I can't imagine the police or the media just buying into this story."

"If we all play our parts, I think we can."

I was suddenly very glad that Stella Harding was on our side. After all, her son would lose out if Hugo was universally accepted as Max, but she didn't seem to mind. I might not have been nearly so understanding were it my son losing out on his inheritance.

"Simon, are you sure you are all right with me usurping your inheritance like this?" Hugo asked as if reading my thoughts.

Simon smiled broadly, his eyes lighting up. "I couldn't wait to get away from this old pile when I was a boy—I hated it. You are welcome to the lot, and all the responsibility that goes with it. I want my old life back."

"Speaking of which, whatever happened with Heather?" I asked, curious as to how Simon's escape from his wedding had played out. I could only imagine the scene once Simon returned from the past and eventually faced his jilted bride. I liked Simon immensely, but I couldn't help being sympathetic toward poor Heather, who'd been literally left at the altar when Simon dashed to the crypt moments before the ceremony and plunged into the past rather than go through with the marriage.

I was surprised to see Stella give me a stern look as she shook her head. "Leave it," she mouthed.

"Sorry. Didn't mean to pry."

"I made a terrible mistake," Simon said curtly before rising to his feet and reaching for the keys on the counter. "Shall we go then? It's best if we leave tonight, before anyone sees you."

I stood up reluctantly, suddenly apprehensive. I hated saying goodbye to Hugo. I knew he was safe, but after all that'd happened to us over the years, any separation seemed frightening. And who knew when we'd see each other again.

Hugo pulled me into an embrace and whispered in my ear, "Everything will be well. I promise. Just take care of yourself and the children. I'll call you as soon as I can."

I nodded, afraid that I might cry. Hugo and I had been

reunited for less than twenty-four hours, and I simply wasn't ready to let him go.

Simon and Hugo left the kitchen to get the children and settle them in the car, while I busied myself with clearing away the tea things.

"I'll do that," Stella Harding said as she got to her feet and slipped into housekeeper mode. "Don't fret. Simon will take good care of you," she added when she noticed my distress.

"I just don't like to be away from Hugo," I complained.

"It won't be for long. A few weeks, at most. Just keep yourself busy and focus on helping your children through this change. They'll be bewildered and scared and will look to you to put their fears to rest." Stella set down the cups and gave me a one-armed hug.

I nodded in agreement, surprised by Stella's motherly attitude. I remembered her as a cold, judgmental woman, but perhaps I'd misjudged her. Still waters ran deep, as my foster mother was fond of saying, and Stella's waters were certainly deeper than I ever expected.

"Thank you, Stella. I must admit that I hadn't expected your support."

Stella Harding looked at me for a long moment before her face split into a grin. "This is actually kind of fun," she said, surprising me yet again.

TWENTY-EIGHT

I gripped the seat of Simon's SUV as it sped down the motorway toward London. I tried not to let Simon see my nervousness, but I was breaking out in a cold sweat as my heart fluttered against my ribcage. It had been years since I'd been in a car or traveled at such a speed, and everything inside me seemed to rebel. Oncoming lights all blurred into one continuous stream, overwhelming my senses and making me feel dizzy and confused. I felt the bile rise in my throat as Simon swerved to avoid a car that had barreled into our lane without so much as using a turn signal.

"Simon, can you please slow down?" I pleaded.

Simon gave me a look of surprise, but seeing my panicked face eased his foot off the gas pedal. "Are you all right?" he asked, realizing that I was anything but. I felt clammy and nauseous.

"I'm just a bit overwhelmed, that's all. It's been a while."

"I'm sorry, I should have realized. Perhaps it would help if we talked of mundane things," he suggested.

"At this moment, nothing seems mundane. I've been gone for over three years, which might not seem like a long time, but, believe me, it feels like a lifetime. I hardly know where to begin reclaiming my life after all this time. And then there are the children. Can you imagine what it will be like for them when they awake tomorrow?"

Simon nodded. "Children are very resilient. As long as you remain calm, they will believe that everything is all right. Turn it all into a game," he suggested, surprising me with his wisdom.

"Been studying child psychology, have you?" I joked.

"No, but growing up at Everly Manor with frosty Lady Everly, her wily husband, and my mum taught me a lot about adult behavior. No one ever told me anything, least of all the truth, so I learned to gauge the situation by listening less and studying their body language. Sometimes, that which is left unsaid actually speaks volumes."

"Yes, I suppose you're right. I just need to remain calm and try to make this transition fun for them."

"I'd start by going to the zoo. Children love animals, and since your children have never seen any exotic animals, they'll be too mesmerized to notice that they are in a different world."

"That's a great idea, Simon, but getting them to the zoo might be a problem. They've never seen a car or a bus, or electric lights, for that matter. The trip to the zoo might overwhelm them," I said, trying to envision the journey step by step. Valentine might be lured by the promise of seeing animals she'd only heard of, but I was sure that Michael would have an absolute meltdown in the face of London traffic and blaring noise.

"Why don't we start slow then? I'll spend the night in London, if that's all right with you, and tomorrow we'll take the kids for a little drive. We'll show them the sights, perhaps visit a toy store, and feed the ducks in the park. Finish that off with a slice of pizza and they'll think they've landed in an enchanted kingdom," Simon said with a smile.

"Simon, thank you," I said. "You've been amazing. Why do you even want to bother with us?" Grateful as I was for Simon's help, I couldn't quite put my finger on what made him so eager to lend a hand. He'd spent the night at Everly Manor after his wedding escapade, but other than providing him with food and shelter, we'd done nothing out of the ordinary. I suppose he felt he owed us something, but he'd already done more than I could dare hope for.

Simon looked pensive for a moment, his eyes on the road as he considered his answer. "Neve, I made the biggest mistake of my life when I ditched Heather at the altar. I thought that I'd lose my freedom and never have any control over my life again, but it was after I came back and Heather wasn't there anymore that I realized what a fool I'd been. I had a woman who loved me for who I was and was willing to dedicate her life to me and our future family, and I acted like a complete wanker. All I did was prove what Heather already suspected, that I'm a selfish and spoiled child who isn't even man enough to tell the truth and accept the consequences. I ran away and hid like a frightened toddler, and I am ashamed."

"Have you tried to get her back?" I asked, already guessing the answer.

"I did try to talk to her and beg for forgiveness, but she wouldn't listen. She was too hurt to see my side of things," Simon complained. "So, I've kept my distance."

"Will you try again?"

"What's the point?" Simon shrugged. "She's done with me, not that I can blame her. I hear she's seeing someone. He's older and a bit more settled. Probably ready to settle down and start a family. He took her on a holiday to Morocco. We were meant to go there on our wedding trip. I see she wasted no time in doing it with someone else," he added bitterly.

I refrained from pointing out that he'd been the one who'd bolted, not Heather, and that she was entitled to go to Morocco, or anywhere else, under the circumstances. But I didn't really see what Heather's new relationship had to do with Simon's desire to help us. Did he think he was atoning for his mistake in some way by playing the Good Samaritan?

"I've done a lot of soul-searching these past few months," Simon continued, dismissing Heather's love life. "On reflection, I realized that I'd never done anything for anyone. I took and I took, but I hardly ever gave anything back. I resented my mother for never telling me who my father was until it was too late, and left as soon as I could afford to live on my own. I never bothered to understand what she might have been feeling; I was too angry. So, I've been spending a lot more time at the manor, helping her deal with the estate and the museum. And even with Max, I accepted his friendship, his money, his support, but I never really went out of my way to do anything for him."

"Are you helping us because you feel that in some way you're repaying Max?" I asked, needing to understand Simon's motives.

"Yes and no," he replied, his expression pensive as he tried to put his feelings into words. "Neve, you are really brave. You gave up everything for the man you love, a man you knew could have been arrested and executed at any time. You remained by his side without any thought to your own safety or comfort. I suppose what I am trying to say, very clumsily, is that I admire you both. I know that Max would have wanted me to help you, so I will do everything in my power to make this easier for you. It's too late for me to do anything for Max. He's gone, and I can never go back and rewrite our relationship, but I can turn over a new leaf and help the people he cared about. And you know what?" he added, his eyebrows lifting in surprise. "It actually feels really good to do something without expecting any kind of return on investment. It feels noble."

I reached over and squeezed Simon's hand for lack of anything to say. He was about my age, but in some ways he was so achingly young, so immature. A man his age in the seventeenth century would be very different, and a lot less selfish. It was a different life, and it bred different men. I suppose that when human life was as fleeting as it was in a time when a reasonably healthy person could be carried off within days from some infection or unexpected illness, people valued love more. Modern medicine, uninhibited travel, and the internet had inadvertently managed to strip away some values of the past.

A man who might have had only a handful of eligible women to choose from in a seventeenth-century village now had thousands of women at his fingertips and could travel much farther afield if the situation called for it. Having so much freedom of choice made people callous and fickle. They were always searching for the next best thing and failing to see the specialness of the people in front of them. It was easy to give up on someone when you never fully committed to them. Few people married their first loves anymore, and even fewer people were willing to make significant sacrifices for someone they thought of as disposable. Perhaps Heather would take Simon back after enough groveling, but he'd be absolutely fine if she didn't. There were plenty of fish in the sea, and Simon's bout of remorse wouldn't last long. It'd only been a few months since his aborted nuptials. Simon might romanticize our situation, but despite his inherently good nature, he didn't have the moral compass or nobility of spirit that separated the men from the boys in times past.

I felt great relief when we finally parked the car and carried the children upstairs to Simon's flat. They were still sound asleep, having been lulled into even deeper slumber by the motion of the car. It was a relief not to have to deal with their reaction to the big city at this moment. It would come soon enough, but for now, I was tired and on edge, and the only thing I truly craved was a few hours of uninterrupted sleep.

The flat was rather posh, with windows the whole length of the living room, and a spacious bedroom with a king-sized bed and flat-screen TV. Everything was very modern and minimalist. There wasn't an ornament, family snapshot, or a book to be seen, the only decoration being the colorful abstract prints on the beige walls.

I took off the children's shoes and tucked them in before following Simon into the kitchen. The granite counter gave off a dull gleam, as did the stainless-steel appliances; so clean, they looked as if they'd never been used.

"Tea?" Simon asked.

"I'm exhausted," I replied, yawning. "I think I'll turn in. I'll just sleep with the children. Would you have a T-shirt I can borrow?"

"Of course. Bottom dresser drawer. I'll take the couch."

Simon walked over and put his arms around me in a brotherly way, which reminded me of Archie and nearly made me cry as a sharp-edged pain suddenly sliced through my already sore heart. I knew that for a long time to come, I would constantly think of Archie and Frances and try to envision what they were doing on the other side of the veil of time, going about their business as if they didn't die hundreds of years ago. In time, the pain would dull, and I would learn to live with the separation, but at this moment, especially since I'd just been torn from Hugo, it was as visceral as a sudden death.

"It will be all right, Neve."

I nodded into his shoulder, unwilling to let him see my tears.

TWENTY-NINE

APRIL 1689

Surrey, England

Frances pushed aside the bed hangings and slid out of bed. She felt achy, tired, and out of sorts. Her sleep had been fitful, disturbed by dreams of Neve and the children as they tried to reach out to her and cried pitifully for help. Frances had woken up several times during the night, her cheeks wet with tears. She tried to shake off the feeling of dread by telling herself that all was well, and the Everlys were safe in that faraway world that she couldn't even begin to imagine. She hoped that wherever they were spending this first night, they were all together and well looked after, and would awake to a new dawn, one that was filled with possibilities and choices.

Archie had come in sometime after one, having delivered Max's casket to the gravediggers and overseen the burial. He'd felt no great pity for Max, given the role Max had played in all their lives, but even Archie, stoic as he was, couldn't help but be affected by what he saw. He refused to tell Frances about it and tried to feign sleep, but she could just imagine what it must have felt like to stand by and watch the desecration of a corpse.

Frances despised Max with single-minded passion after his ill-fated kidnapping attempt in Paris, but at this moment, she felt nothing but pity for the poor, misguided man. He had died under mysterious circumstances far from home and anyone who might have loved him, and even in death, he would not be given a Christian burial or sent on his final journey in his own name. No one except Frances and Archie would know the identity of the man buried this night, and sadly, no one would care. Max would be swallowed by the earth, and quickly forgotten.

She didn't want to think about it, but all she could see in her mind's eye was the eerie light of the three-quarter moon spilling onto the crossroads as the gravediggers drove a sharpened spike into Max's heart. The gravediggers were coarse men and would have made jokes at Max's expense, deriving whatever pleasure they could from their gruesome task. Tales of the burial would be told at the tavern for weeks to come, the details relished with ghoulish delight by villagers who'd known Lord Everly all their lives and had benefited from his kindness.

Frances was sickened by the thought that everyone believed the desecrated corpse to be Hugo. His reputation was in tatters, his legacy now forever tainted by whatever had taken place in the Tower the night Max died. Hugo was gone, but she knew him well enough to know that he would carry the shame in his heart for the rest of his life, and chafe at the helplessness he'd feel at his inability to tell the truth about what had really happened to Max.

Frances was relieved when dawn finally came, and she was able to abandon all hope of rest and get out of bed. The house was deathly quiet on this Sunday morning—the first of many mornings when the Everlys would no longer be there at the start of the day.

"Come back to bed, Franny," Archie called out softly. "It's early yet."

"I know, but I just can't lie there anymore," Frances replied irritably. "I must do something."

"What do you need to do?" Archie was sitting up in bed now, watching her with concern. He would miss the Everlys too, but unlike Frances, he would just bottle up his feelings and place them on the highest shelf of his mind, the bottle left there to collect dust until he eventually forgot about its existence. It was not that Archie was unfeeling, but he simply had a different way of dealing with loss. He would see giving in to melancholy as having little point. His expression did soften with compassion as he watched her. He understood. Archie swung his legs out of bed and reached for his shirt.

As soon as Watson discovered that Neve and the children were gone, all hell would break loose, so Frances had to find a way to distract him for as long as she could.

"Just tell Mark Watson that Lady Everly is too upset by the events of last night and has taken to her bed. That will buy a few hours."

"And the children?" Archie asked as he continued to dress hastily.

"Mark Watson never even looked at the children. He'll just assume they are with their mother. Give the servants the same excuse," Frances added, considering all aspects of her plan.

Archie planted a kiss on Frances's lips and left the room.

Frances chose her most somber gown, dressed, pinned up her hair, then slipped out of the room, dashing toward Neve's bedroom before any of the servants could see her. She locked the door, then pocketed the key. If anyone went in search of Neve, they'd assume that she'd locked herself in, giving vent to her grief.

Frances considered going downstairs, but she had no appetite this morning, and had no desire to deal with the servants. Archie would take care of all that. Instead, she retreated back to her room and pulled a chair up to the window, throwing it open to get some fresh air. She felt queasy and weak, probably due to her restless night. The fresh air felt good on her face, the smell of grass sharp in her nose. She took deep breaths until she began to feel marginally better. Today would be a difficult day, but tomorrow would be the beginning of the new normal, and in time, she would learn to accept her loss and begin to move forward. After all, the most important person was still here, and she owed it to Archie not to give in to her grief. The Everlys weren't dead, just gone, and who knew, maybe one day they would return.

Frances finally rose to her feet with a sigh, shut the window, and headed downstairs. Mark Watson looked sleepy and confused after his drug-induced slumber, but a scowl appeared on his face as soon as he saw Frances on the stairs.

"Lady Everly best be ready to go to church this morning. If she ain't, I'll break down the door and drag 'er out by the hair. Ye can just tell 'er that," he spat out. Mark Watson had clearly recovered from his fright of the other night. Once he escorted Neve to the church for the trial, his duties as guard would be over, but Frances had no doubt that he'd be first in line to build a pyre or throw a rope over a stout branch if she were condemned to death.

"She'll be ready," Archie replied as he came out of the dining room. "And if you speak to my wife disrespectfully ever again, we'll just see who will be dragged out by the hair," he added, his tone menacing.

Despite her general misery, Frances couldn't help rewarding Archie with a smile of gratitude. It still amazed her how readily he always came to her defense, and how loved and protected it made her feel. The knowledge that Archie would be there to look after her for the rest of her days was the only ray of sunshine on a day which promised to be trying at best, awful at worst.

Frances turned her back on Mark Watson and made her

way to the kitchen. The queasiness had passed, and she was suddenly hungry. She'd need a little something to get her through the morning. The servants were all gathered around the wooden table, their demeanor subdued as they broke their fast on porridge and buttered bread. Frances could hardly blame them for feeling glum. Their future was uncertain and would become even more so once they found out that Lady Everly and the children had fled, and Clarence Hiddleston would be coming to take possession of the estate. He might decide to keep them on, or he might just dismiss the lot and leave the running of the estate to Godfrey Bowden, visiting Everly Manor only to collect rents and review the books. At seventeen, Clarence had little use for the house itself. He currently resided at his estate in Kent, and might continue to do so until he took a wife.

Frances had never met Clarence, but she'd heard enough about him from Jem to share some of the servants' trepidation. She didn't imagine for one moment that Clarence Hiddleston would welcome her and Archie. He'd known Archie when he was a boy, and viewed him as nothing more than a servant and Hugo Everly's puppet. Their days of living in the manor house were over, but Frances didn't mind in the least. Now that the family was gone, there was no reason to remain. Once Archie saw to any outstanding business, they would leave and set up their own household.

Frances tried to imagine what it would be like to have her own home. She'd been mistress of a great house before when she was married to Lionel, but never had any say in anything that went on, save the supper menu, and sometimes not even that. Lionel had been very particular about what he liked to eat. This time, everything would be different. She would be the mistress in every sense of the word, even if the house was a modest one, and she only had one servant. It would be more than enough. She intended to do much of the work herself. She

wasn't so high and mighty that she couldn't change the bed
linens or darn a few pairs of socks. The idea of a home was
strangely appealing, and Frances allowed herself a moment to
daydream while Cook fetched her a bowl of porridge with
honey and butter and poured her a cup of ale.

The servants finished their breakfast and scrambled to their
feet, eager to finish the washing up so that they could get ready
for church. They conferred between themselves as they filed
out of the kitchen, wondering if they might be called to testify
against their mistress. Ruby looked horrified by the prospect,
but Cook and Harriet looked as if they might enjoy their
moment in the sun. They would be affected by the outcome of
the trial one way or another, but they wished to have their say,
and suddenly Frances wasn't sure which way their sympathies
lay. Harriet had been a friend of Liza's and might have been
swayed by her venom, but Cook had a good, secure position at
Everly Manor, which she would surely hate to jeopardize. Polly
hoped that she would not be called on, but clearly stood in
support of Neve, whom she admired. But whichever way the
servants leaned in their support, they were all looking forward
to the trial and the entertainment it would bring to their otherwise dull and dutiful Sunday.

Frances looked up as Jem walked into the kitchen, sat down
at the table, and reached for a slice of bread. He began to butter
the bread with single-minded concentration while staring at the
whorls in the wood as if they might reveal some insight on how
to get through this day. He looked downtrodden and pale this
morning, his eyes glazed by melancholy and lack of sleep.

"Are you all right, Jemmy?" Frances asked gently.

Jem nodded silently, but Frances saw him blinking away
tears as he took a long pull of ale, probably in order to hide his
face behind the large pewter tankard. He was older now and
deeply embarrassed of his emotions, especially if they made him
look weak and less than manly. He was at that awkward age

where he was too old to be treated like a child, but too young to be accepted as one of the men, and it pained him because he was lost in his own misery, unable to share it in a way that made him feel mature and respected.

Frances could understand his loneliness and isolation, but there wasn't much comfort she could offer. Now that Hugo and Neve were gone, there was no reason for Jem to stay, and it had been agreed that he would start for home first thing tomorrow morning. Frances would be sorry to see Jem go; he was another member of her adopted family who would now be lost to her, but it had been Hugo's wish that Jem return to his father, and as much as Frances and Archie both loved the boy, they knew that sending Jem on his way was the right thing to do. Come Monday, it would be just her and Archie left, and they would be on their way soon enough.

THIRTY

Frances came down the stairs, ready for church. A heavy silence weighed on the house, giving her a dull headache. Never had it felt as empty as it did at this moment, not even when they'd returned from France and found the house shut up and freezing cold. There were no sounds coming from the kitchen or from the bedrooms where the Everlys would be getting ready for church as they did every Sunday. Archie had stepped outside with Jem, and the staff had left for church a few moments ago. Mark Watson paced the foyer like a caged animal, glancing at the stairs every few seconds to see if Lady Everly was coming down. Despite his earlier bravado, he had no desire to confront her, for fear that she would summon her black magic and curse him for all eternity.

"Well, where is she?" Watson snarled at Frances.

"They'll be down presently," Frances replied calmly and went to join Archie and Jem. They walked silently toward the church, amazed by the number of people streaming through the lychgate. This was an occasion not to be missed, a witch trial in Cranley. The atmosphere in the church was almost festive, as if people had come to see a play rather than a legal

proceeding against a person they all knew, a person who had
been nothing but good to them. People were talking between
themselves, exchanging predictions for the outcome of the trial,
and telling tales of their own run-ins with the witch. The three
men of the ecclesiastical committee were sitting in the front
pew, their carriage erect, and their gaze unwavering. They
would take the floor after the Sunday service, but, for now,
they were keeping their own counsel. Frances strained to catch
a glimpse of their faces, but they resolutely faced the front,
wishing to have no dealings with the parishioners until the trial
began.

Bradford and Beth Nash sat in their usual place in the third
pew on the right. Beth seemed to be fixated on her hands, which
were folded in her lap, but Bradford's head kept swiveling from
side to side as he watched the door. He was as much in the dark
as everyone else in the church and would continue to be until
Archie passed on Hugo's message to him after the service.
Brad's gaze met Archie's, and the two men nodded to each
other, acknowledging the sad events of this day.

Frances scrutinized the congregation looking for Liza
Timmins. Was she here? Archie was confident that Liza
wouldn't dare show her face, but Frances had her doubts. Liza
was just insolent enough to defy Archie and try her utmost to
turn the situation around to her own benefit. Of course, her
accusation no longer mattered since there would be no trial, but
Frances sincerely hoped that Liza got her just desserts. If
Archie had scared her enough to make her leave these parts, so
much the better.

Reverend Snow glanced anxiously at the door, his forehead
creased with worry. He wanted to make sure that everyone was
in attendance before starting the service, not wishing to be
interrupted midway. He periodically glanced at the three
bishops and shook his head.

The crowd began to grow restive, but there was still no sign of the accused. Every head turned toward the sound of the opening door as Mark Watson burst into the church.

"She's gone," he cried. "The house is empty."

"And the children?" Reverend Snow asked, concerned.

"They're gone, too."

"How is this possible?" one of the judges roared, finally turning to face the congregation. He looked livid, his eyes bulging with fury. "She was under house arrest since returning from London, watched day and night. How could she have escaped, and with two young children?"

"I don't know, your eminence," Reverend Snow replied, his voice laced with uncertainty. "We'd seen the other members of the household coming and going, but Lady Everly never left the house other than to take a stroll in the garden, where she was clearly visible."

"This just proves she's a witch," Bishop Cotton screeched. "Find her."

Several men erupted from their seats and ran down the nave and from the church. The mood had turned ugly; people now baying for blood rather than just hoping for entertainment. Women talked loudly, their comments malicious and cruel. Frances clearly heard one woman saying that the children were possessed by the Devil and should be put through some form of exorcism. Archie squeezed Frances's hand in reassurance, gently reminding her that Neve and the children would never be found.

The other two bishops were now on their feet, moving down the nave, studying the faces of the villagers, who were looking around in confusion. They were bishops of the church, but there wasn't an ounce of kindness or forgiveness in their demeanor. Their skin was mottled with rage, and their eyes scanned the parishioners, looking for anyone who appeared frightened or afraid of making eye contact. They knew how to use their power to intimidate, and they rightfully assumed that someone knew something.

Frances looked up and stared into the eyes of the youngest bishop, daring him to question her. Oh, how she would love to tell him the truth and watch him explode with rage.

"Does anyone know where the witch is? Speak now, and you will be rewarded in Heaven for your piety. But if you withhold knowledge of the witch's whereabouts, you will burn in the fires of Hell for eternity, subjected to endless torture and suffering at the hands of Satan."

The buzz of conversation ceased, leaving the church in ominous silence.

Reverend Snow looked around the congregation. "Please, remain calm," he entreated. "Has anyone seen Liza Timmins?"

"That's the witch they should be trying," Frances muttered under her breath.

"Why don't we hold the service while the men are out looking for Lady Everly?" Reverend Snow asked, directing his question to the three bishops.

"Yes, that sounds like a fine idea. Proceed, Reverend Snow."

The reverend leafed through the prayer book until he found the right page, then waited for silence to descend before he began. After a few minutes, the usual somnolent atmosphere settled on the congregation as Reverend Snow began to preach, his voice lulling even the most robust churchgoers into drowsiness. Reverend Snow was a fine preacher, but his soothing, melodious baritone did little to rouse Christian fervor. He was about halfway through the sermon when the doors of the church burst open again, revealing three men who were heavily armed.

The reverend stopped speaking, his expression going from one of calm to one of apprehension. The three bishops turned to face the newcomers, their hope of seeing Lady Everly replaced by ire at the service being so rudely interrupted.

Reverend Snow opened his mouth to say something when the man in front held up his hand to silence him. "Forgive me for interrupting the service, Reverend Snow. My name is Giles Worthington, and I am the constable of Haslemere. I'm here on important business."

"What important business can you have in church on a Sunday other than the business of the Lord?" one of the bishops barked, clearly annoyed. "Say your piece and get out."

"Liza Timmins, the woman who was due to testify at this morning's trial, according to her sisters, had been found dead by a passing farmer on Saturday morning."

"Good God," Reverend Snow mumbled. "How did she die?"

"The witch smote her," someone called out, but instantly fell silent as the constable glanced in their direction.

"She was strangled with the reins of her horse and left in the woods by the side of the road. The animal was found grazing not too far from the body. Mistress Timmins's sisters said that she was due back Friday evening, so it would seem that she was killed on Friday night while bound for home."

The constable began walking the length of the nave, studying the faces of the parishioners, much as the bishops had done only a short while ago. His gaze finally stopped on Archie, who was looking at Constable Worthington with undisguised interest.

"A tall man with red hair and light eyes was seen on the road to Haslemere on Friday evening, a man identified by several residents of this village as Archibald Hicks."

Archie made to protest as the other two men seized him and hauled him to his feet, twisting his arms behind his back. "Master Hicks, you are under arrest for the murder of Liza Timmins," Constable Worthington announced, his face aglow with satisfaction at having found his man. "You will be taken to the gaol in Guilford, where you will remain until the trial."

"I didn't kill Liza," Archie hissed, his eyes blazing with anger, but no one was listening. The church was in an uproar as Archie was hauled out.

Frances pushed her way through the crowd, but by the time she finally managed to make her way outside, she saw the wagon rattling away from the church, the constable driving and the two men flanking it on horseback. Archie sat in the bed of the wagon, his eyes anxiously scanning the road for any sign of Frances. He smiled reassuringly when he saw her. Frances stared at the departing wagon until it disappeared from view, barely aware of Jem at her side.

THIRTY-ONE

APRIL 2015

London, England

I collapsed on the sofa, weary to the bone, and gratefully accepted a cup of tea from Simon, who looked equally knackered. I couldn't recall the last time I'd had such a hectic day. Simon and I started by feeding the children breakfast and then taking them for a ride on the double-decker bus to the zoo at Regents Park. After the initial shock, both Valentine and Michael began to enjoy the ride, their heads swiveling from side to side as they took in the sights. Michael put his hands over his ears to drown out the noise of the traffic, but Valentine seemed oblivious to the smells and sounds as she looked around, eager to take it all in. I expected a million questions, but, instead, both children were silent with awe, their eyes wide with wonder.

Simon had been right; the zoo proved a huge hit. The children were so overwhelmed with seeing exotic animals that they forgot all about the fantastical change in their environment and the strange clothes they were wearing. I'd run out as soon as the shops opened and picked up a change of clothes for myself and the children using Simon's credit card. They could hardly walk around in the clothes I'd made, which were ill-fitting and looked strange. Both children protested getting dressed until Simon began to describe what they were about to see, and then their resistance melted away. Simon had a natural way with kids, and they warmed to him as soon as they got over the shyness of being around a strange man.

Simon and I exchanged amused glances as both kids jumped in front of the monkey cage, imitating the screeching chimps. They were laughing and making faces as they danced before the cage. I had never seen them so happy, and I desperately wished that Hugo could be there to see his children's joy. Simon pulled out his mobile and took a few snaps which he forwarded to his mother. She would make sure Hugo got to see what his family was up to, and I was grateful to him for his thoughtfulness.

"Can we bring Archie and Frances here?" Valentine suddenly asked, instantly deflating my spirits. "I want to show Archie the giraffe. He would like it," she added.

"Maybe someday, darling," I responded, hoping that, with time, the memory of Archie and Frances wouldn't be as vivid as it was right now.

"How about some ice cream?" Simon piped in, eager to change the subject.

"What's that? I've never had ice cream." Michael said, earning me a judgmental look from a mother next to us.

"It's cold, and sweet, and oh-so-yummy," Simon said, lifting Michael up and settling him on his shoulders. "What flavor would you like? There's vanilla, chocolate, and strawberry."

The children looked blank, so we got two vanillas, one chocolate, and one strawberry, and allowed the children to try all the flavors. Michael liked strawberry, Valentine claimed the chocolate, so Simon and I were left with vanilla cones.

"You have no idea how good this tastes," I said to Simon as I licked my ice cream.

"I bet. You look as happy as the kids," Simon commented.

"Life without ice cream is not worth living," I joked. "But I do wish Hugo could be here. He loves ice cream," I added wistfully.

"You will be together soon; just give it a bit of time. I'll drive back to Surrey tonight," he added, "unless you need my help."

"I think I can manage. I have a lot to do, but I can pace myself. Getting the children acclimated was the first priority, but they seem to be less traumatized than I expected. I know there'll be an avalanche of questions once they have time to process everything they've seen today, but we're over the worst of it."

"They're acclimating remarkably fast. I think we'd better find the washrooms," Simon added with a chuckle.

The children's faces and hands were covered in melted ice cream, their faces aglow with glee.

"Where's Papa? I want him to try this," Valentine announced as I led her to the ladies' room. She blinked at the fluorescent lighting but followed me inside. "How do they make the water come out?" she asked loudly as I turned on the tap and began washing her face.

"It's rather complicated," I replied.

"And it's warm," she oohed. "I like it here, Mama."

"I'm glad, but it's time for us to go back to Simon's house. I think a nap is in order."

"I don't want a nap. I want to see the elephants again," Valentine whined. "And the tigers."

"All right, another hour and then we leave."

Valentine seemed satisfied with that, and we spent the next hour walking around the zoo and studying various animals. By the time we got back to Simon's, the children crashed. I took off their shoes and covered them with a warm blanket, glad to have a little time to just rest.

"Pizza for dinner?" Simon asked. "I'm too tired to organize anything else."

"Oh yes, please," I answered. "Pizza and ice cream in one day is my idea of Heaven."

Simon gave me a tired smile. "Am I to understand that you missed food the most?"

"There are too many things to mention, but I did miss the food. But what I missed most was access to news publications and entertainment."

"Really?" Simon seemed intrigued. "Like what?"

"Like films and books. There were books, of course, but they weren't exactly page-turners, and new books were in short supply, especially in the countryside. And I missed going to the cinema and watching television," I added. "Modern-day people spend hours of their day staring at their phones, watching TV, reading, listening to music, and playing games. All those things distract the mind, which is not always ideal, especially when they should be concentrating on work or study, but the diversion provides a buffer, keeping reality at bay and allowing the person to take a break from their worries and fears. There were times when I thought I'd scream with frustration or go mad with worry, and a book or a movie would have helped me escape from my thoughts, if only temporarily."

"Yes, I see what you mean," Simon replied. "I spent a lot of time playing video games after Heather and I split up. I just couldn't wrap my mind around anything for a while. It was mindless, but in some small way it helped me to finally deal with the situation and move forward."

"Have you?" I asked.

"Yes, I think I have. Loss teaches us to appreciate things, and having lost Max and then Heather helped me realize how careless I've been of other people's feelings. I plan to do better next time. I will be the best boyfriend anyone's ever had. And I will be a good friend," Simon added. "I promise."

I was about to reply when I heard Valentine's voice coming from the bathroom. "Mama, I need help."

Valentine was staring at the toilet with deep suspicion. I'd helped her in the morning, but she wasn't sure how to approach the toilet on her own. She was used to a chamber pot which she was comfortable using herself since it was low to the ground.

"And what's that?" she asked, glaring at the shower while she did her business. Simon didn't have a tub, only a sleek, modern shower stall. Bathing the children tonight would be an experience to remember.

"Come, let's wash your hands and go have some supper. Simon has ordered us a pizza."

"What's a pizza?" Valentine asked as she gave me a sidelong glance. "Is it as good as ice cream?"

"It's different, but very good. I think you'll like it."

"Will Michael like it?"

"I'm sure of it. Let's go see if he's awake," I suggested.

Michael was sitting up in bed, his wooden horse held tight in his hands. He smiled when he saw me, obviously relieved that he wasn't alone.

"Are you hungry?" I asked cheerily. Michael nodded. "Come on then, sleepyhead."

I cut the pizza into small squares and set it in front of them. They weren't accustomed to eating with their hands or with forks, so I gave them spoons, which they used to pick up the squares of pizza to bring to their mouths. This seemed to do the trick. Simon had ordered some Coca-Cola as well, but I wasn't ready to let the children try it. They weren't used to sweets like modern children and didn't crave them. I gave them each a glass of milk instead.

"This is good," Valentine observed as she chewed carefully. "I want to take some home to Archie."

I tried to picture Archie sitting on the sofa with a beer and a slice of pizza, and an involuntary smile appeared on my face. He would fit right in. Frances might not like either, but I was sure that Archie would take to modern food like a fish to water.

THIRTY-TWO

MAY 2015

Surrey, England

Detective Inspector Robert Knowles hurried to his car and got in before the throng of reporters outside Everly Manor had a chance to get a clear picture. He had no desire to appear in some rag, cited as the investigating officer. Had this been a favorable outcome to a homicide investigation he might have been proud to have his role acknowledged, but this particular case had been a disgrace from start to finish.

DI Knowles put on his sunglasses and drove through the gates faster than he should have, but the explosions of camera flashes left him disoriented and angry. He pulled over just as he entered the village and took out his mobile, dialing the constabulary.

"Chief Superintendent Cummings's office," a perky voice answered.

"Hey, Jess. I need to see the Super. Is she available at any time this morning?"

"Oh, hi Bobby. Let me take a look at her diary," Jess said.

"She has a small window in about forty-five minutes. That do ya?"

"Thanks, sweetheart. See you then."

Bobby's anger dissolved after hearing Jess's voice. She was fresh out of the academy, only twenty-two, and cute as a button. These days, she was the only bright spot in this otherwise stressful life. He knew it was wrong, especially since they worked together, but some stubborn part of him simply couldn't give her up. They'd been seeing each other since the Christmas party, when he'd found himself in the back of his car with Jess's dress pushed up to her waist and her long legs on his shoulders as she raked her nails down his back. What a rush that had been. Bobby assumed that Jess would sober up and hate herself in the morning, or worse, hate him, but she'd called him on his mobile and asked him out for a drink instead, a meeting which resulted in another round of wild shagging.

For the first few weeks, Bobby had wondered what Jess saw in him, but forced himself to stop overanalyzing. Whether Jess liked older men or sought some sort of father figure didn't matter. She wanted him, and that was enough for him. Eventually, the infatuation would wear off and he'd be exactly where he started, as long as Carol never found out about the affair. He was a happily married man with a second baby on the way, a son this time. It was just a fling, nothing more, he told himself.

DI Knowles drove to the constabulary in Waverly after making a quick stop at a local bakery, where he picked up a couple of scones and a decaffeinated cappuccino, then presented himself at CID. Jess was at her desk, her pert smile laced with hidden desire. Bobby was shocked anew by the lewd thoughts that always seemed to spring to mind upon seeing Jess, but they had to keep their association out of the office.

He smiled noncommittally as he handed Jess the box of scones and the cappuccino. "Just the way you like it," he teased. "Decaffeinated, extra foam."

"Oh, Bobby, you shouldn't have," Jess replied, blushing prettily.

"It pays to keep the Super's assistant sweet," Bobby said, inwardly cringing. He really had to control his desire to flirt with Jess at work. It was unprofessional and dangerous. Carol, in her current hormonal maelstrom, would cut his bollocks off if she caught a whiff of his interest in a girl young enough to be his daughter.

Jess picked up her ringing phone. "Okay, I'll send him right in," she chirped. "She's ready for you."

Bobby smiled at Jess and stepped into the inner sanctum. Chief Superintendent Joyce Cummings was his boss; an intelligent, efficient woman who was as comfortable with interdepartmental politics as she had been in the field when she'd been a DI herself. She tolerated no crap from her underlings and could administer a bollocking that left one completely eviscerated. And she was damn attractive.

Joyce Cummings was in her early fifties, but she had that inborn chic that few women achieved naturally. Her salt-and-pepper hair was cut into a neat bob, and her navy-blue suit was accessorized with a silk scarf in shades of lavender, gray, and turquoise, giving her just enough color to make her appear more stylish than severe.

"Good morning, ma'am," Bobby said as he settled into the proffered chair.

"What brings you here, Detective Inspector?" the Super asked. "I thought you were working the Everly case again. An embarrassment for this department if I ever saw one," she added with disgust.

"That's why I'm here, ma'am. I've just come from Everly Manor, having spoken with Lord Everly at length about his little jaunt."

"What say you, Bobby?" Joyce Cummins asked, leaning forward with undisguised interest. They'd all been shocked to find out that Maximilian Everly was back, having given him up for dead. It was always good to see a case solved, but not when they weren't the ones to solve it.

"He answered all my questions, a little more vaguely than I would have liked, but he was able to paint a clear picture of his movements."

"A nervous breakdown?" Joyce Cummings asked, shaking her head in dismay. "How could he have had the presence of mind to elude such a widespread investigation in his condition?"

"I'm not sure, but what I am sure of is that the man I spoke to is not Max Everly."

The Super gaped at him, her composure shaken for once. "Are you certain?"

"I am. I grew up with Max Everly. We were at school together until he went off to Eton. We played on the same cricket team in Cranleigh, had pints at the pub after every game. I know Max Everly, and the man claiming to be Lord Everly is an impostor," Bobby Knowles said hotly.

"Do you have any proof?"

"No, but I have my gut instinct. I've been a copper for nearly twenty years, and I know a lie when I hear it."

Joyce Cummings shook her head in disbelief. She didn't need to hear this right now but had no choice but to address DI Knowles's concerns. "Spell it out for me, Inspector. What exactly led you to believe that the man is not Max Everly? I need more than a gut feeling. This department dedicated count-less hours of manpower and a great deal of funds to this case, and came up empty-handed, to our great shame. I can't allocate any more resources to this, Bobby, not unless I have proof. Are there people who are ready to vouch for Lord Everly's identity?"

"The housekeeper, Mrs. Harding, and her son, Simon

Harding, who is actually Max's half-brother, both swear that the man is who he claims to be."

"Bobby, Simon Harding has much to lose now that his half-brother has returned. It would be in his best interests to prove the man an impostor, if that were the case. There's a title and the Everly fortune at stake."

"I think they are house-rich and cash-poor, ma'am, but I see what you mean."

"Bobby, what evidence is there that this man is not who he says he is? Does he look like Max Everly?"

"He does resemble him a great deal, and he seems to know much about Max's life and habits, but there's just something not right. His mannerisms have changed, and he'd forgotten I had a daughter; a child whose baptism he'd attended shortly before going missing."

"Is that all?"

"There are other things as well. His voice is different, and pronunciation of certain words. He just feels wrong, ma'am."

Superintendent Cummings leaned back in her chair, her gaze lingering on Bobby's face. She seemed to be considering something, but then shook her head as if she'd come to a decision.

"I can't authorize an investigation based on a hunch. The man had suffered a nervous breakdown and spent over three years living alone in the Highlands. Of course, he's different. He's bound to be. Had I been banished to the Highlands for such a long period of time, I'd be different too," she added with a comical shudder. "Can't abide the place. It's like going back in time, especially in some of the more remote areas. Leave it be, Bobby. There are more important cases we are working at the moment. There's been a string of bank robberies throughout Waverly and Godalming. Six robberies, similar MO, and not a single clue. I'm assigning you to the case."

"Yes, ma'am," Bobby Knowles said as he took his cue to leave.

"Oh, and Bobby. I wouldn't look kindly upon a sexual harassment complaint coming across my desk. Is that understood?"

DI Knowles stared at his boss, his mouth open with shock. Had Jess accused him unofficially of sexual harassment? She couldn't have.

"No, she hasn't," the Super replied as if he'd spoken out loud. "But I do have eyes in my head. Give my regards to Carol," she added for good measure.

"Yes, ma'am."

Bobby picked up what was left of his pride and made his way out of the office, walking past Jess as if she were invisible. Cummings had hinted that he was sexually harassing Jess, so either she didn't know about the affair, or she did and hadn't wanted to embarrass him further. Either way, the cat was out of the bag.

"Thanks for the scones, Bobby," Jess called after him, but he didn't respond. He felt humiliated, and angry. The warning about Jess was fair enough, under the circumstances, but the way his boss had dismissed his supposition was maddening. He knew he was right about Everly; would stake his career on it. The Super might not authorize any more funds or uniforms to the case, but she hadn't forbidden him from making inquiries on his own time.

THIRTY-THREE

MAY 1689

Guilford, Surrey

Frances awoke early in the morning, as was her custom these days. She used to like sleeping in, but the noise from the door-yard and her morning nausea prevented her from staying abed. The inn was small and shabby, with only two private rooms on the uppermost floor, and one room on the first floor where travelers slept six to a bed, but it was cheap and provided decent meals, which was all she needed. Frances had come to Guilford nearly two weeks ago now and spent her days waiting around at the prison to see Archie. Some days, she wasn't allowed to see him at all, but there were certain guards who were kinder and more open to inducements. She got to see him about three times a week, but she never asked him about Liza.

Archie said that he hadn't killed Liza and Frances believed him. Archie was a man of violence; she knew that. He'd killed that man in Paris, the one who had tried to shoot Hugo, and would just as easily kill Liza Timmins if he felt there was no other choice, but Archie wasn't a liar. He took responsibility for his actions, and would take the consequences as well, if it came to that.

Frances did not condone murder, especially one of a woman who was the sole parent of a small child, but she couldn't say that she was sorry the woman was dead. Liza was a parasite, a leech who'd bleed you dry till there was nothing left. Whoever killed her must have had their own motivation, since it stood to reason that Lady Everly was not the only person Liza had tried to extort money from.

Of course, with Liza being the key witness against Neve and the person on whom the entire trial rested, it was easy to point the finger at Archie since Lord Everly was presumed dead and couldn't be responsible for her death. No one but Archie Hicks would have a motive for killing that conniving slattern. Killing Liza was a way to protect Lady Everly and her children from what was to follow, for if Neve were found guilty, the children would be condemned by association, especially without their father to protect them. They might be sent to live with that nasty little turd Clarence Hiddleston, who would want no part of them. Valentine would be safe enough, but Michael, who stood to inherit the title and estate, would be in grave danger, the only person standing between Clarence and his heart's desire. Children died all the time, and if a little boy never lived to see adulthood, no one would wonder or care.

Archie didn't wish to discuss the future during the few minutes Frances was allowed to see him, but they both knew that the case against him was solid; too solid for the constable to even bother seeking anyone else who might have a motive for killing Liza. His job was done, the dispensation of justice left to the courts. And justice for an accused murderer meant only one thing—death by hanging.

Frances bolted from her narrow cot and retched violently into the chamber pot. Her breathing was ragged, her stomach heaving as it tried to force out contents that weren't there. She wasn't eating much these days, and what she did eat, she could barely keep down. Frances took a sip of ale and sat on the bed until the nausea passed and she felt well enough to get up, get dressed, and begin another day. Since coming to Guilford two weeks ago, Frances had lived life day by day, hour by hour, never looking past waking the next morning and doing it all over again. Archie kept imploring her to return to Cranley, but he didn't realize what he was asking. There was no going back, not now, not ever.

Returning to Everly Manor after Archie's arrest had been something of a shock. Frances had stood in the road long after the wagon taking Archie away from her disappeared from view. She felt rooted to the spot, instinctively realizing that once she walked away, reality would set in, and she would be on her own. She stood by herself as the villagers left the church, some ignoring her, others hissing insults under their breath. A few women even brushed past her, pushing her just enough to let her know that it wasn't accidental. Frances was the companion of a woman who was now widely believed to be a witch, and the wife of the man arrested on suspicion of killing her accuser. There was only one person she could turn to for help, but there was nothing Horatio Hicks could do either for her or his son.

Frances finally tore her eyes away from the road and looked around. Jem had been at the church earlier, but he must have gone back to the house. There was nothing for her to do but follow suit. Frances walked up the ridge slowly, suddenly too exhausted to make the climb. She stopped several times to rest before finally reaching the gates of the manor house.

The door was partially open, and Frances walked into the foyer. The silence enveloped her like a thick blanket. Even Mark Watson was gone from his post, his services no longer required. Frances shrugged off her cloak and started up the stairs, eager for the sanctuary of her bedroom. She needed to think things through and come up with a plan, but first she needed to lie down for a bit. She felt like she might faint.

Frances looked up as she saw Harriet coming down the stairs. She looked unusually tense, her face pinched and pale. Polly was behind her. The two maids blocked the way, forcing Frances to take a step back.

"Let me pass," Frances said, but neither girl moved.

"Come into the parlor, if you please," Harriet demanded. "We'd like a word."

Frances had no choice but to do as they asked. She held on to the banister for support and returned downstairs, where Cook and Ruby were already waiting. Frances took a seat and leaned back, looking up at the angry women towering above her. She could understand their uncertainty and suspicion, given the morning's events, but she'd never expected the type of hostility that emanated from people who'd been nothing but subservient and polite until that day.

Cook had been elected as the spokesperson, being the most senior and the eldest. She stepped forward, hands on hips, facing down Frances as she would never have dared had Lord or Lady Everly still been there. Abigail Fowler was normally a quiet, reserved woman, one who never spoke unless spoken to. Frances was taken aback by the change in her demeanor, and the fury she saw in her eyes. "Is she really gone then?" she demanded. "For good?"

"Yes," Frances replied, hoping that would pacify the woman.

"That's as good as an admission of guilt, that is," Cook stated, looking to her minions for support. They nodded, their hostility growing. "And who is to pay our wages if their lordships are gone? You?"

"You can apply to Master Bowden for your wages. He's been paying them up till now, hasn't he?" Frances replied, referring to the estate agent who saw to the wages of the staff. Rumor had it that Abigail had not only worked for Godfrey Bowden in the past, but shared his bed before he went and married a woman half her age. Abigail had lost not only her lover, but her employment as well. She thought she'd be safe working for Lord Everly, but now the situation had changed again, and the woman was understandably bitter and angry.

"And what's he going to pay us for if the family are gone?" Cook spat out.

"I understand that you're angry about losing your position, but it wasn't my decision to make, Abigail," Frances said, standing up to the cook. "Lady Everly had to do what was best for her and the children."

"Gone back to France, has she? Might as well have gone back to the Devil, if you ask me. Those foreigners have corrupted her. Both of them. A traitor and a witch, a fine pair. Well, he's good and dead, and she won't be far behind, if there's any justice in the world."

"She was in league with the Devil long before that," Harriet chimed in. "Liza always said there was something not right with her, and now Liza is dead. She told the truth and died for her pains."

"I think you'd best leave now, and go the way of your murdering husband, Mistress Hicks. You are no longer welcome here, it not being your home," Cook said, snarling at Frances.

Frances finally had enough and sprang to her feet, advancing on Cook until they were face to face, their gaze level. "I'll leave when I am good and ready," Frances retorted. "You don't scare me, Abigail Fowler. You are no better than you should be, and don't think that the man whose bed you warmed will protect you. Godfrey Bowden is married now, and you're about as appealing to him as week-old porridge," Frances spat out. She was really angry now, the color rising in her cheeks. "And same goes for you all. Lord and Lady Everly had been good to you, and you have business speaking ill of them."

"We are lucky to be rid of them and their spawn," Harriet cried indignantly. "Come, Polly, let's pack our belongings and leave this den of iniquity before our mortal souls are corrupted by their ungodly filth."

Cook, Harriet, and Polly left the room; only Ruby remained. She was the youngest and the kindest of the lot. Losing her employment would hurt her as much as the others, if not more. The Henshalls were poor as church mice, and equally numerous.

"I'm sorry, Mistress Hicks. Is there anythin' I can do for ye afore I go?"

Ruby's eyes swam with tears, and Frances felt an overwhelming urge to hug the girl. It wasn't the done thing to hug servants, but it made no difference now. She put her arms around Ruby, and they clung to each other for a moment, drawing comfort from each other.

"I don't believe anythin' they say about their lordships, an' I loved those children. Now I have to return to me family," Ruby sobbed. "Me mam will be that upset."

"Here, Ruby," Frances said as she pressed a coin into Ruby's palm. "Keep that for yourself. Don't give it to your mother. You might have need of it before long."

"Thank ye," Ruby mumbled, stunned by Frances's generosity. "I will keep it in a safe place. Do ye need me to help ye pack yer things?" Ruby asked.

"I can't carry much," Frances replied, her mind already on her journey to Guilford. She planned to leave tomorrow anyway; now it would be that much easier. "Perhaps a change of linen and a serviceable gown or two. And a change of clothes for my husband. Oh, and Ruby, the enamel box on my mantel. It was a gift from Archie."

"O' course. I'll do it now."

Frances sighed as she threw one last look about the room. They'd spent many happy hours here: talking, sewing, and playing with the children. She stiffened her back and her resolve and left the room, shutting the door firmly behind her.

Jem was hovering outside the door. He looked nervous and ill at ease, probably because he felt guilty for leaving her alone by the church.

"I'll come with you to Guilford, Frances. I can help."

"No, Jem," Frances replied as firmly as possible. "You must return to your family. I'll be better off on my own."

That wasn't strictly true, but she had no right to take Jem away from his life and involve him in her troubles. He had a future to think of, and a father who would be worried about him. No, she would go alone. Archie had looked after her since she was fourteen years old, and now she would look after him.

THIRTY-FOUR

Frances finally found the strength to get going. She splashed some water on her face, tidied her hair and covered it with a linen cap, then dressed in the sack gown she wore at the convent. She quickly found that it was better to be invisible. Dressing like a fine lady attracted too much attention, and not of the good kind. The first guard she'd approached when visiting Archie had unlaced his breeches and ordered her on her knees if she wanted to see her husband. Frances had fled, and waited until the gaolers changed before trying again. There were one or two kind guards who didn't harass her, and today one of them, named Lawry Gibbs, actually answered her questions—something no one else had been willing to do.

"Well, you see, Mistress Hicks, there are quarterly assizes, and the last one was during Lent. Now, the next court session will be in the summer, with Guilford being last on the list after Lewes and Croydon. Your husband will be tried then."

"Is the judge just?" Frances asked, her voice shaking with fear for Archie.

"Justice is swift, if not always merciful. Few of the accused are ever found innocent, if any," Gibbs replied, scratching his head. "The executioner is very busy just then. There're several hangings a day."

"But what if the accused is innocent?" Frances persisted. There had to be some way of helping Archie, and the only way she could figure out how was to understand as much as possible about the process.

"The accused is not allowed to speak for himself. Witnesses are brought in, but not for the purpose of defense. They are there to give evidence against the accused," Lawry explained patiently. He was clearly interested in the law and had attended many hearings.

"So how does one defend oneself?" Frances asked, confused by this odd system of justice.

"One doesn't. The verdict is based on the strength of evidence presented."

"In other words, everyone is guilty as long as there's someone to testify against them," Frances concluded, finally understanding what Lowry had been trying to tell her all along.

He nodded sadly. "There's not much chance of a pardon," Lowry said. He reached out and took her hand, smiling at her kindly. He was a nice-looking lad of about twenty, his fair hair tied back and his hazel eyes sympathetic, unlike the other guards Frances had encountered. "I know now is not the time, Mistress Hicks, but perhaps in the future, we might get to know each other better."

"You mean once I'm a widow," Frances snapped, outraged.

Lowry had the decency to look contrite, but didn't withdraw his hand. "You'll be needing a friend when the worst happens, and I can be a good friend," he said. "I have nothing but the most honorable intentions toward you, Frances. I am not proposing anything lewd or indecent. I have a good position here, and a wage that would support a family. I'm a patient man, and I would wait for as long as it took for you to come to terms with your loss," he added.

Frances swallowed back an angry retort, having thought better of it. Lowry was right, she did need a friend, and a man who was enamored of her was that much easier to manipulate than some lustful, middle-aged guard. Giving Master Gibbs false hope was unfair, but the only way she could help Archie was by using her wits and charms. She would do anything it took to save his life.

"I thank you for your proposal, Master Gibbs, and I will consider it most carefully should the worst come to pass. In the meantime, I must do what I can to make this time easier for my poor husband. Would you aid me in that? I would always remember your kindness."

"I will do what I can," Lowry promised, smiling at Frances with renewed hope.

"May I see him now?" Frances asked. "I brought some food."

"Ten minutes, Mistress Hicks, no more. I shouldn't be letting you in at all, but I can't refuse you, so be quick about it."

"Bless you, Master Gibbs," Frances said, giving him the warmest smile she could muster.

The guard escorted her through the narrow, dark corridors of the prison toward Archie's cell. Many prisoners shared large, filthy cells as they awaited the trial that would send them to the gallows, but their crimes were of lesser importance. Most were thieves and forgers. Those accused of murder got their own cells, their hands and feet fettered and chained to the ring high in the wall, which enabled the gaolers to pull them to their feet by jerking on the chain.

The stench inside the prison was so overwhelming that it made Frances's eyes water. There were no chamber pots, so the prisoners pissed and shat right on the floor which was covered with moldy straw. No water for washing was provided, nor any food. The prisoners depended on their family to bring them something to eat, otherwise they starved or ate the rats which were so abundant in the cells. Feeding them was an unnecessary and pointless expense to the Crown, considering that most of these men would not see the end of summer.

The inside of the prison was strangely quiet. Most prisoners were too hungry and desperate to converse with each other. They sat silently, dark husks propped against damp walls, their matted hair and long beards making them indistinguishable from one another.

Archie was sitting on the stone floor which was strewn with vermin-infested straw. His wrists were chafed from the fetters, and his bare feet were covered in muck up to the ankles. After only two weeks in this hellhole, his clothes were nearly in tatters and his hair was filthy from lack of washing and brushing. The smell in the cell was overwhelming, but Frances hardly noticed. She knelt in front of Archie and kissed his face, oblivious to the grime and reek of his clothes.

"I'm here, love," she whispered as she took out some bread, cheese, sausage, and a jug of ale. Archie tried to ration his food from visit to visit, but Frances could see in his eyes that he was ravenous.

"Thank you, Franny. Can you perhaps bring me some stew next time?" Archie asked as he tore off a chunk of bread and ripped off a piece of sausage with his teeth. He barely chewed the food before swallowing, desperate to fill his growling stomach.

"Of course," Frances replied. "But it will be cold by the time they let me in."

"It doesn't matter," Archie replied as he smiled at her. "What would I do without you, Franny?"

"They won't try you until the summer, Archie. Master Gibbs said that the assizes are quarterly, and then they put everyone on trial within a few days," she added.

"And they pronounce them all guilty and execute them the following morning," Archie finished for her.

"There's still hope. Isn't there?" Frances asked desperately.

Archie cocked his head and gazed at her as he continued chewing. "Franny, there's always hope, but I want you to promise me that you will take the money Lord Everly left for us and start a new life should the worst happen. When I face my executioner, I need to know that you will be safe and comfortable. I will die a happy man if I know that you are all right."

"Don't talk like that," Frances pleaded. "I can't bear to think of losing you."

"Franny, there's something I wish to tell you before I go to trial," Archie said, laying his dirty hand over hers.

"What is it?"

"I know that you haven't asked me if I'm guilty for reasons of your own, but I want you to know that I didn't kill her. I did meet her on the road, and I did threaten her, but I didn't kill her. I let her go."

"Were you planning on killing her?" Frances asked.

"Yes, I was, but when I held my dagger to her throat, I just couldn't bring myself to do it. I've never killed a woman, Franny, and I'd seen her with her boy. Whatever evil that woman might have harbored, she loved her son, and he adored her. I just couldn't take his mother from him, no matter how much she deserved it. Do you believe me?"

"Yes. But if you didn't kill her, who did, and why?"

"I don't know. Perhaps it was the farmer who saw me that evening, but I can't imagine what his motive might have been. Liza didn't have anything worth stealing on her, and they found her horse grazing by the body. Surely, if theft had been the motive, the horse would have been taken. No, it was someone who targeted her specifically, but for the life of me, I can't figure out who that someone might have been."

"Do you think it might have been Hugo?" Frances asked. Hugo would kill to protect Neve and his children, but what would be the point of killing Liza if he planned on leaving with his family? Liza's testimony could only do damage if Neve were to actually stand trial.

"Hugo was with my father at the time Liza was killed. He never left the farm. And he'd asked me to take care of her, so why would he kill her?"

"Because you didn't."

"No, Franny, it wasn't him. It was someone who was most likely unarmed."

"Why do you say that?" Frances asked, confused. She hadn't considered that possibility.

"Because a person who was armed would have either cut her throat or shot her. Why strangle her with the reins of her horse if you have a better weapon?"

Frances shrugged, unable to come up with an answer. She collected the empty bottle and got to her feet, ready to be escorted outside. Lowry Gibbs was already waiting outside the cell, his pale face visible through the metal grill.

"I'll try to get in tomorrow, but if I'm unable, make the food last. You hear?"

"Yes, my love. But do bring me some stew next time," Archie asked again.

"I will; I promise."

THIRTY-FIVE

MAY 2015

Surrey, England

Hugo gave a low whistle, summoning Tilly to his side. The dog had sniffed him suspiciously when he'd first arrived, but seemed to accept him as the new master. The Lab was getting old, but she was always eager to go for a walk through the countryside, trotting alongside him faithfully. Hugo was nearly as eager as the dog to get outside. He was vibrating with nervous energy that he could barely suppress. He'd been cooped up in the house for two weeks, put through a rigorous training course by Simon and Mrs. Harding. He was shown photos, told anecdotes from Max's past, given a list of people in the village with whom he'd been somewhat friendly, and taught to play cricket. Simon had also spent hours explaining the rules of rugby and made him watch several matches, his running commentary driving Hugo out of his mind.

It was not that Hugo wasn't grateful for what the Hardings were doing for him; it was that the more they talked about Max, the guiltier he felt. Max was dead because of him, and he would carry that knowledge with him for the rest of his life. Had Max just gone on to Surrey as he'd originally planned, he'd be the one walking with his dog and enjoying the warm welcome from family and friends. Hugo still couldn't comprehend what had induced Max to come to the Tower and offer to exchange places with him, but that fateful decision had cost Max his life. Archie had assured Hugo that it was some form of divine justice, but Hugo didn't believe that for a moment. If Max had found God and repented, wasn't that enough? Why would God reward him by taking his life, and in such a way that he was denied salvation?

Or was there another reason for Max's actions?

By committing suicide in the Tower of London while presumed to be Hugo Everly, Max had, for all intents and purposes, stolen Hugo's life. He had set Hugo free but made it impossible for him to continue on as Hugo Everly in his own time and place, forcing him to go to the future. It might have been a generous gesture, but it might also have been a trap. If Simon and Mrs. Harding refused to acknowledge Hugo as Max and denied him help, he'd never be able to pull off this ruse and wind up being as much of an outcast in this society as in his own. Was Max really so twisted with hatred that he would go to such lengths to destroy Hugo?

Hugo would never know the answers to any of these questions, but the uncertainty gnawed at him day and night. How could he inhabit Max's life when he was an impostor and a fraud? Perhaps another man would simply enjoy his ill-gotten gains, but Hugo couldn't bring himself to accept this perverse gift from the universe without much soul-searching.

He crouched next to Tilly and looked into the kind, brown eyes. "Even you accept me," he said ruefully. "Can't you tell I'm not your master?"

The dog just wagged its tail, eager to get going.

Hugo put the dog on a lead and headed toward the gates. Only two reporters were still hanging about, and he dismissed them with a curt, "No comment" as he walked away from the manor house. The story that Simon had fed to the press had worked wonders. It wasn't the type of sensational tabloid fodder readers would be hoping for. There was no kidnapping, no unsolved mystery, and no leads to pursue. A middle-aged man had a breakdown and went off the grid for a few years, using the time to write a novel that would never be published. Having worked through his issues, he finally decided to return, angering the British public by wasting police time and funds spent on the search. Very disappointing and forgettable, which was exactly what Simon had been hoping for.

There was one area of concern, however, Hugo mused as he walked briskly down a wooded lane. Detective Inspector Robert Knowles had come to interview him a few days ago, once Simon had let it drop that Max Everly was back. The detective was polite and respectful, but there was a watchfulness in his eyes and a hint of sarcasm as he welcomed Lord Everly back. Hugo was fairly certain that the policeman suspected the truth. He'd not only investigated Max's disappearance, but had known Max personally, had spent time with him, and played cricket on the same team. His trained eye could pick up what others had missed, and it had; Hugo was sure of that. Would he initiate an investigation or just ignore his hunch?

Hugo walked faster, almost jogging. He hated this whole charade, and missed Neve and the children more than he could say. Neve sent numerous pictures of the children, but seeing them enjoying themselves and learning about this new world without him only made him feel more isolated. *I'm doing this for them*, he thought over and over again, but somehow the thought felt hollow.

Perhaps it was time for a reunion. Simon said that Hugo needed to wait a few weeks before being seen in London, but no one would think anything of him visiting his brother's flat. He needed to see Neve and the kids. The need was like a physical pain that only got worse with every passing day.

Hugo abruptly turned around and began walking back toward the village, Tilly at his heels. Whatever DI Knowles was planning to do would just have to be dealt with. It was time for real life to begin.

THIRTY-SIX

I checked on the children to make sure they were all right before returning to Simon's office. We'd been in modern-day London for two weeks now, and I couldn't believe how quickly the children had adjusted to their new life. They were sitting on the sofa, watching *Boohbah* with intense concentration. Television was like a drug, or a free childminder. I tried to spend as much time with the kids as I could, taking them on daily outings and walks to the park, but I had much to do now that I was back.

The first order of business had been to visit my bank. I'd left a safety deposit box with my passport, birth certificate, driving license, credit and bank cards, and some cash. Recovering those documents was the first step in reclaiming my identity. My bank and credit cards had expired, but it was easy enough to get new ones issued and sent to Simon's address. I was happy to discover that I had a tidy sum waiting for me at the bank.

I had sublet my apartment in Notting Hill when I made the decision to leave, arranging for my tenants to pay via PayPal on a monthly basis. Had I never returned, they would eventually figure out that no one was claiming their money and stop paying, but I hoped that hadn't happened yet. I told them that I would be leaving the country for several years, but would return eventually.

The lease agreement was in my deposit box, left there for the sole purpose of collecting outstanding rent should the need arise. I hadn't planned to return when I went to the seventeenth century with Hugo, but if I'd had learned anything from my time there before, it was that anything could happen, and one should always be prepared for any eventuality. Burning bridges was never a good idea, and I was glad I'd had the foresight to prepare for my return. I was happy to see that my tenants had been paying faithfully each month, unwittingly making sure that I wasn't in dire financial straits when I returned.

Having taken care of the more pressing issues such as banking, credit cards, and a new mobile phone, I had to move on to the more difficult areas, such as establishing an identity for the children. They needed birth certificates in order to get registered with the NHS, and, of course, I had none. Even if I spun some story about the documents perishing in a fire or being lost, the children would already be in the database, accessible by name and National Insurance number. I would also have to provide the name of the father, and listing Maximilian Everly as the father of my children would create a media storm if the information were leaked to the press, considering that he'd just returned from his self-enforced exile and claimed to have been on his own all this time. Questions would be raised, and our lives would be probed, scrutinized, and splashed across the tabloids.

There was one person from my past who might be able to help me, but I was reluctant to ask for such a big favor. What choice did I have though? My children hadn't been immunized, and were susceptible to the more advanced viruses and strains of the twenty-first century. They would also need to go to school in the not-so-distant future, and I needed to be prepared.

Reluctantly, I flipped through my list of contacts, so thoughtfully downloaded onto my new phone from their records by my mobile phone provider. I stared at the name for a few minutes before pushing the call button, hoping that the number was still operational. A lot could have happened in three years.

Glen Coolidge was a friend from my old job at Legendary Productions. He was the head of the Special Effects Department and an absolute computer whiz. He was also an American expat who had been embroiled in a bitter custody battle with his ex-wife and living with a sexually fluid couple as part of a triad, which didn't help his chances in court. Glen was the most uninhibited, morally elastic, out-of-date flower child I'd ever met. But he was also loyal, sensitive to the feelings of others— except his ex-wife's, of course—and eager to help when he could.

Glen came on the line after about five rings, his voice sounding uncharacteristically annoyed at seeing an unfamiliar number. "This better not be a sales call," he growled. "I'm sick and tired of people trying to sell me solar panels and holiday cruises, especially during business hours."

"Glen, it's Neve. Neve Ashley."

Glen's demeanor underwent an amazing transformation, his voice now crackling with amusement. "Well, well, Neve Ashley of all people. Fancy getting a call from you after a deafening silence of several years. What can I do for you, my lovely?" he asked, flirtatious as ever. I could almost imagine him sitting in his office, leaning back in his chair until it nearly flipped over, his feet dangerously close to his state-of-the-art equipment, a cup of strong black coffee in his hand.

"Glen, I know it's been a long time, and I'm sorry to bother you," I began.

"Hey, it's no bother. Always good to hear from an old friend, even if the friend in question blew you off without so much as a 'See ya, Glen,' but hey, I'm not one for holding grudges."

"Well, I'm happy to see you are not harboring any negative emotions," I said, smiling to myself, "or this would be really awkward."

"Neh, I'm just busting your chops, kid. How've you been?"

"Well," I replied vaguely. "Glen, could I tempt you with some extra spicy curry?" I asked. When I'd worked with Glen, he used to get Indian takeaway at least once a week, stinking up the entire floor with the smell. I didn't mind it too much, since I could always go for some myself, but many of Glen's employees ran for the door as soon as the food was delivered. I was actually kind of glad Hugo wasn't there. Curry was not a favorite of his.

"Sure. I'm free for lunch tomorrow. How about that place we used to go to? They changed owners twice since the last time I saw you, but the curry is still just as good."

"Actually, I was hoping you'd come round. I have no one to mind the children."

"Children? As in multiple children? My, you've been busy. Okay, give me the address."

I gave Glen the address, smiling when he whistled into the phone. "Very swanky. Did you find yourself a sugar daddy, or what?"

"Not exactly. I'll fill you in tomorrow."

"Okay, see ya," Glen said before hanging up.

I was actually looking forward to my lunch date since I hadn't had much adult interaction of the social kind. I hadn't rung anyone from my past life yet. I wanted to, but the idea of having to explain away my lengthy absence and two children put me off. I simply wasn't ready. Glen was the first, and I was curious to see how our reunion would go.

At some point, I would have to call Deborah. She'd been a good friend when I was in a relationship with her ex-husband, Evan, but Deborah, unlike Glen, who could take a hint, would ask a million questions, and feel the need to tell me all about Evan since she was still in touch with him because of their daughter, who was likely at university by now. I'd loved Evan once, and hoped for a life with him, but the thought of hearing about his selfishness and self-absorption left me cold. Having been married to Hugo, I now knew what real commitment was, and the memory of my misguided love for Evan made me cringe.

Having known Frances and Archie, I now also knew what real friendship was. It wasn't just about guzzling wine and complaining about the men in one's life; it was about knowing that the person you called your friend would do anything for you should the need arise, even dig up a dead body in the dead of night and replace it for a live one, as Archie and Hugo had done when they broke me out of Newgate Prison. So, calling Deborah would have to wait—maybe a year or two.

THIRTY-SEVEN

Glen showed up a half-hour late, but he did come bearing gifts. He correctly deduced that my children couldn't be older than four, and brought several coloring books, crayons, and two adorable stuffed teddy bears that were exactly the same and wouldn't cause a fight between the kids. Valentine and Michael were charmed, hugging the bears as they leafed through the books. They looked really sweet as they sat at the kitchen table, their heads bent over the coloring book, working on a picture together, rather than choosing to work in separate books. Valentine was berating Michael for coloring outside the lines, but I could see that she didn't really mind. She was enjoying playing the role of tutor.

I left the kids to color and invited Glen into the dining room where I'd set the table for lunch. I had also prepared a bottle of good Sauvignon Blanc, remembering it as Glen's favorite. I'd studied him discreetly while he met the children and presented them with the gifts. He was the same old Glen: tall, lanky, with spiky black hair and horn-rimmed glasses. But there was a new wariness about him which hadn't been there before, and a few tiny wrinkles now bracketed his eyes and mouth when he smiled. He still smelled good though. Glen had been a huge fan of cologne, and always left a lingering trail of delicious scent after he passed by.

"So, where did the little rugrats come from?" Glen asked as I set the takeaway on the table and opened up the containers, releasing the smell of the food into the air. I could see Glen salivating as the pungent and spicy aroma filled the dining room.

"Want a glass of wine?" I asked as I uncorked the bottle.

"Sure." I could feel Glen's eyes boring into me as I poured us each a glass. "You look good, Neve, but different somehow. Are you going to tell me where you've been all this time, or is it a secret?"

"I've been undercover for MI5," I replied with mock seriousness. "I can tell you, but I'd have to kill you."

"You Brits are always so secretive," Glen complained as he took a sip of the wine. "Americans love to talk about themselves, but you hold your cards close to your vest."

"Tell me about you instead," I invited, validating Glen's observation.

"Not much to tell. I get to see my daughter twice a month on Sundays. We have lunch, go to the movies, or hang out at the playground. She calls me Glen," he added bitterly. "My ex remarried, and now her new husband is Daddy. I suppose she's better off; I never was cut out for marriage."

"Do you regret it?" I asked.

"I regret the marriage, not the child. I wish I could see Poppy more often. I enjoy being with her, and I hope that once she's a little older we can be real buddies."

I decided not to point out that teenage girls were rarely buddies with their dad, especially a dad who was sexually confused and still played with toys. I had been a sort of stepmom to Evan's teenage daughter and although a good kid at heart, she was the most sullen, hormonal, irrational human being I'd ever met. Glen was in for a surprise once Poppy hit puberty.

"And your flatmates?" I asked, unsure of what to call Glen's lovers.

"Oh, they left about two years ago. I think they're living in Berlin now. I've been on my own for a long while."

"What? No new love interest?" I asked, teasing. Glen was always in love with someone.

"There was someone, but it didn't last."

"I'm sorry, Glen."

I had to admit that, for all his eccentricity, I really liked Glen. He was real, which was something that wasn't easy to come by in any century.

We chatted easily while we ate, eager to catch up, but eventually Glen came around to the purpose of his visit.

"So, what can I do for you, candy girl?" Glen asked, grinning at me in that knowing way. "I know how appreciative you've always been of my talents."

"Glen, my children don't have birth certificates. They were born in odd circumstances, and I have nothing legitimate to show the powers-that-be. Val and Michael need to be immunized and will eventually need to be registered for school."

"I see," Glen replied. "Where were they born, if you don't mind my asking?"

"France."

"They don't issue birth certificates in France?" he asked, watching me closely.

"Not in the seventeenth century, they don't."

Glen put down his fork and gaped at me as if I'd just told him that my children were sired by Darth Vader. "Come off it, Neve. Just because I happen to be a fan of science fiction, and have attended every Comicon in the last ten years, doesn't mean I'm buying that one."

"Too bad, 'cause it's true." I knew that if anyone believed

my story, it would be Glen. And I had to tell him the truth because that's the only way he would feel compelled to help me.

"So, that dude who needed a passport a few years back was from the past?" Glen asked, intrigued.

"Yes. He is the father of my children, and I have lived in the seventeenth century for the past three and a half years. Can you help me, Glen?"

"Only if you tell me, in excruciating detail, how you managed to go back in time, and then come back. You know that traveling through time has always been one of my ultimate fantasies. But I have no desire to go back. God, can you just see me in the seventeenth century?" Glen had a good laugh as he accepted another glass of wine, no doubt picturing himself dressed as Charles II. "I want to go into the future. I want to fly a spacecraft, travel to as yet undiscovered galaxies, and meet people from alien races." Glen's face was glowing with excitement, and I wished I had it in my power to grant him his wish, but I had no idea how to travel forward.

"All right, put your light saber away and concentrate on the problem at hand," I quipped in an effort to redirect him.

Glen leaned back in his chair and glanced toward the kitchen, where an argument over what color to make a monkey had just erupted.

"Well, they are cute little kiddies, I'll give you that. It is easier to establish a false identity for children than it is for adults. Less to invent. Since your passport doesn't show that you've left the UK or entered France in this century, I think it's best if we forge a British birth certificate," Glen suggested, his gaze thoughtful. "I suppose I can create a file for these two, but it might be best if you go with the Earth Mother routine."

"What in the world do you mean by that?"

"I mean that any normal British woman would have taken her precious offspring to the clinic for checkups and immunizations. I can falsify a birth certificate, but not health records—too risky. So, if you explain your aversion to modern medicine by saying that you believe in the holistic approach, it might be easier to avoid suspicion."

"So, what do you suggest?" I asked, unsure of where Glen was going with this.

"I suggest that we find a midwife, preferably someone who is far away from London and is of advancing years and forge her name to a birth certificate. I doubt anyone would bother to check if she has any record of the births. People tend to believe what they are told, or what they see, in this case. If they see a document signed by a registered midwife, they'll accept it."

"So, why does she need to be of advanced years?" I asked, still confused. Glen's mind was usually about ten steps ahead of my own.

"Because if some eager beaver does decide to do their civic duty and check with the midwife, they might be led to believe that being an older woman, she simply forgot you and your babies, or has misfiled the records. Some old people are sharp as tacks, but people tend to believe that you start going senile at forty. I'm well on my way," he added.

"Can you put your senility on hold long enough to do this for me, Glen?"

"Sure thing. I'm a master forger. I'll find the right candidate and print off a generic birth certificate, which I will fill out by hand. No worries, my pretty. Your children will be legit by the end of the week. Now, what about that husband of yours?"

"He died," I choked out. I was willing to tell Glen about the time travel since no one would believe him anyway if he shared the story, but divulging that Hugo had taken Max Everly's place and was now the master of the house was risky. Glen loved to gossip, and this story might be too good to keep to himself. He might not tell people that the impostor was from the past, but selling the story to some publication claiming that the man who returned was not the man who'd left could open up a nasty can of worms and make Glen a rich man. I had it on good authority that the divorce and subsequent custody battle had left him skint, so it was best not to give him anything which might be too tempting to share with the world.

"I'm sorry, Neve. Is that why you came back?"

"Yes. My husband died in the Tower of London last month."

"What was his name?" Glen asked casually, but I could see the insatiable curiosity in his eyes.

I knew that Glen would do a search as soon as he got back to work, so it was imperative that he believe me. I was sure that he would find some mention of Lord Everly's death in April 1689, and that would help my cause. I hated being conniving and false, but this was a unique situation, so I had to come up with unique explanations for my motives.

"Hugo Everly," I finally replied.

"Why was he in the Tower?"

"He was accused of treason."

"Ho ho," Glen cried out. "Married a rebel, did ya? Was he a Catholic then? A Jacobite? I just read a great series about the whole Jacobite thing. Very diverting when you can't sleep."

I was partially grateful for Glen's flippant attitude. I couldn't bear to go into the ins and outs of seventeenth-century politics and Hugo's role. If Glen wanted to believe Hugo was a Jacobite, then that was fine with me. I wasn't even sure if the term had existed in the seventeenth century, or if it became popular later on, but Glen didn't seem to care, so neither did I.

"Thanks for lunch. Gotta dash. We're working on a big project, a sort of rip-off of *Doctor Who*, so my department is working overtime. Are you thinking of returning to work? Perhaps Lawrence Spellman could be convinced to give you your job back. We have two location scouts now, but they are not nearly as good as you were. You always had that special feeling for a place."

"Thanks, Glen, but getting a job is not a priority right now. I must be here for my children."

"But how will you support yourself?" he asked, always practical. "And whose place is this anyway?"

"It belongs to a friend."

"Ah, you've got a new man already. Good for you. Don't let the grass grow under your feet, I always say." Glen was being a bit insensitive, but his comments weren't mean-spirited, just thoughtless. He gave me a peck on the cheek as he turned to leave. "I'll stop by on Saturday with the docs. See ya."

I shut the door behind Glen, feeling ashamed and excited at the same time. Could I really pull this off?

THIRTY-EIGHT

Hugo turned out the light, threw open the window, and sank into a comfortable armchair. Sitting in the dark was soothing somehow, a reprieve for the senses after the glaring light of electricity, which he still found harsh after the soft light of candles. A pleasant breeze caressed his face, and the smell of spring was in the air like an intoxicating elixir beckoning one to abandon the apathy of winter and embrace life and all it had to offer.

The brief trip to London to see Neve and the children had been heartbreakingly joyful, but it made Hugo feel his isolation more acutely after leaving them. They'd only had a few hours together, reminding him of how much he was missing every single day that he wasn't with them. Valentine had barely let go of his hand, and Michael had clung to him as if he'd come back from the dead. The children had chattered incessantly, their need to fill him in on all the new things they'd discovered overwhelming after weeks of separation.

They'd changed so much in such a short time. Valentine seemed more grown up somehow, suddenly interested in all the girly things a child her age would be. And Michael seemed much less timid than he had been in the past. He asserted himself when Valentine tried to cut in on his time with Hugo, and proudly showed Hugo his new favorite toy, a motorized police car with doors that opened and closed, real flashing lights, and a siren. The carved wooden horse that Michael never parted with since Archie gave it to him in France lay forgotten on the bedside table.

Hugo had barely had a chance to talk to Neve but was glad to see that she seemed to be adjusting well. She looked more animated, more relaxed than he'd seen her in months. Things weren't necessarily simpler, but her mood was much improved. Neve had things to accomplish and was rediscovering what it was like to be able to have some control over her daily life again. She'd often complained of having to wait around helplessly while events took place which had the power to change her life. That had been the role of a woman in the seventeenth century, but now she had the power to make decisions and fend for herself.

She'd started wearing make-up again, which made her features appear more dramatic and exaggerated. Hugo knew he'd get used to the change in time, but for the first few minutes, Neve seemed like a stranger, some other man's wife who vaguely resembled his own. Gone were the gowns, hose, and elaborate hairstyles. Neve was wearing a comfortable pair of jeans paired with a silk top, her wavy blonde hair loose about her shoulders. She looked young and graceful without the voluminous skirts and full sleeves. Hugo supposed that he looked different to her as well. He felt different, and would have liked to talk to Neve, and share with her all the things he was learning and going through, but the children barely gave them a moment of peace, so the conversation would have to take place over the telephone and not in person, as Hugo had hoped.

All too soon, Simon had returned. He'd gone out to run some errands in order to give the Everlys some private time, but he came back for dinner, which consisted of pizza and juice, the kids' favorite new food. Simon opened a bottle of wine for the adults, and they finished it off while the children watched a little television before bedtime. Valentine and Michael clung to Hugo when he tried to say goodbye, their good spirits dissipating into a flood of tears. Only the promise of a long hot bath finally distracted them from their misery, and after a hasty goodbye, Hugo and Simon were on their way back to Surrey, and back to the deception. Only that morning Hugo had fantasized about reuniting the family, but it was too soon, given the circumstances.

Hugo had decided to buy some picture books for the children before setting off for London that afternoon. He'd walked into the village with Tilly on his heels, glad to see that people no longer stared at him as if he were a curiosity. Several people called out a greeting, while others nodded in acknowledgment. It seemed the village was beginning to accept him as one of their own.

Hugo was just about to enter the bookshop when DI Robert Knowles stepped out with his little girl. The child was about a year older than Valentine, a sweet little thing named Lucy.

"Hello, Bobby," Hugo said, feeling self-conscious at addressing the police officer in such a familiar way, but that's what Max would have called him.

Knowles just nodded, not bothering to respond.

"Hello," Lucy said as she smiled up at him. "I got a new book," she shared, showing him the beautiful book Knowles had just bought for her.

Hugo almost blurted out that he was there to buy books for his children, but bit his tongue just in time. DI Knowles was watching him carefully, his gaze missing nothing. He'd noticed that Hugo was holding something back.

He leaned forward ever so slightly and spoke in a low voice, meant only for Hugo's ears. "I don't know who you are, but I mean to find out, and when I do, I will take you down."

"Come, sweetheart," he said to Lucy in a completely different tone. "Mum will be expecting us back in time for lunch."

"Bye," Lucy called out as she waved to Hugo and trotted off after her father.

Hugo spent a few minutes browsing the children's section before choosing several books he thought the children would enjoy, but Bobby's words stayed with him the whole day.

"You all right, mate?" Simon asked as they set off for London an hour later. "You seem preoccupied."

"Just eager to see my family," Hugo had replied, reluctant to tell Simon of his run-in with Knowles. Simon had done more than enough for him already, and Hugo didn't intend to burden him with this.

Now that Hugo was alone, he needed to think of a way to deal with the situation. Had it been just him, he would have gone off somewhere and began a new life, but he had Neve and the children to think of. They needed a home and a future.

A gentle rain began to fall outside, the pitter-patter of raindrops strangely soothing to Hugo's frayed nerves. His mind strayed to Archie, as it so often did. He could almost feel Archie's presence in his mind.

"I wish you were here, old friend," Hugo said into the darkness. "Between the two of us, we could have figured this out."

But he was alone, and he needed to find a way to get one step ahead of DI Knowles.

I need to simplify this, Hugo thought. He didn't know nearly enough about how things were done in the twenty-first century, but he did know something of human nature, which hadn't changed much over the centuries. Everyone had weaknesses which made them vulnerable, and everyone made mistakes. Now all he had to do was find Knowles's.

THIRTY-NINE

Bobby Knowles tiptoed from his daughter's room, having just read her a story from the new book. She loved fairy stories, his Lucy, just like her mother. Carol was a dreamer, a fantasist, a woman who didn't like dealing with the ugly side of life. Bobby supposed that's what drew him to her in the first place, but sometimes he wished he could be with someone who understood him better. Where Carol chose to see rainbows and butterflies, he saw motive, opportunity, and method. It made talking to her about his job difficult, and at some point during their fifteen-year marriage, he'd stopped. Carol didn't want to hear it, and he grew tired of talking to someone who wasn't interested. He had his mates for that, guys he'd known since he was in the academy and who provided the support he needed.

Carol was in the kitchen doing the washing up after supper. She put her hands on her lower back and arched backward to ease the tension. "Give us a back rub, Bobby," she said with a smile. "You have magic in your hands."

Bobby came up behind Carol and began to rub her back. She made sounds of contentment, making Bobby think that she might be amenable to other ideas. He kissed her neck lightly, then moved on to her earlobe as Carol leaned back into him. Her belly bulged in front of her, their son kicking up a storm as if he resented his father's presence. Lucy had never kicked so fiercely. Bobby wrapped his arms around Carol and placed his hands over her belly in an effort to connect with the baby, but the moment was gone, and Carol swatted him with a tea towel.

"I'm going to bed. Can you finish up here?"

"Sure," Bobby replied, disappointed and angry. They hadn't made love in weeks, possibly even months. Carol had been more than willing when she'd decided she wanted to have another baby, but once the test came back positive, she seemed to lose all interest. She was hormonal and tired all the time, especially with Lucy being so demanding and threatened by the new baby, but he was still her husband, or so he liked to think.

Carol had loved him once, he was sure of that, but now he couldn't really say what she felt for him, other than dependency. They hardly talked anymore, and the few times they went out, Carol insisted on inviting her sister. Bobby liked his brother- and sister-in-law well enough, but although they always had a pleasant time, it prevented him and Carol from reconnecting.

He'd hoped that having another baby would get them back on track, but Carol was so wrapped up in Lucy and the pregnancy that she barely spared him a few minutes. He left before she woke in the morning and came back just in time for supper, after which Carol usually went to give Lucy a bath and then toddled off to bed. He supposed that he was trying to justify his reasons for having an affair with Jess. He felt guilty when he was at home, but as soon as he was alone with Jess, all feelings of wrongdoing fled, and he was pumping with desire—something he hadn't felt for Carol in at least a decade.

Bobby finished the dishes and retired to his office. It was his man cave, and the only place in the house not yet invaded by

Barbies, stuffed toys, and Carol's pregnancy manuals. Bobby turned on the desk lamp and opened a manila folder marked "Everly". He'd respected the Super's decree and not done anything on work time, but no one said he couldn't dig around on his own. He'd been conducting his own investigation over the past few days, and was as suspicious as ever.

According to his findings, Max Everly had not accessed his bank account in over three years, nor had he used his mobile phone or credit cards. He had never phoned home during the time he was missing, unless he used the landline at the cabin, if there even was one. Bobby would have to check on that. And how in the world did he get to the Highlands when he left Everly Manor without his wallet or car keys? Did he take a wad of cash with him? Did he hitchhike? If so, why did no one come forward when his face was plastered all over the telly? Someone must have seen him. And, if the man claiming to be Lord Everly wasn't actually Max, then what had happened to the real Max, and who was this impostor? How could he bear such a striking resemblance to Maximilian Everly? None of this made any sense at all, and all these questions were driving Bobby crazy. Max had been a good friend, and he couldn't rest until he answered at least a few of them.

Bobby absentmindedly spun his globe on its axis, watching the colorful countries speed by. He jabbed a finger at the orb, stopping it dead. He glanced at the map of England, then allowed his eyes to travel northward to Scotland. That's where the answers were. He had to go see the place where Max had been hiding out, talk to the people in the area, and demand to see CCTV footage. If Max had been there for over three years, someone would have seen him, and spoken to him. He must have bought groceries, gone to the pub, went for walks.

Bobby leaned back in his chair, his eyes still on the map. He'd make a long weekend out of this inquiry, and take Jess for a much-deserved getaway. No need for her to know that he was working. He'd be discreet, and find out what he needed to know. Then, if his suspicions hadn't been allayed, he would go back to Superintendent Cummings and present his case. She could order a DNA test, and compare dental records. If this man was an impostor, modern science would prove it.

FORTY

MAY 1689

Essex, England

Jem vaulted into the saddle, happy to have escaped the strained atmosphere in the house. The baby was teething, his miserable cries echoing down from the nursery on the top floor. Jem's stepmother was in a state, and his father was irritable and angry, unable to bear the incessant crying and the nervous condition of his wife. He'd told her to visit the village wisewoman and get a remedy for the child, but she refused, claiming that no ignorant peasant was going to give some evil concoction to her baby. Jem had to admit that he felt sorry for the poor mite and wished that his stepmother would relent. The village women swore by Mother Goode's skills and knowledge. But this was no concern of his, and he was glad to be out in the fresh air, galloping on his horse, wind in his hair and sun on his face. It was the only place he felt truly free.

Jem had gotten quite a thrashing for running away and not leaving word of where he was going, but his father grudgingly forgave him after a few days, happy to have Jem back home. Mistress Marsden, however, wasn't nearly as pleased to have him back. She felt that Nicholas had been too lenient with Jem, and a more severe punishment was called for. She'd made Jem's life a living hell for the past two weeks, finding reasons to punish him and cause him pain. His knees were permanently scarred by kneeling on hard peas for hours, and there were marks on his hands where she'd hit him with the riding crop when she'd caught him trying to saddle his horse when he should have been at his lessons.

It was while reading with his tutor that Jem had hit on a plan for the future. Jem was certain that the estate would go to his baby brother—the legitimate son, conceived and born in church-sanctified wedlock. There was no point in rebelling or aggravating his father out of sheer spite. Seeing the relief on Nicholas Marsden's face when Jem finally showed up at home had ultimately convinced him that despite his bastard status, his father did care for him, and now that Lord and Lady Everly were gone, there was no one left in this world he could turn to anyway. The wisest course of action was to bide his time, keep his father and stepmother happy, and then, in a few years, ask his father to get him a commission in the army. Of course, Jem could simply join up, but he had no wish to be a regular foot soldier, or cannon fodder. He wanted to become a great general, like the Roman generals he read about in his books. He wanted to command legions, not march for days until his feet were sore and his stomach growled with hunger. Perhaps with his father's money and influence, he could start out as a captain and make his way through the ranks.

Archie would have made an excellent soldier, Jem thought wistfully. Archie had what it took not only to kill but to lead men into battle. He had presence of mind, keen intuition, and the ability to strategize, which most common soldiers lacked.

Jem's mood turned sour when he thought of Archie. He so wanted to accompany Frances to Guilford, and was sure that Lord Everly, had he been there, would have wished him to go with her. Archie needed his help, and he wasn't there. Of course, he could do nothing to free his friend, but he could go places Frances couldn't, which was sometimes very helpful, and offer Frances his company and support. Instead, he was here; reading Latin and Greek, listening to the incessant crying of his baby brother, and trying to maintain a fragile peace with his father.

Jem tied up the horse by his favorite spot and sat down on a fallen log, watching the stream flowing past, the water sparkling in the May sunshine. *What if Archie were executed?* Jem thought miserably. Archie had been like a beloved older brother, who taught him how to shoot and fish and approach a skittish horse. Archie had never babied him or comforted him the way Lord Everly had, but he'd taught him many a valuable lesson, and always treated him like a person, not a pet or an asset. Archie wasn't one for gushing with approval, but when he bestowed that rare smile and clapped Jem on the back, Jem felt as if he could take flight, knowing that he had managed to please the toughest of masters. Archie's approval meant more to Jem than even Lord Everly's because it was that much harder to gain.

Jem knew that his father loved him, but Nicholas had never hit on that magic combination of love and respect that a boy Jem's age needed. He still treated Jem like a child, and tried too hard to prove that bringing him back from France hadn't been a colossal mistake. Sometimes Jem wished that his father would simply talk to him the way Hugo and Archie used to talk to him. He needed to be seen and heard, not merely looked after. Perhaps his father would have a better relationship with his younger son, having learned the hard lessons of parenting with Jem.

Jem suddenly froze, a new idea settling into his head with a deafening thud. His stepmother wasn't so emotional because of the teething baby. She'd been pale and prone to tears, and her already ample bosom seemed to have swelled of late. And Jem hadn't heard his father visiting her bedchamber even once since coming back home. She was with child again, Jem thought with disgust. His father certainly hadn't wasted any time. How many more babies would there be before his stepmother either grew too old to bear children or died in childbirth? Well, it didn't matter. Another three years and he'd be gone from this place forever.

Jem picked up a handful of pebbles and began to throw them into the stream. Silent tears of misery and dejection flowed down his cheeks. Thankfully, no one would see him cry in this place, and even if they did, no one would care.

FORTY-ONE

MAY 1689

Guilford, Surrey

A lashing rain beat at the window, engulfing the room in perpetual gloom. It was nearly the end of May, but it was freezing cold, and the bedclothes were damp without a hot brick to warm them. Frances yanked the coverlet over her head and pulled up her knees in a desperate effort to get warm. Eventually, her teeth stopped chattering and she was able to relax slightly, but sleep wouldn't come. She'd been in Guilford for a month now, and her days consisted of the same routine: get up, wash and dress, have breakfast, go to the prison, wait, either gain entrance or not, then come back to her room and fret. On fine days, she took walks by the river, just to keep from going crazy within the four walls of her tiny garret.

Thanks to Lowry Gibbs, Frances got to see Archie at least a few times a week, but he had become silent and withdrawn. Archie's eyes were always fixed on the door, and he kept asking questions about who had let her in and how many guards she'd seen. What did it matter? They were all the same, for the most part, except Master Gibbs, who was at least kind to her, if for his own selfish reasons. Although even he didn't seem as interested in her these days, since she gave him no elicit encouragement. He'd asked her for a kiss, and she'd nearly slapped the silly fool. She was a married woman, a woman whose husband was still alive. But Lowry assumed it wasn't for long, and in her heart, she knew that to be the truth.

By nightfall, she'd have some supper, then go to bed. She barely spoke to anyone, and no one paid her much mind either, not even the landlord. As long as she paid, she was invisible. And in a way, she was. She drifted through the town, ate in the dining room from time to time, but no one noticed her. She'd lost weight, her face was pale and drawn, and there were dark circles beneath her eyes caused by worry and sleepless nights. She might have stopped eating altogether if it weren't for the babe growing inside her. Archie's babe. She hadn't told him yet. It seemed too cruel to tell him of a child he might never get to see or hold.

Frances had no illusions; she knew what the assizes would bring. The thought of losing Archie cut so deep that she couldn't bear to think of it. She lived life one day at a time. Thinking of the future only brought her pain. Sometimes she dreamed that she was walking down a long, winding road through some barren landscape, with not a house or tree in sight. The lowering sky looked thunderous, and a thick fog swirled about her feet, making her falter and stumble. She clutched a small bundle to her chest, but the baby within wasn't showing any signs of life, its form still and silent. Frances woke up from her dream with tears streaming down her face. Perhaps if the baby kicked, she might have had some reassurance, but it was too soon to feel movement, so she had no idea if the child was thriving.

A few months ago, Frances would have been beside herself with joy to know she was pregnant again, but now the baby was a sad reminder of a life that would never be—a future stolen.

She had no one to turn to, no one who would care for her or take her in besides Archie's father. She would return to him after the trial and await the birth of her child. At least she would have a roof over her head and someone there to talk to about Archie and the man he had been. Frances didn't think that Horatio Hicks would last out the year, but perhaps the thought of seeing his grandchild would force him to hold on.

Some days, Frances almost wished that Jem had come with her. She knew it would have been wrong to encourage him, but he was someone she could trust, someone she could talk to and reminisce with about the days when they were happier. Funny how a person forgot all the trials and worries of the past and only remembered the moments of joy. Frances often thought of sipping chocolate in a brasserie in Paris or sitting in the garden with Neve as Valentine slept next to them on her blanket. Even the trips to Versailles now seemed full of romance and excitement, the days brimming with music and color.

Frances rarely thought of Luke Marsden or the baby she'd self-aborted, but Jem said that his uncle had married while in Constantinople. Perhaps the posting with Sir Trumbull hadn't turned out as badly as Luke had expected. She hoped he was happy. She hadn't been fair to him, and for that she was sorry. Could God be punishing her for what she'd done? He'd offered her a good man and a baby, and she threw both away. And now she might lose another man and another baby, and these two she wanted to hold on to more than to life itself.

Thoughts of France always culminated in memories of the house outside Rouen where the love between her and Archie had truly blossomed. She cried silently as she remembered the lazy afternoons and long talks over picnics by the stream. They had shared their hopes and dreams, believing that the golden days would go on forever. She'd never been as happy as she had been in Rouen. And then they came back to England.

If only she could turn back the clock, to even a month ago.

They should have gone to the future with Hugo and Neve. She should have insisted. Archie would have listened to her; he always did. At least they would still be together, and not torn apart by time and space, scattered across the universe like distant stars. Whatever hardship they might have faced couldn't be nearly as awful or heartbreaking as her everyday reality.

Frances gasped as a sharp pain tore through her belly, followed by another.

"Please don't leave me," she whispered to her baby. "Please."

FORTY-TWO

MAY 2015

The Highlands, Scotland

Bobby Knowles walked out of the little market, a shopping bag in his hands. He had bought a bottle of wine, some cheese and grapes, imported pate, and a loaf of bread. The food was for the picnic he was planning, but the motive for going to the shop had been something else entirely. He'd chatted up the woman behind the counter, the owner's wife, who was only too happy to talk. He'd never been to the Highlands before and expected the people to be taciturn and dismissive, but everyone had been very friendly and eager to have a chat, especially the American couple who owned the guest house. Those two seemed starved for conversation. For all their friendliness, the local folk hadn't been as welcoming as the Americans would have liked, and their only real source of social interaction came from their paying guests. That's how Bobby had learned about the shop. If Max had lived in this area for over three years, he would have had to visit the McLeods' shop at some point.

Mrs. McLeod was friendliness itself. She was a wholesome-looking woman in her early sixties, whose tightly permed gray hair was the only sign of advancing age. Her eyes sparkled with mischief, and her rosy cheeks were punctuated by deep dimples. She wore a serviceable pinafore over her blue jeans and pretty jersey. It took Bobby nearly ten minutes of small talk to finally get around to what he wanted to know. Bobby had casually asked if they had a CCTV camera since he'd been unable to spot one while browsing through the store.

"Och, no. What for?" Mrs. McLeod laughed, throwing up her hands. "We haven't had a violent crime hereabouts in donkey's years. A local lad stole a pack of gum; that was the extent of our crime wave."

"Do you get many strangers in these parts?" Bobby asked as he examined the bottle of wine.

"Sometimes the folk from the guest house stop in to buy a drink or a snack, but no, not really. All locals. Been here since God was a baby."

"What about Lord Everly? I heard he'd been staying nearby. A real recluse, I take it."

"That he was," the woman said. "My Angus made a delivery out there once every few months, but never saw hide nor hair of the man. Said the place looked deserted. But someone took the groceries in, and someone paid the bill, so I reckon someone was in that cottage."

"Did he place the order himself?" Bobby asked, still trying to work out the logistics of the operation.

"No. He left a note pinned to the door with a list of things he needed in the next delivery. Angus would just take it and fill the order."

"Do you have any of his notes lying about?" Bobby asked, sensing a lead, but the woman suddenly clammed up, her face going from friendliness to anger in a matter of seconds.

"Now, listen up, laddie. We run a respectable business here, and people's preferences are their own affair. How'd you like someone to scrutinize your shopping lists? If you're quite finished here, you should be on your way. I have customers to attend to." Mrs. McLeod was referring to a young man who'd been browsing the shelves while Bobby chatted her up. The young man had approached the counter, ready to pay for his purchases.

"Point taken, Mrs. McLeod," Bobby relented, not wanting the woman to get her knickers in a twist. A note would have been useful, but it didn't really prove anything.

Bobby took his groceries and went out into the sunshine. It was a glorious day, and he had a lovely spot picked out, not too far away from the cottage where Max was said to have spent the past three and a half years.

Bobby waved happily when he saw Jess emerging from the guest house. He'd snuck out early to get the supplies, letting her sleep in, but she was ready, a spring in her step as she walked toward him, a smile lighting up her lovely face.

"Hey there, handsome," she said, linking her arm through his.

"Good morning, my beautiful. I have a surprise for you."

"Better than the surprise you had for me last night?" Jess asked innocently.

Bobby could barely hide his smug smile. When at home, he lasted a good while but was never really up for another round. Last night, he'd made love to Jess three times in quick succession, leaving her quivering like a bowl of jelly and too exhausted to get up in time for breakfast. Being away from Carol made him feel young and carefree, and he felt the telltale stirring in his loins as he looked at Jess's sweet young face. He was having a lovely time, and he had Lord Everly to thank for it.

FORTY-THREE

MAY 1689

Guilford, Surrey

Archie willed himself to remain perfectly still and silent as Lowry Gibbs escorted Frances from the cell. He wanted to call out to her, to ask her not to leave, to talk to him for just a few more minutes, but, of course, she couldn't stay. The guards only allowed short visits, long enough for family members to bring food to the inmates and line the pockets of the guards, who charged them for the privilege. If the visitors refused to pay, the guards refused to pass on the food. No one cared if a prisoner died while awaiting trial. It happened all the time. A fresh corpse was carried out by the guards at least once a week. Of course, the guards were in no rush to remove the newly deceased, leaving the corpses in the cell for a few days to put the fear of God into the other prisoners who begged their loved ones to pay any bribe necessary to bring them food and drink. Thank God Frances had enough money to keep bribing the guards, since many women didn't. They had to make a choice between spending all their money on sustaining a condemned man, or feeding their children.

Frances looked dreadful this morning, and Archie had only himself to blame for the state she was in. Frances had always been so lovely, but now she looked haggard and tired, the bloom gone from her cheeks from worrying about his sorry self.

Archie leaned his head against the wall and closed his eyes. A pounding headache started behind his eyes and had now spread into his temples. He needed to sleep for a bit. He managed to stay awake for Franny's visits, but he was really tired during the day since he wasn't sleeping much at night. After a month of being chained to the wall, his muscles were weakened, and his beard and hair crawled with lice. He couldn't even remember the last time he'd had a wash, and his clothes were nothing more than tatters. He'd make a fine impression when brought before the judge. Good thing he had no intention of standing trial.

He needed to be well rested for tonight. Thankfully Frances had been allowed in today. Having food in his belly was a definite plus. He was as weak as a newborn kitten, but at least he wasn't about to faint from hunger. Archie allowed his mind to drift until the pain began to ease and he sank into a deep sleep. There were benefits to having a cell all to himself. At least it was relatively quiet, and no one could rat him out to the guards.

Archie slept until nightfall, then finished off the food Frances had brought that morning and began his preparations. He'd been watching the guards for the past few weeks, timing their rounds and trying to estimate how many people there were and where they were situated. It was hard to do since he couldn't see any of them through the tiny opening in the door; he could only hear. Frances wasn't much help in gathering information. She couldn't understand his interest in the gaolers or their habits since Archie hadn't shared his plan with her for fear of disappointing her should it fail.

As far as Archie could tell, there were eight guards in total, who worked in teams of four and alternated every other day. There seemed to be only two people on duty during the night. One guard did a final check of the prisoners around midnight, and then all was quiet until daybreak. The two guards probably slept through their shift, but it was hard to tell since the snores could have been coming from other cells. The doors to the cells were locked unless a visitor came to bring food.

The guards never opened the doors at night, not even if someone called for help. There had been a brawl a few nights ago in one of the cells, and the guards had ignored the cries, allowing one of the inmates to be killed. They had just left him there until all four guards were assembled and armed. Only then did they take the body out. Archie had heard someone crying softly as the corpse was carried away. The man must have been someone's brother or son.

After a month-long incarceration, Archie noticed that there was only one reason for the guards to open the door. They feared infectious disease, and if anyone died of something they suspected to be anything other than malnutrition, they got rid of their carcass pretty quickly and threw the body into a pauper's grave behind the prison, denying the family the comfort of burying their dead.

Archie finished his preparations and waited patiently for midnight. He needed to conserve his strength, so he remained perfectly still, going over the details of his plan again and again. He normally saw the light of the lantern as the guard set off down the corridor just after midnight, and once he saw the light it'd be time to act. He had to get out of this hellhole and get to Franny before she starved herself to death or died of a broken heart. He'd promised to love and cherish her, and he would keep his promise until the day he died, which, if his plan failed, might be sooner than anticipated.

Archie finally saw a glimmer of light and slid down onto the floor, rattling his chains as he convulsed. He moaned pitifully and moved his head from side to side, as if he were delirious with fever. The effort of rattling the chains made him break out in sweat, which suited his purposes just fine.

It took a minute or two for the guard to reach his door, and then the opening grew dark as the guard blocked the tiny window with his face. He peered inside, trying to ascertain what was wrong with the prisoner.

"You there, what's wrong with you?" he growled.

"Chills," Archie groaned as he made his teeth chatter. "Something under my arm."

That did it. The fear of the plague was enough to force the guard to open the door. He set the lantern on the floor and put a handkerchief over his face as he cautiously approached Archie. Archie hoped that he could see the sweat glistening on his brow in the glow of the lantern.

"Oh, God," Archie moaned. "Get me a priest. Please."

The guard was clearly annoyed that this calamity had happened during his shift. Archie could almost hear him debating whether he should do something or just leave Archie and move on, but the fear of the plague kept him from leaving.

The guard drew a little closer just as Archie stopped convulsing and grew absolutely still. He knelt down in an effort to hear if Archie was still breathing. Normally, the guard would just check for a pulse, but to touch someone afflicted with the plague was as good as infecting yourself. No matter, the guard was close enough.

Archie allowed the sharpened spoon to slide out from his sleeve and drove it into the man's neck. Warm blood spurted over his fingers, but he didn't care as long as the guard died quietly, which he did. He barely made a sound; just slumped over Archie like a sack of turnips. Archie pushed the man's body off and reached for the ring of keys, trying each one in turn until he found the one for his fetters. He removed them as quietly as possible and slipped out of the cell, walking on silent feet toward the door of the prison where the second guard waited.

Archie was glad to see that the man wasn't Lowry Gibbs. Gibbs desired Frances, that was plain to see, but he had been kind to her, and for that, Archie was grateful. He didn't want to repay Gibbs by taking his life. The guard by the door was Norman Weeks, a man renowned for his brutality and meanness. Weeks was one of the guards who demanded more than money from visiting wives. The poor women had no choice but to submit if they wished to see their husbands and bring them food. He did give them an alternative, though; they could either lift their skirts and bend over the table or get on their knees and pleasure him that way. He was happy with either option. He was a thickset man in his forties with a bushy black beard and guileless blue eyes that belied his ugly nature.

Weeks sat at a scarred wooden table, a jug of wine in front of him and a pair of dice in his hands. He threw the dice absentmindedly, waiting for his partner to return.

"Hey, what took you so long?" he grumbled.

Archie appeared in front of the man like an apparition, making the guard gape with astonishment. He didn't have long to ponder how Archie had escaped, since Archie killed him in much the same way as his partner before the man even had a chance to rise to his feet. Weeks fell back with a thud as the chair overturned, his legs remaining up in the air and making him look even less dignified in death than he had in life. Blood flowed freely from his neck onto the stone floor, pooling beneath his head and seeping into the cracks between the slabs. Weeks had an expression of utter surprise on his face, his eyebrows raised and his mouth slightly open. His blue eyes stared heavenward, as if calling for divine intervention.

Archie was about to flee when he thought better of it. A few more minutes wouldn't make much difference to his escape since there was no one left inside the prison to alert the authorities and the door was locked from within, but a change of clothes would do wonders for his chances once on the outside. Archie quickly stripped off his filthy rags and used water from a bucket in the corner to wash. He didn't have any soap or enough water to wash his hair, but at least he didn't stink as badly as before.

Weeks had been stout about the middle and shorter than Archie, but his clothes were the only ones available. Archie slid the chair out from beneath the corpse and carefully undressed the man so as not to get any blood on the doublet and shirt. Miraculously, the shirt was almost clean since Weeks had fallen over immediately after being stabbed in the neck. The blood flowed backwards instead of down onto the fabric. The doublet was smeared with blood at the back, but it was leather and easily cleaned off. Weeks would have been astonished to learn that he'd been left naked in a pool of his own blood.

Archie sniffed the shirt. It smelled of stale sweat, and the hose were far from clean, but he had no choice. He ignored his revulsion and dressed in Weeks's clothes. The boots were a bit tight, but they would have to do. Archie lifted Weeks's purse and felt the weight of it in his hand. It wasn't much, but enough to get him through the next couple of days. He then removed the thong out of the leather pouch, pulled back his hair, and tied it before jamming a hat onto his head. He wouldn't pass for a fashionable gentleman, but he'd pass for a respectable citizen, especially in the dark.

Archie found the key for the door, let himself out, locked it from the outside, and slipped out into the night. The air outside was intoxicating after the unbearable stench of the prison. Archie took a long moment just to take a couple of slow breaths, enjoying the tang of the river, the smell of new grass, and the cool freshness of the night. He felt weak and lightheaded after maneuvering Weeks's body, but now was not the time to rest. He walked toward the river and threw the keys into the murky water. No one would be able to get inside the prison until sometime tomorrow, which gave him enough time to make his escape from Guilford.

Getting out of the prison had gone according to plan, but now came the hard part. He had to get to Frances without rousing the whole inn. The landlord knew that her husband was in prison awaiting trial. If he showed up in the middle of the night, they'd know exactly what he was up to and alert the authorities. Archie walked toward the inn, contemplating his next step. Franny's room was on the top floor, so throwing pebbles or climbing up was out of the question. He needed her to come out on her own, but waiting for her to emerge after breakfast was too risky. They needed the cover of darkness to get out of the city unnoticed.

Archie briefly considered leaving Frances in Guilford and coming back for her once the manhunt for him had died down, but once his escape was discovered, Frances would be the first person they'd come after. She might even get arrested for supplying him with a weapon, unwittingly, of course. He'd asked for stew just so the guard would allow Frances to bring him a spoon. He'd kept the wooden spoon and sharpened it a little each night until he'd worked the handle into a sharp point, sharp enough to pierce a man's neck without much resistance. It took a while, but his weapon had been effective. However, this meant that he had to get Franny out tonight.

Archie stopped as the church clock struck one. He had to act fast, but to walk into the inn as he was would attract too much attention, especially since he'd have to knock on the door and wake the innkeeper to gain entrance. Then he had an idea. All places of business were closed, but there were houses in every city which stayed open throughout the night, houses where anyone's coin was welcome. Archie found a publican who was just closing up for the night and asked for the best brothel in town, then made his way to the address. There was enough money in Weeks's purse to gain access to the establishment.

Archie knocked on the door and was instantly admitted. He was shown into a well-appointed parlor, where he was met by a handsome middle-aged woman who sized him up in a matter of moments. He must have passed muster because she invited him to sit down and offered him brandy, which he politely refused. He would have loved some, but he needed to keep his wits about him, and the combination of a month-long abstinence from strong drink and his nearly empty belly was sure to work against him and either make him sick or drunk, or both.

It seemed to be a slow night, and the proprietress was all smiles, happy to have a paying customer. "I have five young ladies for you to choose from, fine sir," she said as she motioned for the girls to come and stand in front of Archie. "We try to appeal to every taste. And if there's something special you require, well, perhaps we can accommodate you in that regard as well," she added meaningfully.

"Oh?" Archie asked noncommittally, curious what the woman had in mind.

"I have a young lad on the premises, if that's your pleasure."

"No, thank you. A girl will do just fine."

Archie looked at the girls. They ranged from very young to about mid-twenties. Two were buxom and lush. Two were thin and willowy, and the last looked like a child. She reminded Archie of Frances when he'd first met her. The girl looked terrified and was clearly new to this kind of life. The proprietress noticed Archie's gaze and was quick to sing the praises of the girl.

"I'm sorry to say that Jane is no longer a maid, but she's only just turned fourteen and doesn't have much experience. If it's innocence you crave, then she's the one for you."

"I'll take her," Archie replied gruffly.

The poor girl blanched but didn't say a word and forced a wobbly smile to her lips.

"This way, sir," she said and shyly took his hand.

Archie followed her up the stairs and to a room at the back of the house where a single candle glowed on a nightstand. Archie took a closer look at Jane. Her cheeks were still childishly round and her skin supple and clear. She had small high breasts and a tiny waist. Another few years and she would lose her bloom and become one of the countless whores who were drawn to every city in England in search of patrons or just a means of survival. The breasts would sag, the waist would expand from countless unwanted pregnancies, and her gaze would become hard and calculating. He felt sorry for the girl, but her plight had nothing to do with him; he had his own problems at the moment.

The girl invited him into her room and shut the door behind them. It was small, but clean and prettily furnished. Archie spotted a ewer and basin next to a hunk of scented soap. Jane was already unlacing her bodice, but Archie held up his hand to forestall her.

"Jane, I've been traveling for some days and could use a shave. Would you mind terribly if I shaved first?"

"I don't got nothin' to shave with," she replied, surprised by the request.

"I just need a bit of water and soap," Archie said.

"All right," the girl agreed. "Here." She poured some water into the basin and handed Archie the bar of soap. "Will this do?"

"Splendidly." Archie lathered his face and shaved off his lice-infested beard with Weeks's dagger in mere minutes. He gazed into the small mirror hanging above the washstand, glad to see his own face again. His red hair was always a dead giveaway, so the beard had to go, and it was nice not to feel so itchy anymore. "Is there a privy out back?" he asked.

"Aye," she said. "But I have a chamber pot if ye have need of one, sir."

Archie took out a coin and handed it to her. He'd already paid the proprietress downstairs, but this would keep the girl quiet and happy for the next few minutes. "Now this coin is just for you. Hide it and don't show it to anyone," Archie instructed. It wasn't much, but it might help her in her hour of need.

Jane's eyes grew round with incomprehension, but she nodded and clutched the coin in her hand.

"I'll be back in a moment. Just wait for me," Archie said as he slipped out the door into the darkened corridor. He'd counted five rooms besides Jane's when he'd followed her earlier. Archie tiptoed down the corridor trying every door until he found one that was unlocked. The client was spread-eagled on the bed, the young whore riding him like a stallion. Her head was thrown back, her eyes closed in concentration. The man had his hands on her hips and was urging her to go faster as he panted with pleasure. Archie didn't bother to stay and watch. He reached in and grabbed the man's wig, hat, and coat off the chair, before shutting the door quietly and making his way down the back stairs and out into the street toward the River Wey where Franny's inn was.

Archie changed in a dark alleyway, then sauntered out in his new finery. The wig hid his red hair, and the plumed hat and fine coat immediately identified him as a gentleman of stature. He hoped that Jane would take advantage of the respite and wait for him as long as possible before going back downstairs to face her mistress. The proprietress might be angry and beat the girl, but he hoped she would be understanding since there was nothing Jane could have done to stop him from leaving. The woman had gotten her money, so perhaps Jane would be left alone.

Archie banged on the door of the inn, brazen as you please. "I need a room for the night, my good man," he drawled, amused by the shocked expression on the innkeeper's florid face.

"Ah, yes sir," the innkeeper muttered, his eyes lighting on the coins in Archie's fingers. He might have asked if Archie had a horse, a manservant, of any luggage, but the sight of the money rendered him momentarily speechless.

"I prefer the upper floor, if you please. Enjoy the view," he added by way of explanation.

"Yes, yes, of course. I have one room left on the top floor. It's not overly spacious, but it does have a fine view of the river."

"I hope the other room is not occupied by someone garrulous," Archie complained. "I like to sleep until noon at the very least, so keep the other occupant quiet."

"There's only a young woman on that floor, and she's quiet as a mouse. You've no reason for concern. She usually leaves early in the morning to go see her husband."

"Her husband? And where is he?" Archie demanded.

"In prison, sir. Accused of murder. She goes every day to bring him food. Her time would be better spent looking for a new admirer, if you ask me. The man is sure to hang as soon as the assizes are in session. She's a fine-looking girl, or was, until recently. Her husband's incarceration is taking a toll on the poor thing."

"I think you mistake me for someone who cares, my good man," Archie replied haughtily. "All I care about is my peace of mind. Just tell the wretch to keep quiet."

The innkeeper unlocked the room and showed Archie inside. The room was small and shabby, but it was next door to Frances.

"Hmm, I suppose this will do. I was told that you keep a fine inn here, but I can see they were overselling it a bit. I'm used to more luxurious accommodations."

"I'm sorry, sir. Perhaps you'd like a room on the ground floor. It's bigger and has been recently redecorated."

"This will do for tonight," Archie replied, his voice laced with resignation. "You can show me the other room tomorrow. I'm simply too exhausted to bother with any of that now." He reclined on the bed without bothering to remove his boots. "Well, what are you waiting for? Go!"

"Sorry, sir. Sleep well."

"Here," Archie held out the coins to the man, then waved him away as he pretended to fall asleep. He would have given anything to sleep for a little while but couldn't afford to waste any time. Dawn came early in May, and in a few hours, the streets would come alive with delivery wagons, servants going about their business, and boatmen setting off on the river.

Archie waited until all was quiet before leaving the room in his stockinged feet and knocking lightly on Frances's door. He heard a sharp intake of breath, but Frances didn't answer. He knocked again.

"Franny, it's me," he whispered. "Open the door."

A moment later, the door flew open. Frances was clad only in her shift, with a thin blanket thrown about her shoulders. She threw herself into his arms as he kissed her tenderly.

"Archie, how did you manage to get out of prison?" she whispered. "What are you doing here?"

"Franny, get your things. We need to leave before the town begins to wake. Wear your drabbest gown."

Archie watched as Frances threw her few possessions into a valise. She quickly dressed in the sack gown from the convent, pinned up her hair, and covered it with a cap before throwing on her cloak. Gone was the beautiful woman, replaced by a girl who could easily pass for a servant or a fisherman's wife. Archie took the valise from Frances and motioned for her to wait while he pulled on his boots and replaced his wig and hat. They slipped out into the night and walked along the bank of the river. If anyone saw them, they'd appear as a gentleman and his maid.

"Archie, where are we going?" Frances asked as she hurried after Archie.

"Shh," was all Archie said. His gaze seemed to be fixed on the river, watchful and darting from one boat to another. He finally spotted what he was looking for. Most boats were open, but this one had a wooden storage compartment, probably used for protecting precious cargo from the elements. Archie helped Frances onto the boat, forced open the door of the wooden cabin, and bid Frances to hide inside. He untied the boat from the dock and pushed off. The boat rocked back and forth gently as it began to move slowly, carried along by the current. Archie found a punt and used it to maneuver the boat into the middle of the river where it could move along faster and with no obstructions. He then removed his wig, hat and coat, and changed into a leather doublet and plainer hat, going from a fine gentleman to a simple oarsman.

Frances watched Archie from her hiding place, her heart filled with quiet joy. She had never really believed that Archie would accept his fate and allow himself to be tried and executed. Archie was clever and resourceful. Lord Everly always said so. She supposed she should feel nervous and scared, but instead she was strangely calm. Archie knew what he was doing and would get them away from Guilford safely. She made herself comfortable and settled in to wait. Light pink streaks began to appear on the horizon, the inky black sky of only half an hour ago now a deep blue and getting lighter by the minute. A pleasant breeze blew off the river, caressing Frances's face and lulling her to sleep as the boat gently rocked beneath her. She felt happy for the first time in over a month, and smiled to herself as she drifted off to sleep.

Archie was still steering the boat when she awoke sometime later. It was now fully light, and the sun shone brightly in a cloudless sky, the light reflecting off the water and creating a playful rainbow of color on the normally muddy waters of the river. The bank was thick with trees. Ancient willows dipped their branches into the water and created a tunnel of green along the riverbank, the peace of the countryside shattered only by birdsong and the lapping of water against the hull of the boat. Archie turned to face Frances and smiled happily. His eyes were dancing with merriment, but Frances could see the fatigue in his pale face and the tension in his shoulders.

"Archie, are you all right?" Frances asked. He still hadn't told her how he'd managed to escape, but she didn't for a moment imagine that it had been easy or nonviolent.

"Franny, I killed two men last night, two guards. The authorities will be looking for me. If they find me, I'm a dead man. We must get as far away from Guilford as we can, then abandon the boat and make our way on foot."

"Where are we going?" Frances asked as she rubbed sleep from her eyes. "Do you have a plan?"

"We can't go back home; that's the first place anyone would look for me, and I don't want to endanger my father. The only place that's safe for the moment is the convent. I don't know if the nuns will allow us to stay for more than a night, but we must go there first. They will give us enough provisions to last us till we get to London."

Frances nodded in understanding. Archie knew what she was thinking and feeling, but there was no choice. The convent held painful memories for her, first of her escape from her vicious husband, and then of the birth and death of her baby, but there was little choice. It was a safe haven.

FORTY-FOUR

MAY 2015

Surrey, England

Detective Knowles paid for his pint of stout and settled into the snug in the corner. The pub would be packed later, everyone there to watch the match between Manchester United and Arsenal, but at the moment, it was nearly empty with only a few tables occupied by people having a late lunch. Two attractive women sat by the bar nursing glasses of white wine, but Bobby didn't even spare them a glance, as he normally would have. His weekend with Jess had left him feeling unusually conflicted. He had gone into this affair with the understanding that it was nothing more than a fling. Jess knew his domestic situation, and at the age of twenty-two, she wasn't interested in any kind of long-term commitment. She never made mention of a future, nor did she put any pressure on him to see her more often or choose between her and Carol.

The problem lay with him. After spending a few carefree days with Jess, coming home was harder than he expected. He'd missed Lucy, of course, but Carol went on a rant as soon as he walked through the door, and it took all his determination not to turn around and walk right back out again. Being with Jess made Bobby realize that whatever he'd felt for Carol had died a long time ago. After dropping Jess off at her flat in Haslemere, Bobby had taken the long way home, working up the courage to face Carol after an adulterous weekend. He'd had a few one-night stands, but he'd never indulged in an actual affair, and had certainly never gone away with any of his lovers. This was uncharted territory, and he wasn't sure how to proceed without a map.

The thought of Carol finding out about his indiscretion made him break out in a cold sweat, but he had realized on the drive home that what he feared wasn't the loss of Carol, but the impact a divorce would have on his children. He wanted to be there for Lucy, and he wanted nothing more than to be a good father to his son. If he left Carol, or if Carol chucked him out, he'd never get a chance to be the kind of parent he wanted to be. No judge would give him joint custody when faced with proof of adultery. And did he even wish for a divorce?

He certainly didn't want to marry Jess. She was a bit of fun. A symptom of his midlife crisis. She was young and idealistic, and required more enthusiasm and energy than he could muster on a regular basis. There was no way he could keep up with her lifestyle. She was always on the go, getting together with friends, clubbing in London, hiking in Scotland, and going to music festivals in Ireland. He couldn't pin her down if he tried. She was enjoying their trysts now, maybe because they were clandestine and forbidden, but how would she feel about him in a few months when the baby was born, and Bobby rushed home to change nappies and read stories to Lucy, instead of telling Carol that he was working late and going to Jess's place instead?

Perhaps the cost of this weekend was turning out to be too high. For the first time in fifteen years, Bobby was questioning the very fabric of his life, and he wasn't ready to deal with the answers. Carol was due in two months. This wasn't the time to even contemplate leaving her. She was his wife, for better or worse, the mother of his children. Most couples grew bored and restless after years of marriage, but if they stuck it out, it was well worth it. They had a loving companion in their twilight years. What would he have if he left Carol?

After a few years, he would become one of those ridiculous middle-aged men who were always trying to pick up younger women and made fools of themselves more often than not. Sure, it was exciting to have sex with new partners, but only when one had a loving family to come home to. What would it be like to live alone after all these years? Bobby wondered. He couldn't begin to imagine. He'd actually never lived alone. He had lived with his widowed mother until he married Carol, and then they had moved just down the street from his mum. She doted on Lucy and couldn't wait for the new baby to be born. His mother would cut his bollocks off if she ever found out he'd been unfaithful to Carol, and she would be right. Besides, he probably wouldn't even be able to afford a flat. He'd have to move right back in with his mother since most of his salary would go to pay alimony and child support for two children. Carol would get to keep the house and the car, and he would have to start over with nothing more than a suitcase full of clothes and a few books and CDs.

I have to break it off with Jess before my life implodes, Bobby thought miserably. *The risk just isn't worth it.*

Bobby went up to the bar and ordered another pint. Perhaps he was in a foul mood because he was agitated by the upcoming meeting. Everly—he couldn't bring himself to refer to that man as Max—had called and asked to meet, his reasons unclear. Bobby had been a copper too long to believe that he was about to confess to anything. If he wanted to meet, it was for an entirely different reason.

Bobby glanced anxiously at his watch. Everly was late. What if he didn't show up at all? He'd be angry at being stood up, but not knowing what Everly wanted would eat away at him. He'd wait another quarter of an hour at least, then leave.

Bobby watched with some relief as Everly finally entered the pub, ordered himself a pint, and brought it over to the snug. He slid in, nodded to Bobby in greeting, and took a sip of his beer as if this was nothing more than a friendly drink between friends. It annoyed Bobby no end to see that Everly was wearing Max's shirt. He'd seen Max wear that shirt several times; it had been a favorite.

"You're late," Bobby pointed out.

"I apologize. Couldn't be helped, I'm afraid." Everly looked completely unruffled, as if he met with police inspectors all the time. If the man was an impostor—and he was—how could he remain so cool when faced with exposure? Bobby wondered as he watched the man drink his beer.

"What do you want, Everly?" Bobby finally asked, unable to stand the tension any longer.

"How was Scotland? Was the heather in bloom?" Everly asked. "It's quite beautiful, don't you think? It's like a purple quilt covering the ground. Reminds me of lavender fields in France."

Everly's tone was conversational, but Bobby could almost feel the underlying menace. He felt a traitorous clenching of his stomach muscles. How did the bastard know he'd been to Scotland? He had told Carol that he was going to a police conference in Liverpool; something he couldn't get out of. He'd been to conferences enough times over the past few years for Carol to take his absence in her stride. She knew there were certain obligations which couldn't be avoided, especially once Bobby made Detective Inspector.

"I was in Liverpool," Bobby replied neutrally. "For a conference. Miss me?" He could hear the acid in his voice, but couldn't keep his personal feelings out of the conversation. He hated this man.

"Hmm," Everly replied noncommittally as he set down his pint.

"Why did you ask to meet?" Bobby asked. He hated that Everly was controlling this meeting. It was time to turn the tables on him. "I'm onto you, you know. Once the case is reopened, I will leave no stone unturned to find out who you are and what happened to Max. So, don't get too comfortable."

"Perhaps you shouldn't get too comfortable either," Everly replied as he pulled his mobile out of his pocket. He turned it on, found what he was looking for, then slid the phone across the table toward Bobby.

Bobby stared at the little screen. There was a picture of him and Jess, sprawled on a tartan blanket on a riverbank, their picnic forgotten. Bobby was lying on his back as Jess straddled him, her bare breasts in his face, and his hands grabbing her hips for deeper penetration. He stared at the picture for a few seconds, shocked.

"You followed me?" he hissed as his eyes finally met Everly's dark ones.

"No. That's not my style."

"So, who did?" Bobby suddenly remembered the young man in the shop. He'd overheard the entire conversation between himself and Mrs. McLeod, and had followed him out into the street where he'd met up with Jess. Bobby had taken him for a tourist, the expensive camera around his neck a dead giveaway of someone who wasn't local. Bobby hadn't noticed anyone following them to the river, nor had he felt anyone's presence while he poked around the locked-up cottage and selected a spot for the picnic. And he wouldn't have noticed if aliens had landed their mothership right across the river once Jess got a hold of him. The young man must have chosen his hiding place well, and that zoom lens sure came in handy.

"There are a few more," Everly said casually as he took back the phone and replaced it in his pocket.

"What do you want?" Bobby Knowles said, his voice hoarse. If Carol saw this picture, his marriage would be over, as well as his career. The Super had warned him about Jess, and if this evidence somehow made it to her desk, he'd be finished. He wouldn't do too well in the custody department either. Cheating on his heavily pregnant wife wouldn't win him any points with the judge. The things he'd been speculating about only a few minutes ago were now a cold, hard reality.

"I want you to back off. I won't send these pictures to anyone. I have no desire to ruin your life, Bobby, but I will use them if necessary."

"You fucking bastard," Bobby spat out. Everly had him over a barrel, and they both knew it.

"We all have our secrets, Bobby."

"Just answer one question, will you? Did you kill Max?" He didn't expect an honest answer, but he needed to see the man's face as he answered. That would tell him much of what he needed to know. He was surprised to see a look of anguish in Everly's eyes. Was that guilt? Remorse?

"No, I didn't kill him, but he is dead. I never meant him any harm, Bobby."

"Who are you?" Bobby demanded, desperate for answers. The man had just admitted to not being Max Everly, but how could he bear such an uncanny resemblance to his friend? The only person he'd ever seen who even remotely resembled Max was that ancestor of his, whose portrait hung in Everly Manor. Max had often saluted him as he went past.

"That's two questions." Everly finished his pint and slid out of the snug. He smiled at Bobby, his expression now insolent rather than contrite. "See you around, Inspector."

Bobby watched as Everly left the pub. He normally allowed himself only two pints, but he sauntered over to the bar and asked for another one. He needed it and had no desire to go home just yet. For all her preoccupation with Lucy and the coming baby, Carol had an uncanny sense when it came to his moods. She'd know something was wrong as soon as he walked through the door. He needed to calm down and organize his thoughts.

Whoever this man was, he was no fool, and he'd preempted Bobby's investigation by initiating one of his own. And he'd fallen right into the trap. How easy did he make it for Everly to catch him out? Now, here he was, prick in hand, completely at the man's mercy. All he had to do was forward those pictures to his wife or to Superintendent Cummings, and Bobby's life was finished. For good.

Bobby took a deep pull of beer and closed his eyes. He'd been outmaneuvered, masterfully so. If he breathed another word about this case, Everly would use the photos. His every instinct told him not to provoke the man. He had a certain kind of old-fashioned nobility about him, but he'd strike if pushed. He'd made that clear enough, and Bobby had no desire to test his resolve. The man admitted had outright that he wasn't Max Everly, but any further action on Bobby's part would open a can of worms which would take him down as surely as it would take down Everly, or whoever he was.

Bobby finished his beer and got to his feet. It was time to go home to Carol and Lucy. Tomorrow he would finish things with Jess.

Case closed.

FORTY-FIVE

I stood before the manor house, thrilled to be back home at last, but my eyes strayed from the impressive façade of Everly Manor and slid to the old manor house which was now a museum. A busload of tourists had just arrived, and everyone was chatting excitedly about the house and gardens they were about to see. A part of me felt a pang of resentment as I imagined these people trampling through what was once our home, taking pictures, and commenting on the furniture and costumes displayed on the first floor. I still felt possessive of the place. It hadn't been used as a full-time home since the end of the eighteenth century, but it had been my home only a few weeks ago.

Hugo took our bags out of Simon's car and carried them into the house, but Valentine made a beeline for the house as soon as she saw it, calling for Archie and Frances. She stopped before I could catch her, suddenly aware of the large group of people and the modern-day tour guide who came out to greet them ready to begin the tour. Valentine instinctively understood that Frances and Archie weren't there, and her eyes filled with tears as she looked to me for an explanation. How could I explain to a three-year-old child that a house that had been her home only last month was now a museum, a relic of another time, and that Frances and Archie had died hundreds of years ago? Or that her father was to be called Max from now on and not Hugo.

I hoped and prayed that someday Valentine would forget the past and believe that it had been nothing more than a dream, but it would take some time. At the moment, she was full of questions, and I had to consider carefully before answering them because each answer led to another question, and by the end of the conversation, Valentine usually managed to back me into a corner.

Michael was much easier to divert. At only one and a half, he wasn't nearly as inquisitive and took everything he saw in his stride. He was so excited about his new toys and the television shows I allowed him to watch that all thoughts of the past fled from his mind. I did catch him looking around sometimes, as if he were searching for someone, and I knew he was looking for Frances. He'd loved her, and she had showered him with the love and attention she would have shown her own son had he lived.

"Mama, why are those people going into our house?" Valentine asked tearfully. "Where is Archie?" She ran back to me and wrapped her arms around my legs, her face pressed into my thigh.

I tried to comfort her as best I could, but Michael was in my arms and was beginning to cry as well. He always picked up on his sister's moods and often began to cry just to feel a part of things. I set Michael down and hugged both children at once as their wails grew louder.

"Valentine, Michael, come and see what I have inside. I think you're going to like it." Simon looked as mischievous as a little boy as he skipped down the front steps.

The children were instantly distracted from their misery, their tear-stained faces raised to gaze at Simon.

"What?" Valentine asked.

"I'm not telling. You have to come and see for yourself. It's a surprise. Unless, of course, you want to stand out here and cry. You're right, that's much more fun," Simon teased.

"I don't want to cry," Valentine protested. "I want my surprise."

"Well, come on then." Simon scooped up Michael and took Valentine by the hand to help her up the steps. "Take as long as you need," he called to me over his shoulder.

I had no idea what Simon had planned, especially since he'd just brought us from London and had only been inside the house for a few minutes, but I'd learned not to underestimate his resourcefulness, or his affection for the children. I couldn't help thinking that my children were very lucky to have people who cared for them not only in the seventeenth century, but in this one as well. I had been a lonely little girl with an absentee father and a mother who drank herself to death. Seeing my children surrounded by so much affection gladdened my heart.

I stole one more peek at the old house, melancholy stabbing at my heart as I thought of Archie and Frances. There were moments when I longed to go online and see if I could find any information about them, but something stopped me. I suppose I was afraid that I would either find nothing at all, which was likely since they were just common people and had no reason to be mentioned in any historical account unless something dreadful had happened to them, or something which would break my heart. I wanted to remember them as they were, young and beautiful... and in love. Once the children and I had settled into life at Everly Manor, I would go to the cemetery and search for their graves. Perhaps I would even find graves of their children and have physical confirmation that their life went on long after we left. I needed to know that they'd been happy.

I finally turned away from the horde of tourists and walked into the new manor. The children were already occupied, playing a video game with Simon. They were hooting with laughter and jumping up and down as they tried to follow the instructions on the screen. Simon jumped with them, being deliberately clumsy and falling from time to time just to make the children laugh.

"Papa, come play," Valentine called out when she saw Hugo. "Simon is being silly," she added.

"I can be silly, too," Hugo replied as he joined in.

I watched from the doorway for a moment, smiling with contentment. It amazed me sometimes how many different emotions a person could experience in a short time. Since we'd left London, I had gone from anticipation to apprehension to dismay to gratitude to melancholy and then to utter contentment. Only a month ago, I had lived in terror of losing Hugo and being condemned for witchcraft, and now I was back in the future, watching my husband jump around with the kids as if he didn't have a care in the world. I smiled at Simon, who collapsed on the sofa in mock exhaustion. None of this would have been possible without him.

I left the parlor and headed for the kitchen to say hello to Stella Harding, who was busy preparing lunch. She nodded in greeting and went back to her task.

"If you'd like a cup of tea, help yourself," she said. "I've got flour on my hands. Come to think of it, I wouldn't say no to a cup myself."

I filled the kettle, put it on the hob and took out two cups. I had to admit that I actually enjoyed performing domestic tasks. After years of having servants and spending hours of my day just being idle, it felt good to feel needed, even if it was just to make a cup of tea or cook for my children.

Stella put two pies in the oven, washed her hands, and took a seat at the table.

"Steak and kidney pies," she announced. "Hugo likes my

pies," she added proudly. "There're a couple of biscuits in the tin."

I arranged a few biscuits on a plate and set them between us as I handed Stella her tea. It was at least an hour until lunch, and she was fond of her elevenses.

Stella dunked a biscuit in her tea and took a bite. "So what now?" she asked. "Have you worked out a plan of some sort? Simon has been awfully tight-lipped these past few weeks. He's carrying on like an undercover agent," she added with a chuckle. "I am glad to see him taking an interest, though. He hadn't been himself since that sorry business with Heather. He seems to be coming out of his depression."

"I'm glad. He's been such an incredible help. The children love him."

"Oh, he loves them too. I think he's come to realize that having children is not all burden and responsibility. He's coming round to the idea." Stella smiled wistfully. "I do long for a grandchild. I loved it when Simon was little. He was such a joy. Simon doesn't believe it, but I'll spoil his kids something rotten. In the meantime, I can enjoy those two," she said, glancing in the direction of the parlor. "I hope you won't mind me playing granny since they don't have grandparents on either side."

Stella quickly changed the subject when she saw me choke up with emotion. I never imagined that my children would have a grandmother. Stella wasn't a blood relative, but her son was, and if she wanted to be a grandmother to my children, I would be more than happy to accept.

"Right, then. So, what's the long-term plan?" she asked, her tone now more businesslike.

This was my first time back since the night we'd returned from the seventeenth century, and it felt odd to be in this house where Max had grown up. Very soon, this place would be our home, but for now, we had to settle for a weekend visit. To suddenly spring a family on the village would fan the flames of gossip, so we had to go slow.

"Simon will take us back to London on Monday morning," I replied. "It will be difficult for the children to part from Hugo again, but hopefully it won't be for too long. Now that the village has accepted Max's return and the media has lost interest, we can introduce Max's girlfriend and her children into the equation. We'll come back for another visit in about two weeks, then eventually move into the manor," I replied.

"And then?" Stella asked, giving me a shrewd look.

"I already have birth certificates for the children listing Maximilian Everly as their father. Hugo and I will eventually get married to legalize our union."

Stella nodded in approval. "Don't rush things. That Bobby Knowles is still suspicious. You know, Lady Everly used to quite dislike him. She said he was an irritating child who grew into an even more irritating adult. Always used to get into trouble, that boy. Good thing he turned his penchant for nosing around and getting under everyone's feet into a career."

"You knew him as a boy?"

"Oh, yes. His mother owns the beauty salon in the village. Bobby and Max used to be thick as thieves when they were children. Then Max went off to Eton, of course, and Bobby remained at the village school. But Bobby always felt loyal to Max, and I know he's been sniffing around, until about a week ago."

"You think he suspects?" I asked, suddenly worried. Bobby Knowles wasn't just an old friend; he was a Detective Inspector. If anyone could prove that Hugo wasn't Max, it'd be him. All he had to do was request Max's medical and dental records, and he'd have the proof he needed.

"I'm sure of it. But he won't pursue it."

"How can you be so sure?"

"Your husband is a clever man," was all Stella said as she finished her tea and went to check on the pies, which were filling the kitchen with a delicious aroma. "I think I'll make a nice green salad to go with those. Care to help?"

I rose to my feet and went to get some vegetables from the refrigerator while Stella took out a large bowl. Stella wasn't my mother, but it felt strangely comforting to be preparing lunch with her in the kitchen. It reminded me of those long-ago days when I used to help my foster mother, Linda. She used to call me her sous-chef and make me do all the menial work, like cutting vegetables and washing the pots. Afterwards, Linda used to tell my fortune by reading tea leaves. It was a tradition of ours.

I wished Linda was still there for me, but Alzheimer's had claimed her mind many years ago, leaving her unable to recognize me. On my return, I'd called the nursing home where she spent the last decade of her life, only to be told that Linda had passed away two years ago.

"We're hungry," Simon announced as he poked his head into the kitchen. "How long till lunch?"

"Five minutes," his mother answered. "Here, take the silverware and set the table in the dining room."

"I'm too tired," Simon moaned, sounding suspiciously like Valentine.

Stella gave him a look that could wither flowers and Simon reluctantly complied.

"Work, work, work," he mumbled as he took the silverware and left the kitchen.

* * *

After lunch, I put the children down for a nap and followed Hugo out into the garden. It was a lovely May afternoon, fragrant with the smell of blooming roses and newly cut grass.

The clouds floated lazily above our heads, their fanciful shapes a wooly white against the startling blue of the spring sky. Hugo took my hand, and we walked in silence for a few minutes, each lost in our own thoughts. I knew him well enough to see that something was troubling him, and I wondered if that pesky detective had been harassing him.

"Hugo, is everything all right?" I asked, concerned by his silence.

"Yes, sweetheart. All is well," he replied, almost too brightly.

"Are you going to tell me what's on your mind?" I had a fairly good idea, but I needed to hear it from him. Putting aside Hugo's guilt over Max's death and his reluctance at having to claim his identity by fraudulent means, I knew my husband well enough to figure out what was bothering him.

Hugo turned to me and smiled ruefully. He'd changed over the past few weeks, going from a seventeenth-century nobleman to a modern-day man. I'd seen him in modern clothes before, but it was still strange for me to reconcile this man who was wearing a hoodie and jeans, to the seventeenth-century lord all dressed up in his finery and sporting a wig, the curls of which fell halfway down his back. Hugo hated wearing wigs, but certain situations had called for full regalia. I had a sudden picture of him as he had been at Versailles, conversing easily with King Louis, the picture of a seventeenth-century courtier.

It wasn't just the appearance that had changed. There were moments when Hugo seemed more relaxed, as he had been when dancing around with the children only a short while ago, but at other times, he seemed pensive and remote. In the seventeenth-century, Hugo knew his place and accepted his responsibilities. He wore his duties like an old comfortable mantle. There was his family, his estate, his tenants and servants, and his duty to the king. In coming to the future, Hugo had shed a lot of those obligations. He no longer had to see to the estate or the tenants or bend the knee to a monarch. Now, there was the museum with its gift shop and tearoom, and several properties in the village, but the museum was overseen by Stella Harding, and the properties looked after by a management company.

At this stage, Hugo's only responsibility was to us, and he was doing his best to help us transition easily into the future which lay before us, but judging by the lines bracketing his mouth and the pensive expression in his eyes, he wasn't transitioning quite as easily himself. He ran his hand through his hair. It had grown longer in the past few months, and he hadn't bothered to cut it. The longer hair and modern clothes made him look trendy, and more like Max.

I smiled up at him as I cupped his cheek. "I like seeing you like this," I said, pressing my face against his chest as his arms encircled me.

"I miss seeing you all dressed up. Women look so different now," he replied, his tone wistful.

I was dressed much like Hugo, in a thin sweater, the color of cherry blossoms, a pair of jeans, and tall suede boots. I had enjoyed shopping for clothes these past few weeks, especially since I could see my legs again and wear comfortable undergarments. I'd even ventured out to get a haircut while Simon minded the children. When I first arrived in the seventeenth century, my hair had been shoulder-length, but I'd let it grow out since it was worn up all the time anyway. I never wore my hair down, not even at bedtime, since it got all tangled without the benefit of conditioner. I usually brushed it out, then plaited it before going to sleep. My hair was halfway down my back, and I felt like Rapunzel when I left it loose about my shoulders. Now I was back to a long bob with some long layers thrown in for texture. I liked the way my hair framed my face and bounced when I walked. I felt lighter and younger.

Hugo pulled me to a bench, and we sat down, looking for all the world like a courting couple. Hugo had his arm around me, and I rested my head on his shoulder, content to be with him, if only for a few hours. Hugo absentmindedly played with my curls, letting the silky hair slide through his fingers.

"Tell me, Hugo," I prodded gently. I could tell he needed to talk but was looking for an opening.

"I could tell you that I feel like a murderer and a fraud, but that's neither here nor there. I know we must move forward. Max is gone, and DI Knowles will no longer be a problem."

"Oh God, what have you done to him?" I asked with a chuckle.

"He did it all to himself," Hugo replied cryptically.

"So, why so glum?"

"Neve, I have no idea what to do with myself," Hugo finally admitted. "All my life, I've had a clear notion of my duties. I had an estate to run, a sister to care for, a king, a country, and political ambitions. Then I had a family to support and protect. And now, I have no clue where I fit in. Most of the estate lands have been sold off over time, so there's not much that's required of me. Mrs. Harding enjoys running the museum, and Simon has taken on all financial responsibility and seems to be doing rather well. He's been explaining his investment ideas to me, but I must admit that a large part of what he said went over my head."

"You still have us," I reminded him.

"Of course I do, but I need something to occupy my mind, and my time. I can't stand not having a purpose."

I knew this moment would come sooner or later, although I was surprised that it had come as soon as it had. But while I had been dealing with reestablishing my life and acclimating the children to their new surroundings, Hugo had been stuck at Everly Manor learning about Max's life and trying to look inconspicuous while doing it. I'd actually given this some thought and had an answer all ready for him. I knew Hugo well enough to understand what he needed, and how to go about it. I hoped he'd like my plan.

"Hugo, at this moment, you have the world at your feet. You have the time and the financial independence to pursue whatever goals you wish. No one says you have to play lord of the manor. The time of noblemen looking after their estates and paying court to a king is over. You can have a career," I said, watching Hugo for his reaction.

"A career?" He stared at me in surprise, his face transforming before my eyes as the notion began to sink in. "You mean I can work?"

"Yes, why not? Max had planned to stand for Parliament before he disappeared. You've always rather enjoyed politics." For someone who had nearly lost his head several times for his convictions, that was the understatement of the year, but I had to start from afar.

"I've had my fill of politics," Hugo replied. "Besides, my well-documented 'nervous breakdown' would not help me win any supporters. Perhaps I can do something else."

"What would you like to do? Have you given it any thought?" Once upon a time, Hugo had remarked that had he been born in the twentieth century, he would have liked to become a doctor, but at nearly forty, he was too old to pursue that dream. However, if he wished, he could do something else in the medical field which didn't require going to medical school.

Hugo stared off into the distance, a dreamy look on his face. "I have to give this some thought," he finally said. "What was Max's field?"

"He had a degree in Political Science."

Hugo pulled me close again, and I felt his lips brush my temple. "You know me so well," he whispered in my ear. "My clever little Neve."

"Have I successfully planted the idea?" I quipped.

"Oh, you have. But, first, I need to become computer literate and learn to drive."

I looked up at him and saw the glimmer in his eyes. I'd pointed him in the right direction; he would do the rest. He was already planning the first steps, which was exactly what I'd hoped for.

FORTY-SIX

MAY 1689

Surrey, England

The forest was just coming to life, the birds singing their hearts out in tribute to the rising sun, and leaves whispering high above, the brilliant green of new foliage forming a crown overhead. Frances trudged wearily after Archie, putting one foot in front of the other in a desperate effort born of sheer determination. She was tired, hungry, and terribly thirsty. They'd abandoned the stolen boat just after midnight and continued on foot since. By Archie's estimation, the next shift of guards would have discovered the bodies no later than midday and organized a manhunt for the escaped prisoner. Eventually, someone would connect the missing boat to the fugitive, and the search would spread out, possibly as far as London.

Walking through the night and avoiding main roads was the safest way to get to the Convent of the Sacred Heart. Frances understood that, in theory, but, in reality, walking at night was more of a trial than she could have imagined. With no trail to follow, they had to rely on the feeble light of the moon which filtered through the thick canopy of leaves above their heads.

The ominous silence of the forest was occasionally disturbed by the hooting of an owl or the breaking of a twig as it snapped off from a branch. A cool wind moved through the trees, moaning like a woman in pain as its frosty breath caressed Frances's face and made her shiver. The forest floor was a treacherous mass of fallen branches, pine cones, invisible dips and hollows, and scurrying animals. Frances's feet were not only sore from walking, but raw from stepping on hard pine cones and sharp twigs. The thin soles of her shoes did nothing to cushion her tread, and she felt every step in the sensitive skin of her soles.

Archie held her hand the whole time to keep Frances from losing her balance, but she tripped and nearly fell several times, scratching her hand as she tried to grab on to a low branch for support. With no light to see by, she felt like a blind man stumbling through a hostile terrain with no sense of direction or a visible goal in sight.

"Come, Franny, we are almost there," Archie urged. He'd offered to carry her part of the way, but he was so thin and wasted after weeks of hunger and forced immobility that Frances couldn't bear to agree. She could sense that he was exhausted, but he just forged ahead, ignoring his physical needs. They continued on until the barest lightening of the sky indicated the approach of dawn.

"Just give me a moment to rest," Frances pleaded as she sat down on a fallen log. She still felt nauseous in the mornings, but as soon as the nausea passed, she became ravenously hungry, her body demanding sustenance for her and the baby. Her stomach growled, sensing that it was nearly time for breakfast.

Archie sat down next to her and pulled her against him. Frances could feel him trembling with fatigue and hunger. She wished she'd had the presence of mind to stop by the kitchen and grab something edible before they left the inn.

Archie leaned against the trunk of a tree and closed his eyes. His face looked gaunt and waxy in the gray light of dawn, and the copper stubble which usually gave him a golden glow in the mornings underlined the sickly pallor of his skin. The past month had taken a toll on him, and Frances suddenly wondered if Archie would have even made it to trial. The food she'd been able to bring him wasn't nearly enough to sustain a grown man, especially when she wasn't even allowed in every day. Archie had averaged one meal a day, if that much, and his body had wasted away rapidly. And if not for the kindness of Lowry Gibbs, he would be in an even worse state.

Archie's breathing became shallow as he fell into a deep sleep. Frances glanced at him guiltily. She still hadn't told him her news. She wanted to, but the right moment hadn't presented itself. All his energy was directed toward making their escape and keeping her safe, so the added strain of knowing she was with child would only make things more difficult, since Archie would feel wretched about forcing her to endure physical hardship when she was in such a delicate condition.

Frances smiled ruefully when she remembered how Hugo fussed over Neve when she was pregnant and his terror when Neve was in labor with the twins. He hadn't said a word, but it had all been there in his eyes, the terrible fear that God would take her away from him, as if he had Neve on loan and it was time to give her back.

Dear God, where would she and Archie be by the time this baby was ready to come into the world? Frances wondered. She still had at least six months to go, and a lot could happen in that time. Right now, she couldn't even think as far as next week. They were taking things day by day, hour by hour. The past month had been one of the worst months of her life. Surely, things were bound to get better. She refused to consider the alternative. Yes, everything would be all right once they got to the convent.

The forest no longer looked sinister. It was filled with a

peachy light which shone through the canopy of leaves and chased away the last of the shadows. Birdsong filled the air, and the wind had died down, leaving behind a lovely freshness scented with pine needles and resin. Frances reached out and tore off a few dew-covered leaves and used them to wipe her face. The cool dew felt good on her skin, and she felt marginally refreshed.

Frances touched Archie's face gently. "Archie, it's time to get going." She might have let him sleep, but she felt vulnerable in the woods now that the sun was up.

Archie woke up with a start and rubbed sleep from his eyes. He nodded, smiled, and helped her to her feet. Archie pulled Frances into an embrace, kissing the top of her head.

"I know you're tired and hungry, love. Just a little bit further and we'll be at the convent. You'll have a hot meal and water for washing, and then you can sleep for the rest of the day. Won't that be nice?" he asked, his voice cajoling.

Frances nodded in agreement. Yes, it would be nice, but after they'd eaten and rested, they'd need a plan, and so far, Archie had been mum on what he intended to do.

Frances smiled happily when she saw the high wall of the convent finally come into view at mid-morning. The sharpened logs of the wall pierced the morning sky, and several birds were already perched on the wall, singing joyfully. Frances was looking forward to seeing some of the sisters, if not others. Sister Angela, who had been the soul of kindness, and Sister Julia, who was also Archie's sister and a particular friend while Frances lived at the convent. She didn't relish a reunion with Mother Superior, who had been more than happy to see the back of her when she'd left with Archie, desperate to accompany Lord Everly and Neve to France.

And, of course, she longed to visit Gabriel's grave. She could barely recall his face now, the baby who'd died only a day after being born. Frances closed her eyes momentarily, trying to summon the image of her son's face, but all she could recall was a tiny, pink blob, its features lost to the ravages of time. He would have been three and a half now, a few months older than Valentine.

Frances sighed. There was a hole in her heart where the Everlys used to be. She knew it would shrink in time, but at the moment, it was a dark, gaping chasm.

Frances barely noticed that Archie had stopped walking, his face suddenly alert as he held up his hand for her to stop. His eyes were fixed on something just above the wall.

"Archie, what is it?" Frances whispered, even though there was no one to hear her.

Archie didn't respond, but looked around until he found a tree stump. "Sit and rest for a moment while I take a look."

"What's wrong?" Frances tried again.

"It's too quiet," he finally replied.

Frances glanced at the forbidding wall and finally understood what had put Archie on his guard. It was around eleven, normally a busy time at the convent. The sisters would be at their morning tasks before stopping for midday prayer. There would be sounds of activity, smoke from the kitchen chimney curling into the sky, the smell of food wafting over the high wall as the sisters on kitchen duty prepared dinner and baked fresh loaves of bread. Instead, there was near silence. All Frances heard was the sound of crows circling over the convent and the weak lowing of a cow coming from the barn just beyond the wall. Something was very wrong.

"Archie, what's that smell?" Frances whispered, suddenly aware of an undertone of putrefaction beneath the smell of flowers, pine, and sun-warmed earth.

"It's the smell of death."

FORTY-SEVEN

Frances spread her cloak on the grass and sat down with her back to a stout oak, glad to have a backrest. Her back ached something awful, her belly growled with hunger, and her feet were on fire, but physical discomfort was nothing compared to the terrible sense of foreboding she felt as she watched Archie walk toward the convent.

Archie put his ear to the door for a moment, listening intently before raising his fist to knock. Sister Angela's hut was closest to the door, so she'd be the first to hear the knocking. She usually worked in the stillroom in the mornings: grinding, boiling, stewing, and mixing potions for the various ailments of the nuns.

Archie knocked again, but he clearly didn't expect an answer. Instead, he began walking around the perimeter of the wall, looking for a crack to peer through. There were none. The logs had been tarred in between, leaving no gaps. Archie finally found what he was looking for; a tall oak whose branches extended over the wall. He deftly climbed the tree and inched his way along a thick branch until he was over the wall. Frances heard the thud of his boots hitting the packed earth when he landed on the other side.

A moment later, he unlocked the door and peered out. "Franny, stay there and do *not* come inside. Understand?"

Frances nodded, her heart pounding with apprehension. She remained where she was, listening intently, but all she heard was ominous silence and the ever-present crows cawing like mad and circling above the compound. Her eyes closed of their own accord as fatigue finally overtook her. She was so tired.

* * *

"Franny, wake up," Archie urged gently. "Sweetheart, open your eyes."

Frances forced herself to open her eyes, but her thoughts were muddled, her mind still caught between wakefulness and dreams. She finally shook off her lethargy and looked at Archie. His face was pale, his mouth pressed into a thin line framed by the coppery stubble of a two-day beard.

"What is it?" Frances asked, alarmed anew.

"We must leave this place, Franny. Now."

"But I'm tired and hungry," Frances pleaded. "What's happened?"

Archie sat heavily on the ground next to her and stared at the walls of the convent. "I don't know what happened," Archie replied warily.

Frances waited for an explanation, but Archie remained mute, just staring into space for a moment before rising and pulling her to her feet.

"Come."

"Where are we going?"

"Away from here."

Frances rose laboriously to her feet as Archie picked up the cloak and draped it over her shoulders. She was full of questions, but the closed look in his eyes warned her not to ask them now. Whatever he'd seen inside those walls had made a deep impact, and he needed to get away from this place before he could talk about it.

They walked on in silence for about an hour before Archie allowed them a break. He found a sheltered spot beside a fast-flowing creek, made a small fire, and took out the last of the bread and cheese they'd bought from a passing farmer the day before. The bread was stale and the cheese a bit moldy, but Frances fell on the food, her body desperate for sustenance. Archie just stared into the flames, his meal forgotten.

"They're all dead, Franny. Julia, too," he finally said. "I found her in her cell."

Frances reached for Archie's hand and squeezed it. What was there to say? His sister had lost her five children and her husband in the space of a week, the children to sickness and the husband to suicide. He simply couldn't cope with the loss, and had hanged himself in the barn, leaving Julia to grieve for them all. Julia had spent nearly a year alone in her house, barely eating or sleeping, just staring into space, her grief impenetrable. She would have died too had it not been for her parents and neighbors who came by, brought food and drink, and wouldn't leave until they were sure she'd eaten at least some of it.

Julia had finally found some semblance of peace after leaving her parents and brother and joining the secret convent in the woods. Since the dissolution of the monasteries during the reign of Henry VIII, there were few religious communities for women in England, and most existing convents were located in either Ireland or France, and only for those of the Catholic faith. The sisters feared interference from the outside world but were still under the jurisdiction of a bishop. Reverend Engel, who presided over the local parish, came to visit the convent once a month to bring some necessary supplies and see to the physical and spiritual well-being of the sisters.

There had been sixteen nuns and Mother Superior at the time of Frances's stay. Most of the women were twenty-five or older, and had come to the convent for reasons of their own. Some sought a place where they could serve God unobstructed, and others had simply fled from a life which was no longer bearable. Sister Angela had been a midwife once, but she'd come to the convent with Julia, eager to escape the suffering of the outside world. She'd used her skills as a healer to look after the nuns and had cared for Frances during her pregnancy. Sister Angela had delivered Gabriel, and helped lay him to rest. And now she was gone.

Frances felt a terrible sadness wash over her at the thought of those women. Most of them had been kind to her in her hour of need, and some had grown to care for her. Sister Angela took Frances under her wing and nurtured her as she would a wounded bird until the bird was well enough to fly again. Frances had noticed the twinkle in her eye when Archie came to collect her all those years ago. The older woman had spotted something that took them much longer to see. How happy she would have been to see Frances married and with child once again. Frances had hoped that Sister Angela would examine her and confirm that the pregnancy was progressing well. Frances experienced sharp pains from time to time, there'd been some bloodstains on the sheets a few weeks ago, but she hadn't lost the baby, of that she was sure. Perhaps once they settled somewhere, Frances would seek out a midwife.

"Tell me what you saw in there, Archie," Frances invited, although she didn't wish to hear the tragic details. She wanted to remember Sisters Angela and Julia as she had known them, kind and serene, but Archie needed to talk about what he'd seen to unburden himself, so she would listen.

"There must have been some pestilence, Franny. I saw a

number of fresh graves. The sisters weren't all taken ill at once. Some died first, and were buried, but others died later, alone in their cells. It can't have been too long ago, since the beasts were still alive, if weakened from lack of sustenance. I set them free. I couldn't just leave them to starve."

"Was there no food left at the convent?" Frances asked, wondering what they would eat now that their meager rations had run out.

"There was. There was flour for baking, cheese, and oats, but I was afraid that the supplies might be contaminated by the sickness that carried the sisters off. And the animals might have been infected as well. I thought it best not to risk it. You know how Lady Everly always went on about infection and germs. I had no way of knowing what the nuns had touched or breathed on."

"And the sisters?" Frances asked, meaning Julia in particular. Had Archie really left his sister's body to rot?

Archie shook his head in despair. "I was afraid to handle their bodies, Franny, in case the contagion was still live. And there were too many to bury. I thought of setting the place on fire, but it isn't safe to start a fire in a forest. So, I left them there, and may God forgive me." Archie buried his face in his hands. He was overcome with guilt, especially about Julia. "What will I tell my father?"

"Archie, you've done the right thing. You might have contracted whatever illness they had and passed it on to us," Frances said quietly as she reached for his hand.

"Us?"

"I'm with child, Archie. Perhaps it's selfish of me, but that's the only thing that matters—us and the baby. We must survive. We must find a safe place before this baby is ready to be born."

"Oh Franny, what wonderful news!" Archie breathed as he held her closer and splayed his hand over her still-flat belly.

"So, you're pleased then?"

"Of course, I'm pleased. I wish I could have told Julia. She would have been happy for us, as would Da, but we can't go back to Cranley. Not now."

"Archie, where will we go?" Frances asked carefully.

"To London, I think. We're too conspicuous out here in the country. A populated place like London is the perfect cover. We'll find a room and bide our time for a while. Eventually, the authorities will stop hunting me, and I will be able to find some sort of employment. I think we'll be safe there, but it's getting to London that's the hard part. We must not be seen, and get through the gates unnoticed. It will take several days, Franny. Are you up to it?"

She wasn't, but what choice was there? They were too exposed in the countryside, and any village they walked into would be instantly aware of strangers in their midst. With his red hair, Archie stood out in a crowd, and would get arrested sooner rather than later, especially if there was a reward, which there was bound to be. He'd been accused of killing Liza Timmins, and now he had the deaths of two guards to answer for. The reward would be substantial enough to break the bonds of loyalty and decency. Every red-headed young man within fifty miles would be a suspect unless the parish clergyman and neighbors could vouch for him.

The journey to London would take days, possibly even a week at the rate they were going. They'd need rest and food before they set off again. Perhaps they could find some remote farm where Frances could buy some food. Alone, she wouldn't arouse as much suspicion.

FORTY-EIGHT

The nighttime sky was strewn with stars, the branches overhead a living dome with a skylight into the heavens. The air was balmy and sweet-smelling, the cold ashes of the fire no longer smoking or giving off the acrid smell of burned wood and grease from the rabbit which had been the first hot meal they'd had in days. Frances slept quietly next to Archie, her cheek pressed to his side. They'd walked for hours after leaving the convent, but since learning Franny's news, Archie had made the decision to stop for the night and let her sleep. Frances needed rest and decent food, not endless hours of walking or stale bread and moldy cheese washed down by warm ale. And she needed his love and support. They hadn't had a proper reunion since Archie had escaped from prison, and it was time to slow down and remind her that, despite everything, she was still his number one priority, as was their child.

They'd bathed in a shallow creek before settling in for the night. It was such a pleasure to feel clean again. Frances didn't bother to dress after her bath, just stretched out on her cloak smiling shyly at Archie. Her body glowed like marble in the gathering darkness that had settled on the forest, and her golden curls were spread about her head making her look like the Medusa Archie had seen in one of Hugo's Greek mythology books. Archie lay down next to Frances and gave her a tender kiss. His hand went to her belly. Her waist was still tiny, but there was a barely noticeable swell just beneath his palm where their baby slept.

Franny's breasts were heavier, her pale flesh marbled with blue veins where the blood flowed just beneath the surface. Archie traced them with his finger, marveling at how much her body had changed in only a month. He bent his head and kissed the top of her breast, enjoying the cool feel of her skin beneath his warm lips. Frances lay still, but Archie could sense her arousal. He wanted her badly but wasn't sure that he was allowed to make love to her in her condition.

Frances opened her eyes and gazed up at him. "It's all right, Archie," she whispered, sensing his hesitation. "You won't hurt the baby."

"Are you certain?"

Frances nodded and pulled him down on top of her. He'd meant to wait, to take things slow but forgot his resolve when Frances wrapped her legs around his waist in invitation. Blood pounded in his temples as he slid carefully inside her, savoring Frances's sigh of pleasure. Their lovemaking was slow and tender, not the frenzied coupling of two people who'd been apart for a month, but a marriage of body and soul, a poignant reunion of two halves. It was achingly intense and brought them both an emotional and physical release that shattered the tension and fear of the past few weeks. And for just a few moments, Archie felt whole. He held Frances in his arms until she finally fell asleep, studying the pale moon of her beloved face. She still looked exhausted, but the lines of tension about her mouth and between her brows had smoothed, her mouth slightly open in slumber and not pursed as it had been that afternoon. Her lashes fanned out against her cheeks, her eyes still beneath closed lids. She was sleeping peacefully, which was all Archie could ask for.

Archie wished he could sleep as well, they were safe enough in this part of the wood, but his conscience plagued him, keeping him awake despite the physical fatigue. Archie tore a few blades of grass and crushed them between his fingers, bringing the pulp to his nose. The grass smelled earthy and fresh, but he couldn't get the stench of death out of his nostrils. It haunted him, as did the truth of what he had found inside the convent walls. He'd kept it from Frances for fear of what she might do. She had believed his tale and willingly followed him away from the convent, but Archie couldn't unsee what he'd seen, or assuage the guilt that gnawed at his insides.

He'd stopped believing in God long ago, probably the week that Julia lost her children to the putrid throat. Her husband hanged himself in their barn directly after the funeral, leaving Julia to mourn her loss on her own. Archie had been only twenty then, but he couldn't accept that a loving God would cause a good woman such suffering. Children and husbands died all the time, but usually not within days of each other. He had found himself unable to accept Julia's decision to retreat from the world, but had taken her and Angela to the convent at their request, and left them to forge a new life for themselves. Sister Angela had been a friend of his mother's and had delivered both him and Julia, as well as the twins who came two years after Archie and had been stillborn. She'd been a part of their lives for as long as he could recall, and he had repaid her friendship and kindness by letting her die.

Archie had known what to expect as soon as his feet had landed on the ground within the compound. He'd know that smell anywhere; he'd smelled it before. He'd tied a kerchief over his nose and mouth and pulled out his gloves. Neve always said that contagion traveled through air and touch. Archie wasn't sure where she'd gleaned this knowledge, but it made good sense. He had stood still for a long moment, listening for sounds of people, but all he'd heard were the feeble cries of animals left to starve and unable to get out of the barn without someone unlocking the doors. He walked toward the chapel, hoping that some of the sisters might be at prayer, but the chapel was deserted, as was the hall where the nuns took their meals. The ashes in the hearth were cold and bitter-smelling. No one had made a fire in several days.

Six fresh graves dotted the small cemetery, the shovels left haphazardly next to the mounds. Archie suspected that the graves weren't very deep, since it would take great strength to dig six. These graves wouldn't be disturbed since the wall kept out forest creatures, but a heavy rainfall might wash away the top layer of dirt, leaving the shrouded corpses partially exposed. Clumsily made wooden crosses were stuck into the dirt at the head of each grave, but no names were carved into the crossbar, as if the identity of the occupants didn't really matter.

Archie finally turned his steps toward the building which served as a dormitory. The smell there was much stronger, penetrating even the coarse, densely woven fabric of his kerchief. It was overwhelming and made his eyes burn. Archie pushed open one door after another. The first two cells were empty, but the evidence of the illness was there. Brown and red stains covered the bed linens and the floor, bloody feces over-flowing the reeking chamber pots. The third cell contained a nun who lay face-down on her cot, the back of her black cassock crusted with waste. She was beyond help, so Archie moved on. He found two more women in much the same condition. One was in her night rail, the other still in her habit. It had been the bloody flux and it must have carried them off quickly.

Archie left the dormitory and headed toward Sister Angela's hut. Her dwelling was closest to the gate, and she lived there alone, preferring to remain near to her potions and on hand should one of the sisters take ill and need looking after.

Sister Angela slept in the back room where she kept a spare cot for patients. Archie pushed open the door. The front room looked much as he remembered it when he came to take Frances away after the death of her baby. Dried plants hung upside down from the roof, and a mortar and pestle sat on the wooden table by the window. Several empty stone jars waited to be filled with ointments, and a beaker containing some bitter-smelling solution sat uncorked, the fumes evaporating into the air. The door into the other room was tightly shut, but Archie could smell the putrefaction.

He nudged the door open with his foot and sucked in his breath. Sister Angela lay on a cot by the cold hearth. She was wearing a linen shift, and her hair was uncovered. It was thin and gray, the strands matted on the pillow. Her pale blue eyes were glazed with suffering, her cheeks sunken, giving her the appearance of a living skull. Archie couldn't see the filth beneath the blanket, but he could smell it from where he stood. The chamber pot was empty.

Julia lay on the second cot, her freckled face white and still. Her bright hair framed her face, making her pallor all the more shocking. Her eyes, so like Archie's, were open and staring, but no longer seeing. Archie gently closed his sister's eyes before turning to Angela.

Sister Angela tried to raise her hand but couldn't find the strength. Archie poured some water from a pitcher and held the cup to her chapped lips. Angela drank greedily. The water ran down her chin and onto her shift and soaked the fabric, but she didn't seem to notice. Archie refilled the cup, but Angela shook her head slightly. She'd had her fill. The water would probably go right through her and result in another bout of diarrhea.

"Leave this place, Archie," she whispered hoarsely. "Leave now before you take ill. Everyone is gone."

"I can't leave you like this," Archie protested.

"I'm already dead. Please, save yourself. Don't touch anyone or you'll expose yourself to infection."

"What happened? Who brought this pestilence to you?" Archie asked. It didn't really matter, but he felt the need to ask.

The old nun barely had energy enough to keep her eyes open, but she gathered what strength she had and began to speak. "A new nun came to us two weeks ago. A young girl named Agnes. Reverend Engel brought her on his visit. Agnes said she was feeling poorly, but Mother Superior thought it was just nerves, and dismissed her complaint. The girl fell ill the next day. Bloody flux. The pestilence spread quickly, more so because we couldn't isolate the sick. Someone had to care for them, so everyone was exposed. We managed to bury the first few victims, but then there was no one left to dig the graves. We said a prayer and left them where they were. Julia and I were the last to fall ill."

"When did Julia...?" Archie asked, his voice breaking on his sister's name.

"She breathed her last yesterday. She's at peace, Archie. Let her go."

Archie highly doubted that his poor sister would ever be at peace after what she had suffered during her short life, but it was futile to argue with a woman who likely wouldn't last the night.

"How's Frances?" Sister Angela croaked. "Is she well?"

"Yes, she's well. We're married now."

Sister Angela nodded. "I always knew you two would find your way to each other."

"Please, let me help you, Angela. I can't just leave you here to die alone."

"Go away, Archie. Touch nothing, not even the animals. There's no telling what carries the infection. I have no fear of death. The good Lord will welcome me into his embrace whether I lie in earth or on this cot."

Archie nodded, acknowledging the truth of Sister Angela's words. There was nothing he could do, and handling the corpses would only expose him to infection, and Frances as well. He had to go against his instinct and leave the sisters as he found them.

Sister Angela gave a feeble wave, ordering Archie to leave. He took one last look at his sister's face. She did look peaceful. A small smile was on her bluish lips, as if she were happy to go at last, her trial on Earth finally over. He wished he could bury her at least, but Angela gave him a stern look.

"Look after Frances," she croaked, making him feel guilty for wanting to take the risk.

"God be with you, Sister," Archie said as he left the hut.

He considered finding some laudanum and leaving it by Sister Angela in case she changed her mind, but he knew she'd never take her own life. She'd lie there quietly and wait for death to come and claim her, serene in the knowledge that she would soon meet her beloved Lord and be free of earthly suffering. She was weak and hollow-eyed, but Archie saw no fear in her gaze, only acceptance.

Archie considered opening the barn and letting the animals out. Perhaps they were afflicted, or perhaps this sickness didn't strike beasts, but after one look inside the barn, he changed his mind. There were three cows, two horses, and several goats. The animals hadn't been fed in at least a week and were too weak to move. Only two of the goats looked like they still might be saved since they managed to eat some hay through the slats of their enclosure. Archie herded them through the narrow wooden door and set them free in the woods. At least they wouldn't starve. He then closed the door to the convent, making sure the latch slid into place on the inside. He couldn't bury the sisters, but the least he could do was make sure that the animals wouldn't get into the compound and gnaw on the bones of the dead. He said a silent prayer for them all before removing his gloves and kerchief and washing his hands thoroughly with morning dew. He had rubbed his hands with new leaves until they were raw and cleaned the gloves on the grass before putting them away. Only then did he go to wake Frances.

Archie tucked the cloak more securely about Frances and sat up, still unable to get to sleep. He knew he'd done the right thing under the circumstances, especially now that he knew Frances was with child, but his heart still ached. Julia would have wanted to be buried next to her children; instead, her body was left to slowly decompose in Angela's hut. He couldn't save her from death, but he could have saved her from that. He should have buried Julia, or at the very least made a funeral pyre and burned her body. It would have been more respectful than just leaving her there to rot. But it was too late to do anything, and he would have to live with his guilt for the rest of his life.

Archie poked life back into the fire and stared into the flames. Now there was another problem to consider. If Reverend Engel had become infected with the bloody flux and brought it back to his parish, it was quite possible that there was a raging epidemic sweeping through the nearby villages, but there was no way to get news. Buying food from farmers might be dangerous, which meant that Archie had to either hunt or fish to keep them from starving over the next few days. There was no fish in the stream where they'd bathed, and Archie didn't have anything to hunt with. He'd caught the rabbit quite by chance since the poor creature had broken its paw when it fell into a ditch and couldn't run away. Archie could build a trap easily enough, but that would mean that they had to remain in the vicinity until something was caught, which was out of the question. They had to move on. The sooner they got to London, the sooner they'd be safe.

FORTY-NINE

JUNE 2015

Surrey, England

I slung a basket over my arm and grabbed a pair of secateurs from the shed as I made my way to the museum gardens. Mr. Shilling, the elderly gentleman from the village who tended the gardens had taken a few days off due to a badly sprained ankle, so I volunteered to help out since I had time on my hands. The day was as perfect as only a June day could be, and after three days of miserable drizzle, I was glad to be outside. The sky overhead was a sea of blue, the sun shining brightly and quickly burning off the dew sparkling on the lush grass and delicate leaves. It was just past eight in the morning, but already the air was warm and likely to get much warmer by the afternoon. The smell of roses was intoxicating as I stopped for a moment to admire the colorful bushes and take a deep breath, enjoying the wonderful aroma.

Hugo had been struck by inspiration sometime during the past week and decided to take the children fishing at a nearby stream. He'd found several fishing poles, two of them just right for youngsters, and had spent hours digging for worms with the children in the muddy garden the day before. They'd gone off right after breakfast, armed with their gear, a can of worms, and a basket of goodies prepared by Stella Harding. Simon had gone to London on some mysterious errand, and Stella was busy baking scones in the kitchen, to be ready in time for the opening of the tearoom at ten. She baked several batches every morning, especially if there was a large tour group scheduled to come through. Misty, a young woman who made numerous urns of coffee and tea in the tearoom, was on hand to help, baking her "secret recipe" currant buns alongside Stella. The two women had been up to their eyeballs in flour, so I left them to it. Deadheading some rose bushes in the gardens would keep me occupied for at least an hour and get me out of the house, where I always seemed to be under the watchful eye of Stella Harding.

I couldn't really tell the difference, but Simon insisted that his mother was much happier since Hugo and I had returned from the past. I never felt any undue warmth from the woman, since on some level she probably blamed me for Max's death, but she did seem to make it her life's mission to look after us well. The only time I actually saw an unguarded smile was when she was with the children, Michael in particular. She seemed to have a real soft spot for him, perhaps because Michael reminded her of Simon at that age. Or maybe because she sensed his vulnerability.

Valentine was naturally more independent and opinionated. Michael, on the other hand, was quick to cry and run for the safety of our arms. There were times when I caught him glancing around, a look of confusion on his little face as if he were looking for someone. Perhaps I was reading too much into it, but I'd read something about twins a long time ago. The bond that formed inside the womb was never broken, even by death, and I suspected that perhaps Michael was looking for Elena. They had been very close before Elena's death, and Michael, although too young to really understand, instinctively missed his twin sister.

There had been an incident in London when Michael had spotted a dark, curly-haired girl of about his age walking with her mother. He tore his hand out of mine and went running toward the girl, screaming "Lena, Lena." It nearly broke my heart. Hugo was sure that Michael would get over it in time, especially once he had more children his own age to play with, but I wasn't so sure. I knew that I would never get over the loss of my baby, no matter how many years went by, so it was possible that Michael would feel the loss of Elena for the rest of his life as well.

It didn't take me long to deadhead the roses and pull some weeds from the flower beds. The grass could wait a few days before cutting, by which time Mr. Shilling would be back to work. I took out my secateurs and cut a dozen primroses. They'd always been my favorite, partly because of their sunny color, and partly because of the heady scent. The fishing party had not yet returned with their catch, so I wasn't immediately needed back. I walked through the gates and made my way down the ridge toward the church. I hadn't been back to St. Nicolas church since the night we returned, and my heart thumped painfully as I approached the wall, reminded of that day.

To anyone who looked at the two lichen-covered graves in the churchyard, the occupants would mean nothing, having died hundreds of years ago, but to me, they'd died only months ago, and the pain was still raw. I involuntarily glanced toward what once was a crossroads outside of Cranley. Max had been buried there, but there was no sign of either the road or the marker. Were his remains still beneath the ground or had they been moved or desecrated when they built the new road? Perhaps not, since the road would have been paved over rather than dug up. I had to admit that I was surprised that a marker had been erected in the church cemetery. Perhaps it was proven in time that Max hadn't committed suicide as was initially assumed, but had actually been murdered in the Tower of London. We would never know, and perhaps it was for the best. Hugo would feel even guiltier if he had to live with the knowledge that Max's murder had gone unsolved and unpunished.

There *was* a little mystery that Hugo had managed to clear up. Ever since meeting Max in the twenty-first century, Hugo had wondered why the family name had remained Everly if Clarence Hiddleston had indeed inherited the title. It had taken him nearly two weeks of searching through dusty boxes in the attic, but he did find an old family bible from the 1700s which had been started by Clarence once he took possession of Everly Manor. Clarence married in 1691, and the marriage was recorded in the Bible as having taken place between Clarence (Hiddleston) Everly and Marjory Cartwright. Clarence and Marjory went on to have five children, three of them boys, whose names were recorded as Thomas, Edward, and John Everly, completely eliminating Clarence's surname.

"What do you think that means?" I'd asked Hugo as I looked at the fragile Bible over his shoulder. There were several generations of Everlys listed, but the name Hiddleston never cropped up again.

Hugo had shrugged. "I suppose we'll never know, since we can hardly ask Clarence, but I would think that he decided to drop the name of the man who was never really his father and died in such disgraceful circumstances. Sharing a name with an accused traitor would bring him notoriety, which Clarence had probably enjoyed. So, he became Clarence Everly and eventually sold off Ernest Hiddleston's estate in Kent and moved permanently to Cranley."

That explanation had a ring of truth to it. Clarence had been a sullen and selfish boy, one who would have enjoyed going from a nameless nobody to being recognized as the

nephew of a notorious rebel and spy. It would have been interesting to learn more of his life, but it seemed that Clarence
never did anything notable, therefore vanishing from history as
a puddle vanishes once the sun comes out.

I passed beneath the low arch and looked around. The
graveyard was quiet and still, the stones basking in the mellow
sunshine, the grass rippling in the warm breeze. I approached
the graves slowly, almost reluctant to see the neglected plots.
Max's stone was taller, with only the name "Lord Hugo Everly"
and the dates etched into it. Elena's grave was smaller, her name
almost invisible. It was overgrown and sad. I set down my basket
and began to clear away the dead leaves and weeds and tear off
the ivy until the stone was clearly visible. I closed my eyes and
ran my fingers over my daughter's name. "Elena," I whispered,
hoping to feel something of her spirit, but all I felt was a melancholy emptiness. My baby wasn't there. Not anymore.

I laid five primroses on Elena's grave and five on Max's.
He'd been an enigma, a thorn in my side, a threat, but also a
blessing. If not for him, Hugo would be dead, and I would be a
widow. Perhaps Max's sacrifice hadn't been intentional, but it
was a sacrifice, nonetheless. It was a life for a life, and he'd inadvertently gifted me the life of my husband.

I said a prayer for Max before walking on through the cemetery. There was one more thing I had to do today—something
which I knew would be painful. I walked slowly among the
graves, reading the names and dates, the remaining two roses
still in my basket. They had to be here somewhere. I found
headstones for Anne and Horatio Hicks, Archie's parents, and
one for Reverend Snow and Godfrey Bowden, who had been
Hugo's estate agent. I had stumbled upon a cluster of stones
belonging to Clarence's family and some of his children's
descendants, and wandered among the graves of the Henshalls,
who had been numerous, but there were no headstones for
Archibald and Frances Hicks. That was perplexing. Unless

Archie and Frances had left Cranley for good, this would be their resting place, as well as that of their children, if they had any.

Of course, it was completely within the realm of possibility that Archie and Frances had moved on. Archie hated farming and had no desire to take on his father's farm after his death. He might have sold up and moved his family someplace else, possibly even to London. He'd go to a place where there was potential employment, since I couldn't see Clarence taking Archie on, but somewhere deep inside, I didn't buy that hypothesis and the absence of gravestones left me deeply disturbed. I wasn't sure why I was so upset; perhaps it was the lack of closure. Finding out when Archie and Frances died would have told me something of their life after we left and would have allowed me to find out if they ever had children. Not finding any trace of them didn't necessarily mean anything sinister, but it was worrying, and my gut instinct whispered urgently, telling me that something had befallen them not long after we left.

The peace of the graveyard was suddenly disturbed by the sound of an engine and the voices of men. I looked around to see what the commotion was all about. A construction vehicle had pulled up in front of the gate, and several men exited the church, carrying buckets, a ladder, and various tools. They seemed to be leaving for good. Reverend Lambert came out after them, his round face glistening with perspiration. He seemed upset and retreated back into the church after exchanging a couple of terse words with the workers. The men walked toward the truck, joking and laughing as they loaded up the tools and the ladder. The reverend exited the church shortly after the truck pulled away and walked off without so much as a wave in my direction.

I waited for the coast to be clear before entering the church and descending to the crypt. I wasn't really sure what I hoped to find, but some unseen forced dragged me down those steps.

The crypt smelled of fresh paint and cool stone. The ceiling had been painted white, and the walls had been repaired, fresh mortar drying between the ancient stones and new blocks of stone visible here and there where the original ones had cracked or crumbled. I moved toward the effigy of Bruce the Crusader, and stared at the spot on the wall which normally displayed the six-petaled flower used to open the passage to the past. The stone had been replaced, the flower gone, the passage closed forever. I sank onto a small bench worked into an alcove at the back.

Some small part of me had hoped and prayed that Archie and Frances would come in their own time, but now it was too late. The portal between our worlds was closed for good, and the physical connection broken. We would remember them for the rest of our lives, but we'd never see them again, or hear their voices. I felt an overwhelming sense of loss as I stared at the wall, willing the flower to reappear. Perhaps it was better this way. No unsuspecting person could find themselves in the past, or lose their life while trying to return, like Max. And, Hugo and I were here for good; there was no going back.

I laid my two primroses at the feet of Bruce and left the crypt, knowing that I wouldn't return. I walked out into the morning sunshine and through the archway in the wall. Whatever my personal feelings, this was closure of sorts, and I had to accept it. There was nowhere to go but forward. I suppose that was the case for all people, except when they went backward as I had done. I smiled when I saw my children running down the ridge, laughing and waving their arms like windmills as Tilly ran after them, wagging her tail and barking happily. Hugo was chasing the children, a huge grin on his face when he spotted me. The children flew into my arms, blissfully happy on this summer day.

"Mama, we caught two fishes," Valentine gushed as she

spread her hands to show me how big the fishes were. "Mrs. Harding is going to cook them for lunch with some potatoes."

"I don't like fish," Michael said petulantly. "I want ice cream."

"Well, I suppose it's early enough. If we get ice cream now, it won't spoil your lunch," Hugo said as he swung Michael onto his shoulders. Michael instantly brightened, happy to get his way.

"I want chocolate ice cream," Valentine announced. "Mama, are you coming?"

"Ice cream, Mama," Michael reiterated, in case I wasn't feeling enough excitement at the prospect.

"All right, ice cream it is. What about Tilly, what flavor does she like?"

"Tilly likes strawberry," he replied, because that was his favorite.

Hugo linked his arm through mine as we walked into the village. Several people eyed us in surprise, not having seen us together before, but we no longer cared. They'd have to get used to the sight. We were here to stay.

"Did you find them?" Hugo asked after we settled the kids on a bench with their cones.

"Who?" I asked innocently before taking a lick of Hugo's ice cream. He never passed up an opportunity to get ice cream. He'd discovered on his first trip to the future that he had quite a sweet tooth and was no better than a child when it came to sweets.

"You know who," he replied as he offered me the cone.

I shook my head. One lick was more than enough for me.

"No, I didn't, but I wish I had. Now we'll never know."

"No, we won't," Hugo agreed. "I do miss them. And Jem."

"Me too."

FIFTY

JUNE 1689

Surrey, England

"Would you like to rest for a bit?" Archie asked after several hours of walking. He found a nice shaded spot by a stream and settled Frances on his cloak before going to get some water. The days were getting warmer, and although it wasn't as cold and uncomfortable at night, Frances found herself feeling over-heated and drowsy during the afternoons. Her limbs seemed to turn to lead around midday, and her eyes began to close of their own accord, her body demanding rest. The sharp pains she'd experienced in the early days of her pregnancy seemed to have passed, replaced by an occasional feeling of stretching as her womb grew to accommodate the baby. She still didn't feel it move—it was too soon—but despite the inadequate diet, her belly had grown a bit larger. If her calculations were correct, and she did indeed conceive in March, then she would be nearing her fourth month and due to give birth sometime in December. She was still terribly anxious, but it had been more than a week since Archie's escape, and perhaps the manhunt had been called off.

Frances gratefully accepted a cup of water and drained it in one gulp. It was cold, sweet, and refreshing. She held out the cup for more, and Archie poured her some from the bottle he held.

"Are you feeling all right, Franny?" he asked as he knelt in front of her. "You've gone over all pale."

"I'm just tired, Archie. We've been living like vagabonds for nearly two weeks now. I long for a hot bath, a clean bed, and a decent meal. I feel like I could sleep for a week, given the chance."

"It won't be long now, love. Another few days and we'll be in London. Once we get into the city, it'll be that much easier to lose ourselves in the crowd. We'll find a place to live and just lay low for a few weeks. You'll be able to rest then. And I'll go out every day and get you fresh pies, oyster stew, and maybe even some syllabub. Would you like that?"

Frances smiled sadly. "Syllabub reminds me of Jemmy. Remember how he used to love it? I do hope he's all right, Archie. He wanted to come with me, but I just sent him away. He looked so forlorn. He lost everyone he cared about in the space of a day."

"I miss him too, Franny, but you did the right thing," Archie replied gruffly as he sat down next to Frances. "Jem belongs with his family now. He might not be very happy, few boys his age are, but he'll grow up to be a fine gentleman. His father will see to that. He will have an education and the means to have a life of his own choosing. Even if Jem's brother inherits the estate, being Master Marsden's firstborn within wedlock, Jem will still be better off than he would have been."

"I think he wanted to go with Lord and Lady Everly and was hurt that he wasn't asked," Frances said wistfully. "Of course, he assumes they went to France."

"France or not, he wasn't theirs to take. He has his father

now, and it would have been wrong to drive a wedge between them."

"I think his father is doing a fine job of that himself," Frances argued as she settled her head in Archie's lap. She was so tired, all she wanted was to sleep for a bit. At this moment, the thought of an actual bed made her giddy with anticipation.

"Franny?" Archie's tone made her put the feather bed out of her mind and focus all her attention on him. Whatever he was about to say was not going to be something she wanted to hear.

Frances opened her eyes and looked up at Archie. His face had that stubborn look he got when he'd made up his mind about something and wasn't about to be diverted from his course of action. Frances felt a pang of apprehension. What plan had he been hatching these last few days when he'd been unable to sleep and sat by the dying fire long into the night, brooding while she slept?

"I need to see my Da before we head for London."

Frances's stomach lurched with fear. "But, Archie, it's not safe to go home. You said so yourself."

"It's not safe to remain there, but I think that passing through Cranley is safe enough. No one would expect us to go there for fear of being recognized and arrested, so it's probably one of the safest places at the moment, especially if we go at night."

Frances didn't quite agree with Archie's reasoning but decided to try another tack. "Why do you need to see him?"

"I have to tell him about Julia's death," Archie explained. "He has a right to know."

Frances shook her head in dismay. "Archie, your father is an old man. Would it not be kinder to leave him in ignorance? He's lost so much already, why break his heart?"

Frances didn't add that she didn't think Horatio Hicks had much longer to live. Perhaps what Archie really wanted was to say goodbye. He knew his father was ill, and probably wouldn't last to see the year out or to meet his grandchild. Archie wanted to assure his father that he was alive and well and put his mind to rest about Liza. Telling him about Julia's death was just an excuse, or was it?

Archie nodded at the wisdom of her words, but she knew he wasn't dissuaded. He'd been distant and silent the past few days, his sleep disrupted by bad dreams. There was nothing she could do to help him forget the horror he'd seen or come to terms with it; all she could do was be patient and let him deal with his feelings of guilt and grief. Perhaps talking to his father about Julia would make it easier for him to accept her death.

"Franny, my father is the type of man who'd rather know the truth and suffer the pain of that knowledge than be lied to. In some ways, Julia was lost to him already, but he deserves a chance to mourn her properly, and perhaps ask Reverend Snow to pray for her soul. I wasn't able to give her a proper burial, and I will have to live with that knowledge for the rest of my days, but at least I'll know that her death didn't go unnoticed and unacknowledged."

"Archie, your sister is in Heaven with her beloved children and your mother. Her death is not unacknowledged. She's with the Lord, whom she'd served faithfully despite all the suffering she'd been through."

"I hope you're right, Franny. I'd like to imagine her reunited with her babies. I still dream of them sometimes. They were such sweet children, and so affectionate. I used to think that once I got married, I'd like to have a family just like Julia's. That was until they all died, and then I swore I'd never marry or have children of my own." Archie's hand rested on Frances's belly, his face suddenly tense. "Franny, if anything ever happens to you or our baby...."

He didn't finish the sentence, but Frances knew what he was feeling. She wanted to reassure him, and opened her mouth to say that nothing would happen, but then changed her mind. To make a promise like that was to tempt fate. Things happened all the time. There wasn't a family in England that hadn't been touched by death and loss, and no man who didn't fear losing his wife and baby in childbirth.

Archie helped Frances to her feet, and they resumed their journey. They walked in silence, but it was a companionable silence, the silence of two people who didn't need to talk all the time to feel connected. Archie held Frances's hand, his own hand warm and solid on hers. Archie was no careless fool. If he thought stopping in Cranley was safe, then most likely it was. He'd never endanger them or their unborn child.

Frances smiled as she thought of the baby. Archie laid his hand on her stomach every day before they fell asleep, the gesture one of love, blessing, and the promise of protection.

FIFTY-ONE
JUNE 2015

Surrey, England

Detective Inspector Knowles pushed Lucy on the swing at the playground, her squeals of delight gladdening his heart. She'd been a little upset the past few days, her initial joy at having a baby brother overshadowed by sudden jealousy. She wanted her mum, but Carol was busy with the new baby, catching a few hours of sleep between feedings and nappy changes. Baby Justin was only four days old, but it was obvious that he was going to be a fussy baby, not at all like Lucy had been when she was a newborn. Justin slept lightly and cried when he was awake. Colic, Carol said.

Bobby was so proud to have a son, but he was too tired and sleep-deprived to feel any actual joy. And poor Lucy seemed lost, her little face full of confusion as she was constantly told to wait or be quiet because the baby was asleep. Bobby pushed the swing harder, eager to make her happy. He would take her for an ice cream after the playground and then perhaps go visit with DS Johnson's wife Sarah for a playdate with their little girl. Lucy would love that, and it would give Carol some much-needed alone time with Justin. She said they needed to bond, so Bobby would bond with Lucy in the meantime.

Bobby's benevolent mood dissipated when he saw Everly walking toward the playground with two children. The girl was a little younger than Lucy, but there was a determination in her step and a glimmer in her eye which instantly made him feel protective of his own daughter. The little boy held on to Everly's hand, an old-fashioned wooden horse in his other hand. He looked excited to be at the playground, but held on to the man's hand as if he were intimidated by the swings and slides. Bobby had heard that Everly's girlfriend had moved into Everly Manor with her two children. To others, it would seem strange that a man who'd been missing for over three years would get involved in a serious relationship so quickly, but knowing what he knew, Bobby realized that this relationship was anything but new.

"Good morning," Everly called out politely as his girl made a beeline for the swings and climbed on next to Lucy.

The two girls eyed each other like prizefighters taking each other's measure. Lucy seemed a bit put out, but the other girl suddenly smiled beatifically.

"My name is Valentine. What's yours?"

"Lucy," his daughter mumbled.

"I just loooove swings," Valentine said, as if she'd never been on a swing before.

Everly walked over to the slide with the boy, who climbed to the top and waited for Everly to walk around to catch him when he came down. The child finally let go and slid down with a squeal, only to have Everly catch him at the bottom and toss him up into the air to the delight of the boy who screamed, "Again, again."

"Are you visiting Lord Everly?" Bobby asked Valentine, hoping that the child would reveal something important. Surely she was too young to have been schooled in a lie by Everly and her mother.

"We did before, but now we're going to live here with Papa. We lived here once before, but it was a long time ago, and we stayed in the other house then," Valentine volunteered.

"What other house?"

"The one where we can't go anymore. Archie and Frances were there too, but we had to leave them behind."

The child didn't make much sense, but she'd called Everly "papa." That was interesting.

Bobby gave Valentine a push, making her giggle happily.

"Thank you, sir," she said formally, startling him.

"What's your papa's name?" Bobby asked conversationally as he continued to push both girls, watched by Everly from the slide.

"Lord Hugo Everly."

Bobby was about to ask something else when he saw a woman walking toward the playground. She was attractive, with blonde curls framing her face and large brown eyes, so like Valentine's. She waved to Everly, a warm smile on her face. "You forgot your wallet. The children will be wanting a treat after the playground."

Bobby stared at the woman. He'd seen her before. She came to the village a few years ago to scout out the location for a historical series about Charles II that was to be filmed at the old Everly Manor. Max had fancied her, but then she'd disappeared. Must have gone back to London once her job was done. Bobby stared at Everly and the woman. This made no sense. Where did she come from? What was her relationship to this man, and were these their children? What was her connection to Max? Was she somehow responsible for this twisted charade?

She smiled at Bobby as she walked over. "Thank you for pushing her. Valentine loves swings."

"Yes, she told us. Have you recently moved to the village?" he asked, trying to sound nonchalant.

"In a sense. We're here to stay with Max for a while." The woman seemed on guard now, her demeanor one of wariness.

Bobby's mind teemed with questions, but he couldn't very well interrogate this woman. Everly, whoever he was, could destroy his life at any moment, so he had to abide by their peace accord. They would leave each other alone, but that didn't mean that Bobby was pleased with the arrangement. Most people would not recall this woman from before, but he did, and the children were clearly hers and Everly's since they resembled them in looks and coloring. They looked more like the woman, but there was something in Valentine's facial expressions and strange formality which reminded Bobby of Everly.

Bobby helped Lucy off the swing. "Are you ready to go, love?"

"I want to play with Valentine," she whined. "Want to go on the slide?"

"All right," the other girl answered regally. Valentine took Lucy's hand and led her to the slide. She was younger, but there was no question who was the leader.

Bobby walked over to a bench and sat down, his mind going in circles. The child had said her father's name was Hugo. As far as he knew, there hadn't been a Hugo Everly since the seventeenth century, but this man had to be an Everly to resemble Max as much as he did. Only a few days ago, Bobby had seen fresh roses laid by the grave of Hugo Everly and Elena Everly, both of whom had died in the late seventeenth century. The child had mentioned that they used to live in the old house but couldn't go there now.

Bobby shook his head. This line of thought was absurd. Whoever this man was, he was likely some distant relation Max had never mentioned. Perhaps he had met the woman at some point, and they'd conspired to get rid of Max and take his place. Bobby sighed with frustration. His detective's instinct was on fire, every fiber of his being convinced that these two had murdered his friend. Bobby strode over to the slide, scooped up a protesting Lucy, and practically ran from the playground. He'd never felt so helpless in his life.

FIFTY-TWO

JUNE 1689

Surrey, England

A hazy gibbous moon hung above the village of Cranley, the stars barely visible in the balmy sky. Despite the warm temperature, most windows were shuttered for the night, the villagers fearful of the ill humors the night air might bring. A stray cat slithered along the wall of a house, its fur bristling with alarm when it saw two strangers walking hand in hand, but it appeared to be the only inhabitant awake at this late hour. It was well past midnight, and the street was deserted.

Frances sighed with sadness as she glanced at the shadowy bulk of Everly Manor, sitting proudly on the ridge. The estate manager, Godfrey Bowden, most likely had the house shut up, and the staff dismissed until such a time as a new Lord Everly took up residence, be it Michael or Clarence Hiddleston who was next in line. Michael would not be coming, so eventually, Clarence would get his clutches on the estate his mother had so desired for him. Frances felt a pang of despair when she thought back to last November. Had the Everlys not decided to return from France, they might still all be together, Elena still alive, and herself and Archie not on the run from the law. How life changed when you least expected it, and rarely for the better.

"Come, Franny," Archie cajoled, seeing her forlorn expression. "It's not far now. We'll visit with Da and be gone from here before the sun rises."

"I'm so worn out, Archie," Frances moaned. She knew it wasn't safe to stay near Cranley, but her back ached, and her feet were sore from days of walking. What she wouldn't give for a hot bath scented with rose oil and a soft, feather bed with clean linen and a fluffy pillow. But that life was gone forever. Frances slid her arm through Archie's, desperate for support. Archie was alive, and that was all that mattered. They would make a life for themselves and be a family.

The village was almost behind them now, the ribbon of road winding toward open fields and the forest. A few more miles and they would reach the Hicks farm. Archie suddenly stopped, his face tense. "Shh," he whispered, but it was too late. They'd been seen.

Jacob Wilmot, the blacksmith, sat in front of the smithy, tankard in hand, and a jug of ale at his side. A faint glow lit up the doorway, illuminating the man's belligerent expression. Strong drink mellowed some men, but Jacob was a mean drunk, the kind who sought to brawl, and often took out his fury on his long-suffering wife, who wore the marks of his ire more often than not. He'd been thrown out of the tavern often enough, and warned not to return, unless he could contain his temper and keep the peace with hardworking men who came into the tavern to enjoy a tankard of ale with their neighbors after a long day.

Jacob Wilmot and Archie didn't get on, for reasons that Archie never elaborated on, but if Frances had to hazard a guess, Archie had probably either beaten the man to a pulp at some point or humiliated him in front of his cronies. If angered,

Archie wouldn't hesitate to belittle the dimwitted, bullish blacksmith and make him a laughingstock, something that he richly deserved in Frances's opinion.

She looked around frantically, praying that Mark Watson wasn't nearby. She didn't see anyone else about, but the blacksmith was enough. Wilmot was on his feet in seconds, surprisingly steady for someone who'd been drinking heavily. He charged Archie like a mad bull. Archie pushed Frances out of the way, simultaneously dodging a blow.

Frances took a few steps back, but refused to go any further. Her heart was hammering in her chest, her breathing shallow as she watched the two men facing each other in the dusty road, murder in their eyes. Having Archie arrested would be bad enough, but at the moment, her fear was of a more immediate nature. Wilmot weighed at least twenty stone and was all hard, ropey muscle from endless days in the smithy. After almost two months of near-starvation, Archie was probably half that. He was thin and weak, his body depleted from weeks of walking and not eating properly. Archie's only advantage was his agility, something that was in short supply in a man the size of a small mountain.

"Ye," Wilmot growled as the two men circled each other. "How dare ye show your face 'round 'ere? They should 'ave strung ye up when they 'ad the chance, the fools. They say ye killed two guards with a sharpened spoon; a killer will always find a way, I always say, but I must admit, I admire yer ingenuity." Wilmot said that last bit slowly, savoring the unfamiliar word on his tongue. He must have overheard it somewhere.

"I'm just here to see my father," Archie spat back. He clearly had no wish to fight Wilmot, but the blacksmith wasn't about to give him a choice. He was enjoying himself too much.

"Yer poor father was so ashamed of the son he'd raised that 'e dropped where 'e stood when 'e learned of yer killing spree.

Dead as a door nail, 'e was." The blacksmith smiled gleefully, baring crooked teeth stained with tobacco.

Archie's stricken expression told him everything he needed to know, and Wilmot savored his brief moment of triumph, having blindsided Archie with news of his father's death. Frances doubted that Horatio had "dropped where he stood," but if Wilmot was going for a fatal blow, he'd succeeded. Archie looked shattered, all fight gone out of him.

"There's a goodly price on yer head, and I mean to collect it," Wilmot announced.

He charged Archie again and landed a hard blow on Archie's cheekbone. Archie staggered and nearly fell, but regained his balance quickly and backed away from the blacksmith. Blood welled beneath Archie's eye and began to flow from a cut made by Wilmot's heavy silver ring. The blacksmith struck out again, but Archie ducked out of the way and punched the man in the chin, hitting him from beneath and managing to unbalance him for just a moment. Wilmot let out a roar of rage and threw himself at Archie, knocking him off his feet. The two men tumbled into the dirt, a tangle of limbs as they struggled, grunting with effort. Archie had his hands around Wilmot's throat, but the blacksmith's neck was too thick for Archie to do him any actual harm. Wilmot clearly had the upper hand, and Archie knew it. He tried to press his thumbs into Wilmot's Adam's apple to cut off his air supply, but Wilmot punched Archie in the side again and again, forcing Archie to release the pressure on his neck.

Archie was on the ground, gasping with pain, his strength ebbing as he tried to fight off a man twice his size. While Frances stood frozen with indecision, Archie managed to bring up his knee and kick Wilmot in the groin, which gave him a few seconds' reprieve, but completely sent Wilmot over the edge. Wilmot's eyes rolled in his head, and he roared like a wounded animal. He grabbed Archie by the throat with his left hand and straddled him, pinning him down. Archie gasped for breath and tried to throw the man off, but his efforts were in vain—he was helpless.

Wilmot paused and grinned at Archie, his smile a grimace of victory as he released Archie's throat. Archie was panting, his face white in the moonlight, the blood on his cheek a black smudge, but there was nothing he could do to dislodge the blacksmith who was sitting on his chest.

"Fortune seems to be spreadin' 'er legs for me tonight. I get the reward whether ye're alive or dead," Wilmot informed him, his tone gloating. "And I will take great pleasure in killin' ye, ye worthless whoreson." Wilmot bent down lower and whispered into Archie's ear, his voice still loud enough for Frances to hear: "And after ye breathe yer last, I will mount yer whore and ride 'er till she bleeds."

Archie seemed to find some last reserve of strength born of unbridled fury. With a roar, he managed to throw the blacksmith off and jumped on top of Wilmot, pounding his face like a madman. Archie's fist became slick with Wilmot's blood as he continued his frenzied assault, but Wilmot was still the stronger of the two, and tossed Archie aside like a rag doll. He was on Archie again in seconds, blood from his broken nose dripping into Archie's eyes.

Frances cried out in terror when she saw the glint of a dagger in Wilmot's right hand. Archie howled with pain as the knife found its mark. She couldn't just stand there, she had to do something, or Archie would surely die. Frances dropped her valise and sprinted into the smithy. As her eyes adjusted to the crimson light of the dying fire, she stared around wildly, frantically searching for anything she might use as a weapon. Her eyes stopped on a hammer lying next to an anvil. The hammer was heavier than Frances expected, but she grasped it with both hands and hefted it outside.

Archie was still fighting back, but his shirt was soaked with blood, and his forehead was beaded with sweat. The blacksmith held the dagger to Archie's throat, ready to finish the job. He was breathing heavily, the lower part of his face covered in blood from Archie's beating.

Wilmot spat out a glob of blood-tinged saliva and grinned at Archie. "Mayhap I should keep ye alive for a little while longer; so that ye can watch me enjoying yer wife. She is a pretty little thing, I'll grant 'er that. I hear she's used to rough treatment. She might even enjoy it. 'Twill be like old times," he cackled. "And then I'll pass 'er on to Mark Watson. Friends should always share in their good fortune."

"Don't you lay a finger on her," Archie snarled.

"Or what? Ye'll kill me?" the blacksmith laughed.

Frances didn't wait to hear any more. She approached Wilmot on silent feet and lifted the hammer. Her arms trembled with the effort, but she gathered all her strength and brought it down hard on Wilmot's head. There was a sickening crunch as iron met bone. Wilmot lost his balance and fell on top of Archie, roaring with pain, but he was still very much alive and conscious. Frances had a few seconds to strike again before Wilmot regained his bearings. She struck again as hard as she could, and then again and again. Wilmot's head split like a ripe melon. He seemed to shudder for a moment before going completely still, his lifeless body sprawled on top of Archie.

Frances threw the hammer to the ground and went to Archie. His eyes were wide with shock and gratitude. It took both of them to push the blacksmith's body off. He was even heavier in death than he'd been in life. The man's face was slack, and his sightless eyes reflected the light of the moon. Frances tried not to look at him, but couldn't help staring at the man she'd just killed. She began to shake, her teeth chattering in her head as the reality of the situation finally sank in. Frances fell to her knees next to Archie, who tried to sit up, but couldn't manage it on his own. His face was glistening with sweat, and his skin was unnaturally pale. He was shaking violently.

"Archie, are you badly hurt?" she sobbed.

"Yes," Archie breathed. "Help me, Franny."

It took all of Frances's strength to help Archie to his feet, but he could barely stand.

"Can you walk?"

Archie mutely shook his head. Even if he could walk, Horatio's farm was at least two miles away. Archie would never make it there. He seemed to be bleeding in more than one place. The blacksmith had stabbed him several more times while Frances was searching for a weapon. The few moments of indecision had cost Archie dearly. Archie leaned on Frances and took a few tentative steps, but the effort nearly made him pass out.

Frances looked wildly around. She needed to hide him before someone who'd been woken up by the commotion decided to investigate. The smithy was on the outskirts of Cranley, but not far enough that no one would have heard the scuffle. Frances leaned Archie against the wall, where he was lost in shadow, and grabbed their things from the road. Archie's breathing was shallow, his eyes closed as he leaned against the wall for support.

"Franny, take me to Everly Manor. We can hide in one of the outbuildings," Archie mumbled as he slid down the length of the wall.

Frances grabbed him about the waist. "Put your arm around me. Come on, Archie. One step at a time."

Archie did as he was told, but Frances sank under his weight. He was barely conscious. The uphill walk to Everly Manor seemed impossible. Frances swallowed a sob as she tried to move Archie forward only to stop after two steps. Going to Everly Manor would only forestall the inevitable. How long could they hide in an outbuilding? They would be quickly discovered once Wilmot's body was found in the morning.

Archie was leaving a trail of blood in the dirt, and someone only had to follow the blood to find them.

And now she was a murderess too. It would be the gallows for them both. They'd reached the end of the line. No place in Cranley was safe, and there was absolutely no way they could get to London. They had a few hours at best, and then they would be apprehended and turned over to the authorities. They would either hang her right after the assizes or allow her to live long enough to give birth, and then hang her. Their baby would have no chance of survival if no one claimed it, and no one would, since neither of them had any family to speak of.

Frances looked around wildly. There was only one place they could go—the church. It was closer than the manor house, and they could claim sanctuary, much good would it do them. Archie would die if he didn't get help, and even if she managed to stop the bleeding and get him through the next couple of days, they would go hungry unless Reverend Snow showed them mercy and brought them food and drink. Some people managed to remain in sanctuary for months, but they had people on the outside willing to help them. Either way, they would have to emerge sooner or later and face the king's justice. The villagers would not allow them to escape, not this time. Jacob Wilmot was not well liked, but he was one of them, and his death was yet another nail in the coffin which was already nailed shut.

Frances knew that Archie would try to take the blame to spare her and the baby, but her life was forfeit anyway. She had no wish to go on, not without him. With men like Jacob Wilmot and Mark Watson around, she didn't stand a chance on her own, even if she were allowed to leave. The villagers would tear her to pieces. No, she would stay with Archie until the end, and then die alongside him if it came to that. At least she would be dying on her own terms.

Frances got her arm more securely about Archie and began

to walk him very slowly in the direction of the church. Their progress was laborious, and she breathed a sigh of relief when they finally passed beneath the arch of the lychgate and out of sight of the village. It took Frances another half-hour to get Archie into the church and down the steps to the crypt. She spread her cloak on the floor and helped him lie down before running back up to get some water from the baptismal font. Jesus would just have to forgive her. Frances cleaned the wounds and bound them as best she could. The bleeding seemed less now that Archie was lying down, but he was cold and clammy to the touch, and his lips were dry as he tried to speak.

"Franny, save yourself," Archie whispered. "Leave me and go. Get to London. There's enough money for you to live on comfortably for a long time. You can remarry after I'm gone," he added.

"Stop talking daft nonsense, Archie," Frances admonished him. "I'm not going anywhere without you."

"Franny, I need to know that you and our child are safe. I can die a contented man then. Please, go."

But Frances wasn't listening. She was looking frantically around the crypt as the light of the candle she'd taken from the church cast eerie shadows on the walls. Bruce the Knight looked as if he were moving, but Frances knew it was just a trick of the light. She got to her feet and walked around the perimeter of the crypt, searching, but no matter how hard she looked, nothing looked like a door. But the passage had to be here somewhere. Neve and Hugo had left and didn't come back. It still worked; she just needed to figure out how to open it.

"Archie, how does it work? How do you open the passage?" she asked as she knelt by his side. She should have asked Neve when she had the chance, but Archie's mind had been made up, so there had seemed no point. Now, that was the only way out. "Archie, how does it work?" she repeated more urgently, shaking Archie's shoulder to keep him from losing consciousness. "It's our only hope."

"Six-petaled flower," Archie mumbled. "Press the center."

Frances got to her feet and began to search every inch of the crypt. The walls were heavily carved, the flower and vine motif repeated throughout.

"Next to Bruce," Archie croaked.

Frances made her way to the far end of the crypt and began searching by the sarcophagus of Bruce the Knight. It couldn't be behind him, so had to be either at his head or feet. Frances finally located what she was looking for. It was the only six-petaled flower anywhere, the rest only had five. Her heart pounded with fear and excitement, her breast swelling with hope. Whatever they found on the other side had to be better than this. Perhaps someone would help them, and then they'd look for Hugo and Neve. All she had to do was get Archie up and through the passage, if it opened, and then out the other side.

"Archie, we must go," Frances pleaded, but Archie was unconscious.

Frances put her ear to his chest. Archie's heartbeat was faint and erratic, his breathing shallow. He didn't have long.

"Archie, please," she wailed, trying to rouse him, but Archie wouldn't budge. She tried to lift him, but he was a dead weight in her arms. There was no way she could manage to get him through the passage on her own. "Oh, Archie," Frances begged. "Please wake up. We need to go." Frances suddenly felt overwrought. The events of the evening crashed over her like a tidal wave, and something inside her simply shut down. She sank to the floor and curled up next to Archie before falling into a dreamless sleep.

FIFTY-THREE

JUNE 2015

Surrey, England

I walked slowly toward the church, my basket swinging over my arm, the heads of the roses swaying lightly as if nodding in agreement. It was early in the morning, the village of Cranleigh just coming awake, the residents preparing for another workday. I liked this time of day; it was a time when the mist began to dissipate, and dew sparkled on every leaf and stalk of grass. The sky was a riot of color, bands of fuchsia and peach streaking the heavens, the sun fading from a ball of shimmering scarlet into an orb of gold as it rose majestically into the sky. It was also a time when no one was in the graveyard, and I could have a little privacy while I visited my daughter's grave. Passersby wouldn't understand why a modern woman came to stand by an ancient grave every day and left an offering of yellow roses, but those few moments alone with Elena brought me peace. Time and space didn't matter when it came to a love between a mother and child; it remained unbroken.

I hadn't told Hugo I'd been visiting the grave every day, but I think he knew. He'd been there as well. We never spoke of what happened when Elena died, never returned to that awful time when we blamed ourselves and asked over and over if we'd done the right thing, but now that we were here, in the future, it was hard to justify not having grabbed Elena and brought her to a place where she might have been saved. We should have done it, should have risked everything to save our little girl, but it was too late for recriminations, and I had never been one to lay blame. We were both at fault, and we would both live with that knowledge for the rest of our lives.

I never wanted to return to the past, but I would if there was a way to navigate through time and go back to that moment just before Elena got ill. I would give anything to turn back the clock to keep her from coming in contact with Hugo when he returned that night, already carrying the infection. I would quarantine all the children and then, if Elena still got sick, would have taken her straight to the future and to the nearest hospital. Or to Doctor David Lomax, who would have prescribed a dose of antibiotics and saved my baby. That's all it would have taken, just a dose of antibiotics.

I shook my head as if to chase away my awful thoughts. There was no way to go back. There was no way to save Elena; death was final. And then there was the second death, as described in a poem by Thomas Hardy, "The To-Be-Forgotten." Well, there would be no second death for Elena as long as Hugo and I were alive. She would live in our hearts and never be forgotten.

I began to recite the poem in my mind as I made my way down the ridge, amazed that I still remembered the words, but it had struck a chord in me when I'd read it at school. The poem made me realize that although it had never been a conscious decision on my part, I had allowed my parents to die in my mind. There came a point during my teenage years when I'd stopped thinking about my mother, stopped missing her, and even stopped blaming her. I'd forgotten about my father as well,

let go of the man who'd abandoned me when I needed him
most. The poem sprang to mind again just after my baby died.
No, there would be no second death for Elena.

I heard a small sad sound,
And stood awhile among the tombs around:
"Wherefore, old friends," said I, "are you distrest,
Now, screened from life's unrest?"

—"O not at being here;
But that our future second death is near;
When, with the living, memory of us numbs,
And blank oblivion comes!

"These, our sped ancestry,
Lie here embraced by deeper death than we;
Nor shape nor thought of theirs can you descry
With keenest backward eye.

"They count as quite forgot;
They are as men who have existed not;
Theirs is a loss past loss of fitful breath;
It is the second death.

"We here, as yet, each day
Are blest with dear recall; as yet, can say
We hold in some soul loved continuance
Of shape and voice and glance.

"But what has been will be—
First memory, then oblivion's swallowing sea;
Like men foregone, shall we merge into those
Whose story no one knows.

"For which of us could hope
To show in life that world-awakening scope
Granted the few whose memory none lets die,
But all men magnify?

"We were but Fortune's sport;
Things true, things lovely, things of good report
We neither shunned nor sought... We see our bourne,
And seeing it we mourn."

I approached the grave, removed the wilted flowers and replaced them with fresh ones, glad to see that the grave was tidy. I crouched by the stone so that Elena's name was at eye level, and spoke to her the way I did every day. I'd never know if she heard me, but I hoped that on some spiritual level she knew she was loved and missed. I wished that I had a picture of her, even a sketch, just something I could look at to help me recall the tiniest details of her features. No matter how hard I tried to keep her in my heart, the memories were becoming fuzzy, her sweet face fading just a little more with every passing day.

Having finished my one-way conversation, I finally got to my feet, but felt reluctant to leave. The graveyard was so peaceful, especially on this warm June morning. The birds sang, bees buzzed from flower to flower, and a gentle breeze moved through the leaves overhead and made ripples in the grass. I walked over to a bench and sat down, enjoying the profound silence. There were times when silence was ominous, but this silence was rejuvenating somehow. It was almost as if I could hear a voice on the wind telling me that everything would be well, everything would fall into place. A few more weeks and it would be as if we'd lived here always, just another couple raising their children in a sleepy English village, making plans and dreaming of the future.

I would remember the happy times, of course, but I would

finally be able to let the nightmares recede into my subconscious. I would be able to file the snapshots of my seventeenth-century life into the album of my mind, not to be taken out again for fear of stirring up the past. There were so many things I wished to forget: my incarceration in Newgate; Hugo, barely holding on to consciousness after the shooting in Paris; Frances, white as a sheet as the lifeblood flowed out of her after her abortion; saying goodbye to Jem, saying goodbye to my baby, saying goodbye to Archie and Frances; and finally, standing over Max's lifeless body, unable to call him by his real name or give him a proper burial. So much tragedy in such a short time.

Things would be different now. There would be no fear of arrest and execution, no accusations of witchcraft, no more goodbyes. Hugo and I would be just an ordinary couple. The thought made me smile. Would we ever be ordinary? Could I ever really be the person I used to be? "Yummy Mummy." That's what Simon had called me in jest. I suppose the silly term was better than "traitor's lady," "witch," or "whore." I'd heard those often enough in the past four years.

I sighed and rose to my feet. It was time to return to my new life. By the time I got back to the house, the children would be up, demanding breakfast, running downstairs barefoot to watch their favorite show, and basically turning the house on its ear. After breakfast, Hugo would devote an hour to his online computer course, and then we would leave the children with Stella and go out for a drive, switching off as soon as we reached a deserted stretch of road. Hugo's driving set my teeth on edge, but I guess that could be said about anyone teaching someone to drive. He kept comparing cars to horses, which made me want to strangle him. He was growing more confident though, and in a week or two, I'd take him onto the motorway and let him cruise for a few miles as a reward for all his hard work.

I actually loved seeing him behind the wheel. When Hugo and I had visited the future several years ago, Hugo had had no desire to learn to drive or hone his computer skills since, deep down, he always knew he would be going back to his real life. Now this was his real life, and his desire to learn everything a man of this age would know was a kind of reassurance that he had no regrets, which was a blessing really since the passage was now really and truly closed, the choice taken out of our hands forever.

I was so lost in my thoughts that it took a moment for me to realize that something in the atmosphere had changed. I hadn't seen anyone enter the churchyard, nor had I heard anything other than the sounds of nature, but I was suddenly aware with unwavering certainty that someone was watching me. I looked around, seeing nothing but gravestones, their occupants slumbering peacefully in the morning sunshine. Then I heard something like an intake of breath coming from the church porch. My head swung around like a pendulum, my heart suddenly racing with fear. I don't know why I was afraid, but I suppose it was just the surprise of realizing that I wasn't on my own as I had imagined. I set my basket on the bench, my eyes trained on the church porch. I thought I saw a flash of something, but it was no longer there. All was still and quiet, but I was sure that I wasn't alone.

"Hello? Is anyone there?" I called out as I approached the church cautiously. I should have run the other way, but something compelled me to find out who'd been watching me. My heart nearly stopped when I saw a figure step forward, an apparition in a filthy blue gown with a dirty face and limp curls. It gave a cry of anguish and hurled itself into my arms, the dirty urchin transformed into Frances. She smelled of stale sweat, fear, and blood.

"Is it really you?" Frances sobbed. "Have I really found you?"

I wrapped her in my arms, and we stood clinging to each other for what seemed like an eternity. My heart was thumping with joy and apprehension at the same time. How did she come to be here? The stone with the six-petaled flower had been replaced, the wall reinforced. How was this possible? And what had happened to make her come? Where was Archie? Whose blood was on Frances's gown and hands? She didn't appear to be hurt, just shocked, but something was very wrong. Frances was too overcome to say anything just yet. She was shivering, her body small and slight against me. Frances had always been petite, but she'd lost weight since I'd seen her last. She was gaunt, but I could feel the slight swell of her belly against my own.

"Oh, Franny," I breathed, my vision blurred by tears. "I'm so happy to see you."

"I need help," Frances finally whispered. "Please, help me."

"Of course, I'll help you. Where is Archie?" I looked around, but no one else came out of the church.

"Neve, he's hurt. He's dying. I left him in the crypt." Frances was crying hard now, her body shaking with sobs. She'd held it together until she saw me, but now she seemed to be coming apart at the seams, the shock of whatever happened finally catching up with her.

"Frances, focus," I commanded as I took her by the shoulders. "Think of Archie."

She nodded in understanding as she squared her shoulders against what was to come and gathered her last reserves of strength.

The two of us dashed back inside the church and down the steps to the crypt. It was dim, the only light coming from above, but I could see Archie lying on the floor, his face like marble. He was completely still, not even the rise and fall of his chest visible beneath the blood-soaked fabric of his shirt. Blood was smeared all over the stone floor, and Archie's hands were red from holding his hands to his wound in a futile effort to staunch the bleeding.

"I dragged him through the passage," Frances said, and I noticed the bloodstains on her gown again. "They would come for him if I didn't."

My mind was teeming with questions, but answers would have to wait. Archie needed immediate help, and the only person who would know how to deal with this was Hugo.

"I'll be right back," I promised. "Stay with him." I raced back up the steps and exploded into the church where I could get cellular reception. Thank God I'd stuffed my mobile into my pocket before leaving the house. "Pick up, pick up," I begged as Hugo's line rang. He was asleep when I left, but his mobile was on the nightstand next to the bed.

"Neve?" Hugo's sleepy voice answered. "Are you all right?"

"It works," I yelled, sounded demented. "It still works. Hugo, come to the church. NOW!!!! It's urgent." I didn't bother to explain, but I heard an intake of breath, an expletive, and then confirmation that Hugo was on his way. I had no idea what he inferred from my garbled speech, but he understood the urgency I was feeling. He heard it in my voice.

Hugo appeared ten minutes later, dressed in jogging pants, a T-shirt, and trainers. His hair was disheveled, and his face shadowed by stubble, but he was fully awake and ready for whatever needed to be done. He gave me a quick once-over to make sure I was all right. I was vibrating with anxiety, my hands clasped in front of me as if I were praying. I could barely get the words out, but Hugo followed my gaze and jogged down the steps to the crypt with me on his heels. I heard a gasp of shock as he was confronted by the horrible sight. Frances was weeping softly as she sat on the floor next to Archie. She was holding his hand, which was limp and white—the hand of a dead man. She stared up at Hugo, no doubt shocked by his sudden appearance, then sprang to her feet and ran into his embrace, burying her face in his chest.

"Dear God," Hugo breathed as he took in Archie's condition.

"Archie is dying," Frances cried, her eyes full of hope and desperation at the same time. "Do something. Please!"

Hugo knelt next to Archie and pulled up his shirt. Parts of the fabric were stuck to the skin with dried blood, but Hugo could get an idea of where Archie had been wounded. Archie's chest and stomach were a striking white, the curly red hair on his chest a stark contrast to the alabaster skin. I stared at his chest, willing it to rise and fall, but saw nothing. Hugo placed two fingers on Archie's neck. He obviously heard a pulse because he looked up at me, eyes hopeful.

"Neve, call Doctor Lomax's surgery immediately. Ask him to come to the church. And take Frances up to the house. It'll be difficult enough to explain Archie without having to explain a seventeenth-century maiden covered in blood. I will stay with Archie until the doctor arrives."

Frances opened her mouth to protest but thought better of it. I could see a look of relief on her face; she was no longer alone. By taking charge, Hugo had lifted the enormous burden off her tiny shoulders. Later, we would find out what had happened, but for now, we had things to do. I pulled Frances along as she gaped at a passing car.

"What...?" she mouthed.

"Later."

Frances could barely walk up the ridge. She was exhausted and confused. The new house standing proudly on the ridge and overshadowing the old manor house in which we'd lived in the past left her speechless, but she was too eviscerated by fatigue and worry to ask any more questions.

Stella Harding didn't bat an eyelash as I pushed Frances through the door and toward the stairs. "Shall I put the kettle on?" was all she asked as she peered at us from the kitchen doorway. The woman was a gem.

"Yes!" came my instant reply.

I sat Frances by the unlit hearth and went into the master bathroom. I hit the light switch and turned on the taps to fill the bath. The bathroom began to fill with fragrant steam as I poured some bath oil into the water and went to fetch Frances. She stepped through the doorway and squinted at the bright light, unused to its intensity.

"Come, love. A hot bath will do wonders."

Frances just stared at the water gushing from the tap. "It comes out hot?" she asked as she reached out a tentative hand and felt the water. "Oh," was all she said. She looked near collapse, so I turned her around and began to undo the laces at the back of her gown. They were all tangled, and I couldn't undo the knots, so I pulled out a pair of small scissors and just cut them in my impatience. Frances stood still as I took off the gown and pulled the shift over her head before rolling down her torn and dirty stockings. Her shoes looked almost completely worn through.

"Come," I said gently as I helped her into the tub.

Frances cautiously sank into the hot water and let out a sigh of pleasure. She leaned back and closed her eyes, too worn out to do anything. I lathered a washcloth and began to wash her as I did the children when I gave them a bath. Frances barely moved. I longed to ask her what had happened, but now wasn't the time. She was too exhausted and distraught. Frances obediently bent her head as I used the detachable shower to rinse off her hair. She stepped out of the tub and just stood there like a child waiting to be dried off, her eyes huge in her face. I toweled her dry and helped her into my softest dressing gown.

"When was the last time you've eaten?" I asked as I took a hairbrush and began to brush her hair.

"Yesterday morning," she mumbled, the steady rhythm of the brush making her drowsy.

"I'll have Mrs. Harding bring up a tray, and then it's off to bed with you. You need to rest."

"I must go to Archie," she protested, but I could see that she was barely functioning. Her speech was slurred, and her hands shook.

"Archie is in good hands with Hugo. He will see to everything." I hoped that were true, but I needed to keep Frances calm. She seemed to be on the verge of a breakdown. God only knew what they'd been through since we left.

Stella was ahead of me, as usual, and appeared only a moment later with a pot of tea and a plate of ham sandwiches; a smart choice, since introducing Frances to new foods at this moment wouldn't bode well.

Frances inhaled two sandwiches and drank a cup of tea before finally succumbing to exhaustion. I tucked her into our bed before going to check on the children, who were already up and jumping up and down on their beds.

"Come, time for breakfast," Stella said brusquely, instantly putting a damper on the festivities. "Let's brush your teeth, get dressed, make the beds, and go downstairs." She scooped Michael up while he was in midair and carried him toward the bathroom. "Go," she said to me, not unkindly. "I'll see to the children, and your guest. I think she'll be out for a long while."

"We have a guest?" Valentine instantly asked, picking up on the one thing that interested her. "Is it someone I like? Can I have Lucy over to play? I met her at the playground with her papa. He's gruff," she added.

"Ah, perhaps another day," I answered vaguely. I wasn't ready to tell her about Frances since Valentine would demand to see her immediately. Frances needed to be left alone for a while, and Stella would see to that. She was amazing with the children, able to make them behave with just a stern look. "Thank you," I mouthed to her. "Be good," I said to the children. "I'll be back soon."

"Can we go back to the playground?" Valentine wailed.

"I'll take you after breakfast," I heard Stella saying as I left the nursery.

I raced down the stairs, grabbed my handbag and car keys and ran outside. Hugo might need my help in dealing with Doctor Lomax. The two men had not come face to face since our return, and the doctor, who'd been Max's physician since his birth, might be suspicious when faced with this new version of Lord Everly. If anyone could spot that Hugo wasn't Max, it'd be Doctor Lomax.

FIFTY-FOUR

Hugo met Doctor Lomax, who arrived on the scene in record time, outside the church. The two men sized each other up, shook hands, and proceeded into the church, where Reverend Lambert was just coming out of the vestry, humming a hymn. Hugo led the doctor down to the crypt without offering any explanation.

Reverend Lambert followed the two men down the stairs, babbling anxiously. "What's happened? Is someone hurt?"

"Yes," Hugo said. The reverend would see for himself soon enough, and the less Hugo said, the better.

Doctor Lomax sucked in his breath when he saw the state of the patient. He threw curious looks at Hugo while he examined Archie but said nothing.

"Will he live, Doctor Lomax?" Hugo asked anxiously as he squatted next to the doctor.

"Call for an ambulance," the doctor barked. "You should have done so immediately."

"Is there nothing you can do for him here?" Hugo asked, hoping the doctor would just patch Archie up.

Doctor Lomax rose to his feet and glared at Hugo with

indignation. "Are you mad, man? He needs a blood transfusion, and surgery, most like. I can't tell if there's any serious damage to his organs in this dark crypt. What happened to him anyway?"

"I don't know," Hugo replied honestly. Archie had never regained consciousness, so there was no way to ask him anything or warn him that he was now in the twenty-first century.

"I'll call an ambulance," the reverend volunteered as he disappeared up the steps.

Hugo continued to watch Doctor Lomax, hoping for a clue as to Archie's prognosis. Archie was strong and resilient, but he'd lost a lot of blood and had been stabbed more than once. The wounds looked fresh, but Hugo had no idea how long ago they'd been inflicted or how much blood Archie had lost in the interim. He refused to believe that Archie wouldn't pull through, not with all the miracles of modern medicine at the doctors' disposal, but a telltale moisture clouded his sight, and he turned away from Doctor Lomax so the man wouldn't see him cry. He should have called for an ambulance. His indecision might cost Archie his life, but Hugo had been afraid of the consequences. Once Archie was taken to a hospital, there'd be no way to keep his presence in the village a secret. Questions would be asked—questions to which he couldn't provide answers.

"About five minutes," Reverend Lambert reported as he came back down the steps.

"Do you know his name?" the doctor asked Hugo, his fingers on Archie's wrist.

Hugo thought frantically. Admitting that he knew Archie would complicate things, so perhaps it was best to stall for a time until he and Neve could figure out what to do.

"No, I don't."

"How did you know he was here?" the doctor asked, persistently.

"I couldn't sleep, so I went for a walk. I came inside the church and heard moaning coming from the crypt. I came down to investigate," Hugo improvised.

The doctor gave Hugo a cold, disbelieving look. Max had not been a religious man. Perhaps going to church was not something he would have ever done. God, he hated lying, but bringing Neve into the equation wasn't a good idea. Doctor Lomax had probably heard through the grapevine that Max's living situation had changed, but explaining Neve and the children at this moment might prove difficult. People just assumed that Neve was Max's girlfriend and the children belonged to her. He planned to keep it that way until they were able to marry legally in the twenty-first century and be a family again.

"Have you ever seen him before?" Doctor Lomax asked, his eyes never leaving Hugo's face. He could see Hugo's distress and rightly assumed that there was more to the story.

Hugo was granted a reprieve by the wail of an approaching siren. Two young medics came down the steps with a stretcher and lifted Archie up, securing him so he wouldn't slide off when they carried him up the stairs. Doctor Lomax was issuing instructions as Hugo silently followed behind.

"I'm going with him," Hugo announced to the surprised medics, but they didn't argue and allowed him into the ambulance. Archie would be in shock when he woke up—if he woke up—and the last thing he needed was to find himself alone in a strange place full of bright lights and beeping machines.

The ambulance took Archie to Cranleigh Village Hospital in the high street, a quaint-looking redbrick structure that looked more like a private residence than a medical facility. Hugo stepped aside as Archie was wheeled into Casualty, where the doctors immediately went to work. There were only two other people in Casualty, and neither one looked as if they required immediate assistance.

Hugo took a seat on a hard, plastic chair and waited, relieved to see Neve when she erupted through the door a quarter of an hour later.

"What's happening?" she asked. "Will he be all right?" Neve looked as if she were about to cry. She needed to hear that Archie would live, but Hugo couldn't lie to her and give her false hope. There was a very good chance that he wouldn't, but Doctor Lomax had assured Hugo that they would do everything they could to save the young man.

"I don't know yet. They're working on him. How's Frances?"

"Exhausted, overwrought, frightened. She's so thin, and Archie looked downright emaciated. What do you think happened to them?" It was a rhetorical question, of course. Hugo had no way of knowing.

They both looked up as Doctor Lomax came toward them. He was attached to this hospital, so Archie would remain his patient throughout his stay. Doctor Lomax's eyebrows shot up at the sight of Neve, but he didn't ask any questions and directed his comments to Hugo.

"The man you found has been stabbed several times. Two of the wounds are not severe, but a third has punctured his kidney. It will need to be removed. He's been savagely beaten and has sustained several broken ribs. He's also malnourished and has lost a considerable amount of blood. They are prepping him for surgery now, but his chances are not good. Did he have a wallet on him, or any other form of ID? We'd like to notify his next of kin."

"Not that I saw," Hugo replied. He tried to keep his voice flat, but it shook, nonetheless. Archie's next of kin was at Everly Manor, and she would be heartbroken if Archie didn't pull through, as would the rest of them.

"How long will he be in surgery?" Neve asked, her voice filled with worry.

"Several hours. He will need a blood transfusion before the surgeon can operate. You can come back in the afternoon," the doctor added. "No need for you to hang about."

"I'll stay," Hugo replied. "Someone should be here."

"Suit yourself." Doctor Lomax gave Hugo a searching look. He suspected the truth, Hugo was sure of it, but he didn't say anything. Instead, he turned on his heel and walked away, leaving Neve and Hugo to confer. "Neve, go home and see to Frances and the children. It's best if you don't bring her here. I will ring you as soon as I know anything. In the meantime, we need to devise some sort of plan. Questions will be asked."

Neve nodded. Her face looked blank.

"Go," Hugo said gently. "You look like you need a strong cup of coffee. I'll see to things here."

"All right," Neve agreed reluctantly as she rose to her feet. "Keep me informed."

"I will."

* * *

The sky beyond the window turned a deep violet, the last remnants of daylight leeched from the world outside. The hospital room was softly illuminated by a bedside lamp that cast a mellow golden light onto Archie's face. It was still pale, but his lips were no longer bluish, and there was just a hint of color in his cheeks.

Hugo reached out and gently squeezed Archie's hand in a gesture of support. The hand was warm and dry, but not unnaturally hot. No infection. Archie was still asleep, the machines overhead beeping quietly and reassuring Hugo with every beep that Archie was still alive. The surgery had lasted well into the afternoon, longer than Doctor Lomax had predicted, and now

Archie looked like a mummy, his ribs bound, and his stomach bandaged. He also had a plaster over his right cheek, a few stitches on his chin, and a cast on his right hand to aid in the healing of his broken fingers. An IV was hooked up to Archie's left hand, the clear liquid meant to hydrate and nourish him. Archie had lost a kidney, but Doctor Lomax assured Hugo that he would recover and lead a normal life. Little did Lomax suspect that what was a normal life for him was anything but a normal life for Archie.

"Max, what's your involvement in this?" Doctor Lomax asked quietly after the nurse had left and they were alone with only an unconscious Archie between them. "Do you know this man? Is he someone you met while...?" He let the sentence hang, but Hugo knew what he meant.

He shook his head. After a few moments of silence and an irritable shrug of the shoulders, the doctor left. He'd done all he could for his nameless patient, and he was off home to his wife and a good dinner.

Hugo ignored his growling stomach. He hadn't eaten all day and didn't have his wallet on him. He should have asked Neve for a few pounds before she left, but he'd been too upset and worried to think about practicalities. Now he was starving.

Hugo looked up as a nurse poked her head into the room. "You must be hungry, love," she observed. "Shall I bring you something from the cafeteria?"

Hugo shook his head. "I left my wallet at home."

"Not to worry. You can repay me later. Cheese and pickle or ham and tomato?"

Hugo would have gladly taken one of each. "Ham please, and a cup of tea."

"Back in a tick," the nurse said and disappeared.

I'd better bring Archie some clothes, Hugo thought as he finished off the second sandwich. The nurse must have realized how hungry he was and had brought two sandwiches, a cup of milky tea, and an almond biscuit. He could have easily eaten more, but there was nothing left.

Hugo leaned back in the chair and looked over at Archie. He was still asleep, but his breathing had changed; it was deeper, not shallow like before. Hugo hoped that it was a good sign. He suddenly realized that he had no idea what had happened to the bloodstained clothes Archie had been wearing, but fervently hoped that no one would look at them too closely. One didn't need to be an expert in history to see that the clothes didn't belong in this century. Perhaps it would be assumed that Archie was an actor. The best-case scenario would be that whoever prepped him for surgery had simply cut off the bloody fabric and tossed it into the rubbish bin. Archie would have nothing to wear when he was ready to be released. If the recovery went as planned, Archie would be discharged in about a week. Keeping Frances away for that long would be difficult, but it was imperative that no one saw her just yet. They would work out all the details once he had a chance to speak to Archie.

Hugo took a spare blanket out of the cupboard and settled more comfortably in the recliner. He had every intention of staying by Archie's side until he woke.

FIFTY-FIVE

I wasn't sure what woke me, but I was jolted out of sleep, suddenly wide awake. I'd fallen asleep next to Frances last night after speaking with Hugo one last time. He had sounded calm and reassuring, but I felt cold fingers of dread walking up my spine. Archie still hadn't woken after the surgery. Surely that wasn't a good sign, but Doctor Lomax seemed optimistic, so I pushed away my fears and tried to focus on other things.

Frances hadn't woken either. She'd slept all through the day and was still out when I'd climbed in next to her. I felt her forehead for a temperature, checked her pulse, and listened to her even breathing. She wasn't ill, just exhausted. Whatever had happened had left her utterly depleted, and the best medicine for her was rest. I'd curled up next to her, but sleep wouldn't come. My mind was spinning, my thoughts going in several different directions. I'd call Simon first thing in the morning. He had proven himself to be invaluable in a crisis, and he would be a great help in dealing with this situation since his feelings weren't involved. In the meantime, there was nothing to do but wait. I must have finally drifted off but felt as if I'd just fallen asleep when I woke.

I looked about the room. Everything was bathed in moonlight, the silvery pall just enough for me to see clearly. Frances stood by the window, staring out at the sky, her arms wrapped around her middle. She was still wearing my dressing gown, and her hair cascaded down her back and framed her face, her pale skin unnaturally bluish in the moonlight. She looked like some mythical creature, bloodless and immune to the ravages of time, but that was just an illusion. Once my eyes adjusted to the dim light, I saw the silent tears rolling down her cheeks and the tension in her shoulders.

I slid out of bed and came up to stand behind Frances. I wrapped her in my arms and kissed her on the temple. Frances leaned into me, but her body was still tense, and the tears continued to fall.

"Tell me," she said quietly. "I need to know." I felt her tremble, her anxiety mounting as she braced herself for what I was about to say. She'd been preparing herself for the worst, and now the moment of truth was here.

"He's alive, Franny," I hurried to reassure her. "He's very badly hurt, but he is alive."

"I have to see him," she cried. "I need to be there."

I gently turned Frances around to face me and brushed a curl out of her eyes. "We can't go to the hospital. Not yet, but Hugo will ring as soon as there's any news."

"Ring?" Frances asked, confused by my choice of word.

"Send a message," I clarified.

I led her to a chair by the hearth and asked her to sit down. I thought of lighting a bedside lamp but changed my mind. To Frances, it would be too bright, too garish. So, instead, I lit a few candles which Hugo kept on the mantel. He liked to sit by candlelight sometimes, preferring it to the harsh light of electricity.

Frances sat on the edge of the chair, tense and silent; her

arms wrapped around her middle, as if she were trying to hold herself together.

"Franny," I began, "you will see Archie very soon, but first, I need to explain some things to you. And you need to tell me what happened. Can you do that?"

Frances nodded mutely. She just stared into the empty hearth for a few moments in an effort to muster the strength to tell me. "Oh, Neve, it all went so wrong after you left," she finally said.

"What did?"

"Liza's body was found by the side of the road the day you'd gone. She'd been strangled with the reins of her horse." Frances sighed and finally turned to face me. "Archie was arrested and charged with Liza's murder. He'd been seen on the road to Haslemere that day, so the constable never even bothered to look for anyone else. In the eyes of the law, he was guilty. They would have hanged him, Neve."

Once Frances began to talk, the words flowed like a torrent of water. I remained silent, just letting her get it all out. She spent the next half-hour telling me about Archie's incarceration, his daring escape, the death of the sisters at the convent, and Jacob Wilmot's attack. I noticed her hand going to her belly several times as she spoke but waited for her to tell me.

"I killed him, Neve. I smashed his skull in," Frances whispered.

"Are you sorry?"

Frances shook her head. "I'm only sorry I didn't do it sooner. He would have killed Archie. He nearly did. But now I'm damned. I will go to Hell for taking a man's life."

A terrible anger welled inside me. I wasn't really sure who I was angry at: God, fate, or maybe just luck, but I was furious. What had this poor girl done to deserve such suffering? She'd lost her mother, was sold to the highest bidder by her father at the age of thirteen, had been horribly abused by her husband, lost her baby, and now this. She would have to live with this for the rest of her life. She'd done what she had to do to save Archie, but she'd murdered a man in the process. Her conscience would never be clear.

"You will *not* go to Hell, Frances," I said with more force than I intended. "You killed a man who attacked you for no reason and nearly killed your husband. You did what anyone would do under the circumstances. You protected the person you love. God makes allowances for self-defense."

"Really?" Frances asked, her voice small. "You think so?"

I nodded. "I'm sure of it." I suddenly understood why Frances hadn't said anything about the baby. She was terrified of losing it. She'd said something a long time ago about God taking baby Gabriel to punish her for leaving her husband, so perhaps she thought that God would take this baby as well as punishment for killing Archie's attacker.

"Neve, what's going to happen?" Frances asked, sounding like a child.

"Hugo will look after Archie, and I will look after you. I will explain some things to you about this century, and then we will find you some clothes and make you look like a modern woman."

"But when can I see Archie?" Frances persisted.

"Franny, things are different in this time. Every crime is investigated by the police in order to punish the guilty and protect the innocent. Archie was stabbed and savagely beaten. Questions will be asked. If I take you to the hospital, the police will demand to see your identification and demand to know what happened, and what you were doing in the crypt. We must keep you hidden for a few days and allow Hugo to deal with the police. Do you understand?"

Frances nodded. "Yes. I will do whatever it takes to keep Archie safe."

"Good girl," I said. "Would you like to go back to bed, or would you like to begin your education?"

Frances smiled shyly. "I would like something to eat. I'm famished."

"Of course, you are. Foolish of me not to guess. Let's go down to the kitchen. I'll make you a cup of hot chocolate, and there's some shepherd's pie left over from dinner."

"Hot chocolate?" Frances asked, a small smile on her face. "I haven't had a cup of chocolate since France." The smile was instantly replaced by a look of sadness. "I wish Jem was here."

"Me, too."

FIFTY-SIX

Hugo carefully folded the blanket and returned it to the cupboard. He'd managed to get a few hours of sleep, but the nurses came in every hour or so to check on Archie. The nice nurse from last night was in the room now, changing the IV bag.

"Sorry, I didn't mean to wake you. I brought you a cup of tea," she said brightly. "Thought you'd need it. We have an electric kettle at the nurses' station. Just come by if you'd like some more."

"Thank you, you're very kind," Hugo replied. "How is he this morning?"

The nurse shook her head. "Not as well as we hoped. He's running a temperature. I've called Doctor Lomax. He should be here shortly."

She finished her task and left the room, closing the door softly behind her.

Hugo looked at Archie. In the bright light of morning, Archie looked better, but Hugo now knew that the blush in his cheeks was due to a fever rather than improving health. His eyes were closed, the auburn lashes fanned out against his flushed skin.

"Archie, can you hear me?" Hugo asked softly. "I'm here, and I will be here until you wake up."

He opened his mouth to tell Archie about Frances when the door opened behind him. Hugo turned, expecting to see the doctor or one of the nurses, instead, he was faced with DI Knowles, who stood in the doorway, surveying the scene.

"Good morning," Hugo said, pitching his voice to sound as civil as possible. He was in no mood to deal with the inspector, but it was inevitable that the police would get involved. Hugo was surprised that no one came yesterday, but he supposed they wanted to wait until the patient was out of surgery and able to answer questions.

"Is it?" the man asked sarcastically as he pulled up a chair and sat down next to Archie's bed. "Do you know this man, Everly?"

"No."

"So, why are you here with him?" DI Knowles asked, his voice dripping with suspicion. "It seems you've gone beyond the call of duty, keeping vigil all night."

"I found him, and he seems to be all alone," Hugo replied. "And why are you here, Inspector?"

"The hospital called me in. This man has been stabbed and beaten; it's standard procedure to call the police when someone appears to be the victim of a violent crime."

"I see." Knowles didn't sound antagonistic, so Hugo just nodded in acknowledgment and sat down, prepared to be questioned.

Knowles opened his notepad and took out a pen. "What were you doing at the church?" he asked.

"I couldn't sleep, so I went for a walk." Knowles took in Hugo's track pants and T-shirt, nodded, then continued.

"Did you see anyone in the vicinity of the church?"

"No, I didn't."

"Was he conscious when you found him?" Knowles asked. "Did he say anything?"

"No."

"Did he have anything on him? Money, wallet, identification of some sort?"

"I didn't rummage through his pockets," Hugo replied calmly.

"Have you ever seen him before?" DI Knowles asked, watching Hugo like a hawk.

"Not that I can recall."

"The nurses mentioned that the man was strangely dressed. What was he wearing?"

"Trousers, a shirt, and leather boots."

"You didn't notice anything odd about his attire?" the inspector persisted.

"I wasn't really paying attention. The man was unconscious and bleeding. His fashion sense didn't seem important."

Knowles scribbled something in his notepad, flipped it shut, but seemed in no hurry to leave.

"Are we done here?" Hugo asked, relieved to see that Knowles seemed to be finished with his questions.

"Not quite. I'm waiting to speak with Doctor Lomax. He should be here shortly."

As if on cue, Doctor Lomax entered the room. He looked tense, his white coat stained with blood. "Sorry to keep you waiting. A little boy fell off the swing and hurt himself rather badly. He needed stitches in his chin."

"Not to worry, Doctor," Knowles smiled expansively. "I just wanted to ask you some questions. I gather you were first on the scene, after Everly, that is."

"Yes."

"What do you make of this case?" Knowles asked. He clearly liked and respected Doctor Lomax, and his tone was one of deference. Hugo was surprised that he hadn't been asked to leave, but Knowles didn't seem to mind his presence. "Anything you can tell me that I don't already know?"

"This case is very perplexing," the doctor began.

"In what way?"

The doctor shook his head, as if unable to believe what he was about to say, then tore his gaze away from the still form of Archie and turned back to the inspector. "This man was beaten and stabbed, but he fought back against his attacker. The broken fingers, torn fingernails, and bloody knuckles are defensive wounds. He saw the man who attacked him. The assailant was right-handed, judging by the location of the blows, and stabbed him in the left kidney with his right hand." Doctor Lomax demonstrated a stabbing motion as he faced the inspector. "But that's not what puzzles me. The victim has multiple lacerations to his back, suggesting that he was dragged, but I saw no blood or bits of his shirt on the steps leading down to the crypt. There was some blood by the tomb of the knight, but that's neither here nor there. He might have crawled toward the wall before realizing there was no way out."

"Are you saying that he was attacked someplace else?" Knowles now looked very alert, his notepad open again.

"The injuries would suggest so, yes."

"There's a SOCO team already searching the area," Knowles assured him. "Scene of crime officers," DI Knowles explained when Doctor Lomax looked momentarily blank.

"There's something else, Inspector."

Doctor Lomax reached for Archie's wrist and held it up gently. "The man is malnourished, and both his wrists and ankles are chafed. The wounds are not fresh, a few weeks old, I'd say, but it looks as if this man was chained and starved."

"Are you certain?" Bobby exclaimed, staring at Archie's reddened wrist.

"Look here," the doctor said, pointing to the wrist, "the scars are wide, too wide to have been made by a rope."

Inspector Knowles bent down to examine Archie's wrist, then pulled back the blanket to expose his ankle. "Good God. Do you think he might have been into kinky sex?"

Doctor Lomax shook his head. "There is no evidence of sexual assault."

"Do you have any other ideas?" Knowles asked, clearly at a loss.

"His hands are calloused. This man is no stranger to physical labor. Perhaps he is a victim of human trafficking. He might have escaped his captors and fought back when they caught up with him. We won't know anything for certain until he wakes up."

"Will he remember?"

Doctor Lomax shrugged. "I don't know, Bobby. He was hit repeatedly about the head. We'll run more tests once he wakes. If he wakes."

DI Knowles scribbled some more and shut his notepad. "I will be posting an armed guard outside the room. This man will need to be questioned when he wakes up, but in the meantime, I need to make sure he's safe."

"Thank you, Doctor Lomax. Good day to you, Lord Everly," he said with mock deference before leaving the room.

Doctor Lomax followed after taking one last look at Archie.

Hugo reached out and took Archie's hand, now very much aware of the chafing on his wrists. "What happened to you, Archie?" Hugo asked quietly. "Who did this to you? Who beat you so savagely?"

He wasn't expecting an answer but was surprised to feel a slight twitch in Archie's hand, which he took as a good sign.

Hugo covered Archie's hand with his own, willing him to feel the contact. He bent down low, speaking directly into Archie's ear. "Archibald Hicks, you are the strongest, bravest man I know. I need you to come back to us. To Frances. Do you hear me? I forbid you to die."

He waited for another twitch, but nothing happened, and eventually he released Archie's hand and leaned back in the chair, staring at the florescent lights overhead. He felt so helpless. He'd known Archie since the lad was seven years old; a skinny, coltish troublemaker with a mane of red hair. He wasn't bigger or stronger than other boys his age, but he had a determination and resourcefulness that Hugo found endearing. The only person who could intimidate Archie was his bossy older sister Julia, who secretly doted on him, as did his mother.

Hugo had watched Archie grow from an awkward lad into a strong, capable man. Archie had true grit. He never ran away from a fight, and never betrayed a friend. And now Hugo felt as if he had unwittingly betrayed Archie. He'd left him behind to face whatever it was that had happened after their departure. Hugo had no doubt that whatever befell Archie was directly tied to the events that forced them to flee, and he felt a gut-searing guilt. Archie had finally found love and contentment after years of aimless womanizing. He loved Frances with a fierceness that came so naturally to his passionate soul, and she loved him unconditionally in return. His death wouldn't only destroy Frances—it would destroy all of them.

And if Archie, God willing, pulled through, there was now the police to deal with. He had expected a detective to show up, but hadn't bet on an armed guard being posted outside the room. It was bad enough that Archie was in a hospital with no identification or National Health Service number, but now there would be an investigation into what happened. The police would want answers. Had this been the seventeenth century, Hugo would have figured out how to manipulate the situation, but he was out of his depth here, especially where the police were involved. And poor Archie would be in for a surprise when he finally came to. If he came to. Hugo had to think of something, and fast. He couldn't get Archie out of here, but the least he could do was buy some time.

He continued to stare at the light, emptying his mind of all other concerns and focusing on the problem at hand. He would make sure Archie was safe no matter what, even if he had to blackmail Detective Inspector Knowles with the photographs from the private investigator.

FIFTY-SEVEN

Archie tried to force his eyes open, amazed by how difficult such a simple task seemed. An overwhelming darkness kept dragging him under, making him feel as if he were trapped somewhere between life and death. A steady sound came from somewhere to the left, the annoying beeping never-ending. Archie tried to open his eyes again and was blinded by the bright light shining down from the ceiling. It was almost white and filled the room with its unearthly glow. *Am I dead?* Archie suddenly wondered. He couldn't recall anything past the fight with Jacob Wilmot, the blacksmith. He remembered the agony of the dagger piercing his side and the metallic smell of blood. Had Wilmot killed him?

Archie attempted to turn his head but couldn't find the strength. He felt hot, the heat coming from the inside, as if he were fevered. His mouth was very dry, the tongue thick and unwieldy. Archie tried to take a deep breath, but his ribs groaned in protest, making him gasp instead. They were tightly bound and there was a throbbing pain in his side. Every bit of him hurt, even his prick felt strange. Something was inserted into it, something hard. Was this some form of torture? Where was he? Archie tried to focus, but his mind seemed to wander, as if alternating between reality and a particularly fantastical dream.

A strange tube appeared in front of his face, and a familiar voice said something, but it sounded distorted. Archie tried to see who was speaking to him, but the bright light blinded him, making the person's features indistinguishable. He closed his eyes to block out the glare.

"Drink, Archie," the voice said again. Archie allowed the tube to be inserted into his mouth but didn't know how to drink through it. "Suck the water up," the voice instructed. Archie did, and cool water squirted into his mouth. He drank all the water and was disappointed when nothing more came out.

"More," he croaked.

He heard a rustle and then the tube appeared again, the drink refilled. He could have drunk a bucket of water; he was so thirsty. When had he last eaten? His stomach felt completely empty, but he wasn't really hungry.

Archie suddenly felt a jolt of anxiety. Where was Franny? What had happened to her? Was she hurt?

Archie finally managed to turn his head, amazed to find Hugo watching him with a small smile.

"Welcome back, or should I say welcome forward?" Hugo joked, but his voice sounded shaky, almost tearful. He reached for Archie's hand and gave it a reassuring squeeze.

"Where am I? Where's Franny?" Archie managed to ask. His lips were still dry, and it was difficult to form the words.

"Don't worry about anything. Frances is safe with Neve and the children. You were badly injured. This is a hospital, and you've had an operation. They had to take your kidney, Archie, but you still have one healthy kidney left."

"They took my kidney?" Archie gasped in shock. "Why?"

"You would have died, Archie. You were bleeding internally, and your kidney was damaged beyond repair. How do you feel?"

"Bloody awful," Archie muttered. "What's wrong with my cock?"

"Nothing. It's still fully functional, probably the only part of you that is. What you feel is a catheter. It's used to empty your bladder of urine without you having to get up."

Archie's eyes widened in amazement, but he didn't comment.

"Archie, who attacked you, and why?" Hugo already knew the answer, having spoken to Neve earlier, but he wanted to see if Archie recalled anything of what took place before Frances dragged him through the passage. He had no idea what he expected, but it wasn't the terrible story Frances had finally shared with Neve. The fact that Archie had survived was truly a miracle. If not for Frances's quick thinking, Wilmot would have surely killed him, and then he would have turned his rage on the helpless girl. Frances would not have escaped unscathed. According to Neve, she was terribly shaken and shocked by her new surroundings but seemed physically unhurt.

Archie shook his head. He didn't want to talk about it, not yet. The blackness was still pulling at him, coaxing him to go back to sleep. All Archie heard as he began to drift was Hugo's voice. "If anyone asks you anything, just say that you can't remember."

"All right," Archie mumbled as he stepped into the darkness.

FIFTY-EIGHT

"Frances," a soft voice whispered. "Wake up, Frances."

Frances decided to ignore it. She was still dreaming. She'd fallen asleep sometime before dawn, having spent several hours trying to absorb all the things Neve tried to tell her. Most of what Neve had said seemed too fantastical to be true, but she'd experienced electricity and running water firsthand, and watched in amazement as Neve heated up the shepherd's pie without lighting a fire. She'd made a cup of chocolate the same way, just emptying a packet into a mug, and pressing a few buttons on a strange machine which beeped when the drink was ready. Miraculous.

"Frances," the voice whined. "Wake up."

Frances felt something wet on her cheek, like the tongue of a puppy. The puppy continued to slobber, covering her face with wet kisses. Frances opened her eyes carefully and came face to face with Valentine, who was holding Frances's face in her small hands and covering it with kisses.

"Oh, you're awake," Valentine squealed. "You've finally come. I've been waiting for so long. Where's Archie? I want to show him my new toys."

Michael peeked out from behind his sister. He didn't say anything, but he was smiling widely.

Frances opened her mouth to reply, but a sob tore from her chest. She was overcome by the love of this family. She'd felt so alone after they left, so abandoned and scared after Archie had been arrested. And suddenly, magically, she was with them again. Loved and cared for.

"Frances, why are you crying?" Valentine asked petulantly. "Aren't you happy to see us?"

Frances just nodded. "I'm too happy."

"There's no such thing. Now, get up. I helped Mrs. Harding make breakfast. You are to have scrambled eggs, sausages, fried mushrooms and toast. Coffee or tea?" she asked, as if taking an order.

"Leave Frances be, Valentine," Neve said as she entered the room. "I asked you and Michael to let Frances sleep."

"But we wanted to see her," Valentine protested as she climbed off the bed. "We missed her."

"Missed her," Michael chimed in. "Archie?" he asked as Neve scooped him up off the bed.

"You will both see Archie in a few days. He's not feeling well."

"We'll make him better," Valentine said. "We'll give him hugs and kisses."

Frances began to sob again, completely disarmed by the love of the children. She'd missed them so desperately. If only Archie were here, everything would be all right.

"Say goodbye to Frances and go have your breakfast; it's getting cold. Frances will be down in a little while, you can show her your toys then," Neve admonished as she handed off the children to the woman Frances had met yesterday.

Frances wiped her eyes and tried to smile at Neve, but she couldn't quite get her lips to cooperate. "Any news?" she asked, her heart racing.

"I spoke to Hugo a few minutes ago," Neve replied as she sat down next to Frances on the bed. "Archie woke up for a few minutes this morning. He remembers what happened, and he asked about you. The doctor is giving him a special medication to combat the infection. He's on the mend, Franny."

Frances nodded, unable to speak. She'd been so terrified that Archie would die. Neve had said that modern medicine could do wonders, but Archie was barely alive when she'd dragged him through the passage. He would have died had Frances not seen Neve in the cemetery. She'd thought it was a vision caused by distress and fatigue, but there Neve was, as if she'd been waiting for her.

"I brought you something to wear," Neve said once Frances recovered. "Would you like to try it on?"

Frances stared in shock at the summer dress laid out for her. It was scandalous. She held it up and glanced at Neve. "Where's the rest of it?"

"This is how people dress in this century. You put on a bra and panties beneath the dress. I think my bra will fit you. Here, try it on."

Frances pulled off the nightie and fumbled with the underwear. The bra fit almost perfectly now that her breasts were swollen, but the underwear felt strange between her legs. She longed to take it off, but Neve shook her head. "You'll get used to it." She held the dress over Frances's head as she slid her arms through.

Frances looked down, her expression one of disbelief. The dress came down to her knees and had cap sleeves, but Frances felt as if she were naked. Her legs were pale and bare, sticking out from beneath the skirt, if you could call it that, in a most ridiculous way. There was nothing beneath the dress, so it felt more like a shift. Frances's belly pushed against the fabric, stretching it a little around the middle.

"I can't wear this," she breathed. "Can I have what you are wearing?" Neve was wearing men's breeches and a linen shirt, but at least she was covered up.

Neve just smiled and went to the wardrobe. She rummaged in a drawer and produced a pair of similar breeches, and a cotton top the color of moss. "How's this?" she asked. "These are called jeans. Everyone wears them, men and women. They can be worn with anything."

"Better, I suppose." Frances changed but had some trouble with the zipper.

"Here, let me help you," Neve said as she easily pulled the metal tab upward. "Now, let's find you some shoes. Your feet are smaller than mine, but a pair of trainers should fit you if you wear thick socks."

"Trainers?" Frances asked, staring at Neve's feet, which were clad in some sort of open shoes with straps. They were strange, but kind of pretty at the same time.

Neve pulled out a pair of clunky, colorful shoes from the wardrobe. They almost looked like wooden clogs but were made of a softer material. "Sorry, that's all I've got. We'll get you some proper clothes as soon as we can."

Frances pulled on the socks and pushed her feet into the trainers. They were surprisingly comfortable. Soft and snug. Much better than clogs.

"Come, the children made you breakfast."

Frances took one last look in the mirror and shrugged. When in Rome....

"This is wonderful," Frances said through a mouthful of food. "Even better than that pie you gave me last night. May I have some more?"

"Of course. You must eat and rest, that's your only job," Neve said as she refilled Frances's plate and poured her a fresh cup of tea, to which she added sugar and a splash of milk.

Frances would have preferred ale, but tea was all right too. Her stomach was beginning to feel pleasantly full, so she took a few more bites and pushed away the plate. She was just about to take a sip of tea when a sharp pain tore through her abdomen, leaving her breathless. Frances cried out, her hand going to her belly, and all color draining from her face.

"Frances, what is it?"

"I get these sharp pains from time to time. I haven't had one in a few weeks, but dragging Archie might have hurt the baby." Frances began to cry softly. "He was so heavy, so unresponsive. It took me a very long time to get him to the other side, and then the door wouldn't open. It held fast. I left Archie on the floor and worked my fingers into the crack. I kept pulling until it opened enough for me to squeeze through. Then I got into the wedge, leaned against the frame and pushed with my hands and feet until the gap was wide enough to pull Archie through. I laid him on the ground, and then the pain came. It enveloped my belly and felt like a vise. I lay there, praying that Archie and the baby would survive, but if God wanted one of them, then I would rather keep Archie."

"Oh, Franny," Neve said as she enveloped Frances in a hug. "How long have you known?"

"Only a few weeks. I think it's all right now. The pain has subsided, and there is no bleeding. Is there a midwife here?"

"Yes, we'll find you a midwife," Neve replied soothingly. "Taking you to the hospital is out of the question. I'll talk to Mrs. Harding about ringing Doctor Lomax. If anyone has sway over him, it's Stella Harding. In the meantime, let's get you back upstairs. I'm no doctor, but bed rest can't hurt. You can watch some television."

Neve had mentioned television last night, but Frances couldn't wrap her mind around the concept. Neve said it was like a stage play, but available anytime and in everyone's home.

And, there were many different plays to choose from, according to personal taste. It sounded intriguing and would help distract her from her worrying while she awaited news of Archie and a visit from the midwife.

FIFTY-NINE

David Lomax unwrapped his lunch and reached for the newspaper. It had been a hectic morning, and he looked forward to his lunch break, which he usually took in his office away from the bustle of the cafeteria. Clare had packed him a tuna salad sandwich today, his favorite. She'd included a container of cut-up vegetables. He would have much rather had a bag of crisps, but his wife was always mindful of his cholesterol. "Doctor, heal thyself," she said with that holier-than-thou look, which annoyed him no end since he knew all about the stash of chocolate in her hosiery drawer. A bag of crisps wouldn't kill him, not after being on his feet all morning, seeing one patient after another.

David scanned the headlines, but couldn't concentrate on the news, his mind straying to the nameless young man from the church. He'd woken up for a few minutes this morning, which was a very positive development under the circumstances. David had been pondering the case ever since he'd first examined the young man and seen his odd injuries. He felt relieved at having been able to share his suspicions with the police. At least the man was now under police protection. A young constable had been placed just outside the door. The policeman had looked tense and uncomfortable every time Doctor Lomax passed by the room, but at least he seemed alert. David wondered how long it would take for him to appropriate every magazine in the building and start chatting up the nurses.

David tossed aside the newspaper and stared out the window. Having worked in Cranleigh for the past thirty years, he'd become blasé, lost his edge. He spent his days stitching up kids who had accidents at the playground, lecturing middle-aged patients on the dangers of their sedentary lifestyle and unhealthy diet, and performing minor outpatient procedures. He'd forgotten what it was like to deal with true emergencies, the type he'd had to deal with while working at The Royal London when he was just starting out. He'd forgotten how vicious human beings could be to each other, and the harm they could inflict, usually intentionally.

He'd realized, guiltily, that he missed those days, missed feeling as if he were really making a difference and saving lives. Getting away from it all had been something of a relief at the time, especially since Clare was pregnant and they had no wish to raise their family in London. And coming home to Cranleigh was the natural next step, when David's father was ready to step down and hand the practice he'd built over forty years to his son. It had been a good, happy life, if not a very exciting one. Everything in life was a trade-off, and this had been his. No regrets. But he'd fought tooth and nail to save that young man's life, and now he had a vested interest in his well-being. He'd give Bobby Knowles a call later and see if any leads had presented themselves.

David was startled out of his reverie by the trilling of his mobile. Few people called him on his mobile during the day. Patients called the surgery, and his wife waited for him to get home. She never called him at work unless it was an emergency. David stared at the little screen. Stella Harding.

"Stella, how are you?" he asked, wondering why Stella would call him now. She knew he'd be at the hospital. "Are you ill?"

"David, I need to ask a favor of you," Stella said, her tone hesitant.

"Yes, of course. How can I help?"

"Do you think you could come by the house after your shift? Bring your medical bag."

"Stella, are you ill?" he asked again. Stella was hardly ever unwell, and she rarely asked for favors. She was always careful not to overstep the boundaries of their friendship out of respect for Clare. Stella had nothing to worry about. Clare was secure in their marriage and never once questioned her husband's friendship with his first love. She had no reason to. David was content with his life, and would never do anything to jeopardize his marriage, not even get an unauthorized bag of crisps.

"No, not me. Will you come?" she persisted.

"Yes, of course. I finish here at four."

"Thank you, David."

David opened his mouth to ask more questions, but Stella had already rung off. She'd sounded very mysterious, which was unusual for her, leaving David rather intrigued. He glanced briefly at his watch. It was nearly two, time to return to his patients.

* * *

Stella was waiting on the front steps when David pulled up in front of Everly Manor at ten past four. She was dressed somberly, in a dress of dark green with an apron tied around her middle. Her hair was scraped into a bun at the back of her head, but her face was still youthful, the girl he'd known just beneath the surface.

She smiled warmly. "Thank you for coming."

"Are you all right?" David asked as he followed Stella into the kitchen, where the kettle was already whistling on the hob.

Stella poured two cups of tea and set one in front of him, clearly inviting him for a chat.

David set down his bag and took a seat at the table. "So, what's going on, old girl?"

"David, we've known each other for a long time," she began, her eyes on her tea. If David didn't know better, he'd say she was blushing.

"Yes," he replied, confused.

"I would never ask anything of you if I didn't think it important."

"You're being awfully secretive."

"There's a young woman upstairs who requires medical attention. She's frightened and traumatized. Promise me you won't interrogate her."

"Why would I interrogate her? Who is she?" David asked, his curiosity piqued.

"Neve Ashley found her in the crypt with that young man."

"What?" David sprang to his feet, nearly spilling his tea. "Stella, the police need to speak to her. She might have information about who attacked him."

Stella looked away and shook her head. "No, David."

David stared at the woman he'd known most of his life. What was she hiding from him, and why in the world was she protecting this girl from the police? "Stella, did she stab him? Was it self-defense?"

"No, of course not. She dragged him to safety."

"From where? There were no traces of blood anywhere inside the church or on the steps leading down to the crypt."

Stella just made a vague gesture with her hand, as if the girl had conjured up the injured man from thin air. "David, she's pregnant, and she's having abdominal pains. She's terrified of losing her baby. Please, be gentle with her."

"I'm always gentle," David replied defensively. He was utterly confused by this turn of events. Why were they hiding this woman from the police, and what was Stella's involvement in all this? Lord Everly said that he'd found the young man while out walking. Now Stella was confessing that Neve Ashley had been on the scene and had taken the girl away before the doctor had arrived.

"Do you know her? Does Ms. Ashley?" David asked.

"My Simon was at their wedding," Stella replied, her face suddenly going pale. She looked up at David, daring him to ask and dreading having to answer. He'd never seen her like this.

"When?"

"January 1689."

David's first reaction was to fly off the handle, but he knew Stella too well. She wasn't some fanciful young girl; she was a sensible middle-aged woman. He took a sip of his tea to give himself a moment to calm down, set down his mug, and faced Stella across the table.

"Please explain."

"David, Max Everly is dead. He died in April 1689 at the Tower of London."

"I just saw Max Everly at the hospital."

"Are you sure?" Stella asked, watching him slyly.

David thought back to his interaction with Max. He hadn't actually seen him up close since his dramatic return nearly two months ago. He'd expected Max to make an appointment for a physical after his return, but Max never rang. Yesterday was the first time they'd come face to face. He did notice that something about Max was off, but he'd been through a lot and was bound to seem different. Any type of breakdown always left its imprint on the person, even if they managed to recover and soldier on.

"Are you saying that man is not Max?" David asked, finally realizing what Stella was trying to tell him.

"I'm saying that there are some things in this world which

don't always make sense. Digging into this case will not help anyone. Now, do you promise to be kind to the girl?"

"Will you not tell me what's going on?"

"Not right now. Tend to her first, then we'll talk."

David got to his feet, feeling utterly perplexed. Stella was talking in riddles—1689—what utter rot. He'd have to convince her to come by the surgery for a checkup. Perhaps this was a symptom of something, early onset of what?! Raving lunacy? But right now it was his duty to help a woman in need, and whatever all this was about had no bearing on that. He would refrain from asking questions, as promised, but he would glean whatever information he could, nonetheless, tactfully.

David followed Stella up the stairs, medical bag in hand. Stella had always been in good shape, but she stopped on the second-floor landing, as if to catch her breath. David stared at the portrait hanging directly above him. The insolent dark gaze fixed on him as if the picture were alive. He felt something shift in his gut, but refused to acknowledge what he was seeing, at least out loud. The man in the portrait was the man he'd just left behind at the hospital.

SIXTY

Doctor Lomax gave me a look that could curdle milk, but refrained from expressing an opinion on the strange goings-on of the past two days. He was clearly confused by whatever Stella had chosen to tell him. She said she'd have a chat with him before taking him up to Frances, and judging by the pinched look on the man's face, I'd say it didn't go as well as expected.

The doctor looked away from me and focused on Frances, who was lying on the bed, her eyes round with worry. I was relieved to see his expression soften. No one could be cross with Frances.

"Would you mind waiting outside?" he asked me, but Frances instantly grew agitated.

"I'd like her lady—Neve to stay, please," she pleaded.

I was glad that Frances asserted herself. She'd feel somewhat more relaxed with me there, and I could make sure that Doctor Lomax didn't put any undue pressure on her to tell him more than she had been coached to. I hoped that everything was all right, though. The poor girl had been through enough, and to lose a baby she'd longed for so badly would be a blow she might not be able to recover from. Random pains were normal during pregnancy, but given the amount of stress Frances had been under, and the fact that she'd practically carried Archie, there was definitely cause for concern.

Doctor Lomax nodded, then sat down next to Frances on the bed. "I'm Doctor Lomax, and you are?"

"Frances," she answered shyly.

"And how old are you, Frances?"

"Eighteen."

He didn't seem in any rush to examine her. Instead, he took her hand and measured her pulse. I noticed that he looked very carefully at her wrist, before turning to look at her ankles. I suppose he needed to see if they were swollen.

Doctor Lomax opened his medical bag and withdrew a stethoscope and a blood pressure armband. "You're awfully thin, Frances. Have you been eating normally?"

"Not recently, no. We didn't have much food after we left Guilford," she replied guilelessly.

"Why is that?" the doctor asked gently, but Frances didn't elaborate.

"You need to eat for your baby."

"I know," Frances replied. "Mrs. Harding has been feeding me what seems like every hour," Frances supplied. "I've never eaten such marvelous things."

"Do you know when you might have conceived?"

"Sometime in March."

Doctor Lomax nodded and began to palpate Frances's stomach. "And you've been having some pains?"

"I didn't have any pains the first time, but this time, I keep getting these sudden, sharp pains," Frances said. Her eyes flew to my face as she realized what she had just said.

Doctor Lomax stopped what he was doing and looked at her closely. "Do you have another child, Frances?"

"No."

"But you said..." Doctor Lomax asked, watching her intently.

"He died."

"What was the cause of death, if you don't mind my asking?"

"He came early. He wasn't strong enough." Frances looked like she was about to weep, so Doctor Lomax patted her hand gently and changed the subject.

"May I examine you now, Frances?"

"Yes," Frances whispered.

Doctor Lomax pulled on a pair of latex gloves and performed an internal exam. Frances exhaled audibly when he finished, as if she'd expected him to cause her pain.

"Is my baby all right?" she asked, her voice shaking badly.

I could see that Doctor Lomax, who was normally a calm, cool presence, was deeply affected by Frances. His eyes were gentle behind his rimless specs, and he looked as if he were fighting the urge to give Frances a fatherly hug. He opted to take her hand instead and give it a reassuring squeeze. "I think it's just fine. You need to rest and eat well. May I see you outside, Ms. Ashley?" Doctor Lomax said to me as he packed up his gear.

He motioned for me to follow him downstairs to the front room, and turned on me as soon as I closed the door, his anger palpable.

"I don't know what you're playing at, but whatever it is, keep me out of it. That girl is malnourished and most likely anemic. It's a wonder she hasn't lost her baby, and there's no guarantee she won't if she doesn't get proper care. Not to mention that she looks like a minor. She doesn't look a day over fifteen. Who is she, and what is her relationship to that young man? Is she the one who stabbed him? I have a good mind to go to the police."

"Doctor Lomax, please," I pleaded. "She is not the one who

stabbed him. She's his wife, and she's frantic with worry for him. They are migrants, and the last thing they need is to come to the attention of the authorities. Lord Everly wishes to help them, so please, allow him to do so. We'll look after the girl and make sure she gets the care she needs."

Doctor Lomax didn't look happy, but he gave a slight nod. Turning Frances over to the police would probably result in a miscarriage, and as a doctor, his first priority was to do no harm. I knew he was burning to ask prying questions but was too polite to do so. No doubt he'd interrogate Mrs. Harding later. They had an odd relationship, and if I didn't know better, I'd say there was something more than just friendship between those two.

"What can I do for Frances?" I asked in an effort to distract him.

"Plenty of rest, fluids, good nutritious food, and fresh air. Once she feels stronger, she should take daily exercise. A half-hour walk would do for a start. She's about four months along, so, at a guess, she's due mid-December. Of course, I can't be more specific without bloodwork and a scan. Bring her to my surgery on Monday. I will treat her pro bono after hours, so no one need know she was ever there. I will also supply her with prenatal vitamins, which she desperately needs."

He looked as if he were about to say something else but changed his mind and stalked from the room.

"Thank you," I called after him, but all I heard was the slamming of the front door.

SIXTY-ONE

Detective Inspector Knowles nodded to the uniformed guard in greeting and let himself into the hospital room. The young man was lying back against the pillows, his bright hair framing his face. He appeared to be awake, but still a bit drowsy from all the painkillers coursing through his bloodstream. Everly sat in a chair by the bed thumbing through an old magazine. The young man's eyes slid over Bobby, but his face didn't register any expression.

Bobby couldn't help noticing that the young man was surprisingly attractive, in that rugged kind of way that was popular in American film stars. He didn't look American though, not with that coloring. Irish, maybe. He was awfully thin, and Doctor Lomax had mentioned that he was malnourished, borderline anemic. The doctor thought he might be a druggy, but no sign of narcotics was found in his blood. Perhaps he was just down on his luck. Out of a job.

"Hello, how are you feeling?" Bobby asked as he walked toward the bed. He smiled at the man in an effort to put him at ease.

"Better, thank you," the man replied cautiously.

"My name is Detective Inspector Robert Knowles, and I'd like to ask you a few questions. Is that all right?"

The man glanced at Everly before replying, which annoyed Bobby no end. He didn't need Everly's permission to talk to the police. Perhaps it'd be better if Everly left them to talk privately.

"All right."

"Everly, would you mind waiting outside?" Bobby asked as politely as he could.

Everly started to rise to his feet when the young man forestalled him.

"I'd like him to stay."

Bobby gritted his teeth but nodded to Everly to sit back down. He had no official reason for expelling Everly from the room, so stay he would. The young man was obviously more comfortable with him there; perhaps Everly's presence would help.

Bobby pulled out his notepad and pulled up a chair to the bed, his actions as casual and non-threatening as possible. "What's your name?"

"Archie," the man replied with childlike innocence. There was something about him that Bobby just couldn't put his finger on, something not quite right. He was just different somehow.

"Archie what?"

"Archie McDonald." Now they were getting somewhere.

Bobby glanced at Everly before continuing. What was the relationship between these two? Clearly they'd met before, even if Everly continued to deny it.

"Can you tell me what happened to you, Archie?"

The young man's shoulders slumped as he considered the question. He looked upset, which was, of course, understandable under the circumstances. He'd been viciously attacked, and the last thing he wanted to do was relive those moments.

"Take your time," Bobby offered, hoping he wouldn't take too long.

"I was down in the crypt, looking at the effigy of the knight when someone accosted me," Archie finally said.

"Were you alone?"

"Aye."

"Were you robbed?" Bobby asked.

"I must have been since my possessions are gone," Archie answered gruffly.

"Where are you from, Archie?"

"Scotland," Archie replied.

"Whereabouts in Scotland?" He didn't sound like a Scot, but then again, many Scots who lived and worked in England lost some of their brogue.

"I can't recall."

That was odd, but persisting would just antagonize the man.

"Did you see the person who attacked you?" Bobby asked, hoping for some clue as to who might have done this.

"No, not really," Archie replied. He was starting to get agitated. Probably upset at not being able to remember clearly.

"Was there only one person?"

"No, I think there were two of them."

"Archie, if I might ask you just one more question. Why were you wearing period clothes?"

The young man looked embarrassed for a moment, his pale cheeks turning pink. "I can't remember."

Bobby was sure that he could, but suddenly the reason seemed unimportant. Probably some kind of history buff or fetishist.

"I'll leave you to rest now. Please ask the nurse to ring me should you remember anything else."

"Aye, I will," the young man replied curtly.

Bobby couldn't see the expression on either Archie's or

Everly's face as he left the room, but he had the distinct impression that he just had the wool pulled over his eyes. The young man appeared sincere enough, but when all was said and done, he gave Bobby nothing. He had a name, but without even checking, he knew that there were probably at least a thousand men in Scotland named Archie McDonald, or MacDonald, whichever it was. What Bobby did know was that the man wasn't telling the truth. The forensics team had confirmed that the attack had not taken place in the crypt, and if Doctor Lomax was correct, which Bobby had no reason to doubt, Archie had faced his attacker, so had to have seen him. The fight took place somewhere else, and the men most likely knew each other, which brought Bobby right back to square one.

He'd had his men go door-to-door in the village, but no one could remember seeing anyone fitting Archie's description. No one saw any altercation or noticed anyone suspicious in the village the night before Archie was discovered. The young man's clothing was made from good fabric, but bore no labels or markings of any kind, nor did his boots. Bobby had the lad fingerprinted while he was asleep, but no match came up in the database. The man was a phantom, and Bobby would have a hell of a time identifying him without more information. It did seem pointless to keep an armed guard outside his door. He was clearly the victim, not the perpetrator, so wasting police time and funds would not be appreciated by the Super.

Bobby sighed as he walked down the corridor and out of the hospital.

* * *

"How did I do?" Archie asked once he was sure the policeman had gone. Hugo had schooled him in what to say, and Archie had gone along with it, not questioning Hugo too closely. He was still in too much discomfort to think clearly, and the only thing he wanted was to see Franny.

"Brilliantly. Now get some rest. I'll be back in a few hours. I must go home for a bit."

"Don't rush back. I'm all right. Really," Archie said. He wasn't, but he didn't want to impose. Hugo had been at his side for the past twenty-four hours, and he needed a break. All Archie wanted to do was sleep anyway. The doctor gave him something for the pain, and the medication made him feel sluggish and sleepy. He couldn't even eat, but he wasn't hungry anyway. Hugo said they were feeding him intravenously, whatever that meant. "I'm all right," Archie repeated stubbornly.

"I know you are. You're in good hands, Archie McDonald. I'll see you soon, and I'll bring you something that will make you happy."

* * *

Hugo left the hospital and turned for home. Archie would be all right for an hour or two, and Hugo needed to shower, shave, change his clothes, and get his wallet before he returned to the hospital. He was eager to see Frances as well. He had so many questions.

Hugo pulled out his mobile as he walked down the high street and dialed Neve.

"Well? How did it go?" she asked, her voice anxious. "Knowles puts me on my guard. Stella says he's like a dog with a bone, which is what makes him good at his job, I guess."

"It went just as you predicted," Hugo replied, smiling to himself. Neve's idea had been simple, but clever. "Wild goose chase initiated, and the guard has been removed."

"Excellent," Neve replied. "Now we just need to bide our time until Archie is better. How is he? Frances is desperate to see him."

"He's even more desperate to see her. I hate keeping them apart like this, especially after what happened, but it's necessary. Archie is a bit better, but he's still in a lot of pain. The infection seems to be clearing up, and the incision is healing nicely, according to Doctor Lomax. He'll need a few more days at the very least before we can even consider moving him."

SIXTY-TWO

Bobby Knowles parked the car and headed toward the constabulary building. At this moment, he would have rather walked over a bed of hot coals, but he couldn't ignore the summons from the Super. Bobby braced himself as he approached her office, praying that Jess had taken a sick day, but, alas, there she was, tapping away on her keyboard, a look of such loathing on her face that he felt as if she'd physically punched him. He'd had no choice but to break it off with her, but she was angry and hurt, and bent on giving him hell. Bobby had a feeling that she would have broken it off with him in time anyway, but he'd taken the decision out of her hands and cited his family as the reason. Jess had called him every name in the book, some too vile to repeat even to himself.

Perhaps Everly had unwittingly done him a favor. He'd saved him from the biggest mistake of his life. Now that the affair was over and Bobby could look at it more objectively, he realized that he'd been an absolute wanker, a man who permitted his prick to do the thinking for him. He'd risked losing not only Carol and Lucy, but Justin. Bobby's heart turned over at the thought of his precious little boy. The love he felt for him was the purest thing he'd ever experienced, and no piece of ass, no matter how delectable, was worth losing his son for.

Already he saw Jess in a different light. He'd been attracted by her innocence, sense of fun, and natural sensuality, but now that the glittering veil of infatuation had been lifted, what he saw was a hard, unfeeling woman, who'd been with dozens of men before him and would probably go through dozens more before even considering anything permanent. She hadn't felt anything for him other than a kind of perverse pleasure in having the power to take him away from his family and make him break every vow he'd ever taken. Jess was completely devoid of morals and not given to guilt. She wouldn't have felt an ounce of remorse had he left his family for her. Carol, Lucy, and Justin simply didn't exist for her—they were completely irrelevant.

Bobby had never considered himself an overly sentimental or religious person, but at the moment, he felt the kind of self-loathing he'd never experienced before. He could blame Jess all he wanted, but, ultimately, the responsibility lay with him. He was the one who was married, the one who risked his family for a tawdry little tryst. He would beg God for forgiveness and pray that Carol would be spared knowledge of his affair. She might forgive him for the sake of the children, but she would never forget. Her love and trust once lost were lost forever.

"Morning, Jess," Bobby said stiffly as he took a seat in the waiting area, as far from her as possible.

"I hope your bollocks shrivel up and fall off," Jess replied pleasantly, looking like a praying mantis who was about to bite his head off. "Go in," she added with a bright smile which scared him to death. What if she decided to tell Carol just to punish him? God, he'd mucked things up for himself.

Bobby walked into the inner office and took a seat. Superintendent Cummings gazed at him over the rim of her fashionable specs, her expression difficult to read. She looked as stylish as ever, but there was a weariness about her that hadn't been there before, showing in the lines bracketing her lipsticked mouth and in the bags beneath her eyes. She was under tremendous pressure from above to provide a good result.

"So, what have you learned about the stabbing at St. Nicolas, Inspector?" she asked in a tone that said, "you'd better give me some good news, or I'll hang you by your testicles." His balls were very popular today.

"In a word—nothing."

"Care to reconsider that answer? It happened three days ago, and we've got nothing? Look harder."

Bobby stared down his boss, suddenly outraged. It wasn't fair. He'd done everything he could, left no stone unturned, but there really was nothing. Bobby sucked in his breath and quickly counted to ten to cool his rage. Lashing out at the Super would do his career no favors.

Once he felt calmer, he finally replied, infusing his tone with all the respect he could muster at the moment. "Ma'am, the victim's name is Archie McDonald, which might as well be John Smith. He has no ID of any kind, so we have to take his word for it—a word I don't trust for a second, since I am positive that he's either lying or simply holding something back. He claims to be from Scotland, but can't recall exactly where, having been hit on the head, or just using his injuries as an excuse to withhold information." Bobby ignored the Super's thunderous expression and went on. "Johnson fingerprinted him, but we found no match in the database. We've also found nothing useful at the crime scene. There's no weapon or any other clues. We did find some strands of long blonde hair and a broken fingernail which belong to a woman. Even if the woman in question was not just someone who'd gone down to gawk at the crypt, there's no way the damage McDonald sustained could have been inflicted by a woman. We are looking for a man, possibly two. We've also been questioning the villagers for the past two days, going door-to-door, but no one has seen anything even remotely helpful. So, again, in a word, we have nothing."

"What do Forensics have to say?" the Super asked, unimpressed with his speech.

"Again, nothing, ma'am. St. Nicolas's crypt had been under construction for the past few months. Everyone and their mother has trampled through there."

"Blood?"

"There's only McDonald's blood. No one else's."

"Have you questioned the local 'talent'? I hear Alfie Doggett is out on parole."

"Spoke to Alfie and all his mates. No one has seen or heard anything. Alfie has a watertight alibi for that night. Everything I've tried is a dead end."

"Do you realize how incompetent this makes us look? A young man gets violently attacked in a church, for God's sake, and nearly bleeds to death, and no one—*no one*—knows anything of value. What am I to do with that, Knowles?"

"Do what you wish, ma'am, but the facts speak for themselves. And he wasn't attacked at the church; he was attacked someplace else, which makes this case even stranger, since there's no physical evidence that he was dragged down the stairs or across the floor of the crypt."

"Are you suggesting that he stabbed himself and went to the crypt to die, making sure that he cleaned up all the blood on the steps first before passing out?" Superintendent Cummins roared, now truly furious.

"I'm suggesting no such thing, but we haven't found a single clue as to what happened."

The Super glared at him over her glasses, her color slowly returning to normal. She was usually a very reasonable person, but as any superior, she was under a lot of pressure to perform, or, at least, to take measures when her people weren't performing. She ran a hand through her hair and stared out the window for a moment, deep in thought. "Bobby, I think you should take some well-deserved leave. Spend some time with your family. I'm sure Carol would appreciate an extra pair of hands around the house. Two weeks, say?"

"That's utterly unfair, ma'am," Bobby exploded, feeling cornered and humiliated.

"Is it? Jess has made a complaint of sexual harassment against you. I talked her out of it, but she's angry, and she will act on her anger if nothing is done. You are a good copper, Bobby, and a fine detective, but sometimes it's wise to take a step back and reevaluate the situation. Your personal peccadillos are affecting your judgment and your job. Sort yourself out, Inspector. We'll talk in two weeks. In the meantime, hand over the case to DI Sutherland. Good day."

Bobby stormed from the office. He'd have liked to strangle Jess, but luckily for her, she wasn't at her desk. She'd indulged in their affair with her eyes open. She knew about his family, knew he would never leave his wife. At no time did he make any promises. It was all just a bit of fun. Well, not anymore.

Bobby slammed the door as he exited into the street and made for the nearest bar. It wasn't even noon yet, but he needed a drink quite badly.

SIXTY-THREE

I held Frances's hand as she stared around the examining room, intimidated by all the equipment. Frances had had a lot to absorb over the past few days, her senses on overload as she tried to wrap her mind around all the things she was seeing and hearing. To a person with seventeenth-century sensibilities, this was like magic, and I suppose it was.

I insisted that Frances rest as much as possible, and I think she was grateful for hours of silence in a darkened room, a place where she could push aside all the wondrous and frightening things she'd seen and just be alone. She missed Archie dreadfully and had nearly gotten hysterical when she'd heard his voice on the telephone, but had managed to hold it together and speak to him, although she refused to put the phone to her ear, and I had to set in on speaker mode. I had snapped a few pictures of Frances once she'd calmed down and assured her that Archie would see them within a few minutes, just as soon as I sent them to Hugo's mobile, which made her smile with wonder. She had asked to see the photos and stared at them for a long while, amazed that her likeness had been caught so quickly and accurately.

"This is sorcery, this is," she breathed as she stared at the image.

"Are you frightened?" I asked. "Do you want me to erase the photographs?"

There were some who believed that taking a picture was like stealing a piece of someone's soul, especially if the subject looked straight into the camera. It was perfectly natural for Frances to question and doubt the things she could never have imagined even a few days ago. I remembered Hugo's first foray into the future and the confusing, wonderful, intoxicating journey he'd embarked on in those first days. He had questioned everything, wanted to understand how things worked, but, although at times he was afraid, waded in nonetheless, too caught up in the wonder of it all to allow superstition and ignorance to prevent him from learning and exploring.

Frances shook her head. "If you say it's safe, I believe you. Can I see a likeness of Archie?" she asked shyly.

I knew that Hugo didn't want her to see Archie in his condition, but not seeing him at all was probably more frightening.

"Of course. I'll ask Hugo to take a picture," I had promised, making Frances clasp her hands with joy.

And now she was about to experience something even more magical. Even women born and raised in this time held their breath and cried when they saw their baby for the very first time.

I held Frances's hand as she pulled up her top and unzipped her jeans. She was white as a sheet, her hand gripping mine like a vise. I'd explained to her what was going to happen, but I don't think she fully believed me, her mind refusing to accept the fact that she could see an unborn child moving about inside her body.

She squeezed her eyes shut when Doctor Lomax turned on the machine, and the screen sprang to life.

The doctor squirted some jelly onto her stomach, and

Frances yelped with surprise as he pressed the scanner against her belly and began to move it slowly.

"Don't be afraid, Frances. This won't hurt the baby," Doctor Lomax said gently. "I'll just see how big it is and listen to its heartbeat."

I squeezed Frances's hand in warning not to blurt anything out. She looked as if she were about to flee, but suddenly there was a whooshing sound coming from the monitor, and Frances froze, staring at the little pulsating blob. The image was very fuzzy, but if you looked carefully, you could make out arms and legs, and the head. The baby appeared to be waving.

"There it is. See?" the doctor explained, pointing with his finger to the screen. "You're about sixteen weeks pregnant. You should start feeling the baby move within the next few weeks. It's too soon to tell whether it's a girl or a boy, but it seems to be doing very well. You have nothing to worry about. Just take the vitamins I'm going to give you, eat properly, and get plenty of rest."

Silent tears poured down Frances's face as she stared at the monitor. "It's miraculous," she muttered. "Simply miraculous."

"Would you like a picture?" Doctor Lomax asked.

Frances nodded mutely, unable to speak. She was utterly overcome.

The doctor handed her a printout, and she clutched it to her bosom, sniffling loudly as I handed her a Kleenex.

"My God, you'd think the child had never heard of a scan before," the doctor mumbled as he walked from the room to fetch the vitamins.

"I have to show Archie," Frances pleaded.

"And you will. Very soon," I promised as I followed her out of the doctor's surgery carrying the vitamins and sheaf of brochures about prenatal care. Frances wasn't walking as much as floating, her feet not quite touching the ground. She was ecstatic, and her joy nearly brought me to tears.

My phone buzzed in my pocket, and I checked the caller ID. Hugo.

"How did it go?"

"All is well. Frances is anxious to show Archie the picture of her scan."

"Neve, I think it must be tonight," Hugo said cryptically.

"Why so soon?"

"A new inspector has been assigned to the case, and he's determined to get answers. He came by earlier to speak to Archie and reposted a guard outside the room. He won't allow the hospital to release Archie until they confirm his identity and place of residence. We can't afford to wait any longer."

"Can he walk?"

"Yes, but he's very weak. He hasn't been able to eat much, just dry buttered toast and some soup. He'll be lightheaded, but I think he can manage a short distance."

"All right, I'll take Frances home and have her get ready, and get in touch with Simon."

"Call me after you speak to Simon, and I'll tell you my plan."

"Hugo," I said, my voice full of awe, "I love that you always have a plan."

"And I love that you always go along with it," he said with a chuckle. "I hope this doesn't lead to a brush with the law."

"It probably will," I sighed, "but we don't have much choice."

SIXTY-FOUR

Archie grimaced dramatically as the nurse carefully pulled out the catheter, his face relaxing when he realized this wasn't going to be painful at all.

"There you go, love," the nurse said cheerfully. "Doctor's orders. Perhaps you can try getting up after dinner." She placed a tray of food in front of Archie and removed the lids. "Green salad, roast beef and mash, and a fruit cup for afters."

Archie smiled happily. "I can't remember when I've last eaten meat," he said and tried to pick up the cutlery, which was a challenge with his broken fingers and the IV in his hand.

"Shall I help you?" the nurse asked.

"I'll do it," Hugo volunteered and moved a chair closer to Archie's bed.

"I feel like a baby," Archie complained as Hugo carefully guided a loaded fork toward his mouth.

"Well, open wide then," Hugo quipped.

Archie obediently opened his mouth, his expression torn between happiness at finally eating solid food and embarrassment at being fed.

"So, who do you reckon killed Liza?" Hugo asked, more to

distract Archie than to find out the answer. Based on what Frances had said, Archie had no idea. He'd left Liza alive and well, if a little subdued and seething with rage, on the road to Haslemere, and Hugo had no reason to doubt Frances's word. Archie wasn't the type of man to lie about his deeds. If he had been the one to kill Liza, he would have owned up to it, both to his wife and to Hugo. Archie had told him about the guards he'd killed to escape from prison. He felt no particular guilt at having taken their lives, but leaving Sister Angela to die had weighed heavily on his conscience, as did his inability to bury his sister properly. Archie had whispered Julia's name more than once in his sleep, and Hugo had said a heartfelt prayer for her soul on Archie's behalf, as well as for Archie's father, who went to his grave without ever finding out what happened to his children.

Archie chewed for a moment, swallowed, then shrugged. "I don't rightly know, but can't say I care as long as I don't swing for it. Liza pushed her luck; it was bound to run out. I heard that she'd even approached Josiah Finch; told him her boy was Lionel's bastard."

"Did she?" Hugo asked as he maneuvered another forkful of meat and potatoes into Archie's mouth.

Archie nodded, his mouth too full to speak.

"What?" Archie asked once he swallowed. "You look like you just sucked on a lemon."

"I just can't believe how I misjudged her," Hugo replied, his expression thoughtful. "She was always a bit brazen and unconventional, qualities I found to be diverting at a time when nothing much brought me joy. But I never thought she had it in her to go to such lengths to get her hands on some money."

"You didn't misjudge her," Archie countered as he examined the fruit cup with undisguised suspicion. "Liza was a good girl once, as naïve and hopeful as any other young girl who thinks that a man is the answer to all of life's questions. However, she wasn't content to settle for the life she'd been born into. Some people just accept what's given to them and try to make the best of it, and some bite and claw to better their situation. She tried it on with you, hoping that you would set her up as your mistress and elevate her from the drudgery of service, and then, when her scheme failed, pinned her hopes on that captain, thinking he'd give her the comfortable future she longed for. Had he married her, she might have been content, but he left her pregnant and alone with no means of support. Life and bad decisions forced her hand, Hugo."

"Sounds like you feel sorry for her," Hugo observed as he fed Archie the fruit. He was surprised by Archie's analysis of Liza's predicament, more so because he, himself, had never given it much thought. Perhaps he was in some way to blame for her evolution. He'd taken Liza for a willing participant when it suited him, and assumed that she understood the way things stood, but she'd obviously believed their brief affair to be much more, and harbored hopes that Hugo had dashed without ever pondering the consequences of his actions.

"Liza nearly got us killed by betraying you to Finch, and would have been happy to see her ladyship burn, so, no, I don't feel sorry for her, but I can understand how she spiraled out of control. She had few options. She gambled and lost."

Hugo suddenly understood Archie's logic. He wasn't just speaking of Liza, he was speaking of Frances. Had Gabriel lived, the nuns would have eventually asked Frances to leave, and she would have been cast out into the world—a young, helpless woman with a child to support and no one in the world to turn to. Frances wasn't the type of girl to turn to blackmail, but if desperate enough to feed her baby, she might have been forced to rely on the kindness and generosity of some man, or a string of men. There would be few choices open to her, especially since, at the time, her husband was still alive, and she couldn't legally remarry.

"You saved her," Archie said, as if reading Hugo's thoughts. "And now you saved me, too."

Hugo set aside the tray and gave Archie a stern look that made Archie smile impishly. "Now, don't go getting all maudlin on me, Archie. I haven't saved you yet."

* * *

Hugo glanced at the clock on the wall, then left Archie's room to go get some coffee. He didn't really want coffee; this was more of a reconnaissance mission. The uniformed guard outside the door was a young man who seemed nervous and inexperienced, and sprang to his feet as soon as Hugo opened the door. Hugo didn't envy him getting this particular assignment. The policeman wasn't allowed to read or play on his mobile, so he just sat there, bored stiff, too shy to even chat up the nurses.

"Just getting some coffee," Hugo explained to the young man, who sank back into his seat, relieved that he didn't have to take any action.

The two nurses at the nurses' station smiled at Hugo as he passed by, having become accustomed to his presence. There was a vending machine at the end of the corridor, so Hugo strolled over and purchased two cups of coffee. He mixed a white powder into one cup and carried it over to the young guard.

"Fancy a cup of coffee, Trevors?" Hugo asked in a friendly manner.

"Thank you, eh, Your Lordship," he stammered. "Very kind of you."

"Think nothing of it," Hugo replied as he took a sip from the other cup before returning to Archie's room, looking as innocent as he could manage. He felt awful about having to drug the young officer, but things would go much easier on him if his coffee had been tampered with, rather than if he allowed Archie to escape while on duty. The crushed sleeping tablet would render him unconscious for a few hours, and the residue in the cup would get him off the hook with his superiors. Hugo would, of course, deny any knowledge of how the sleeping powder got into the officer's cup.

Archie was lying back on his pillows, the TV tuned to a rerun of *Britain's Got Talent*. Archie was absorbed in the program, laughing joyously at some particularly silly performance.

Hugo sat down and drank his coffee at a leisurely pace, helping himself to a biscuit from a tin by Archie's bed. The nurses really took to the young man, bringing him snacks and magazines to read, their compassion making Archie uncomfortable.

Archie held out his hand for a biscuit and popped it into his mouth whole, his eyes glued to the TV. "Will there be a telly in London?" he asked hopefully.

"Yes, there will."

"Never in my life have I seen anything so entertaining. Imagine, folk just sitting there in their parlor watching what they like when they like. What a life. How do they manage to get anything accomplished with so much to distract them? I do wish my da could have seen this. He would have busted a gut laughing."

Hugo smiled and glanced at the clock again. He loved seeing Archie enjoying himself for a change. He deserved to be distracted from his pain and worrying for a few minutes. Twenty minutes had gone by since Hugo had given Trevors the coffee; another ten and it would be time to go. Hugo carefully disconnected Archie's IV, then took out some clothes from a plastic shopping bag and handed them to Archie.

Archie dressed as quickly as his injuries would permit. He pulled on a pair of track pants, a T-shirt, socks, and trainers. He couldn't manage the laces on his own, so Hugo tied them and helped Archie brush his hair and tie it back. It was odd to see him in modern dress, but he looked comfortable, if not relaxed.

"Ready?" Hugo asked.

"Aye. As ready as I'll ever be."

Not for the first time, Hugo was grateful that the Cranleigh Village Hospital was located in an old building. Had this been a modern hospital, Archie would likely have been on a higher floor and would have to navigate corridors and elevators before making his escape, but his room was on the ground floor, the old-fashioned window easy to open. According to Neve, there were no CCTV cameras on that side of the building since it faced nothing but some shrubbery, so Archie's escape would not be caught on camera. Hugo helped Archie climb out the window and watched for a moment as he disappeared into the darkness where Neve was waiting to collect him.

This is almost too easy, Hugo thought with some regret as he locked the window from the inside and arranged a couple of pillows beneath the hospital blanket. He turned off the light, exited the room, and walked past the soundly sleeping Trevors.

The nurses were talking quietly at the station so as not to disturb the hush of the hospital.

"Are you off then, Lord Everly?" one of them asked. She'd been trying to flirt with him for days. She was pretty, with huge brown eyes that fixed on his own in open invitation.

"Yes. He's asleep," Hugo added as he returned her smile.

"Oh, good. Poor man, all alone with no family or friends to look after him," the second nurse said. She was motherly and warm, her concern genuine. "You've been an angel taking care of him the way you have," she added. "Not many strangers would care about someone they'd found bleeding half to death. Would probably step over them and keep walking. A real gent you are, Lord Everly."

"Thank you, Nancy," Hugo said, giving her a warm smile.

"It's no trouble. I'll see you ladies tomorrow. Will Archie get discharged soon, do you think?"

"Oh, no," Paula said as she leaned forward, giving Hugo a tantalizing glimpse of cleavage. "They won't release him until they access his medical records in the NHS database and find out his address. No rush though; he still needs a few more days to recover. I'm sure they'll find what they are looking for by then."

"I'm sure they will," Hugo replied before bidding the nurses goodnight and walking out through the front door. He walked a few paces to the Three Horseshoes Pub and ordered a pint. Several people called out a greeting, and Hugo joined a group of men at the bar who were discussing the latest developments in the Middle East. It was important for him to be seen tonight, so no one could accuse him of aiding in Archie's escape.

SIXTY-FIVE

I buckled Archie into the back seat and gave his hand a reassuring squeeze. "Hold on, cowboy," I joked, smiling at Archie's look of surprise as the car began to move. He tried to look unimpressed, but I could tell that he was torn between delight and apprehension. Hugo had told him about cars, but riding in one was vastly different than seeing a picture in a magazine. We drove for several minutes before coming to a stop by the church gate.

Frances slipped out and climbed into the car. She moved as close to Archie as she could and gazed up into his face, her hand cupping his cheek. "Archie," she breathed. She only said his name, but there was a world of meaning in that one word. It was imbued with endless love, worry, relief at seeing him alive, regret at not having been able to do more, and boundless hope for the future.

"I'm all right, Franny, really. Still a bit sore, but much recovered. How've you been, my angel?" He kissed Frances tenderly, his face aglow at finally seeing her in the flesh. They looked so young and happy, and lost in each other.

"Archie, look," Frances whispered as she held a picture to his nose.

Archie squinted at the black-and-white picture in the dim light, trying to understand what he was looking at.

"Ah, what is that?" he finally asked, taken aback by Frances's obvious delight.

"It's our baby. Look here; that's the heart. I heard it beating. It went whoosh, whoosh. It was amazing."

Archie took the picture and held it to his face, turning it this way and that. "I can't make out anything, but that sounds wonderful. I wish I'd been there. Oh, Franny, I'm so glad you're all right."

"Neve took good care of me. Valentine will be upset not to have seen you."

"I miss her too, the little madam," Archie said smiling. "And how's Michael?"

"He's grown so much," Frances replied. "Neve has pictures on her telephone. Oh, Archie, can we get one? I want pictures of our baby too."

"Yes, of course, as soon as we have ourselves sorted, however long that takes," he added, unsure of what was going to happen.

"I'm going to take you to London. You'll stay at Simon's flat tonight, and then he'll find a place for you to stay since we're afraid the police might come looking for you."

"What about work?" Archie asked, his voice tense. "How will I be able to support us?"

"Don't worry, Archie. Everything will work out in time. For now, you just have to give yourself time to heal and acclimate to this life. Hugo and I will see to the rest."

"Thank you, Your Ladyship," Archie said, his voice hoarse with emotion. "I'd have died without your help."

I smiled to myself as we drove away. I hated seeing Archie hurt, but in some perverse way, I was glad things had worked out as they did, since it brought us all together again. I wasn't sure exactly what would happen, but I had no doubt that, in time, everything would turn out okay. Archie and Frances weren't on their own the way Hugo and I were when I brought him over. They had us, and Simon, and I'd involve Glen Coolidge again if I had to.

"Good God, what is this place?" Frances breathed as she pressed her face to the window and stared at the bright lights of London, her eyes huge with wonder, her hand clutching Archie's.

"Wonderland," was all I said with a smile. "Welcome home, Alice."

SIXTY-SIX

CHRISTMAS EVE, 2015

Kingston, Surrey

Archie let himself quietly out of the room and walked on silent feet down the dimly lit corridor. It was decorated with tinsel and pretty ornaments for Christmas, and a fake tree stood in pride of place by the nurses' station, several wrapped parcels with colorful bows carefully arranged underneath. Christmas music played softly, so as not to disturb the patients, its joyful tones needed to lift the spirits of those who couldn't be with their families tonight and had to remain on duty.

A young nurse smiled at Archie and asked if he needed anything, but he shook his head.

"I'm all right, love," he replied.

"Can't stay away, can you?" she asked with a knowing smile and went back to whatever she was doing.

Archie walked over to the nursery and looked through the Plexiglas window. There were about five newborns sleeping peacefully in their tiny cots, a night nurse feeding one of them as she crooned to it soothingly. Archie's eyes swept over the cots, stopping at the one where a baby with an orange halo slept wrapped in a pink blanket. He hadn't realized he'd been holding his breath until he felt lightheaded and sucked in some air. She was so perfect, his little girl, so precious. She came a week late, but had been so worth the wait.

Hugo had generously arranged a place in this private maternity hospital, making sure that no one would ask any prying questions or inform the police that they were illegals. Archie had been terrified of the birth, but it had been fairly quick and, although not painless, very routine according to the obstetrician. Mother and child sailed through and were now resting after their ordeal.

Archie was startled when the night nurse tapped him on the shoulder. She was an older woman who looked at him with motherly kindness. "Would you like to hold her?" she asked.

"May I?"

"Of course. Come in and sit in that comfortable chair. I'll bring the baby over. Have you got a name picked out yet?" she asked as she placed the pink bundle in Archie's arms and made sure that he supported the head.

"No, but I know what I'd like to call her. I'm sure my wife will not object."

The nurse nodded and went back to her own chair, all the while keeping an eye on Archie and the baby.

Archie gazed into the little round face, wishing that his daughter would wake up and look at him, but she continued sleeping, her mouth pursed as if she were displeased at being disturbed. Archie bent down and kissed her fuzzy head. The skin felt like velvet, the hair like corn silk beneath his lips. He caught the nurse smiling at him and smiled back. She had no idea what this meant to him. He wasn't just any new father marveling at his baby. He was a man who had no right to exist, a man who should have died hundreds of years ago, probably on the night that Frances had dragged him into the future.

The past few months had been the best and worst of his life.

He alternated daily between amazement, wonder, joy, frustration, fear, and self-pity. This world wasn't for the faint of heart, or light of brain. What came so easily to children was a challenge for Archie, and he spent hours walking around London just to defuse some of his frustration at not being able to grasp the simplest of ideas. He felt like a newborn who'd come into the world knowing nothing. He had to relearn everything and unlearn those things which held him back. For the first few weeks, the world was a frightening, spinning vortex of color, sound, and motion. There were times when he felt physically ill from all the activity around him, but gradually the effects began to decrease.

Under the careful tutelage of Simon, Archie had learned to use the phone, the computer, and even to drive a car, although he couldn't drive one legally without a license. Simon seemed to get real pleasure from showing Archie around and teaching him as if he were a child. He was a kindhearted soul, Simon, and Archie's first twenty-first-century friend. Simon enjoyed taking him out to the pub for a boys' night out and explaining to him the intricacies of football and other strange modern sports. Archie didn't really enjoy watching grown men chasing after one ball, but kept his opinion to himself and basked in the camaraderie he felt with Simon and some of his mates who accepted Archie as one of their own.

Frances went through an adjustment of her own, although hers seemed to be easier than Archie's. She took to modern life like a fish to water and was watching birthing videos on YouTube and dancing to Lady Gaga before Archie even knew how to turn on the machine. She was always researching things, her face alight when she learned something she deemed important and worth sharing with him. Frances was suddenly filled with purpose and curiosity, her world having transformed overnight. Truth be told, Archie felt a bit resentful and off-kilter at first, but seeing the change in Frances made him happy. She went from being a cocoon to finally changing into a butterfly, and her colors were more brilliant than he could have ever imagined.

Archie gasped with surprise when the baby wrapped her little hand around his finger. Her eyes were open now, and she was studying him with an intensity which was almost disconcerting in a newborn.

"Hello, Julia," Archie whispered as his vision blurred with happy tears. His daughter would have the best this world had to offer; he would make sure of that.

EPILOGUE

SEPTEMBER 2016

Surrey, England

I tried to hide my smile as the chaos washed over me. Hugo was dashing from room to room in search of his briefcase, which Valentine had most likely absconded with since she coveted his laptop with a passion bordering on obsession. Michael had just knocked over his bowl of cereal and was howling with frustration. Valentine and Stella Harding were in the middle of an intense discussion about what color tights would best go with Val's outfit. Frances was nursing Julia while eating a piece of toast as Archie expertly flipped an omelet onto a plate and set it in front of his wife.

"Anyone else? I'm taking orders," he announced.

"I'll have one," I replied. I was always hungry these days. "Mushrooms and cheese, please."

"Coming right up."

"Valentine!" came a roar from the corridor. "Where in the name of God is my briefcase? I have a class in forty-five minutes."

"Valentine, stop torturing your father," I admonished her.

"I only wanted to play a game," she pouted, having decided on white tights with pink flowers. "It's under my bed."

"Under Val's bed, Hugo," I called out, biting my lip in order to keep myself from laughing.

I heard Hugo pounding up the stairs.

He appeared in the doorway a few minutes later, dressed for work with his briefcase in his hands. "Are you ready, Princess of Evil?" he demanded.

Valentine gave him a look of disdain. "I'm ready, Papa. Bye, Michael," she added spitefully, knowing that Michael would cry all the harder if he thought he was being left behind. I helped Michael out of his chair and wiped his face before planting a kiss on his nose.

I walked them to the car and strapped the children into their car seats. Hugo would drop them off at nursery school on his way to work. This was his first semester teaching history at a prestigious school for boys located near Guilford. He was teaching a course on the seventeenth century, and no doubt bringing the past to life.

Hugo maneuvered the car out of the driveway and disappeared through the gates, taking the chaos with him.

I waited on the steps as Frances and Archie came out with Julia. Frances reluctantly handed me the baby, whose halo of tangerine curls remained untamed despite Frances's best efforts. At nearly nine months old, Julia had four teeth which she displayed while smiling and was the sweetest baby in the world. Her round blue eyes regarded me calmly as I settled her on my hip.

"Off you go," I said to Frances. "Wave goodbye to Mum and Dad, sweetheart."

Julia obediently waved, which was the only instruction she could follow on demand, but we were working on that.

Frances turned back for one last kiss before finally tearing herself away and walking off hand in hand with Archie. She wore a pair of jeans, high-heeled suede boots, and a short leather jacket the color of ripe cherries. Her beautiful hair was artfully arranged in a bun on top of her head, and her makeup was skillfully done.

Even in heels, Archie still towered over her, his physique back to what it used to be before his ordeal. He ran a hand through his cropped hair. He'd cut it a few months ago and it suited him. It made him look more modern. Archie was dressed casually in old jeans, leather boots, and a denim jacket.

Hugo and I always joked that Archie and Frances had a long commute to work. They walked briskly in the direction of the manor house museum, Frances toward the front door and Archie toward the stables. A large coach full of tourists was already pulling in through the gates and Frances took her place by the door, a brilliant smile on her face.

"Good morning, ladies and gentlemen, and welcome to Everly Manor Museum, the home of the notorious seventeenth-century double agent, Lord Hugo Everly. Today you will see the place where he lived and plotted, first with the Duke of Monmouth and then with the king of France, until his death under mysterious circumstances in 1689. After the tour, we invite you to stop for a cup of tea at our rustic tearoom and perhaps browse for some souvenirs. Please feel free to explore the lovely gardens, or go for a ride. The stables are open. You can enjoy a ride down the scenic lane where the wicked lord himself was often seen galloping on his Arabian stallion. Please see Archie if you're interested in hiring a horse. Now, let's get your tickets sorted and begin our fascinating tour."

I shook my head in wonder as I hoisted Julia higher on my hip. "Shall we go visit Elena, my love?" I asked as I turned my steps toward the church. I didn't go every day anymore, and once the new baby arrived in six months, I'd have a lot less time, but I still went at least once a week and spent a few minutes telling Elena all our happenings. Julia enjoyed the walk, and we often went into the church after visiting Elena to look at the funny little gargoyle carved into the pillar of the church, said to have been Lewis Carroll's inspiration for the Cheshire Cat. She always reached out and touched it, gazing at it with all the seriousness a nine-month-old could muster.

I stood in front of Elena's grave, Julia in my arms. I'd had a lot to tell her this past year. It had been a whirl. Hugo had finally found his calling in teaching, and I had a sneaking suspicion that in a few years he'd be setting his sights on a seat in Parliament. His disappearance was ancient history now, and his need to meddle in politics was still there, his sense of justice as strong as ever. The children were happy and well-adjusted, enjoying their time at nursery school. Neither one ever mentioned anything about the past, believing it to have been nothing but a dream.

Archie and Frances were still not strictly legal, but since their daughter was born in England and was a British citizen by birth, we'd begun legal proceedings that would give them legal status in this country. Hugo had found a solicitor who had experience in dealing with refugees and illegal aliens and gave him a real cock-and-bull story about the origins of the Hickses, so we were sure that, in time, Archie and Frances would finally get what they longed for. We'd offered them the hunting lodge, but they had politely refused and chose instead to live with us. I had to admit that I was as happy as Hugo with their decision. The house had too many empty rooms before, but now it rang with the laughter of children and was always bustling with activity. Even Stella Harding seemed happier these days despite missing Simon, who'd gone off to New York with Heather. His groveling had finally earned him a second chance, and I was happy to see him wasting no time in starting out on his new life.

Bringing Archie back to Cranleigh after last year's case was a bit of a risk, but to our utter surprise, DI Knowles accepted a job in Brighton and moved there with his family. There was some talk of an affair with a coworker and a threat of divorce by his wife, but I never gave credence to such talk. The DI who'd taken over the case had also been transferred due to the embarrassment Archie's disappearance and lack of progress on the case had caused the constabulary. So, for the time being, all was quiet.

I set Julia on a small blanket beside the gravestone while I weeded the plot and chatted to Elena. I still missed her dreadfully, but on some subconscious level, I had finally accepted her passing and let her go. It was too early to know the sex of the new baby, but I hoped it would be a girl. Perhaps it would be ghoulish to call her Elena, but that's what we would do to honor our baby. She wouldn't be a replacement, but a tribute to a life cut short. And if it were a boy, we'd call him Jeremy, for Jem. I'd scoured the internet, but never found anything about Jeremiah Marsden. Perhaps that was a good thing and meant that he'd lived an ordinary life, as did the Nashes whose graves showed that they'd lived to see old age, as did their children.

I glanced at the church porch as someone walked out of the church. The passage was sealed up for good, at least on this side. There would be no more trips to the past, at least not for us. Our life was here now.

I scooped up Julia and gave her a kiss. "Want to see the gargoyle, darling?" I asked. Suddenly, a poem from *Alice Through the Looking Glass* came to mind and I recited it to Julia as we walked toward the church.

"When the day becomes the night,
And the sky becomes the sea,
When the clock strikes heavy
And there's no time for tea,
And in our darkest hour before our final rhyme,
She will come home to Wonderland
And turn the hands of time."

MAY 1691

Essex, England

Jem looked around his room one last time before picking up the bundle of clothes he'd packed and heading out the door. The house was silent, his beastly baby brother and newborn sister sound asleep. Jem wondered if he should leave a note for his father. He supposed it was the right thing to do and headed into his father's study to pen a quick farewell. He'd never felt at home in this house, and he never would, and now that he was nearly sixteen, there was no reason to remain. Jem caressed the coins in his pocket. He had enough money to live on for a good while if he were frugal, and then perhaps he'd join the king's army. Better to die honorably on some foreign battlefield than to expire of boredom on this remote estate.

Jem left the note where his father could see it and slipped from the house into the darkness, walking briskly toward the stables. He'd take his horse; his father owed him that much. Jem saddled the animal and vaulted into the saddle, eager to get going. Perhaps he'd stop by Cranley first. He knew that Lady Everly and the children were long gone. The accursed Clarence

Hiddleston hadn't wasted any time in taking over the estate. He now lived at Everly Manor, lording it over the servants and tenants, much as Hugo's father had done before his death. Jem had it from his father that Clarence had recently married, and his new wife was a young lady of both beauty and breeding, if of slightly impoverished circumstances. Not many fathers would allow their daughters to marry into a family where both the bridegroom's mother and uncle had had committed suicide, but Clarence's sound financial position and newly acquired title swayed this particular patriarch into overlooking the shame on the family name in exchange for a comfortable and secure life for his daughter. Jem wished them well, as he knew Hugo would if he were still around.

Jem sighed as he reconsidered his plan to visit Cranley. There was no point really, especially since Archie and Frances weren't there. No one knew what had happened to them after they'd fled Guilford, but Jem was sure they'd left England for good. They would never be safe again if they remained, and with their knowledge of French, they could easily settle in Paris where opportunities for someone with Archie's skills would be plentiful. Jem wished he could find them, as well as Lord and Lady Everly. He'd done it all for them, but it all went wrong anyway. Killing Liza had done nothing but taint his soul, and he would have to live with the unforgivable sin of taking a life for the rest of his days.

Jem dug his heels into the flanks of the horse, urging it into a gallop. He was speeding toward an unknown future, but he would not allow one act of evil to destroy his life. He would do whatever it took to make Hugo Everly proud and live a life full of meaning and purpose. Who knew? Perhaps one day they'd meet again.

Jem smiled as he felt the cool spring wind caress his face. A distant star winked at him as he gazed up at the night sky. Jem suddenly felt lighter, his heart no longer as heavy as it had been since the day he'd strangled Liza on that lonely road. He was nearly sixteen—a man in his own right, and he was finally free to choose his own path unhindered by the expectations and mistakes of others. Tomorrow was the first day of the rest of his life, and it would be glorious.

A LETTER FROM THE AUTHOR

Huge thanks for reading *Comes the Dawn*, I hope you were hooked on the epic conclusion to Neve and Hugo's journey. Jem's story continues in *Jem's Journey*, A Wonderland Novella. If you want to join other readers in hearing all about my new releases and bonus content, you can sign up for my newsletter!

www.stormpublishing.co/irina-shapiro

If you enjoyed this book and could spare a few moments to leave a review that would be hugely appreciated. Even a short review can make all the difference in encouraging a reader to discover my books for the first time. Thank you so much!

Although I write several different genres, time travel was my first love. As a student of history, I often wonder if I have what it takes to survive in the past in the dangerous, life-altering situations my characters have to deal with. Neve and Hugo are two of my favorite characters, not only because they're intelligent and brave but because they're fallible, sensitive, and ultimately human. I hope you enjoy their adventures, both in the past and the present, and come to see them as real people rather than characters on a page.

Thanks again for being part of this amazing journey with me and I hope you'll stay in touch – I have so many more stories and ideas to entertain you with!

Irina

Printed in Great Britain
by Amazon